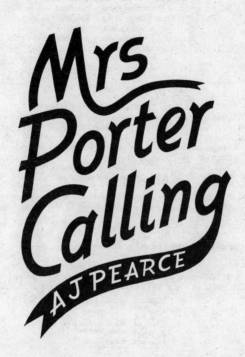

Mrs Porter Calling

A J PEARCE

PICADOR

First published 2023 by Picador

This edition first published 2024 by Picador
an imprint of Pan Macmillan
The Smithson, 6 Briset Street, London ECIM 5NR
EU representative: Macmillan Publishers Ireland Ltd, 1st Floor,
The Liffey Trust Centre, 117–126 Sheriff Street Upper,
Dublin 1, DO1 YC43
Associated companies throughout the world
www.panmacmillan.com

ISBN 978-1-0350-0080-7

1 3 5 7 9 8 6 4 2

A CIP catalogue record for this book is available from the British Library.

Typeset in Plantin MT Std by
Palimpsest Book Production Ltd, Falkirk, Stirlingshire
Printed and bound by CPI Group (UK) Ltd, Croydon, CRO 4YY

MIX
Paper | Supporting
responsible forestry
FSC® C116313

Visit **www.picador.com** to read more about all our books
and to buy them. You will also find features, author interviews and
news of any author events, and you can sign up for e-newsletters
so that you're always first to hear about our new releases.

For my brother

Dear Reader

Welcome to *Mrs Porter Calling*, the third novel in my series *The Wartime Chronicles*. Set in 1943, it continues the story of Emmy Lake, a young journalist living in London during the war. After two years at *Woman's Friend*, Emmy is now an established agony aunt, dedicated to both her readers and the magazine itself.

The series was inspired by a 1939 copy of a women's magazine that I found online. So far I have collected over a thousand vintage magazines, which I realise sounds a little over-committed but honestly, they don't take up as much room as it sounds . . . ! More than anything, they continue to be a wonderful source of ideas for challenges that I can hurl at Emmy and her friends.

If you have read the previous novels, you'll know that the theme running through the series is friendship – its ups and downs, and how sticking together can get you through pretty much anything. In this instalment, Emmy's relationship with her best friends Bunty and Thelma and the team at *Woman's Friend* becomes more important than ever. *Mrs Porter Calling* is a story about finding your chosen family and how that can become the most powerful thing in your world.

The arrival of the Honourable Mrs P definitely gives Emmy her biggest challenge to date. There's also the return of one of my favourite ever characters (no spoilers here, but I love him and am so pleased he is back), and the arrival of Small Winston, a dog who has to choose whether he is on the side of good or evil.

I really hope you'll enjoy them all.

I should also say that if you haven't read the earlier novels in the series, I wrote *Mrs Porter Calling* so that it can be read as a standalone novel. However, if you prefer reading series in order as I know lots of you do, please start with *Dear Mrs Bird* followed by the sequel *Yours Cheerfully*.

As ever, thank you so much for choosing to read my books. That I have been able to write an entire series of novels about Emmy and her world is totally down to the amazing support I have had. I can't tell you how grateful I am.

With best wishes,

London

April 1943

CHAPTER ONE

Happy Birthday, Emmy Lake

MARGARET AND I had been tap-dancing in the garden for nearly twenty minutes, and I was beginning to feel the strain. It was a Sunday afternoon in April and we were celebrating my twenty-fifth birthday. On current performance I was beginning to show my age.

'Keep going, Emmy. TAP, STEP, BALL CHANGE,' bellowed Marg, showing admirable focus for an eleven-year-old. 'Mr Collins, are you watching? I'm being Rita Hayworth, and Emmy is Fred Astaire.'

With the sun shining as if no one in the world had a care, spring had turned into summer for the event and I was enjoying my first day off for weeks. At the house my best friend Bunty and I shared in Pimlico it was so warm that our small party had decamped into the garden, happy to have an excuse to be outside.

Now, our friend Thelma's daughter was putting me through my paces.

'Well done,' I panted, as Guy Collins clapped loudly and Margaret hoofed even faster. She was not what one might call a natural dancer, but since we'd been to see *You Were Never Lovelier* at the Odeon Cinema she had shown the most enormous commitment, and as far as I was concerned, that beat talent every time.

'Excellent work,' confirmed Guy from the wooden

picnic table where he was playing a game of chess with Margaret's big brother, George. 'Although, do you think you may be making yourself perhaps the tiniest bit pink?'

Margaret was an incandescent shade of red.

'It is warm for this time of year,' said George politely, moving his knight. He was nearly thirteen and prone to becoming A Grown-Up in the presence of adults, particularly those he admired. 'Do you know, sir, I think that's checkmate.'

'Again!' laughed Bunty, knowing full well that Guy was a dab hand at the game.

'Good Lord,' said my brother-in-law, taking defeat well, particularly as he had only taught George to play the week before last. 'Well done, old man. And once again, there's really no need to say "sir".'

Stanley, Thelma's youngest child, joined in. 'Actually,' he said, leaning conspiratorially over Guy's shoulder, 'I think Marg's dancing is rubbish. She sounds like a herd of elephants.'

'Who's "*she*", the cat's mother?' said Thel mildly. 'Come on, Stan, everyone has to start somewhere. And remember we're being doubly nice as it's Emmy's birthday.'

Stan nodded and looked thoughtful. He was only nine and an honest lad which was supposed to be a good thing, so he was always baffled when he got told off about it.

'You *are* having a nice time, aren't you, Aunty Emmy?' he asked.

'I certainly am, Stan,' I said, giving up being Mr Astaire, and collapsing into a deckchair. 'Although I think I might need a rest now.'

'And you do like your presents?' asked Stan, who had given me a still slightly sticky balsa-wood model of a Lancaster bomber that he had made himself.

'They're all lovely,' I said. 'Especially the Lancaster.

I'm going to get some thread and hang it from the ceiling in the kitchen so everyone who visits will see it.'

Stanley looked chuffed and I thought what a smashing day it had been all round. Usually there was hardly any time to draw breath, let alone loll about, so today had been a real treat. I'd had lots of cards through the post, and phone calls from my parents and my friend Anne. She and her two small children had crammed into a telephone box to sing 'Happy Birthday' and shriek excitable best wishes until their money ran out. My friend Kath had sent a cable-knit bolero that fitted like a glove, and then Guy had arrived with a large bunch of early tulips and shop-bought chocolate bread pudding which must have taken up all of his coupons. Bunty had made me the most beautiful crocheted purse in my favourite shade of blue, and to cap it all, Thelma and the children arrived with an airgraph that had been sent to her so that she could give it to me on the right day.

It wasn't any old airgraph, either.

It was from my husband, Charles. It still felt funny, calling him that. Even though we had been married nearly sixteen months, we had spent only three days of it together before he had joined his unit in the army and headed away overseas. I missed him like anything and wrote to him almost every day. Sometimes he received my letters, other times he didn't. It rather depended on whether they had moved off to fight somewhere else. But I wrote to him all the same, numbering each letter so he would know if he had missed out.

Despite being so far away and in the middle of goodness knows what (he was always purposely vague), letters from Charles did make it home. They were infrequent though and all the more precious for it.

Today, it was not so much a letter, but a birthday card

5

of sorts as Charles had drawn the most dreadful picture of us both, and put *Happy Birthday* in huge letters underneath. Then he had written,

My Darling Girl,
   Happy 25th!
   Have the most marvellous time with everyone. I shall be thinking of you the entire day — as ever of course.
   My God I miss you, my dearest love. Can't wait till I get to see you again. Won't be long until Adolf gives in!
   Your loving husband,
   Cxxx
   PS: Hope you are impressed with my artistry. No, darling, it's not awful — it's Modern. You'd better hang on to it — could be worth a fortune. Take that, Picasso! Xxx

It made me laugh and cry at the same time, and as much as I adored Stanley, I had not told the truth about the balsa-wood plane. Charles's letter was by far the best present I could possibly have had.

'Does anyone fancy some more cake?' I asked, overly heartily. The children's arms shot up and then Bunty joined in.

'I'd love some if there's enough to go round,' she said. 'That is the best Victoria sponge I've had all year.'

'It's the *only* one,' I said, cutting what remained of the small cake into thin slices so that everyone could have seconds. Thelma said she wasn't hungry, which is what she always said when anything on the ration came up. It didn't matter what you did to try to persuade her, she always gave her share to the children.

'Too late. It's my birthday so you have to do as I say,' I grinned, handing her a piece.

Thelma thanked me and began to tuck in. 'Ooh, before

I forget,' she said, between mouthfuls, 'Bunty, Frank Owen was asking after you.'

Frank was one of the firemen at Carlton Street fire station where both Thelma and I worked. He was quite new and as I was only there part-time, I didn't know him that well. Bunty and I had bumped into him on our way to the grocer's.

'Do I know a Frank Owen?' asked Bunts, spotting a microscopic bit of jam on her plate. After three and a half years of war we had all become experts in sniffing out every last trace of anything sugary or in short supply.

'We saw him by the shops last week,' I said.

'Right-oh,' said Bunty.

'I think he's taken a shine to you,' said Thelma, as if it had only just occurred to her, rather than being a source of furtive discussion between her and me for at least seventy-two hours.

As Bunty started tidying the tea things, Thel threw me a Meaningful Look.

'Oh,' I said, casually. 'Taken a shine? That's nice.'

Bunty stopped what she was doing and gave us both the sort of long-suffering stare a teacher adopts when someone in the classroom has made a rude noise.

'I am entirely fine as I am,' she said, patiently.

'Of course,' I cried.

'I'll say,' said Thel.

Guy, who had been listening quietly, shook his head and then turned his face up towards the sun, smiling to himself behind a pair of clip-on sunglasses.

'I just thought I would mention it,' said Thelma. 'You know. In case.'

Bunty smoothed her hands across her cotton summer skirt. It had been two years since she had lost her fiancé, William, in the most awful of air raids, and while she had now recovered well from her own injuries, the idea of seeing someone again was not top of her list.

'I'm sure Frank is lovely,' she said. 'And I know you worry about me, but I'm perfectly happy as I am. One day perhaps, but . . .' She shrugged. 'I'm just not terribly bothered.'

I nodded in agreement. Bunty had a million years ahead of her to think about chaps.

Thelma, on the other hand, was a little more gung-ho about the idea, and I realised she had stopped listening after 'One day' and was doing all she could not to grab the bull by the horns and march it straight up the aisle.

'Frank's quite good-looking in his way,' she said.

'*In his way*?' said Bunty.

I noticed Guy trying not to laugh.

'It's his teeth, isn't it?' said Thelma, sadly. 'He's gone too far with his teeth.'

'Well, no . . .' Bunty looked over to me for help.

'They're new,' I said to clarify. 'He's still breaking them in.'

At this point, Guy let out a guffaw. Thelma tutted, seeing her chance to sort out Bunty's life slip away. She turned to him and tried to explain.

'They cost Frank a fortune. His front ones got knocked out when he tripped over a hose, but then last month he had a little win on the Pools so he thought, why not? So he had them all taken out and bought himself a smashing new set.'

'My grandmother did exactly the same,' I said. 'Never ate toffee again.'

'Shame,' said Guy, philosophically.

'Thel, I'm terrifically pleased for Frank and his teeth,' said Bunty, calmly, 'but I'm very happy being a spinster. For now at least.'

'So you won't rule it out?' Thel leapt at her chance. 'Even if it's not Frank?'

Bunty sighed, but with a smile. 'I won't rule it out. But I'm not ruling it in, either. Now can we please change the subject?'

'Good idea,' said Guy, rather coming to the rescue. 'Is it too awful of me to mention work on Emmy's birthday? It's just that I have a small piece of news.'

'He's going to give me the sack, isn't he?' I said, not remotely worried.

'Can you imagine?' laughed Bunts. 'It'll be twenty years' time and everyone will *still* be trying not to mention The Time Guy Sacked His Brother's Wife On Her Birthday.'

We all laughed. The fact that I had married my boss's half-brother was always a source of good-natured teasing.

'You do realise that makes it sound as if I only work at *Woman's Friend* thanks to nepotism,' I said. 'Can I just remind everyone that I joined *before* I met Charles? But anyway, yes of course, I'd like to hear some news. What is it?'

Guy took a pristine handkerchief out of his pocket, gave it a shake and then removed his spectacles and began to clean them with it.

'Well,' he said. 'This is probably quite dull, but I've just heard that we're going to be getting a new publisher.'

'Really?' I said, sitting up. 'Do we know who? How did you find out?'

This wasn't dull news at all. Our old publisher, Lord Overton, had been the much-respected and revered owner of Launceston Press and a titan in the newspaper world for over forty years. Two months ago, everyone had been terribly sorry to learn that he had died.

'I heard it through the grapevine on Friday,' said Guy. 'I believe her name is Mrs Porter.'

'That's exciting,' I said. As far as I had seen, publishers were very nearly always men. 'Although it does bring home that Lord Overton really has gone.'

'I know,' said Guy. 'I miss him.' He turned to Thel and Bunts. 'Years ago, Overton gave me a job at a time when no one else would. It could have been a dreadful mistake, but he gave me a chance. It's not something you forget.' He put his glasses back on. 'His lordship was a very decent man. And,' he added, briskly, 'he left us alone to run *Woman's Friend* as we liked. That was also good.'

This was an understatement to say the least. You could have argued that the owner of one of the largest publishing companies in the country had bigger things on his mind than the day-to-day running of a weekly women's magazine, but Guy and I were both well aware that Lord Overton had taken an almost benevolent approach to the publication he had launched nearly fifty years ago. He had stuck by us when things had been difficult, and congratulated us when we'd had success. His were very large shoes to fill.

'Do you have the scoop on Mrs Porter?' I asked, keen to hear more. 'You know everyone who's ever been anything to do with magazines.'

'Thank you, that makes me sound about eighty,' said Guy, who was not yet fifty-one. 'I don't, actually. I'm trying to find out.'

'I wonder what she's like,' I mused. 'Do you think she'll like what we're doing? I hope so. She should be impressed with the business side. It's been going really well.'

As I launched into more questions, Guy held his hands up. 'Hold your horses,' he said. 'We'll know more tomorrow. I have a meeting with the directors. Now, no more talk of work today. My fault for bringing it up. Tell me, Bunty, have you found a new lodger yet?'

Bunty grinned and picked up the hint to get me off the subject of work.

For nearly a year, we'd had a series of paying guests living in the flat at the top of the house. With just the two of us rattling around, it had seemed wrong not to, as there was a huge shortage of accommodation in London. It had all started through a friend of Bunty's who was in the Women's Voluntary Service and keenly involved with billeting and re-housing. When she had mentioned an elderly lady who was struggling to find lodgings where she felt safe, Bunts had immediately offered the flat.

Despite our initial concerns that it was on the top floor, and thus something of a trek, our first guest turned out to have the conformation of a gazelle, and spent a cheery month with us before finding somewhere permanent of her own.

From then on the flat had become temporary home to a succession of women, one or two of whom had become good friends. As Bunty had said, it finally felt as if the big old house was pulling its weight in the war.

'Not yet,' said Bunty. I just hope the next one doesn't have quite such bad insomnia as Mrs Croxton.'

I smiled. Our last lodger had neglected to mention that the only way she could get off to sleep was after a series of rather loud jumping jacks.

'Tricky,' said Guy. 'Mind you, doesn't your next-door neighbour have a lodger who plays the trombone? Isn't that quite a noise?'

'You mean Buzz,' I replied. 'She's wonderful. And she never plays late at night.'

'We like Buzz,' said George.

'She's in an all-girls big band,' added Marg, 'and she's going to give me lessons if I want.'

'Which is very exciting,' said Thelma. 'Fingers out of your ears, please, Stanley.'

'Anyway,' said Bunty, moving on, 'we need to set up some interviews as soon as Emmy and I are both free.'

'Absolutely,' I said. Finding time to do anything was always a challenge. When I wasn't at my job as an advice columnist at *Woman's Friend* magazine, I was working at the local fire station as a telephonist. 'I'm sure we could do it some time this week.'

'I'm on nights this week until Thursday,' said Bunty, as the two of us began to discuss our diaries.

After a few moments, I noticed that Stan was sitting very politely with his hand up. 'Are you all right, Stan?' I asked.

Stan nodded. 'Yes, thank you,' he said, and then paused. 'Um, Bunty, would we be allowed to come, please?'

'To the lodger interviews?' said Bunts, knowing he enjoyed joining in. 'To be honest, love, they're probably a bit boring.'

But Stan shook his head. 'No,' he said, 'I meant could we come and live with you?'

'Stan!' said Thelma.

'It's just that we always have good fun here and you've got a garden *and* a shed which would be ever so good for guinea pigs.'

'I'm so sorry,' said Thel. 'Really, Stanley.'

'Not at all,' said Bunty, 'it would be lovely. But, Stan, you've only been in your flat a few months.'

'I like it here too,' said Marg. 'Ours makes George's chest go funny.'

George nodded. 'Asthma,' he said, seriously, 'but I'm OK.'

'It turns out we've got damp,' admitted Thelma. 'It's entirely my fault. I should have known when we first looked at it in January and the landlord had all the windows open. But it's fine. Now come on, you lot, I think it's probably time to go home.'

'Why on earth didn't you say?' interrupted Bunty, looking as horrified as I felt. 'There's tons of room here.'

'You're very kind, Bunty,' said Thelma, 'but I can't come running to you just because I messed up with our flat.'

'But that's exactly what you should do, you great chump,' I said, giving her a friendly shove with my elbow.

'There are four of us,' said Thel.

'There's plenty of room here,' said Bunts again. 'The boys could have one room in the flat, and if you and Marg don't mind sharing, then . . .'

'I DON'T MIND,' shouted Margaret.

'Or you could use the other bedrooms downstairs,' said Bunty, thinking out loud.

'We'll sleep anywhere,' said Stanley. 'Oh, can we, Mum, please? It'll be good for George.'

George wheezed dramatically.

'Well done,' whispered Guy, adding loudly, 'Dear me, old man, you do sound ropey.'

'We could pool our resources,' I said. 'If we all cooked and ate together.'

'It *would* make the coupons go further,' said Bunty, 'and with three of us it would make shopping easier, too.'

'Six,' said George, miraculously recovered. 'We don't mind queuing, do we?'

'IT'S MY FAVOURITE,' cried Marg, which was news to the rest of us.

'Bunty, would you like a guinea pig?' asked Stan.

'I'll have a think,' said Bunts, kindly. She turned to Thelma. 'Honestly, Thel, please come. It would help all of us, wouldn't it, Em?'

'Gosh, yes,' I said, 'and I can't think of anything more fun than to come home from a long day at work with my awful old boss, and see all of you. It would be lovely. This is the best birthday present ever.'

Guy smiled. 'Mrs Jenkins,' he said, 'would you *please* put us all out of our misery and say that you'll move into the flat?'

We all looked at Thel, as the children held their breath.

'I must admit, it does sound wonderful,' she said. 'We'd obviously pay rent and pay our way on all the expenses the way anyone else would.'

'Hmmm,' said Bunty. 'We can talk about that another time.'

Thelma frowned.

'Hurrah!' I cried, before she could waver. 'Thel, hand in your notice to your rotten landlord tomorrow and move in as soon as possible. You'll be closer to the children's schools, too,' I threw in for good measure.

'Double hurrah!' said Guy, as the children looked unconvinced.

Thelma nodded, thoughtfully. 'If you're absolutely sure?'

'We are,' said Bunty, very firmly indeed. 'Now, I think that's all the questions answered.'

Stanley put his hand up again.

'Yes, Stan,' said Bunts.

'Mr Collins,' he said, thoughtfully, 'are you really eighty?' He was staring at Guy in the same way that people marvel at Stonehenge. 'Eighty,' he said again. 'That's even older than our nan.'

CHAPTER TWO

That Mrs Pye

THE NEXT MORNING, I set off to work, eager as ever to get to my desk. There was no doubt that Guy's news about Mrs Porter had created an exciting start to the week. He said he planned to announce the news to the staff straight after his meeting with the Launceston Press board of directors. Rumours had a habit of racing around the Launceston offices faster than a Spitfire in a dogfight, and he didn't want anyone to hear the news from someone other than him.

I found my favourite spot on the bus and stared out of the window as I wondered what Mrs Porter might be like. It was tremendously exciting that a woman had made it as far as publisher. The only other one I knew of was Monica Edwards, who was absolutely top notch. Bunty had suggested Mrs Porter might be an American, which caused a stir as I envisioned a hard-hitting business mogul, and then Thel said in that case she might well have worked her way up from the wrong side of the tracks and probably enjoyed chewing gum. At this point Guy pointed out that Mrs Porter would be running a woman's magazine, not working for the Mob and perhaps it was better to reserve judgement until the new publisher actually arrived. It was a good point.

Someone pulled the bell to get off the bus, and we

stopped directly outside a newsagent's. The newspaper advertisements on boards outside were increasingly bullish these days, full of celebration about the Eighth Army's triumphs in Tunisia, or how Russia's Red Army was walloping Germany at every turn. The United States was now well and truly involved in the struggle, and even if those of us at home felt that both we and many of our towns and cities were looking far less than our best, there was no doubt that the war was turning in our favour. The belief that Britain and her allies would win was no longer based on patriotism and fear of the alternative. There was a long way to go, but everyone knew Hitler was on his way to running out of steam.

I just hoped he would do so at the double. The Luftwaffe might not be bombing the place to bits every night currently, but people were having a very stiff time of it all the same. The men had been away a long time now, and the women at home were having to fill the gaps in their jobs, step up to war work and keep their families going at the same time. No wonder cracks were beginning to show, in people's relationships, home lives and happiness.

At just before half past eight I sprang up the marble steps into Launceston House and through the entrance hall, calling out a 'Good morning' to Miss Poole at the reception desk and taking the lift to the third floor, before heading to the stairs that led to the *Woman's Friend* offices in a rather poky little corner of the building on the fifth floor.

Opening the anonymous looking double doors that served as the entrance, I smiled at the handwritten sign on a door a short way down the corridor.

Miss E. Lake
Readers and Advice Editor

Although officially I was now Mrs Charles Mayhew, I had kept my maiden name for work. I loved my husband more than anything, but I'd noticed American women journalists tended not to change their names, and I decided to follow suit. Charles didn't mind a bit and quite happily said that he'd never been thought of as Modern before, and anyway, he should have seen it was coming when I'd taken to wearing a beret.

The title *Readers and Advice Editor* always gave me a thrill. Three years ago I'd dreamt of becoming a journalist. Now, here I was, in charge of both our problem page, "Yours Cheerfully", as well as the readers' own section of the magazine where we printed their views about what was wrong with the world and how if women were given even the smallest chance we could sort it all out. Some letters were simply useful everyday tips, while others might be a discussion over whether women should be given the same pay as men. I often thought Mr Churchill and his MPs would be surprised at how much they would learn if they read what our readers thought about things.

Now, I went into the tiny office and hung my hat on the back of the door. My desk was covered in piles of letters that had been opened and put into trays. Without sitting down, I picked up the top one.

Dear Yours Cheerfully

Please can you help? I am recently engaged but my mother has taken badly against my fiancé. She says if we marry, I shall regret it for the rest of my life. My fiancé, who I love very much, says Mother just doesn't want me to be happy, but I'm sure she means well. What should I do?
Yours,
Doreen Anderson, Plumstead

Poor Doreen. If I had sixpence for every letter we had about mothers, I'd have enough money to buy Buckingham Palace.

I put it to one side and ran my eyes over the next.

Dear Yours Cheerfully.

My mother has just got engaged to a man I am in love with. Would it be terribly wrong if I tried to take him away from her?

Could you please answer this asap as they're getting married next month and I need to get a move on.

Yours sincerely,

In Love With Derek

It wasn't always the mothers who were the problem. I wondered if I should write to In Love With Derek's mum and advise her to run away with him as fast as she possibly could?

Before I could think on it further, I was interrupted by raised voices in the office next door. There seemed to be quite a debate going on. Leaving the letters for now, I went to see what was going on.

'All I am saying, is that people can't help their glands,' insisted a forthright voice I recognised as Mrs Shaw. 'If they're up, they're up.'

'Miss Peters' glands are *always* up,' came the sharp reply. 'She's like a human barrage balloon.'

An immediate chorus of outrage made me quicken my step.

'Good morning,' I said, over the din. Everyone went silent. 'Is everything all right?'

'Good morning, Emmy. Belated happy birthday to you. Miss Peters is very sadly off sick,' said Mrs Shaw. 'Not that it's her fault and she should be back tomorrow.' She glared at Mrs Pye, our Fashion and Beauty Editor.

Mrs Pye was looking unmoved. She gave a shrug and said something under her breath in French.

'Poor Miss Peters,' I said, mildly. 'We shall all just have to muck in.'

'I certainly will,' said Mrs Shaw, pointedly.

'Me too, if I'm allowed,' said Hester, who was only sixteen and enjoying being part of a controversy.

'Mais, bien sûr, I am very willing to help,' said Mrs Pye, smoothly. 'Although I am enormously busy.'

'That's handy,' said Mrs Shaw, hotly.

I liked Mrs Shaw. She and Miss Peters were fondly known as the Letters Ladies as they helped me with all the readers' correspondence. They were both excellent sorts, and Mrs Shaw, who enjoyed a robust constitution, was very protective of her friend Miss Peters whose lymphatics had a tendency to go on the blink.

Mrs Pye, however, was unsympathetic. 'I am an Editor,' she added. 'I can't just drop everything. Mon Dieu!'

Hester stifled a laugh.

Pamela Pye, who as far as any of us knew had never been further south than the Isle of Wight, had a partiality for speaking in French. I assumed it had something to do with looking au fait about Paris, but as no one had had the gumption to ask her when she first arrived, we were all still in the dark and it was now too late to ask. As a result, everyone acted as if it was perfectly normal behaviour.

I didn't dare look at Hester, who was easily encouraged, so I tried to find a pacifying comment instead. Neither Mrs Pye nor Mrs Shaw were women to be trifled with.

Mrs Pye's weekly column, "On Duty for Beauty (Pamela Pye Reporting To Help)", was a hugely popular part of the magazine. If anyone could find something stylish to make out of half a yard of lace and a bit of old felt, it was her. Mrs Pye definitely knew her stuff. The only problem was she was also in charge of looking after our freelance contributors, and it was fair to say that her managerial approach had all the finesse of a Sherman tank.

'Mrs Shaw, shall we sit down and work out how to cope until Miss Peters returns?' I said.

Predictably, Mrs Pye walked out of the room.

'We'll be all right,' I said, confidently. Then I dropped my voice. '*Fantastique*,' I added.

Mrs Shaw made a snorting noise. 'The Queen of flipping Sheba,' she said, now sounding more cheerful. 'We'll manage. How was your birthday? Did you hear from your young man?'

I began to tell Mrs Shaw about Charles' makeshift card. Work could wait for a moment. Word from overseas was always cause for a chat because everyone knew how much we all ached for good news. It was an unwritten rule that whatever had been said in a letter would be interpreted by everyone else as indisputable proof that the person who had written it was safe and well, and there was absolutely nothing to worry about.

'Your boy's on smashing form,' confirmed Mrs Shaw. I felt my face light up.

But before I could answer, one of the phones rang.

'Good morning, *Woman's Friend* magazine,' said Hester in her best voice. 'Yes, of course.' She put her hand over the receiver. 'Emmy,' she said, 'it's Mrs Croft. Can I put her through to you, please? She says it's urgent.'

'Of course, thank you,' I said, frowning. Mrs Croft was our cookery expert and writer of the much-loved "What's In The Hotpot?" column. Everyone adored her, and what she didn't know about food wasn't worth knowing. I excused myself from Mrs Shaw and ran back to my office, as Hester put her through.

'Hello, Mrs Croft?' I said. 'How lovely to hear you. I hope you're quite well?'

'Hello, Miss Lake,' she answered, her usually gentle West Country accent sounding upset. 'I am well, thank you for asking. And I'm very sorry to bother you, but Mr Collins is unavailable and I'm afraid this can't wait.'

Mrs Croft was never a bother. I asked her how I could help.

'I've had a letter,' said Mrs Croft. 'It's from that Mrs Pye.'

'Ah,' I said.

'Yes,' said Mrs Croft. 'May I read you what she said?'

'Please do,' I said, bracing myself.

Mrs Croft took a deep breath. '*If someone was to ask me, What's in the Hotpot?*' she read, '*I am afraid I would answer, "Nothing very much".*'

'Oh, Mrs Croft,' I said.

'There's more. *You must also improve your efforts in terms of less fattening foods. All this starch won't help our larger ladies at all,*' Mrs Croft continued with a catch in her voice. 'Does she have any idea how hard it is trying to come up with ways to make rations last? I'm doing my best, Emmy, but there are only so many things you can do with a potato. It's not her job, either.'

Mrs Croft was entirely right. Looking after the magazine's contributors only meant ensuring they delivered their copy on time and sub-editing it if required. Editorial direction was Guy's affair.

'I'm so sorry, Mrs Croft,' I said, speaking carefully. Mrs Pye reported to Guy, not me, and I didn't want to say the wrong thing. 'That does sound like a poor choice of words.'

'It gets worse,' said Mrs Croft. 'She's only gone and sent me a cookbook.'

Mrs Croft sounded as if she had been posted a dead cat. She had been writing "The Hotpot" for nearly thirty years.

'*I am happy to lend you my own copy of* Vogue's Cookery Book *for inspiration*,' she read. 'Inspiration? What does Mrs Pye think I can do about banana ice cream? Six egg yolks? There's six weeks' rations straight off. I'm not being funny but we're in the middle of a war, not lolling about like a lot of flappers on the Riviera. And as for bananas, my granddaughter is seven and thinks they're something I've made up. I'm doing my best,' she finished, sadly.

'Oh, Mrs Croft,' I sighed. 'You more than do your best. You keep the readers and all of us in the office going. Your apple bread pudding is my absolute favourite. I'm so sorry you're upset. Shall I speak with Mr Collins and ask him to have a word?'

'Would you, luvvie?' said Mrs Croft. 'I'm not asking for favours, but she's making me feel as if I'm letting you all down.'

This just wouldn't do. While Mrs Croft made it look easy, coming up with new ideas on extremely limited resources was relentless. The last thing we wanted was for her to feel unappreciated.

I did my best to make up for Mrs Pye's size-twelve feet and promised that Guy would be able to sort everything out.

Mrs Croft began to sound a little happier. 'It's not *Vogue*'s fault,' she said, softening. 'They don't realise normal people don't shop in Harrods. And it was written before rationing, so they weren't to know. There is quite a nice recipe for pheasants in cream if you could get hold of either of them, which you can't.'

'One day, Mrs Croft,' I said. 'When we've won the war. It's something to look forward to.'

'Once your boy gets home,' she replied, 'you bring him over to Bristol and I'll do you a nice roast.'

'We'll never leave,' I said, and as I made a mental note to make sure that the magazine paid for Mrs Croft's phone bill, the two of us fell into a long chat about all the most glorious food we would eat. My stomach rumbled at the thought of buttercream-filled birthday cakes, great big breakfasts with bacon and eggs, and enough custard to fill up a bath.

'It won't be long now,' she said. 'We'll stop old Adolf and then they'll all come home, and we'll have a feast.'

Mrs Croft had two sons who were away, one of them in Africa and one in the Far East.

'To our boys, Mrs Croft,' I said, having promised again to speak with Mr Collins, 'to all of our boys.'

I put the phone down just as Guy appeared at the door. He looked a little flushed, and his hair was even more dishevelled than usual. It meant he had been running his hand through it, something I had come to know as a gesture of frustration on his part.

'How was it?' I asked. 'What's the news?'

'The news,' said Guy, slowly, 'is that we haven't just got a new publisher.' He messed his hair up a little more. 'I have just been informed that the Honourable Mrs Porter is also our new owner.'

'The Honourable who, is what?' I said, like a dimwit.

'Mrs Cressida Porter now owns *Woman's Friend*,' replied Guy, who sounded as shocked as I was. 'Lord Overton has left our magazine, and everything to do with it, to his niece.'

*

Guy was as good as his word. While I was looking like a goldfish with my mouth open, he called all the staff together in our meeting room to give them the news.

'But I believe there are no plans for change. It's just business as usual for the foreseeable future,' he finished, having repeated what he had just told me. 'Does anyone have any questions?'

Multiple arms shot into the air.

'Mrs Mahoney?' Guy turned to our highly esteemed Production Manager first.

Mrs Mahoney got straight to the point. 'It's a bit of a turn-up,' she said, 'but Lord Overton was a very clever and wise man. May I assume that Mrs Porter is from a publishing background?'

'I have no idea, I'm afraid,' said Guy.

'Mr Collins, what exactly is an Honourable?' asked Hester.

'Good question,' said Mrs Mahoney, who other than being a staunch supporter of the royal family didn't tend to hold much truck with this sort of thing.

'It means her father was a baron or a viscount,' said Mr Brand, our Art Director, in his usual quiet voice.

'L'élégance,' breathed Mrs Pye, unnecessarily.

'Is that everything?' asked Guy, deftly heading off one of our Fashion Editor's reveries. 'It's going to be an exciting time for us all, but if you have any other questions or concerns, please come and see me.' He paused. 'Mrs Mahoney is right. Lord Overton was a very wise man, as well as someone to whom many of us, me included, owe a great deal. Above all, I'm sure you will join me in doing everything we can to welcome Mrs Porter to *Woman's Friend*.'

The team needed little encouragement. Mr Newton gave one of his heartfelt 'Hear, hears', and then Mrs Pye overdid it by clasping her hands together and exclaiming, 'Bravo!' as if we had all suddenly found ourselves at the ballet. Mr Brand nodded sagely and Mrs Mahoney gave nothing away with her most beatific face, which only Guy and I knew meant, We Shall See.

We certainly would. Guy had once told me that Lord Overton had always had a soft spot for our much-loved *Woman's Friend*. Now we just had to meet the Honourable Niece he had chosen to carry that on.

CHAPTER THREE

The Honourable Arrives

THE NEWS THAT *Woman's Friend* would be owned by someone different for the first time in its forty-eight-year history had definitely come as a surprise. I for one had assumed the magazine would just be handed down to the late Lord Overton's son along with *The Evening Chronicle* and the rest of the Launceston Press empire. I was not alone in this.

After Guy's announcement, it had been the only thing anyone talked about for the rest of the day. Some of the team were nervous, particularly Mr Newton, but that was all right as he quite enjoyed a good worry, and others, particularly Mrs Shaw, became fixated on details such as whether the office biscuits would change even though there hadn't been any since the start of 1942. Mrs Mahoney and I liked the idea of having a woman owner as it would make other magazines buck up their ideas, and even Guy got involved only to spoil everyone's fun by saying he was sure nothing interesting would happen as long as we kept making enough money. In fact, very little work got done until Hester was found practising saying, 'Good morning, Your Honour,' to herself in front of the mirror in the ladies' lavatories, at which point we all realised we had to pull ourselves together and try to calm down.

When I got home that evening and told Bunty, she

and I decided that all in all the news was A Very Good Thing. As Guy was probably right about nothing much really changing, however, it wasn't half as exciting as the fact that Thelma and the children phoned from the telephone box outside their flat to say that Thel had handed in their notice and would it be all right if they moved in with us over the Easter weekend? From the noise at both ends of the phone, it was hard to tell who was more thrilled about this development – Bunty and me, or Thel and the kids. Seeing as Easter was less than a week away (George's poorly chest having become spontaneously worse since the suggestion that it might mean moving out) it was all hands on deck to ensure the upstairs flat was ready and waiting for their arrival.

I had to admit I was chuffed to bits at how it had worked out. I had first met Thelma when I joined the Fire Service as a volunteer telephonist at the start of the war, and we had become firm friends, working side by side with our friends Joan and young Mary throughout the Blitz. Thel was a few years older than me, and I very much looked up to her. Her husband Arthur had been away at sea for most of the war, and Thel had kept everything going, working long shifts and being both mum and dad for the children. She wasn't slow on enjoying a lark either. Sharing a house was going to be good fun. We all needed some of that.

The next day at the office, due to the fact that none of us had done any work since hearing about the Honourable Mrs Porter, after brief hellos we all got our heads down to make up for lost time until Clarence arrived from the post room with the first delivery of the day.

'Morning all,' he called as he lugged in a large and very full sack of letters. 'There are two more to come. The post boy will be up with them, presently.'

His face wore a look of hard-earned disgust at even having to mention his junior colleague.

Clarence had recently been promoted to Post Room Junior Administrator, and while it was entirely well deserved, it was fair to say the position had gone straight to his head.

'Blinking heck, Clarence,' said Mrs Shaw. 'This will keep us going.'

'The post waits for no man,' he answered, insightfully.

'Get you, Clarence Boone,' said Hester, arriving out of nowhere. 'Quoting people and everything.'

Clarence did his best handsome film-star face at her, which as he was only seventeen tended to be hit and miss. On this occasion it must have worked as Hester turned her back on him and walked off, always a sure sign that she was impressed.

The relationship between Hester and Clarence was a complex one, based on Clarence being an unfailingly decent young man who occasionally made misguided attempts to impress, and Hester talking incessantly about him when he wasn't there while being quite vile to him whenever he was. I went along with it based on the optimistic belief that sooner or later one of them had to crack and tell the other one how they felt. In the meantime, any suggestion to Hester that she and Clarence might want to see each other outside of the office was always met with wild amounts of blushing, fits of hysterical laughter, or the declaration that she would rather be dead.

Sometimes the problems that were sent into the office were easier to solve than the ones going on inside it.

Today though, I needed to finish writing a war-work feature. It was a behind the scenes look at women ship-builders, and having interviewed an absolute top-drawer group of girls the previous week, I was keen to do a good job. Once I had tackled a decent number of readers' letters, I happily bashed away at my ancient typewriter for the rest of the morning until Guy poked his head around the open door.

'Hold the front page,' he said, cheerfully. 'We're having a visitor.'

'Really?' I said, looking up.

'Our new owner,' said Guy. 'I've just been informed she will be here at around three o'clock. I am to receive her in the Launceston boardroom.'

'How grand,' I said, glancing at my desk, which looked as if someone had turned a fan on in a paper factory. 'Will you bring her here? We're going to need to tidy up if so.'

'Oh good grief,' said Guy, who was no friend of tidying. 'I hadn't thought of that. Still, good to know Mrs Porter is keen. I haven't had any luck in terms of gen on her. Not even from Monica.'

Monica Edwards was one of Guy's closest friends. Unflappable, elegant and famously intelligent, she was the publisher of a monthly magazine called *Woman Today*, which under her captaincy had been hugely successful for years. I had been lucky to get to know her through him and was quite sure that if anyone had the inside track on Mrs Porter, it would be her.

Guy looked at his wristwatch. 'We'll know soon enough,' he said. 'Twenty to one. I'll go and tell everyone to look sharp in case Mrs Porter would like to have a look round. It wouldn't do any harm to make a good impression.'

'I'll come and help,' I said, straightening a tray on my desk. I hoped I would look busy rather than out of control.

Just over two hours later, the entire *Woman's Friend* floor was immaculate. The postbags had either been emptied or stacked neatly by desks, Mrs Mahoney had casually placed some of Mr Brand's best cover illustrations just where Mrs Porter might see them, and Mr Newton had had a surge of self-confidence and made new paper labels for his out tray which ostentatiously said, ADVERTISERS and REVENUE. Then he filled both up to suggest thumping great amounts of money about to pour into the magazine's coffers. Even Mrs Pye mucked in by spending an hour on an artistic arrangement of back issues on the meeting room table.

At ten to three we were all at our desks looking the very model of a modern magazine.

At five past three, everyone had become fidgety, and then Clarence brought the second post which meant an All Hands On Deck situation when someone said it now looked as if we were lagging behind due to the unopened sacks.

At a quarter past three, Hester reported that the restaurant at the Dorchester Hotel had just called to inform Guy that Mrs Porter had now finished luncheon and was on her way.

'Most kind,' said Guy.

'That's a blinking long lunch,' said Mrs Shaw.

'Hors d'œuvres,' said Mrs Pye, seizing the opportunity.

I stopped and stared into mid-air. I'd had a meat-paste sandwich for mine.

'Rhubarb cream,' said Mrs Shaw. 'I bet it's all that sort of thing for pudding.'

'Crème de rhubarbe,' said Mrs Pye, now doing it on purpose.

Before Mrs Shaw could respond, the conversation was brought to a halt by Hester, hurtling into the room like a missile.

'SHE'S COMING,' she shrieked. 'MRS PORTER IS NEARLY HERE.'

'Hester, please try to remain calm,' said Guy. 'You're

not trying to get people into the Big Top.' As Hester stopped shouting, he dropped his voice and spoke slowly. 'Are you saying that Mrs Porter is coming directly *here* and not to the board room?'

Hester nodded. 'Miss Poole is bringing her up as we speak,' she whispered, almost inaudibly.

'That's fine,' said Guy. 'I'll take Mrs Porter into the meeting room. Can someone see about making us some tea? Now, if you all can just pretend no one of any interest is coming, and return to your desks, that would be much appreciated. Hester, do you feel up to waiting by the stairs to show Mrs Porter in?'

Hester looked terrified.

'Shall I go?' I said, and she nodded gratefully.

I headed off to the stairs, wondering if anyone had told Mrs Porter that she would have to climb a couple of flights to reach us. Then I stood outside the double doors to *Woman's Friend*, smoothed down my skirt, tucked my hair behind my ears, and waited.

From the stairs below came a high-pitched, rather breathy, almost musical voice.

'Really, Miss Poole,' it was saying, 'I don't mind the climb one little bit. We can pretend we are in a castle. Lovely.'

'It's just up here, Mrs Porter,' I heard Miss Poole say, and then two women appeared around the corner.

Miss Poole was, of course, entirely familiar. The woman with her was undoubtedly the Honourable Mrs Porter. Immaculately, and clearly expensively dressed, Mrs Porter was smiling as if she was in the shadow of the Taj Mahal, rather than having clambered up a battered stairwell in need of a paint.

Aged somewhere in her late thirties, Cressida Porter was picture-perfect. Slim, but not skinny, with dark brown hair and the sort of complexion that makes people talk about peaches, and you instantly understand what they mean, she had a look of wonderment, as if someone had just given her the best Christmas present in the world. Which, if you thought about it, Lord Overton had.

I broke into a welcoming smile.

'Oh good,' said Miss Poole, as she spotted me. 'Miss Lake.'

But before she could begin any form of an introduction, Mrs Porter almost danced towards me, offering her hand and beaming.

'Hello!' she cried. 'How wonderful. I do love your blouse.'

'Oh,' I managed. 'Thank you. How do you do, Mrs Porter?' I said, which already seemed overly formal as Mrs Porter was holding my hand and smiling at me as if we were best friends. It was slightly disarming, but not at all unpleasant, and I found myself smiling even more and wanting to say something nice back.

My blouse was absolutely nothing to write home about and in fact had a small hole which I had hidden with a brooch, but I found myself chuffed that she had noticed it, albeit feeling a little underdressed. In stark contrast to my outfit, which had seen better days, Mrs Porter was wearing a beautifully tailored navy suit with four large buttons in the shape of flowers, and a clutch of what looked like fabric hydrangeas by the lapel. A matching navy hat was simple but exquisite, the front tilted forward just enough to allow her to tip her head down and widen her eyes to gaze out prettily from underneath.

'What a beautiful hat,' I said, which would not have been my first choice of opening remark in terms of making a professional impression. But it was too late and anyway, appeared to go down rather well.

'How awfully kind,' she replied. Then she leaned slightly forward. 'Isn't it just the hugest relief that hats aren't on the ration?'

She seemed even more delighted at her own comment, as if she and I had found the very core of something in common.

'Absolutely,' I said, although I was slightly drowned out by Mrs Porter laughing in a charming way.

I was beginning to feel as if I was being run over by a steamroller made from petals and kittens. It was delightful, but also somewhat immobilizing.

'It's very nice to meet you,' I said. 'Miss Poole, thank you for bringing Mrs Porter up to *Woman's Friend*. Mrs Porter, would you like to come in? Our Editor Mr Collins is so keen to meet you.'

Mrs Porter said that she very much would, and then thanked Miss Poole so effusively I wondered if the younger woman had actually carried her up the stairs.

'I shall take you directly to Mr Collins,' I said, as it began to look as if Mrs Porter was contemplating a hug. I wondered what Guy was going to make of it.

'Yes, please,' she exclaimed, her attention now with me. 'I've never met an Editor before.' She grasped my arm as I opened the door for her. 'Before we go in, you must tell me. Is he very stern? Shall he and I get on? Oh, do say we shall!'

'I'm sure you will,' I said, adding quickly, 'Mr Collins isn't the least bit stern. He's very nice indeed.'

I wondered whether this was a suitable moment to mention that he was also my brother-in-law, but it felt more appropriate that this information should come from him, and anyway, Mrs Porter had now taken on an ad-mirable turn of speed and was already halfway through the door.

I scurried after her, just managing to squeeze in by her side. As the doors to the different offices and rooms were always left open, I quickly directed her towards the meeting room before something untidy caught her eye. As it was, Mrs Porter was staring at the covers of past issues on the walls as if she had just spotted a Matisse.

'I've always loved magazines,' she said to me, mistily. 'My uncle knew that, of course.'

'Of course,' I said, respectfully, then tapping softly on the meeting room door, 'Here we are. After you, Mrs Porter.'

Mrs Porter dipped her head under her hat once again and I followed her into the room.

'Mr Collins,' I said, quite sensibly, and then, as if I had suddenly become head butler to the Duchess of Devonshire, I heard myself say in the most ludicrously important voice, 'may I introduce the Honourable Mrs Cressida Porter.'

CHAPTER FOUR

You Must Call Me 'Egg'

GUY GAVE ME an almost imperceptible raise of an eyebrow, and then stood up to meet his new boss.

'Mrs Porter,' he said, sounding awfully professional and using a slightly lower voice than usual. 'How do you do?'

Mrs Porter looked at him from under her hat and then blinked.

'How do you do?' she said, softly. Then she blinked at him rather quickly twice more. I watched, mesmerised, as she appeared to be batting her eyelashes. 'I thought you might be old and rather frightening,' she continued, 'but your wonderful Miss Lake promised me that you're not in the least.'

I smiled limply.

'Miss Lake is very kind,' said Guy.

Mrs Porter reached across and squeezed my arm as if we were the closest friends. I wondered if I had inadvertently declared some sort of lifelong allegiance to her in the one minute since we had met.

I hadn't a clue what was happening, but it was impossible not to be charmed. I wondered if she was having the same effect on Guy.

'Please, do sit down, Mrs Porter,' he said. 'May I offer you a glass of water?'

He could as well have offered her the finest champagne.

Mrs Porter said how lovely that sounded, but she had just had the most wonderful lunch.

'We had the scallops,' she added.

'Marvellous,' said Guy. 'Now, Mrs Porter, may I . . .'

'Stop!' cried Mrs Porter. 'You must call me Egg. Absolutely everyone does. But I shall call you Mr Collins, because you are in charge.'

She looked thrilled.

'Oh,' said Guy, looking slightly less ecstatic. 'That's very kind of you, Mrs Por—'

'Egg!' cried Mrs Porter, again, sitting down at the table. 'And we shall be friends.'

Guy's expression gave nothing away. We had of course talked about what our new owner might be like, but being told to call her Egg and becoming best friends had not been discussed.

'What a day this is,' Guy said, which could have meant anything. 'Now, I don't know how much time you have, but we thought you might like to hear our current plans for the magazine. I imagine you've been through the financial side, although naturally I can run you through whatever you are keenest to know.'

Mrs Porter laid her hand on his arm. 'Not at all,' she said. 'I'm sure that sort of thing very much looks after itself. I've hardly had a chance to read your darling magazine, yet. Of course, I have the current issue, which is such a delight – the article on making a child's toy out of felt was quite the sweetest thing, but I must confess to a failure on my part not to have been a regular reader to date.' She said *to date* with great sincerity. 'There is one thing,' she added, 'and that is that I should very much love to meet all your staff.' Now she reached over to me and patted my arm again. 'I want everyone to know how super I think your magazine is and what a tremendous job you are all doing. They mustn't worry about a thing. I shall just say hello and then leave you all to carry on doing whatever it is that you do. Oh, it *is* exciting, isn't it?'

Mrs Porter turned her thousand-kilowatt smile on us both.

'Very much so,' I said, strongly. It was impossible not to be swept along with her enthusiasm. I noticed Guy smile ever so slightly at me and then nod respectfully at his publisher.

'Indeed,' he said, standing up. 'Shall we?'

Cressida 'Egg' Porter smiled at him as if she had fallen quite entirely in love.

'Thank you,' she whispered, lowering her eyes.

I leapt to my feet to open the door and Mrs Porter glided into the corridor, leaving Guy to follow in her wake. He had just a second to glance across at me and give the faintest of winks, before guiding Mrs Porter along to her right.

'Might I suggest we begin with the Art Department?' he said, smoothly. 'And two of our most long-serving and highly respected members of staff?'

Half an hour later, it was apparent that the sheer force of Mrs Porter's delight at finding herself the owner of a magazine had knocked the entire *Woman's Friend* team for six. Having been given the full tour, other than Guy's own office, even though Mrs Porter had accused him of not sharing where the 'real magic' of publishing took place, everyone congregated in the old journalists' room so that Mrs Porter could say a few words.

At this point the only word I could find to describe both myself and the general expression of everyone else was groggy, as if I had gone mad on fine wines or loitered for too long in the perfume section in Selfridges. Everything around Mrs Porter was rather giddy and fuzzy and entirely otherworldly.

It wasn't just me. Being with her seemed to make people who didn't usually say things like 'How lovely,' suddenly start saying, 'How lovely.'

Perhaps it was because we had all been expecting someone rather full of themselves, or possibly because despite the odd idiosyncrasy such as Mrs Pye's penchant for French, we were a down-to-earth crowd, and not used to someone wafting in from the Dorchester and telling us how adorable we all were.

Mrs Mahoney was smiley and polite, which I knew meant she was reserving judgement, while Mr Brand looked understandably unsure when Mrs Porter told him his illustrations for next week's lead romance story were worthy of the Louvre. Hester's eyes became permanent soup plates, and at one point I thought Mrs Pye might actually genuflect when Mrs Porter admired her frock.

Mrs Shaw and Miss Peters both lost the power of speech and it was left to Mr Newton to show a hitherto unknown strength of character and ask Mrs Porter if she had enjoyed her lunch. When she confirmed that she had, everyone looked about as glad as if they'd just heard a loved one had been the last person saved off the *Titanic*.

It was the oddest day of my working life.

'Mrs Porter would like to say a few words,' said Guy, who was holding fast against the intoxication going on all around.

Mrs Porter said, 'If I may,' very shyly, even though she was the one who had suggested it and it was the whole point of Guy taking her to meet everyone.

'Thank you,' she said. 'I can't tell you what it has meant to me to meet you all. You have made me feel so very welcome.' The entire team nodded but none of us knew if we were supposed to say anything, so we looked at Guy.

'It is our pleasure,' he said, managing not to add, 'What

is wrong with you all?' which I had a feeling he might be thinking.

Mrs Porter did another of her big blinks at him.

'You have all been so kind to me that I already feel as if . . .' she paused for a moment and then clasped her hands together, 'this is my home. I hope,' she added, while I couldn't help thinking that our tiny little offices were probably absolutely nothing like Mrs Porter's home, 'you will not mind if I pop back to see you another time.' She looked at Guy. 'I am afraid I must fly as I have an engagement. I am so proud to be your new owner even though I can never even dream to come near to your experience and talents. Thank you.'

Mrs Porter ended with a flourish of modesty and we all broke into applause because it felt the right thing to do and anyway we were now so inebriated we had completely forgotten that rounds of applause didn't happen in a normal office on an average Tuesday afternoon.

'Thank you, Mrs Porter,' said Guy. 'Let me show you down to your car. Thank you all.'

Then, and in a cloud of *wonderful*s and *oh it's so lovely*s from Mrs Porter, he escorted her away.

There were a few seconds of silence until we heard the office doors shut.

'Divine,' said Mrs Pye, faintly.

'She liked your frock,' said Hester, sounding impressed.

'Divine,' said Mrs Pye, again.

'A lovely lady,' said Mr Newton. 'If I can say that in the most respectful of ways.'

'Do you think Mrs Porter knows the royal family?' said Miss Peters. 'Only don't you feel that she probably does?'

'Breeding,' said Mrs Shaw. 'That's what it is. They talk to everyone as if they are equals. That's what they say about the King and Queen.'

'We are all equals,' said Mrs Mahoney. 'Other than their majesties, of course.'

A hubbub of opinion broke out with everyone speaking at once and Mrs Porter getting mixed up in a general debate about the aristocracy and how everything in society was going to change after the war.

When Guy returned a few moments later, emotions were high. Guy, though, was a picture of calm. 'Well done, everyone,' he said. 'Mrs Porter said to say once again how very impressed she was.'

I had a feeling Guy had probably reached a full tank as far as excitable hyperbole went for one afternoon.

'Mr Collins, when shall we see Mrs Porter again, do you think?' asked Hester.

'I've no idea,' said Guy, underestimating the impression Cressida Porter had made. 'She said you all put her mind entirely to rest, so perhaps not for some time.'

Hest's face fell as did those of one or two of the older members of the team.

'She did ask if we could send her some back copies,' he added, 'so could you see what we have, please. I have a forwarding address. And now we'd all better crack on. Well done, again.'

Guy then left to go off to a meeting, and it was something of a relief to get back to the quiet of my desk and focus on work. Being in the company of Mrs Porter was rather exhausting.

I sat down in my chair and paused for a moment before starting to tackle the towering piles of letters in front of me. I wondered what Mrs Porter would make of our problem page. I was sure that rich and titled people had their fair share of concerns as the war and the losses it brought meant the most difficult challenges for people from all walks of life. But there was no doubt that while we were all in it together, things were not the same for everyone, not by a long chalk.

Mrs Porter had been delightful and more than generous in her praise for us, but her world seemed a million miles away from the vast majority of problems we received.

I leaned forward and took a pile of readers' letters from the URGENT box, hoping to make a decent stab at getting through them by the end of the day. As I carefully opened the first and read through it, it brought me back to the real world with a serious crash. If Mrs Porter's visit had been like spending half an hour in fairyland, this reader's reality was a horror story.

Dear Yours Cheerfully

I am writing for your help as I am desperate. I am married to a man who has a horrible temper. He is in the army now but posted near where we live and when he comes home, which is most days, he expects little presents all the time and fancy food. I know that might not sound much, but it's impossible to get hold of anything like that these days, even if we did have the money. It takes almost nothing for him to get very angry with me, and then he gets violent.

I have five children and they are all very scared of him. I manage to keep them out of his way as much as I can, but I am so worried he will turn on them.

I have a friend who says I could get away from him and ask for a divorce, but I don't know if I dare. Can you help me? I'm sorry I can't give you my address or real name. I don't know what he would do if he found out about me writing to you.

Yours,

Mrs 'Enid Smith'

It was far from the first time I had read a letter like this, but it made me sick to my stomach, nevertheless. I would make sure we could find enough room to put some advice into the very next issue, and hope that Enid would be able to escape. What I really wanted to do was go round to wherever she lived and get her and her children out as fast as I could. The postmark on the envelope said Northampton, but there was no other clue to her identity.

This was the sort of problem I knew I would never get used to. There was only so much I could do, and there was never enough room in the magazine to help everyone who needed it.

'We can only do our best,' I said to myself, 'and leave it at work when we go home.'

It was something Mrs Mahoney had taught me. Neither of us was any good at the second part. It was the part of my job that I struggled with the most. I hated leaving problems behind. Or rather, I hated having to walk away from women like Enid.

I thought for several moments and carefully typed a reply. More than anything, I hoped that Enid had somewhere safe where she and her children could go. Then I picked up her letter and went off to see Mrs Mahoney. If anyone could squeeze an extra letter onto a page it was her. She and I had worked together on the problem page until I had taken it over, and there was no one more sympathetic to someone in trouble like this. The look on my face as I handed her the letter gave it away.

'Poor lass,' she said, shaking her head as she read it. 'Leave it to me.'

If not being able to help with letters like this was the worst part of my job, working with Mrs Mahoney was one of the very best.

It had been quite a day.

At the end of the afternoon I reached for my hat and bag, and having said goodbye to my work friends, headed home. I would just have time to make a sandwich and quickly change into my Fire Service uniform before heading off to join Thelma on the telephones. If anything would help leave the sadness of the *Woman's Friend* problem page behind, it would be spending the evening with her. I was well aware of how lucky I was, living with Bunty, and now to be joined by Thel and the children. Tonight it was a stark contrast indeed.

Once safely on the bus, I bagged the nearest seat and opened a letter from my friend Anne that I had picked up from the doormat before leaving the house earlier that day. As it was a fat package I guessed it probably included a drawing by her daughter Ruby, who was nearly six and keen on art, but when I turned the envelope over to open it, I noticed that the back had not been stuck down properly and a picture postcard had become wedged inside. The front had a cartoon picture of the outside of some English pubs, and writing that said *I'm taking my medicine!*

Intrigued, I flipped it over and not recognising the handwriting, scanned the card.

Dear Bunty

This in haste to thank you for your kind letter.

I was very pleased that you remembered me from when Bill introduced me to you and Emmy that time. I really am getting better, thank you.

Tea would be terrific! I'm back in London next week and will call you then.

Best wishes,

Harold

I gave a little gasp.

Harold?

Tea? Bunty? Terrific?

This was news!

Feeling guilty for reading a card meant for my friend, but also finding it rather intriguing, I covered it over with my hand.

Harold. I looked at the card again. '*Bill introduced me to you and Emmy*'. I racked my brain, and then it came to me. Just before I met Charles, Bunty and her fiancé Bill had tried to match me up with one of Bill's old college friends – Harold. While he and I had not hit it off romantically, I remembered him as a smashing chap, a huge, friendly mountain of a man. As far as I knew, Bunty had not heard from him after Bill died, but from this postcard I assumed they had recently been in touch.

And now they were going to have tea. This was very cheery news. Romantic even, despite Bunts being very happy as she was, of course.

The only problem was that now I was going to have to sneak the postcard back onto the table at home, pretend I hadn't seen it, and then feign total surprise should Bunty mention it.

Thelma was going to love this.

I looked out of the window and smiled to myself. The bus couldn't get me back home fast enough.

CHAPTER FIVE

False Teeth Frank

THE FIRST PART of pretending I knew nothing about Harold's postcard went without a hitch as I sneaked it into the afternoon post which was lying on the mat by the front door. This was a lucky break as with Bunty working nights it had been delivered when she was asleep, so I left it in a carefully unsorted heap on the console table in the hall and shot off to the station.

There, Thel was as intrigued as me.

'I'm surprised Bunts didn't tell you when she first heard from him,' she said. 'You two know *everything* that's going on in each other's lives.'

I agreed. 'That's why I'm going to pretend I know absolutely nothing. She'll tell me when she's ready.'

'Well done,' said Thel. 'That's very grown up. And do I presume correctly that as soon as she mentions it you'll give her the third degree?'

'Absolutely,' I said. 'We've known each other since we were five and I can only take maturity so far.'

Thel laughed. She knew I'd do anything in the world for Bunty.

'I won't say a word,' she said, 'although it looks like poor old Frank might need to pull his socks up.'

A few days later we would find out if Frank had.

On Easter Saturday morning, Bunty and I headed up

to the flat to add some welcoming touches for Thelma and the children, who were due to arrive at ten. The rest of the week in the office had flown by with Mrs Shaw, Miss Peters and me flat out answering letters, the numbers of which seemed to get bigger by the day.

Despite the initial excitement, there hadn't been a word from the Honourable Mrs Porter, to the point that it was almost as if her visit had been the sort of overly vivid dream one might have after eating far too much cheese before bed.

With us both working all hours, Bunty and I had hardly seen each other, so now we chatted gaily. Bunts laughed her head off when I told her about Mrs Porter batting her eyelashes at Guy, and then we moved on to congratulating each other on how things had turned out with Thel.

'I know they visit all the time,' said Bunty as she put a plate of oatmeal buttons next to a small vase of daffodils in the flat's tiny kitchen, 'but I want them to know that for as long as they want it, this is their home.'

I agreed wholeheartedly. I'd bought comics for the children, *The Boy's Own Paper* for George, *Girls' Crystal* for Margaret, and this week's *Beano* for Stan. I'd put them on each of their beds as a welcome, the boys in one bedroom, and Margaret sharing the other with her mum.

Bunty rubbed at a mark on top of the old walnut music cabinet in the living room. It hadn't come off when my brother Jack put a glass of water on it not long after she and I had first moved to London and into the flat, and it was highly unlikely to come off now.

'Do you remember how badly you told Jack off about this?' grinned Bunty. 'His first leave in weeks and you had the hugest row.'

'Or when I spilt soup all over the rug?' I said. 'And

Bill told me you'd said it was from Persia and your granny would go berserk if it stained.'

Bunty laughed. 'You believed him too. I've never seen anyone scrub at anything quite so hard.'

'He kept a very straight face,' I said, fondly remembering Bunty's fiancé. He had been a very dear friend.

'The swine!' we both said, together.

'I remember Charles coming here for the first time. I was in such a stew,' I said.

Bunty laughed again. 'And you and I had drunk all that bolstering sherry before he arrived and were absolute idiots. I knew then he really liked you.'

I nodded. 'Most chaps would have run a mile.'

Bunty stopped dusting and sat down on the two-seater sofa by the side of the fire.

'It was good fun when we lived up here, wasn't it?' she said, looking around. 'I do hope they'll like it.'

Bunty and I had shared the top flat since before the war. Her granny, who owned the house, had had it modernised so we had somewhere to live when we announced we wanted to move to London. After Bunty had been injured, she and I had moved down to the main part of the house. It had been easier on a practical level for Bunts, but the flat still held an absolute ton of memories for us both.

'It is going to be lovely to have the children here,' I said. 'They always cheer me up.'

Bunty looked at me. 'Are you all right?' she asked.

'Oh gosh, yes,' I said, sturdily. 'It's just that even with the excitement about Mrs Porter we've still been chock-a-block with letters from readers who are having a horrible time. It doesn't matter how fast I answer them, there are always more.' I shrugged. 'Perhaps it's just the anticlimax after her visit. She was so fluffy and flouncy. You could

47

almost forget there's a war on, let alone the readers who are having a wretched time.'

'You do hear about the worst of the worst in your job,' said Bunts. 'You can't be buoyant all the time. I know you try.'

I smiled. I could fool most people, but not her. 'I had a letter this week,' I said, 'from a woman with an absolute stinker of a husband. Very nasty indeed. I've suggested she goes to court and asks for a separation, but she didn't say if she has anywhere to go to get away from him. I hate to think what he'll do if she can't.'

'Can she go to the police?' asked Bunty.

'Only if she accuses him of common assault,' I said, 'but they'd be likely to tell her she's wasting their time: "It's just a row . . . we don't interfere with marriages . . ." That sort of thing. There's no law against hitting your wife.'

'That is awful,' said Bunty.

'Isn't it?' I said. 'Goodness knows what Mrs Porter will think. I have a feeling some of the letters may come as rather a shock. Still, perhaps she won't get that involved. We haven't seen her since she came into the office on Tuesday. Guy says she's gone on an Easter break.'

'Very nice,' said Bunty. 'A break from what?'

We both laughed.

'Don't be rotten,' I said. 'She did say she does huge amounts of charity work. Anyway, we'll see. I think she'll be more interested in the fashion and beauty side of things. But I'm going to show her some of the letters we get from readers who say that we've helped them. That's a nice thing to start her with.'

Bunty nodded. 'Are you still getting letters from that lady with the twins?'

'Oh, yes,' I said. 'The girls are beautiful.'

Last year, one of our readers had been having a tricky time in the marital department with her young husband, but further to one of our *Intimate Know How* leaflets and some encouraging words, things had fallen into place and the couple were now blissfully happy parents. The reader, Mrs Stone, had sent me a photograph of the twins at Christmas, and just this week dressed as chicks well in advance for an Easter parade. I was enormously touched that she had thought to do it, as camera film was now so hard to come by. I had pinned the chicks up on the noticeboard by my desk, which was where I put all the thank-yous from readers.

It was by far my favourite place in the entire office – letters and postcards and sometimes even photographs. On the days where it felt as if we were swimming against a tidal wave of worries and problems, I would look at them all. Knowing that *Woman's Friend* had helped out was the best feeling in the world.

'Actually,' said Bunty, lightly, 'I had a nice postcard this week. Do you remember Bill's friend Harold?'

'Harold,' I said, quickly scrunching up my eyes and pretending to think.

'We met him the same day we first met Charles. Large chap, Royal Engineers Bomb Disposal,' prompted Bunty.

'Oh yes,' I said, doing a good job of amateur dramatics. 'Harold. In the park. Tall. Jolly.'

'That's him,' said Bunts. 'He got in touch and apologised profusely for not writing when Bill died.'

That must have been in the letter Bunty had replied to. I could be genuinely in the dark about this.

'So, why a card now?' I asked, doing quite well at Being Casually Interested.

'Well,' said Bunts, 'he had actually written before Easter and I'd written back. He's had a pretty rotten time. A bomb exploded and he ended up in the same recuperation hospital they'd sent me to when I had my knock.'

I didn't say anything. Bunty's 'knock' had been what most people would refer to as a catastrophe.

'I think he was in there for some time,' she continued. 'Anyway, it turned out that one of the nurses there had looked after me too. She told him to get in touch. I do hope he's on the mend.'

So did I. While I had only met him briefly, Harold had come across as a thoroughly nice man.

'He asked after you, of course,' said Bunty.

'That's very kind,' I said. 'You will give him my best wishes, won't you? I'm so sorry he was hurt.'

'Of course,' said Bunty. Then she fixed me with a hard stare. 'You read the postcard, didn't you?'

'Yes, I did,' I said.

Bunty burst into laughter. 'You are such a rubbish actress. And how on earth have you managed not to say anything? It came days ago.'

'It's been hideous,' I wailed. 'I'm so relieved it's out in the open. I'm not even going to ask why you've been so cloak and dagger about it, although a full explanation is obviously required.'

'Of course,' said Bunty. 'Hold on. Is that the door?'

We both listened as I checked my wristwatch. It was ten o'clock exactly and someone was ringing the doorbell downstairs.

'They're here!' said Bunty, leaping up and heading to the stairs.

'This does *not* mean you're off the hook,' I said. Then I jumped out of the armchair and hurried after her.

When Bunty opened the front door there was a very excited party queuing to get in. Thelma and the children, all holding varying sizes of bags and packages, were lined up on the steps to the house. Behind them, our friends Fred and Roy from the fire station were laden down as well, and behind *them* was Frank. He was carrying more than anyone, but smiling broadly and looking very smartly turned out for a man doing removals. In the street outside, one of the small fire-service vans was parked up.

'Essential war work,' called out Roy, seeing me look at the van. 'All above board. We're on our way to a not very urgent fire. Who's putting the kettle on?'

'Hello everyone, come on in,' said Bunty as we stood aside so they could all troop through. 'Do you want to dump everything here or go straight up? Top floor if you do – you know where to go. Emmy and I can get more out of the van. Go on, Stan, you lead the way.'

'CHARGE!!!!' shouted Stanley, belting past and tearing up the stairs.

'Sorry about that,' said Thel. 'Are you sure you still want us?'

Bunty grinned as we took it in turns to hug her hello, and then each of the remaining children. Then Fred and Roy asked if they got a hug too which was funny, if a bit awkward when we got to Frank.

'You remember Frank,' I said, heartily, as Bunty took a step back and waved at him from somewhere inside the blackout curtains. You couldn't go around hugging people willy-nilly, after all.

'Very nice to see you, Bunty,' he said, making full use of his dentures to give her a blinding smile.

'Go on, mate,' said Roy from the hallway. I couldn't tell whether it was to make Fred get a move on up the stairs, or to encourage Frank in his burgeoning conversation with Bunty.

'Hello, Frank,' said Bunty, politely. 'How kind of you to help.'

Frank beamed at her as if she had just given him the George Medal.

'Are you all right with that one?' I asked, pointing at the enormous box he was carrying. 'It looks awfully heavy and the flat's at the top of the house.'

'Light as a feather,' replied Frank, gamely.

'That's firemen for you. Tough as old boots,' I said, as Frank deserved a bit of praise for helping out. This only encouraged him though, as two minutes later while Bunty and I were taking some smaller boxes from the back of the van, he shot back outside, flashed another huge smile, and bellowing, 'Allow ME, ladies,' made off with a selection of household accessories at such speed that it made him look as if he'd stolen them.

'I hope you're impressed, Bunty old girl,' said Fred as he arrived back outside. 'I've not seen our Gummy move this fast since someone reported a time bomb at one of the breweries.'

'He's doing a grand job,' said Thelma who was close behind. 'I don't know how we've managed to bring so much with us.' She paused. 'Thank you,' she said. 'The children are so excited to be here. They didn't much like the last place.'

'You're doing me the favour,' insisted Bunty. 'Granny was very pleased when I told her. She took a real shine to you and the children at Emmy's wedding.'

'Speaking of shines,' said Thelma. 'What do you think of Frank?'

'I'm putting the kettle on,' Bunty said, firmly.

'What do you think of his teeth?' whispered Thel as we pulled out two odd-shaped packages wrapped in newspaper, and headed inside. 'He won't mind you telling him they're nice.'

'I'm not listening,' said Bunty, putting her hands over her ears as Stan came thundering down the stairs.

'Thanks for *The Beano*, Aunty Bunts,' he said. 'George has got the bed by the window but I don't mind. I like your house,' he added. 'It doesn't smell.'

Thel rolled her eyes and said she gave up.

'That's very kind of you to say,' said Bunty. '*The Beano* is from Emmy, but I've made rock cakes so that you won't like her more than you like me.'

'Did someone say cakes?' said Roy, who was now on another trip from the van. 'Ladies, you put those down here,' he added to Thelma and me. 'You've got three perfectly able firemen at your service.'

Despite our protestations that we were more than capable of lugging things up a staircase, Roy told us you didn't have a dog and bark yourself and then happily set off to the flat again. A moment later we heard him say, 'Steady on, Frank, it's not the Grand National. Why don't you go down to the kitchen? Get the use out of those new gnashers and give Bunty a bit of a smile.'

With Frank arguing that he would carry up the last of Thel's things, Bunty led the way to the kitchen.

For all the many rooms in the house, we spent by far the most time here. It was the warmest room in the house during the winter and the coolest when it was hot, and it was probably the safest too if there was a raid. We could run down to the shelter in the garden, or take our chances that we wouldn't get buried alive in the house, but most of all it was a homey, welcoming room, with a big wooden table in the middle and two very comfortable fireside chairs set up around a wireless in the corner. A tiny hallway led to two smaller rooms which were never used and the scullery which had a sink you could bath an elephant in. It also had the old meat safe which was rarely bothered as whatever meat we had, we ate.

Now, we made Thelma sit at the table while Bunty filled the kettle, and I started getting out cups for the tea. Soon we were joined by George and Margaret who had been rounded up by Stanley, and all of us managed not to start on the rock cakes until the men had finished racing each other up and down the stairs.

'George wants to know if you might be interested in getting a dog,' said Stan, 'but he's worried about asking, and Marg wondered if she can help you with the vegetable patch, and if we can't have guinea pigs I'd like a pet rat but Mum says there are enough of them in London without us adding to the problem and also, will we definitely have our dinners with you because I don't mind counting up all the coupons if we do.' He paused for breath.

Bunty put down her tea towel and as Thelma suggested Stan try to focus on one subject at a time, she went over to him, and leaning against the table, pondered for a moment.

'Well,' said Bunty, thoughtfully, 'I'm not sure about dogs and rats at the moment, although we can see how things go, but I would be terrifically grateful for help in the garden.' She glanced over at Marg, who was watching keenly. 'And counting coupons would be super. But, most of all – and I want you all to know this – as far as Emmy and I are concerned, this is your home, and as long as your mum is happy, we'll just potter along and sort things out together. Does that sound all right?'

The children said, 'Yes,' very seriously and Thelma put her arm round Bunty and said, 'Thanks, love. We're all pleased as punch to be here.'

Roy arrived with the sound of his heavy boots clomping down the stairs. 'Frank's sprained an elbow,' he said, looking delighted. 'He knows it's his own fault and he says he doesn't like any fuss, but he was wondering if *anyone* might like to help put it in a sling.'

He stared meaningfully at Bunty.

'Poor Frank,' I said, getting up and looking in a drawer for a clean tea towel. 'I'll go. Although I'm sure I'm not his first choice so it will be a crushing disappointment.'

Roy roared with laughter and said he doubted it, and as I started the climb up the stairs I heard him ask the children to tell him about their plans for some pets, and then lots of voices speaking at once.

It was the happiest sound and just what the house needed. In fact, what we all needed. Folding the tea towel into a triangle to start making a sling, I smiled and went off to find Frank.

. . . *Charles, darling, they're here! Thelma and the kids have moved in! It is so lovely to have a full (or at least, full-er) house, and the children are thrilled that we have a bit of a garden. Also, if it doesn't fall down first, they've asked if they can commandeer the shed for a secret society. I have a feeling this actually means that when you come back you'll find we have a lot more four-legged friends than in the past!*

I so wish you were here as we all feel we've had rather a boost. But from what the papers say, I think you must be terrifically busy. It sounds as if you boys and the Americans are giving Hitler what for. The Times reckons they're going to give in at any minute now.

I'm so proud of you, darling. Don't worry about writing if you can't. I think about you a million times a day, but you know that, of course. Everyone sends their love and Stan wants to know if you kept guinea pigs when you were his age . . .

CHAPTER SIX

One or Two Tiny Ideas

WE SPENT THE Easter weekend helping Thelma and the children settle in, and as planned, on Saturday afternoon Bunty, Thel and I sat down with our ration books and weekly diaries. Now that there were three of us, or rather, six as George had pointed out, sharing the cooking and shopping would make life a lot easier. Food shopping these days really just meant queuing for ages and hoping there was something worth the wait at the end of it. There wasn't a woman in Britain who didn't have an almighty struggle. It wasn't like the old days where you could dash out to the market in your lunch break, or leave it until convenient during your day. 'Leaving it' meant there wouldn't be anything left to eat.

Now we planned carefully around the three grown-ups' work schedules, enthusiastically looking through cookery books to find easy recipes that fed six and made small amounts of anything go far. ('You *do* like leeks, Stanley, you just haven't realised it yet.') It took no time at all to realise that there was a good chance things really could become easier for us all.

On Easter Sunday, Thelma and I worked a shift at the fire station and came home to parsnip pie, followed by fruit-flavoured junket. Thelma hadn't had to worry because Bunty was at home with the children, and we were all delighted that in turn Bunts had roped in the children to help with the vegetables as well as some of the washing up.

Afterwards we all went out into the garden where, after the triumph of Sunday lunch, morale took a temporary knock. The children were keen to see if the old shed could be put to duty, but when Bunty opened the door one of the very rusty hinges gave way and she was lucky not to get squashed.

'The whole thing's on its last legs,' she said, trying to jam it back shut. 'Sorry kids, we'll have to try to fix it before we can think about anything else.'

If ever there was a call to arms, as far as the Jenkins children were concerned, this was it.

'Don't worry, Bunty,' said Margaret, 'we'll fix it. Were you in the Girl Guides? Do you know the motto?'

'Um, not exactly,' said Bunty, who had been thrown out of the First Little Whitfield company in 1929 for talking.

'I was,' I said, because I hadn't been thrown out and in fact had made it all the way to becoming a highly despotic Patrol Leader. 'Do you mean, *To do my duty to God and the King*?'

'*Be prepared*,' said Marg, patiently.

'I'm getting my woodwork books,' called George, already on his way to the house.

'I'll do a sign,' offered Stanley.

'Do you remember the days when we would have just propped it up and sat down with a sherry instead?' asked Bunty, rubbing her head.

'I did warn you,' said Thelma. 'They're very keen.'

They were an utter delight.

On Tuesday morning, I returned to the office feeling full of beans and with Stan's well-worn copy of *The Wonder Book of Pets* to read on the bus. With things at home sorted in the best possible way, I could focus on work. Guy had said it would be nice to have some idea of how our new owner wished him to report to her with the day-to-day workings of the business, but for my part, I was happy to settle down and focus on writing to and for the readers.

To that end, Guy, Mrs Pye and I sat down together in the meeting room to go through our current plans for the magazine over the next three months.

'If we have space I'd like to propose running a series of features on the most common problems,' I said. 'We're struggling to keep up with them, even though Miss Peters' glands have settled so we're at full strength.'

'Good idea,' said Guy.

Mrs Pye sniffed. 'I am doing my best with the contributors,' she said, 'even though some of them are awfully slow. Mr Collins, are you quite sure I can't look for someone younger to replace Mrs Croft?'

'Absolutely not,' said Guy, sternly. 'You know my view. How are the others getting on?'

Mrs Pye pursed her lips and looked at her notebook. 'Mrs Stevens on knitting is hardly haute couture, but she is good on deadlines. Mrs Fieldwick always sends her copy in on time, Nurse McClay is difficult, and Mr Trevin is a struggle if the moon is in the wrong place. But that's artistic people for you.' She looked at me over her half-glasses. 'Les artistes, you know.'

'Mrs Pye,' sighed Guy. 'Mr Trevin is just making up horoscopes, not writing *War and Peace*, so I would be much obliged if he could brace up. Now, how about your assistant? Have you managed to find anyone who might fit the bill?'

Mrs Pye readjusted her spectacles and put her hand to her hair, checking that everything was in place before she spoke.

'It is very hard to find the right sort,' she replied. 'Miss Lake is lucky – anyone can open envelopes for her. But I need someone with talent and flair and a sense of what is à la mode. That means fashionable, Miss Lake,' she added, for my benefit.

'Thank you,' I said, wondering whether to mention that I'd got a credit in French in my School Cert.

'Well, very good and keep going,' said Guy, as if Mrs Pye was trying to do a four-minute mile. 'We aren't looking for anyone swank and bear in mind we may have to run it past Mrs Porter as she'll be in charge of the purse strings.' He broke off as the sound of laughter came from outside the room. 'Nice to know everyone's happy,' he added, unperturbed.

A mild shriek followed and what sounded like clapping. Guy looked towards the door.

'Have we missed someone's birthday?' he asked.

'I don't think so,' I said. 'If we're finished here I'll see what's going on. I hate to miss out on a hoot.'

'Excellent,' said Guy. 'Mrs Pye and I can nail down the details of an assistant.'

I picked up my notebook and closing the door behind me, headed across the corridor into the old journalists' room. There I was greeted by the sight of Mrs Shaw, Miss Peters and Hester, together with Mr Newton, congregated in a semicircle, their faces a picture of delight as they listened to a woman who was regaling them with what must have been the most entertaining yarn.

'And that is when I said I must pop in to see you all – my team!' she cried, with a flourish of her arms.

'Good morning, Mrs Porter,' I said. 'What a lovely surprise.'

Mrs Porter swung round, her face radiant. 'Miss Lake! Look at you!'

She held out her hand and I shook it, as she clutched mine warmly with both gloved hands.

'And where is your lovely Mr Collins?' she asked.

'He's just finishing a meeting,' I said. 'Might I get him for you?'

'I mustn't intrude,' she said, opening her eyes very wide at me.

Today the Honourable Mrs Porter was in an immaculately cut brown suit, offset with a chic straw boater which was perched on top of her perfect brunette curls.

'He will be delighted to see you,' I said, brightly.

'How kind,' trilled Mrs Porter. She turned back to the others and added conspiratorially, 'I mustn't keep you a moment more from your wonderful work. Do enjoy the sweeties.'

Then she waved gaily, and as I held the door open for her, I was struck by the strange sight of three grown adults and a teenager all holding small paper bags and waving as if Mrs Porter was the local Carnival Queen being driven past on a float.

'Just some treats,' she smiled, 'home-made so they don't count.'

I tried to picture Mrs Porter anywhere near a kitchen, but came up short, so just said, 'How very thoughtful,' and knocked on the meeting-room door, before poking my head in.

'Mrs Porter for you, Mr Collins,' I said as if she had been entirely expected.

Guy and Mrs Pye rose to their feet and Mrs Porter tapped me on the shoulder as a signal to get out of her way.

'Mr Collins,' she sang, floating elegantly over to Guy, where she took his hand and greeted him like the old friend he now was. Meanwhile, I hovered by the door not knowing whether to stay or go, and Mrs Pye watched our publisher as if this was a visitation from her favourite saint. She did not have to wait long for a heavenly sign.

Letting go of Guy, Mrs Porter put her bag down and then clasped her hands to her chest, and as there was a wide table between them which would have meant an unseemly trot around the perimeter to shake hands, she held out her arms towards Mrs Pye rather as if she was about to accept a bouquet.

'Madame!'

If God himself had pointed a finger through the clouds and into Launceston House, it could not have had greater effect. Pamela Pye's face took on the sublime glow of a truly religious experience.

'Mrs Porter,' she breathed. 'Quel honneur.'

Had Pamela actually bowed? Guy closed his eyes. I stared at an ink stain on the wall where Hester's fountain pen had exploded during Any Other Business the week before last.

'Mrs Porter,' said Guy, with commendable control. 'What a delightful surprise. We had no idea you were planning to drop by. I would have ordered us tea.'

'You MUST call me Egg,' cried Mrs Porter. 'And you mustn't dream of treating me any differently to anyone else. I am simply a member of staff. You won't know I am here.'

I wasn't sure about that, but Guy didn't react, and continued to be charming, even if he couldn't quite manage to squeeze out an Egg.

'Mrs Pye and I were just discussing some editorial plans. Would you like to sit down?'

'I won't interrupt,' said Mrs Porter, looking at the chair which was refusing to move on its own.

I stepped forward and pulled it away from the table so that she could sit down.

'Really, Miss Lake, no need,' she said, after it was too late. 'I don't want to be a bother.'

'Should Mrs Pye and I leave?' I asked, which I realised was a mistake as Mrs Pye looked at me as if casting a plague upon my family. 'Or perhaps, stay?' I added.

'How lovely,' said Mrs Porter.

Guy looked as if he didn't care if a herd of elephants was about to join in.

'Did you enjoy your break, Mrs Porter?' he asked, politely.

'So deliciously formal,' sighed Mrs Porter. 'Adorable man. I realise it's a sign of respect.'

'Ah,' said Guy.

'And yes, I did enjoy the break, although it was far from a rest. But that's just me.' She beamed at us. 'Oh, I am glad you are all here.' She opened her bag, a beautiful leather briefcase. 'It was so kind of you to send copies of the magazine. You are all so *very* clever.'

Mrs Porter took out a number of cuttings, together with a large, exquisitely bound notebook. Then she looked at each of us in turn with a very pretty smile.

'Shall I begin? You don't mind do you, Mr Collins? I am the new girl here.'

Guy's smile looked a little more strained than before, but if he was anything like me and wondering what was coming next, he didn't give it away.

'Of course,' he said.

'Wonderful. It's nothing very much,' said Mrs Porter. 'I have a brain the size of a pea so these are just one or two tiny ideas, and of course, you don't have to listen to any of them. *Woman's Friend* is quite splendid in its own way. But let's be honest,' she said, suddenly looking sad, 'and I think I can say this as we're all friends. It could do with a bit of a boost.'

There was a pause.

'A boost,' repeated Guy.

Mrs Porter nodded, and then leaned towards me and dropped her voice. 'I'm sure you've heard this before, but I'm afraid that in parts it does come across as A Bit Mis.'

She turned the corners of her mouth down as if she had come to the part of a children's storybook where a princess goes missing and all the villagers feel rather low.

'I'm so sorry, Mrs Porter,' I managed to say, 'but what exactly do you mean by *A Bit Mis*?' I glanced quickly at Guy.

Mrs Porter became sympathetic. 'Dear Miss Lake,' she said, 'you mustn't be upset. All I mean is that sometimes, things do come across as somewhat glum, don't they?' She whipped out a cutting. 'Look at this. "Woman's Friend to Friend" – such a lovely idea for readers to share their thoughts, and there's a darling tip about stockings. But then the rest of it is taken up with letters about what kind of horrid new houses people will live in after the war, and how some sort of social service could prop up people who can't be bothered to work.' Mrs Porter shook her head, at a loss. 'And that's before we even get to the readers' problems.' She pulled out another piece from the magazine. 'People complaining about their dreary husbands or dreadful mothers, or in a fluster about unwanted babies. It's all just A Bit Mis.' She sighed, heavily. 'Do you see?'

None of us said a word.

It was like being walloped in the face with a powder puff the size of a dustbin lid. It looked soft and fluffy, but before you realised it, you'd been sent flying.

Mrs Porter was looking at us as if we had all just pitched up from a Dickensian orphanage, covered in dirt, and leaving marks on the furniture.

As I was the nearest, she gave me one of her reassuring pats.

'Now, now,' she said. 'You should all be terrifically proud of how well you have done. These tiny offices, awful décor, virtually no staff. It's a wonder you're still going. But You Must Not Despair. Help Is Here.'

'Mrs Porter,' said Guy, who I knew for a fact had, until the last ten minutes anyway, not been despairing in the least.

'No, no.' Mrs Porter raised her hand in its pretty glove. 'It's not your fault. No one could have done more. As much as I loved my dear uncle, and would never speak ill of the dead, I can hardly imagine what he was thinking. I mean, look at the beastly paper you print on. I can almost see through it. And your models! The poor loves. Where *do* you find them?'

At this point, Mrs Pye sat up bolt straight.

'Dear madame,' said Mrs Porter, adjusting a curl that had dared to move from its assigned position. 'It must cut you to the quick. How well you have coped. These awful photographs and ugly mannequins. And "On Duty for Beauty" full of letters about chilblains. This is not fashion.'

'Mrs Porter.' Now Guy spoke just slightly more strongly. 'If I might interrupt.'

Cressida Porter put her hand to her throat and looked injured. 'But of course.'

'Thank you.' He took a breath. 'Mrs Porter, I very much appreciate your interest in the editorial side of the magazine, but perhaps I can suggest we take a step back. It would be my pleasure to talk you through the way in which *Woman's Friend* is run, the audience we write for and how we design the magazine's content specifically for them. And I can go through the publishing side of what

65

we do, the finances – advertising and circulation revenues, the production needs and restrictions – particularly while we are at war – and naturally staffing. Now that's a very simplified summary, but it is at the heart of what you, as our publisher and owner, will want to know. That is, of course, if your plan is to be involved in the day-to-day running of *Woman's Friend*. I do appreciate that you must be very busy already.'

Mrs Porter looked at Guy, her face entirely expressionless. 'That sounds awfully stuffy,' she said.

'I'm sorry,' replied Guy. 'I'm afraid that's rather what being a magazine publisher entails. It's not frightfully glamorous. But we all love it here and very much hope you will too.' He smiled warmly. I had to admire our editor. He was trying hard to bring Mrs Porter on board.

But Guy had met his match.

'The thing is,' explained Mrs Porter, gazing at him with enormous eyes, 'stuffy things are not really my bag.' She blinked her eyelashes several times.

'How about giving them a go?' said Guy.

It was like watching two grand masters at something complicated and dangerous engage in a ceremonial dance before they tried to chop each other up into small bits.

'Mmm, no thank you,' said Mrs Porter, bringing the ceremonial dance to an abrupt end. 'I'd rather tell you all my lovely ideas. I have done research,' she added.

'Really?' said Guy. He ran his hand through his hair. 'Goodness.'

Mrs Porter smiled happily and wrinkled her nose at him. 'Thank you!' she cried as if he'd just bought her an ice cream as a surprise. 'I shall refer to my notes.'

I glanced at Mrs Pye, who was entirely agog, but I was still trying to make sense of Mrs Porter's comments. Had she really just eviscerated almost everything I worked on for *Woman's Friend*? More importantly, was she dismissing the parts of the magazine that were most obviously for and about the readers? I sat forward in my seat, concerned about what might come next.

'It's just one or two little ideas,' she said. 'Just the sort of thing that will cheer the readers up. Here we are. Better fashion – pretty models for a start – more on make-up and less on spots – ghastly. Less dreariness – if we must have careers then might we jazz them up? And far cheerier problems – the ones about affairs give a racier feel which is fun. Now, this is important – less ugly babies in the knitting section, which I can help with as all the ones I know are delightful. Also, please stop mentioning the Government as nobody wants to know, and can we have more advertisements about lovely places like Harrods, rather than dismal pictures of gravy. There,' she finished. 'That was all. But of course, they are only ideas. My friends said I mustn't overwhelm you even though it's not my fault I am creative.'

'Your friends?' said Guy.

'Oh yes,' said Mrs Porter. 'They helped with my research. I asked them all what they thought and they all agreed with everything I said.'

'Are they readers of *Woman's Friend*?' I asked.

Mrs Porter burst into laughter.

'Don't be ridiculous,' she replied.

'In that case . . .' I began.

'But they will be,' interrupted Mrs Porter, her brightest smile switching on like an anti-aircraft searchlight. 'If we could just make these tiny, *infinitesimal* changes. What do you all think?'

I looked at Guy. Mrs Pye looked at Guy. Guy looked at Mrs Porter.

'Well,' he said.

'Hurrah!' Mrs Porter took 'Well' as 'Absolutely'. She clapped her hands together. 'Oh, Mr Collins. Miss Lake. Madame,' she whooped. 'It's all going to be so lovely. Thank you so much. How soon can you start?'

CHAPTER SEVEN

Not In The Least Mis

MRS PORTER TALKED non-stop for the next half an hour about all her ideas, most of which were Gorgeous and Fun and Not In The Least Bit Mis.

'We'll set up a photographic studio at an hotel and all my friends shall model for us!'

'Surely twelve guineas isn't that much for a coat?'

'But if one doesn't visit the couturiers in London, where on earth does one go?'

I could hardly bear to listen.

By the end of the meeting, even Mrs Porter appeared to realise that she had caused something of a stir.

'They are just my little ideas,' she said, 'but I have realised that this is my calling, and I believe that Lord Overton, God rest his darling soul, could see that. It is time to bring *Women's Friend* into a new era.'

'It's *WomAn's Friend*,' I said.

'Is it?' said Mrs Porter. 'Oh.' She paused and then in a forlorn voice, added, 'Miss Lake, is something the matter? Was it my thoughts on the ugly babies? I'm so sorry. It's just I only know ones that are pretty.'

I shook my head. 'Mrs Porter,' I said, 'the features you've pointed out as depressing or dull are some of our readers' favourite parts of the magazine. I'm not trying to blow my own trumpet, but we work awfully hard to write about the things that matter to them. The problem page and "Woman's Friend to Friend", and the war-work features – the response from the readers is always terrific.'

Mrs Porter stared at me.

'Miss Lake is entirely right,' said Guy. 'The new ideas are very exciting and we must of course look into them all. But modesty aside, *Woman's Friend* is currently enjoying its highest circulation for years, and we wouldn't be doing our jobs if we didn't ensure that you know how we've achieved that.'

He was a far better diplomat than me, but it was clear that Guy was completely in agreement.

Mrs Porter gave us both the saddest little smile. 'Oh, you two,' she said. 'Such serious little faces.'

Then she gave me one of her reassuring pats on the arm and before I could come up with something, or indeed *anything* to say in response, she turned to Guy.

'Mr Collins, I am entirely in your hands. I know I am very new here but I feel *so* confident with you by my side.' She paused for a moment, now looking demure. 'Lady Overton, my darling aunt, said you would look after me. "Aunt Victoria," I said, when we learned I would be in charge. "What if I can't do it?" and she replied, "My dearest Egg, Guy Collins has never let your uncle or me down, and I promise he won't let *you* down either."'

Mrs Porter paused and put the back of her hand to her mouth for a moment.

She was laying it on with a trowel.

'We were both tremendously moved,' she finished.

'That was very kind of her ladyship,' Guy began. 'However . . .'

Mrs Porter's eyes had begun to fill with tears. Guy looked aghast.

'I'm fine,' she managed. 'It's very difficult. Now I really must go.'

'Of course. I'm so sorry,' said Guy, unable to say anything much else. 'Can we find you a taxi cab?'

'No, no,' said Mrs Porter, 'my driver is downstairs.' She looked at her wristwatch. 'Oh my word, I must fly or the shops will be shut.' The thought of beating the clock against closing time appeared to give our publisher great solace as she quickly perked up. 'I can see myself out,' she chirruped, 'although, perhaps Madame Pye could accompany me as I would so very much like to chat about millinery. Where, may I ask, do you stand on the visored beret?'

Well and truly outmanoeuvred, Guy and I mustered the necessary goodbyes.

Mrs Pye then fulfilled her life's destiny by finding an unnecessary reason to leave via the journalists' room so that she could flounce off to talk about hats with an aristocrat while the rest of the team stood to attention.

'Mrs Porter is like a Hollywood film star,' whispered Hester as our publisher waved her goodbyes and told everyone off for not yet eating their treats.

'Isn't she?' agreed Mrs Shaw.

It was all I could do to bite my tongue and not blurt out to the team what had just happened. The worst thing was that if you hadn't just heard Mrs Porter crush something you put your entire heart and soul into, Hester was right.

On the surface, Mrs Porter was exuberant – radiant almost – and she dished out compliments faster than she did fudge, although as she did that too it made her even easier to like. While the rest of us had jobs where every day we battled to bring cheer and hope and information to tens of thousands of women who were facing the most challenging of times, Mrs Porter had arrived like a fairy materialising on stage in a puff of smoke, all sparkly and smashing, and completely at odds with the real world.

But the *tiny, infinitesimal* changes she wanted to make to *Woman's Friend* added up to a completely different magazine to the one she had inherited. And more to the point, the one that meant the entire world to me. It wasn't that I was against change, or that I thought everything we did was better than anyone else could do, but to just dump *all* of it?

Because when you got down to it, that's what Mrs Porter was proposing to do.

I was shaken out of my thoughts by Mrs Shaw asking if I was free.

'There's such a lot to go through,' she said, then she nodded towards a large pile of letters on a desk. 'Honestly, the pickles people are in. Still, this is a nice one.' She handed me a postcard.

Dear Woman's Friend,

Thank you for printing my letter about finding friends and getting out of the house. I've joined a sewing group and the ladies are very friendly. I was worried you would think I was wasting your time writing in, but I am very glad I did. The other ladies say their babies drive them round the bend sometimes too, so now I don't feel I'm putting it on. I feel ever so much better now they've said I'm not making a fuss.

Yours,

Mrs R. Bagley, Evesham

Mrs Bagley had said more about what was worth fighting for in *Woman's Friend* than I ever could.

'Of course, Mrs Shaw,' I said. 'I'll be with you in five minutes.'

Guy's office door was open and he was sitting at his perennially cluttered desk sucking on a cigarette while opening a new packet at the same time.

I went in, closed the door behind me, and without being asked, sat down.

Guy said nothing, but continued to smoke thoughtfully. I waited for a while and as the silence began to feel heavy, spoke up.

'Is Mrs Porter serious? You know, about ripping up the entire magazine?'

Guy stubbed out his cigarette, grinding it into the ashtray that was balanced on top of a heap of papers.

'I don't know,' he said, flatly. 'I'm trying to work it out.'

'I was hoping you might tell me I'm overreacting,' I prompted. 'You know, calm down, keep your hair on. That sort of thing.' I was trying hard to bring some levity, but Guy didn't respond. 'She's charmed the team,' I added, 'but then they haven't heard about her Tiny Ideas.'

'Mrs Porter is certainly beguiling,' said Guy, 'and if you like rich, frivolous women who hide their intelligence as a tactical move, then she's an all-round delight. But I fear the Egg is not half as daft as she makes out.'

'Do you trust her?' I said, wishing he would be rather less honest. I hadn't seen him this subdued in a very long time.

He sat back in his chair and narrowed his eyes. 'No. Do you?'

Now Guy lit up another cigarette and took a long drag on it as he tapped his fingers on his desk. The stack of papers threatened to topple over, and he stopped and wedged them up against an Anglepoise lamp.

'I trust that she wants to change *Woman's Friend*,' I said. 'But I didn't quite understand the business about Lady Overton.'

'Mmm. Dramatic, wasn't it?' he said, tapping ash into the ashtray, 'Late last week I had a letter from her ladyship. I'd sent my condolences of course when Lord O died, but it was some time before she replied. I think losing him has hit her very hard.' He paused and then looked at me seriously. 'The letter was brief, but she said she knew there might be some changes when Cressida arrived, and that she hoped I would look after, and here I quote her directly, "my dear old *Woman's Friend*."'

'By which she meant, babysit Mrs Porter?' I said, unsure.

Now Guy shrugged. 'I assume so,' he said. 'And keep the magazine going. I can't imagine Lady Overton speaking in quite the histrionic terms that her niece relayed, but nevertheless, her letter does rather support what Mrs Porter said. I have been here a long time, Emmy, and I've known the family even longer. You know I was in the last war with their youngest son?'

I nodded. Charles had told me the story. Guy and Teddy Overton were good friends. When Teddy was very badly hurt in a gas attack, Guy got him to a field hospital and made sure that he was sent back from the Front. Two months later Teddy died at his parents' home in England. Guy stayed in France in the army until the end of the war. Years later, when Guy was struggling to find work as a journalist, or from what I understood, struggling to find any type of work at all, Lord Overton gave him a job.

'I will find a way to make this work,' said Guy. 'Today may have just been all talk. Half of it was ludicrous so I damn well hope so. But Mrs Porter is our owner. She could get rid of us all on a whim. If she likes us, though, and we try to work with her, perhaps she will listen.'

He gave me a slight, thoughtful smile.

'And if she doesn't?' I countered. 'We can't let her ruin everything. Look at this.'

I handed him the postcard from Mrs Bagley. He read it and looked thoughtful.

'I understand, Emmy,' he said, 'I really do. We'll see if we can limit some of the wilder ideas and encourage Mrs Porter to appreciate that we're here to help people as well as entertain them. If nothing else, hopefully she'll realise we can make her a lot of money by doing what we already do. But we have to tread carefully.'

'Are you telling me I've got to suck up to her?' I replied, managing a grin.

'I'm asking you to try to find some common ground. The others will see through the fudge and the froth soon enough, and we're going to have to keep their spirits up.'

I took a deep breath. 'Right you are,' I said. 'I fully intend to start taking more of an interest in hats.' Now I laughed. 'You'll see. Me and Mrs Pye, fighting over Mrs Porter by talking about berets. It'll be horrendous.'

'Admirable approach,' said Guy. 'Just don't ask me for some sort of expense account in order to keep up.' He smiled. 'We will make this work. Now come on. Let's go and get some of those sweets.'

★

At the end of the day I headed for home. Thel and I were on the late shift at the fire station and I was looking forward to dinner with our new extended family before we needed to leave.

Tonight we were being treated to the result of pooling our coupons. Thelma was in charge of dinner, and the rare and much loved smell of cheese floating up from the kitchen and into the hallway was a more than welcome delight. As ever, I checked the post on the hall table, in case there was something from Charles, which there wasn't. I always told myself that it was quite extraordinary that letters could be sent to and from him when we were a thousand miles apart in the middle of a war, but it didn't stop the stab of disappointment when nothing was there.

I headed downstairs where Thelma was at the cooker, and the children were sitting around the kitchen table in their school uniforms. George and Margaret were doing their homework and Stan was practising his drawing by copying pictures of American airplanes from a pamphlet entitled *Aircraft Identification: Friend or Foe?*. Bunty was in the far corner fiddling with the wireless, while a huge ball of navy blue wool together with her knitting needles sat in the occasional chair next to it. Someone would be enjoying a very comfy pair of thick socks before long.

'Evening all,' I called as I came in. 'That smells like heaven.'

Thelma looked round and grinned. 'It's what you get for using six people's cheese ration for the week in one meal. Close your eyes and pretend it's 1938.'

'You're kidding,' said Bunty, coming over to look in the saucepan and breathing in the cheese sauce. 'That's twelve ounces. I thought it smelled good.'

'I've not used quite that much,' admitted Thel, wiping her hand across her forehead, 'and I've made enough for at least two meals, so it's not pre-war standard. But there's a dose of mustard in there too so it should be decent enough.'

I joined my friends at the cooker and leaned over it, inhaling deeply as Bunty had done.

'Oh my word, you're a magician. Why on earth didn't you move in sooner?' I asked.

Thel laughed.

'Mum's the best cook, ever,' said Stanley, not looking up from where he was carefully colouring in a Curtiss Hawk. 'Everyone says.'

George and Margaret nodded their heads earnestly.

'She certainly is,' I replied. Bunty and I were both pretty handy in the kitchen, but this was a joy.

'It smells so good, I think I might actually weep,' said Bunty, dramatically. 'Can I taste the sauce?'

Thelma handed her a clean teaspoon and told her she was worse than the kids.

I sat down at the table next to Stan and asked the children how school had been, to which George replied darkly that he had had double History, which suggested things had been a bit grim, and Margaret said she had been fastest up the climbing ropes in gym, which it was clear meant a very good day. Stan just said, 'All right, thank you,' and carried on colouring.

'Gosh, Stan, they're good,' I said, looking over his shoulder. 'You must show them to my brother when he's next here.'

Stan looked up. 'Really?' he said in slightly hushed tones. A real, live member of the RAF looking at his aeronautical pictures was a serious thought. 'I've got better ones in our room.'

'He'll want to see those, too,' I said, and Stan grinned as if Christmas had been moved to the week after next.

'Did you open lots of letters today, Aunty Em?' Marg asked. In her eyes, being sent letters by people who I didn't even know was one of the best jobs ever.

'Tons,' I said. 'And our new boss turned up again.'

'Is that the fluffy lady?' said Stan. 'The one that kept touching your arm?'

'All right, Big Ears,' said Thelma. 'Grown-ups talking.'

'It *was* the fluffy lady,' I confirmed, realising that when I had been chatting to Thelma at the weekend my words had been fully overheard. 'Once again she was dressed up to the nines. She looked smarter than I did at my own wedding.'

'You looked lovely,' said Bunty, opening a drawer. 'Didn't you reckon she wouldn't come in very often?'

'I was wrong,' I said. 'Mrs Porter has lots of Ideas. She wants to change *everything*. Oh, and she brought in bags of fudge and still wants Guy to call her Egg. It's been an interesting day.'

'Fudge?' said all the children at once.

'What kind of a name is Egg?' said Thelma, shaking her head at the saucepan.

'Her name's Cressida,' I said. 'So . . .'

'Egg and cress – yes, I get why,' said Thel. 'But still. A grown woman. At work.'

Bunty grinned. 'I wonder if she's ever actually been "at work" before? It's probably a bit new. What do you mean about her changing everything?'

'Ah,' I said, 'apparently, Mrs Porter has decided that *Woman's Friend* is not quite as wonderful as she had first thought. In fact lots of it, especially the readers' letters, is all A Bit Mis.'

'Don't be daft,' said Bunts, looking up from where she was counting out cutlery.

Thel stopped what she was doing and turned round.

'What does A Bit Mis mean?' asked Stanley.

'Go and wash your hands, you lot,' said Thelma, 'but clear that table first, please. Dinner's nearly ready.'

As the three children dutifully got up to do as they were told, she frowned and mouthed, 'Let's talk later,' at Bunty and me.

'You all right?' said Bunty, quietly.

I nodded. 'It'll be fine. Guy says we're going to have to be careful.'

'Cripes,' said Bunty.

Thel said, 'Hmm,' and turned back to the cooker. She fished out a piece of macaroni with a fork to test if it was ready. Biting into the pasta, and happy with its texture, she hauled the pan over to the sink and poured the contents into a colander.

'Egg,' she said again, through a cloud of steam.

'Guy's refusing to say it,' I said. 'You'll get his full review on Saturday. I'm on an early at the station, so he may call round in the afternoon.'

'Oh,' said Bunty and then paused. 'Actually, I won't be here. I'll be out at tea with a friend. Well, one of Bill's friends really. Goodness, this fork's dirty.'

Thel stopped lugging pasta around for a moment before she shook the colander briskly and with a total lack of subtlety, said, 'Who's that then?'

I could see where Stanley got his forthright approach.

'His name's Harold,' said Bunty, going over to where she had left her knitting. 'The chap I mentioned to you, Em. He was one of Bill's friends, Thel. Look at this wool, it's all tangled.'

'That'll be nice,' I said, which was good going as really I wanted to say, 'I can't believe you've let me go on about Mrs Porter when you have vitally interesting information about meeting up with Harold.' Instead, I fixed my voice at a mild level and asked where they were meeting.

'Wimbledon,' said Bunty. 'In the village. He's in lodgings there.'

'Lovely,' I said. 'Did he write to you write again?'

'He did.'

'Smashing,' I said.

'Oh for goodness' sake.' There was a loud crash as Thelma dropped half the macaroni into the sink. 'Blast.'

She whirled round and handed her eldest son a large serving spoon. 'George, can you come and scoop this out and into that pan, please. No one will know.' She put her hands on her hips. 'Right,' she said. 'While George retrieves our dinner, can you two please stop being so bloody polite – close your ears kids, you didn't hear that. Bunty, tell me everything I need to know about this Harold chap, where *exactly* you are meeting him, *what* he said in his letter and *whether* or not we are allowed to get very over-interested about a nice man who is taking you out. And yes, Emmy did mention him to me in absolute confidence, but I'm a hopeless liar and I can't keep it up.'

Other than George who was busy saving the day at the sink, all eyes turned to Bunty, who was now holding her knitting to her chest as if it was her first-born child under an immediate threat.

'Well,' she said. 'He's called Harold and I'm just popping over for tea.'

CHAPTER EIGHT

We'll All Have the Fish

IT WAS LOVELY to have something jolly lined up at home, because as far as work was concerned, since the arrival of Mrs Porter things had taken a turn for the completely upside down. If I had had any concern that I was over-reacting, when I told Bunty and Thelma about the meeting with the Tiny Ideas, their response said I certainly was not.

'But *Woman's Friend* is a raging success,' said Bunty. 'Why change things that people like?'

'More to the point,' said Thelma, 'if she *does*, there won't be much of Emmy's job left.'

Put like that, things felt even worse.

Our new owner had not returned to the office. For the next twenty-four hours, there was complete radio silence.

Then the telephone rang. And didn't really stop.

Mrs Porter had found the *Woman's Friend* offices upset-tingly dreary, with nowhere lovely for her to sit down and think. She felt, she said, better suited to pursue more Tiny Ideas at her London home, a 'dear little terrace' on one of the capital's most splendid squares in Mayfair. As a result, we did not see her for the rest of the week.

Unfortunately, whenever Mrs Porter thought of some-thing, she would immediately telephone Guy, or if he was unavailable, Mrs Pye. If Mrs Pye was not available either, which was unlikely as she had quickly stopped answering the phone to anyone else, then Mrs Porter would move on to Mrs Mahoney or me.

Guy and I had not shared the full details of Mrs Porter's crushing review of the magazine with the rest of the team as we were determined to turn her views round, and to her unusual credit Pamela Pye had managed to keep quiet as well. Morale, therefore, remained high.

It wasn't long, however, before Mrs Porter's constant phone calls began to make their mark.

*

'Mr Collins,' said Mrs Mahoney, in the editorial meeting the following week, 'would you mind explaining to Mrs Porter that we can't change what goes in the magazine right up to the minute it appears in the shops?'

'I'll add it to the list,' said Guy.

'And that our readers can probably wait another week to hear about the Duchess of Somewhere's nice shoes.'

'Russell & Bromley,' breathed Mrs Pye, as if someone had mentioned the Pope. 'In blue and wine calf.'

'I don't care what they are,' said Mrs Mahoney, unmoved. 'I'm not calling the printers and saying, "Stop the press, there's an emergency update about feet."'

There was a knock on the door and Hester appeared.

'Sorry to interrupt,' she said. 'Mr Collins, it's Mrs Porter calling.'

'Of course,' said Guy, getting up. 'Excuse me, everyone. I will return.'

'Mrs Porter has so many inspiring ideas,' said Mrs Pye, 'which she so graciously shared with me during our tête-à-tête yesterday. We share so much common ground.'

Mrs Mahoney rolled her eyes. Mrs Shaw groaned out loud. Pamela Pye had not stopped talking about the previous day's shopping trip since she had come into the office especially early to show off.

'Of course,' I said, and settled back for a short lecture on how none of the rest of us could possibly understand.

Thankfully, Mrs Pye was cut off when Guy shortly returned. 'Sorry all,' he said. 'Emmy, Mrs Porter would like to see us for lunch.'

'That's better than going to the shops,' said Mrs Shaw, pointedly.

Mrs Pye sniffed.

'We'll see,' said Guy, 'Emmy, have you ever been to The Savoy?'

I had not.

The Savoy was one of London's finest hotels and unsurprisingly, Mrs Porter thought it an altogether more desirable location in which to have a meeting. Half an hour later, as Guy and I walked under the grand steel canopy which announced the name of the hotel in magnificent lettering, I had to admit I agreed.

There may have been stacks of sandbags up against the outside of the building, but once through the revolving doors, it was another matter. The Front Hall offered a splendid welcome with its sky-high ceiling and black and white marbled floor, its huge pillars making everything appear even more grand.

I had never imagined myself lunching here, and if I had, I wouldn't have been wearing a darned cotton skirt, sensible cardigan, and crepe-soled lace-up shoes. My hair wasn't up to much either as two night shifts and my National Fire Service cap had done their worst. For the first time ever, I was glad there was a war on as at least I had an excuse for looking somewhat below par.

Guy, meanwhile, was taking everything in his stride. He was one of those people who you felt could go anywhere and they would fit in. It came as little surprise when the gentleman on the reception desk greeted him by name and said how nice it was to see him again. Guy returned the compliment and we made our way through to the Grill.

'The hotel's packed with foreign correspondents,' said Guy to me. 'A couple of drinks here and you find out all sorts of things about what's going on.'

'Do you know *everyone*?' I asked.

'Not at all,' smiled Guy as a very attractive if dishevelled man approached us.

'Good to see you, Collins,' said the man in an American accent.

He and Guy shook hands and then the American said, 'Guy, I gotta run. See you at the bar?' and touched his hat, saying, 'Ma'am,' to me, which was both terrifically transatlantic and also unexpectedly dashing. I didn't know any Americans, and immediately looked forward to re-living the moment with Bunty and Thel, probably repeatedly.

The Grill was busy, full of men in uniform, and a great number of the women as well. Those who were not were far better dressed than me, and several reminded me of Mrs Porter – immaculately tailored, wearing teeny tilted hats and not a hint of knitwear to be seen.

'By the way,' said Guy, after we had taken our seats at what even I could tell was one of the best tables in the house, 'if you see Clark Gable, try not to stare. I understand he hates it.'

'Really?' I said, looking around. 'Are you trying to make me nervous?'

'No, I was trying to help you impress Clark Gable,' grinned Guy. 'Now, I wonder if they have the salted pork? It's delicious, although if this is to become our regular meeting place I'm rather relieved there's the five-bob cap.'

Last year the Government had passed a law so that even the very best restaurants had to stick to three courses and five shillings a head. It had been a good move in terms of trying to make things fairer as now even millionaires couldn't pay their way to culinary excess, at least in theory.

'Look sharp,' said Guy. 'Here we are.'

Mrs Porter had arrived and was being led towards us, a sense of serene belonging etched on her face as she wafted past the other customers. Guy and I rose to our feet, which of course as a man, he would, but I did too because that was the effect Mrs Porter seemed to have. It was ridiculous, but you found yourself opening doors or fussing about with chairs because it felt expected.

Guy and I had agreed that this was our chance to try to get back into Mrs Porter's good books. It had been a friendly overture to ask us to lunch and we were determined to be both delighted and delightful. As Guy said, the more she liked us, the more chance we had of gaining some kind of steadying hand over her colourful ideas and axe-wielding approach to our much-loved magazine.

I would have been a hypocrite not to admit that lunch in the dizzying surroundings of The Savoy was quite an experience. The combination of debonair foreign journalists, the murmured conversations of the great and the glamorous and the steadfast opulence of the hotel itself despite being bombed on numerous occasions was a heady one indeed.

'Mrs Porter,' said Guy keenly, which was not like him at all. 'How lovely.'

It was a strong start. Mrs Porter smiled modestly, somehow managing to imply that the luxury of the venue was her own achievement, and at the same time graciously accepting the fact that Guy may simply have been complimenting her on being divine.

Either way, I couldn't compete, and only managed to say, 'Good afternoon, Mrs Porter, thank you for inviting us,' as if I had arrived at a birthday party expecting jelly and ice cream.

'Dearest Mr Collins. Darling Miss Lake,' said Mrs Porter, which was disarming. 'Will this do?' She looked around the restaurant. 'I'm sure Monsieur Payard will work his culinary magic, despite these difficult times.'

She had decided to be graciousness itself.

'Without doubt,' said Guy, who really was very good at saying things that were both charming and noncommittal. Mrs Porter patted his arm and sat down, as waiters and menus appeared.

I opened my menu with unseemly haste. The Government's Meals in Establishments Order was quoted in a serious manner at the top, but I only had eyes for the liver and sausages in white wine sauce.

Mrs Porter, however, had gone straight to the wine list, declaring that we were celebrating.

'Mr Collins, would *you* decide for us? I'm quite useless at knowing anything.'

As ever, she looked gloriously sure of herself and not remotely useless, but Guy went along with the charade and after a quick glance at the list, ordered something in French and earned an exclamation of 'Perfection,' in response.

Then Mrs Porter caught the eye of someone she knew and started miming a telephone call. Guy leaned over to me and whispered, 'Is there still a war on? I can't tell.'

If she heard him, Mrs Porter chose not to comment. 'May I be honest with you both?' she said. 'You see, I am worried about you, Miss Lake.'

'Me?' I sat up straighter in my gloriously comfortable velvet chair. 'I'm fine, thank you. En pleine forme.'

I had turned into Pamela Pye.

Mrs Porter smiled understandingly. 'You know, I do so hope we'll be friends. Mr Collins has spoken so highly of you. Of course, he may be a little biased. Tell me,' she dropped her voice, conspiratorially, 'are the brothers very much alike?'

To my horror, she broke into a giggle.

Guy looked appalled. I felt the same.

'Oh,' I said, squirming. 'Er. No. Um . . . Charles, my husband that is, he er, he's taller. A little. And quieter I think. Would you say, Guy? I mean, Mr Collins?'

As I stumbled over my words, Mrs Porter looked prettily amused, and I wished like mad that I'd had a better answer off-pat. It was hideous to be asked to compare my boss with my husband.

'Oh no, I've embarrassed you,' she cried. 'I feel dreadful.'

'Not at all,' I managed, not believing her for a second. 'I just don't tend to talk about him at work.'

'Miss Lake is extremely professional about the situation,' said Guy, keeping to our plan and speaking to Mrs Porter as if they were old friends. 'Not easy to keep family and work separate. As I am sure you will understand having inherited *Woman's Friend* from your uncle.'

Mrs Porter blinked at him. I had a feeling she had forgotten that the magazine wasn't actually her own invention.

'A heavy burden,' smiled Guy, 'but one we can share.'

'Hmm,' said Mrs Porter. Unimpressed with the idea of having to cope with a burden, she swiftly changed the conversation back to mine. 'The thing is I couldn't help but notice when I ran through my little ideas, that, well . . . Miss Lake looked A Bit Mis.' Her eyes shone with sympathy. 'So I have come up with things to make you happy. Ah, waiter, there you are. Who's having what?'

'Happy?' I said. 'I *am* happy.'

'I'll have the fish,' said Mrs Porter. 'Are you *really*, Miss Lake? All those down in the mouth letters you have to read. It must be awful. I know, let's *all* have the fish. Waiter, it won't still have its face on, will it? I can't bear it if the poor thing looks sad.'

I couldn't tell if she was talking about me or a sardine.

'Anyway,' said Mrs Porter, brightening up. 'Help Is Here and to that end – and Mr Collins, I haven't told you this yet, but you'll love it – I am bringing in a Mr Elliot as my second-in-command. He's going to look after the funny contributor people so that Madame Pye can spend more time on Fashion and Beauty. So that's super, and now – and this is the most exciting thing of all – Miss Lake, you are going to work in a new area you will ADORE.'

Guy and I waited. Mrs Porter clasped her hands together and took a deep breath.

'Miss Lake,' she said, tremulously, 'I am giving you Weddings.'

I stared at her with my mouth open. The sound of conversations, cutlery on bone china, the soft trickle of wine being poured, continued.

'I know!' beamed Mrs Porter. 'Don't thank me, it's my gift to you.'

'I'm sorry, Mrs Porter,' I managed. 'Weddings?'

'Yes. Everyone's getting married. It's one of the nicest things about the war. I did think about giving it to Madame, but then I said, "No, Egg. No. Miss Lake needs joy in her cheerless life. Let. Her. Live."'

'Which weddings are we talking about?' asked Guy.

'*Society* weddings, Mr Collins,' said Mrs Porter. 'Beautiful brides from the highest echelons. The readers will love it. Miss Lake is going to interview the brides-to-be about how excited they are. We'll have lots of space as I've decided to stop those dreary war-work articles with immediate effect.' Now she looked at me, or rather, at my cardigan. 'Do you have anything nice to wear? I would lend you something, but I don't want things stretched. Never mind. We'll start right away.'

'But the war work . . .' I began.

'Hush – I've not finished. I want you to chop the "Woman's Friend to Friend" page in half as I've decided to write my own column. It just came to me. I intend to call it "Your Publisher's Week" and it will be full of lovely things like art galleries, the theatre, and of course, charity events.' Mrs Porter said *charity events* in a special lower voice which reflected the gravity of the subject. 'It's a lot of work on my part, but I will answer the call. The new *Woman's Friend* will be about cheer, not gloom.'

Finally, she stopped.

I on the other hand, didn't know where to start.

'Society weddings?' I said. 'Galleries?'

'Yes. And far fewer letters because they're awful. There was one just this morning I had to tell Mrs Mahoney to remove. I will say she was most cross. Mr Collins, you must speak with her about that.'

'When was this?' I asked.

'Just before luncheon,' said Mrs Porter. 'A horrid letter about a horrid man. Anyway, it's gone now.'

'You cut a reader's letter?' I said, now moving away from the plan to be a delight. 'It wasn't from someone called Mrs Smith – Enid Smith – was it?'

'I've no idea,' said Mrs Porter. 'Don't worry, Mr Collins, there won't be a blank space. I made up a cheerier problem on the spot and made Mrs Mahoney pop it in. I had to be quite insistent. Miss Lake, whatever's the matter?'

'I'm sorry, but you just can't do that,' I said, feeling

myself go hot. 'That's the first issue we could get it into. It can't wait any longer. You must have seen that this reader is desperate for help. Please, Mrs Porter, we have to print it.'

I turned to Guy.

'Mrs Porter,' he said, 'I agree entirely with Miss Lake. A decision was made to help a reader in some significant distress.'

Mrs Porter looked at him for a long moment, as a small pout appeared.

'Now *you're* cross,' she said, sounding about seven years old.

Damn bloody right, I thought to myself. She didn't have a clue. Guy was keeping admirably calm, but I was beginning to struggle.

'Mrs Porter,' I said, before he could answer her, 'this is what we do. Of course *Woman's Friend* tries to entertain and bring cheer, but we also inform and support and offer help. And no, it's not always very nice. Sometimes these letters *are* horrible, but the problem page is one of the reasons women read the magazine and write to us. They know we try to help. They trust us.'

Mrs Porter looked at Guy, seeming to expect him to come to her rescue.

He held her gaze. 'I'm afraid we do try to offer advice on some rather gritty situations,' he said, quietly. 'Miss Lake knows our readers better than anyone. If she says this letter is important, then I would ask in the strongest possible terms that it stays in.'

Mrs Porter's face hardened for a moment, and then she lifted her chin.

'Well, it's too late now,' she said, airily. 'It's been removed, so there we are. Let's change the subject or we'll spoil our lovely lunch.' She looked around for the waiter, but spotted a friend instead. 'Ooh I say is that Dickie, the Earl of—'

'Mrs Porter,' I interrupted, '*Woman's Friend* isn't a society magazine. There's nothing wrong with those of course, but it's not us. I've spent years learning everything I possibly can to be good at my job. We don't ignore readers when their lives get difficult. People rely on us.'

Mrs Porter gave a small, thoroughly affronted, squeak.

'Emmy,' said Guy, softly.

I stopped talking.

'I see,' said Mrs Porter, in a tremulous voice. 'Here I was trying to cheer you up, inviting you to lunch at one of my favourite places in the world and offering you the most marvellous opportunity to meet all the right kind of people. I must look very silly.'

Now she put her hand to her cheek and looked away, as if terribly hurt. I thought people only did this sort of thing in films, and I couldn't work out if she really was pained by my response, or if it was part of an elaborate act.

Either way, Mrs Porter had the most effective way of making you feel you had done her a dreadful injustice.

Guy and I exchanged looks. The mission to be delightful was not going to plan.

'Come now,' said Guy, gently.

'Oh, Mrs Porter,' I began, realising I had overstepped the mark which was unlikely to help. 'I really am awfully grateful.'

A stern-looking man in a black suit sitting at the table next to us raised a surreptitious finger to ask for his bill. He gave me an idea.

'It's just,' I added hastily, 'that we have a remit.' I paused for what I hoped would be dramatic effect and then dropped my voice. 'From The Ministry.'

Mrs Porter turned her head back to me, although she did not remove her outraged hand.

Two could play at this game.

I glanced around the restaurant as if one of Hitler's spies might be lurking behind a bread roll. 'Mr Collins,' I said, pretending to speak under my breath, 'may we discuss this, even though we are not behind closed doors?'

'Keep it brief,' said Guy, going with me and sounding as if he worked for a secret organisation.

Our publisher's interest was piqued.

'Mrs Porter,' I said, gravely. 'The war-work pieces are written for members of His Majesty's Government. Indeed they are habitually checked by the Censor.'

Guy cleared his throat. 'It has been remiss of me not to mention it. Being part of the Ministry's women war-worker recruitment campaign is our honour.'

It was all true. Admittedly, it was hardly a secret, but nevertheless.

'Why has no one told me this?'

'I have been trying to meet with you, Mrs Porter,' said Guy. 'Telephone calls are not always secure.'

Touché.

'So how do the . . . that is, *they* communicate?' said Mrs Porter, narrowing her eyes. She was many things, but no fool.

'Select briefings at the Ministry,' answered Guy.

Mrs Porter gave a high-pitched 'Ooh,' then, after a few moments' thought, she put her shoulders back and assumed a noble expression. 'You should have told me. We cannot let the Government down,' she said, as if the whole thing had been her idea. 'Miss Lake, you may continue with the war-work articles. Although do try to make them less tedious.'

I breathed a sigh of relief. It wasn't much, but it was a start. 'Thank you, Mrs Porter. I shall do my best,' I said.

Mrs Porter gave a small nod. 'When is the next briefing?' she asked. 'Obviously I will attend.'

Guy looked weary. 'Of course,' he said, without giving a date.

With something exclusive now promised, Mrs Porter forgot that seconds ago she had been traumatised. 'I shall wear my blue suit,' she said. 'And in the meantime, I have some more news. Come on, Miss Lake, cheer up.'

But I didn't feel like cheering up. We may have managed to get her to backtrack on cancelling the war-work articles, but it was pretty small beer.

Mrs Porter's response to Enid's letter had done it for me. I was painfully aware that we received hundreds of letters every week with problems we couldn't fix, from readers in trouble, sometimes even in danger, whom we couldn't help. I hated it, but I accepted it as part of the job. But to pull a letter from someone in a dreadful situation even if there was only the *faintest* chance of it helping? It was reprehensible.

As Mrs Porter now began to talk about herself, I could hardly be bothered to listen. When you cut through the smiles and the 'darlings' and the sugar-sweet voice, it was quite clear that the Honourable Mrs Cressida Porter didn't care about anyone other than herself. She was made of stone, all the way through.

'I have realised,' she was saying, while gazing over Guy's head, 'that Publishing Is My Calling. My ideas must have a life of their own.'

'Yes,' said Guy, his heart not sounding entirely in it.

'I knew you'd agree!' cried Cressida. 'And to that end, I have now told Mrs Mahoney to stop production on all future issues.' Now she gave us one of her most glittering smiles. 'I know you will be very excited when I tell you that I will be re-launching *Woman's Friend* with all my lovely ideas.'

Now I looked up.

'You're . . . you're closing the magazine?' stammered Guy.

'Temporarily. Until I've sorted it all out. In addition I shall be moving into my office after some modest improvements are made over the weekend,' she finished, looking thrilled.

A waiter appeared with our meals.

'This looks perfect,' Mrs Porter exclaimed as she was handed her plate. 'I always think it's so much better when one cuts off their heads.'

CHAPTER NINE

Captain Harold Comes to Tea

I COULD NOT get away from Mrs Porter and the headless fish fast enough. As she moved seamlessly from temporarily closing the whole magazine to saying how the war had been beastly news for tartare sauce, Guy pulled himself together and began a very clear and sensible explanation as to why we couldn't just *stop* the magazine in its tracks.

'The newsagents, Mrs Porter, the advertisers, the readers. If we don't publish, people will want to know what on earth is going on.'

'Exactly!' she cried. 'So when my new, wonderful *Woman's Friend* is launched, they will have their answer. The enigma of silence, followed by the thrill of the arrival. It's called Marketing. I read a book. Well, not an entire book, but enough to get the gist of it. Oh, do say you agree, Mr Collins.'

But Mr Collins did not agree. Not for all the eyelash-batting in London. He held fast, and when Mrs Porter hardly noticed me excuse myself and leave after the main course, he stayed with her to try to negotiate, charm and cajole. I ran to the nearest bus stop to race back to the office as fast as possible and see how the announcement had gone down.

Mrs Mahoney was indefatigably calm. Mr Brand would only quietly shake his head at the madness, and Mrs Shaw and Miss Peters were interrogating Mrs Pye, who didn't help anyone by looking smug and saying how 'merveilleuse' it was now that someone with actual flair was in charge. Poor Mr Newton was nearly in tears at how furious the advertisers would be, and Hester spoke for us all when she innocently said, 'I don't mean to be rude, but Mrs Porter's only been here two weeks. How does she know what she's doing?'

'She doesn't,' I replied. 'But Guy . . . Mr Collins, will sort it. He is with her now.'

'You really don't understand vision, do you?' smiled Mrs Pye. 'Mrs Porter could easily have just let you all go.'

'We understand how to run a magazine, Mrs Pye,' I snapped back. 'And Mr Collins has forgotten more than most of us will ever know. As he always says . . .'

'Think of the readers,' said Hester and Mrs Shaw at the same time.

'Exactly,' I replied. 'You can have all the fancy visions in the world, but it's the readers who matter. Muck them about and there won't *be* a *Woman's Friend*.'

Mrs Pye said, 'Hmm,' glared at everyone, and walked out of the room.

I'd said it in the heat of the moment, but it was a very good point. Mrs Porter didn't have a clue what she was doing. Even worse, she had no idea what that could mean for our magazine. I looked around at my colleagues – my friends. For all her gushing, all the compliments and the sweets, Mrs Porter had now well and truly shown her real self.

*

A few chaotic days later, Thelma was asking me the very same thing.

'Does Mrs Pye have the foggiest idea what a publisher is actually supposed to do?'

It was Friday night and Thel and I were on the overnight shift together at Carlton Street fire station. It was a busy evening and half the boys were still out tackling a nasty kitchen fire started by an over-hot chip pan. It might have sounded mundane in the middle of a world war, but it was still threatening to burn down somebody's home. In between phone calls, Thel and I had been sorting out paperwork as Captain Davies was due to do one of his spot checks to ensure everything was first rate. There was no room for complacency. The Luftwaffe was still enjoying unwelcome visits to Britain, and while the newsreels called them 'nuisance raids' in comparison with the nightly bombardments of the Blitz, they were still vicious and could happen at any time. Only a couple of months previously, a daytime raid near our friend Anne in Berkshire had killed fifteen people, including three children and their teacher on the way home from school. It was mad to think that currently I found working at a fire station a welcome break from the turmoil taking place at a magazine.

'It's bedlam, Thel,' I said. 'Guy's managed to convince the Egg that we can make lots of her Lovely Changes without pulling everything from the printers, but she's spent the whole week calling the office every two minutes telling us to change articles or add one of her ideas . . . I have no idea what the next issue is going to look like.'

'She sounds dreadful,' said Thel, staunchly. 'What's happening about the readers' letters?'

I sighed. 'I managed to persuade her to include Enid Smith's letter in the issue after next, but I had to edit it to the point where the husband sounded hardly more than mildly irritating, so my suggesting she tries for a divorce looks ridiculous,' I said. 'But I used the name Enid Smith and as much of her situation as I could, so I hope she'll see it. And at least I've explained the process of going to the courts, so if other readers are in the same situation, which some certainly are, they know the route to take. But I can't keep giving serious answers to watered-down problems. We'll look like idiots.'

Thelma grimaced. 'Dare I ask, when is your first society wedding?'

Now I let out a hollow laugh. 'Next week. A chat with Miss Wilhelmina Bruce-Roberts before her big day. Actually, she's in the Air Transport Auxiliary so I'm planning to ask her about delivering Spitfires.' Now I smiled properly. 'Mrs Porter gives rich people a bad name. I bet most of the brides-to-be are pulling their weight like everyone else.'

'Did she not fancy joining up and wearing a smart uniform?' asked Thel. 'Officers' bespoke tailoring and all that?'

'She told Guy it wasn't Her Thing,' I answered.

'None of this is Anyone's Thing,' said Thel, drily. 'We're at war.' She looked over to the door. 'What *is* going on in the canteen?'

Loud cheers had broken out in the room above us, and moments later, we heard the thumping of heavy boots on the stairs and Roy appeared in the doorway.

'We've done it,' he roared, not bothering with a hello. 'We've taken Tunis. And Bizerta. They just said on the news. "*An official announcement of Allied victory*". Enemy resistance has gone! I bet they'll surrender within the week. Goodnight, North Africa, next stop Italy. Bloody wonderful!'

My heart nearly leapt out of my mouth, but I didn't know whether to cheer or not.

Charles.

All thoughts of Mrs Porter vanished.

Straight away, Thelma kicked her chair out of the way and put her arms around me, hugging me tight.

'He's fine,' said Thel, throwing Roy a look. 'This is smashing news, Em. It's what we've been waiting for. If Charles is part of it I bet you he's waving a Union Jack as we speak.'

'Of course it is,' I said. 'It's wonderful. Charles may not even be involved, anyway.'

'Me and my big gob,' said Roy, coming over and sitting on the desk next to me. 'Don't you worry, Emmy. We've walloped them. Your lad's probably led the whole thing. That's if he's even there, as you say.'

The fact was, other than knowing he had gone out to North Africa when he left England just days after our wedding and had been there ever since, I didn't know where Charles was exactly, or what he was doing. He never gave details in his letters. None of the boys did. The censors would remove anything sensitive anyway, but mostly letters were crammed with replies to the news we had sent them about home, or how the food was all right, or it wasn't too hot, or what good sorts the other men were, and most of all, how much they missed us and loved us and couldn't wait to get home. Those were the parts of the letters you didn't read out to even your best friends.

. . . Always remember my darling that I think of you all the time. When I am back, I will hold you tighter than you could ever imagine, and I will never let you go . . .

Why talk about the war when you could talk about the future and being together again?

But I didn't live in cloud-cuckoo-land. There was a good possibility Charles had been caught up somewhere in the Tunis operation. It was after all, a huge campaign which was critical to the entire war. It had dominated the news for months. Victory in North Africa meant the Allies could now get into Italy, back into *Europe*. It was the best possible news. But those of us with boys out there watched it more closely than anyone. Battles won were a cause for joy, but there was always a cost. The only way you could keep yourself sane was to assume that he was all right. No news, on a personal level, was good news. Such a crucial military win was a big step closer to getting him home.

I squeezed Roy's hand and smiled.

'You're right,' I said. 'It's bloody wonderful.'

★

The next morning's newspapers were full of details about the Allied triumph.

'Emmy,' called Mr Bone, our newsagent and friend, as Thel and I made our way home at the crack of dawn. 'Here you are!' He was in the middle of sorting out his deliveries, and now he waved a copy of *The Times* as he strode across the street towards us. 'That's shown them,' he said, his eyes shining. 'Well done,' he added, 'well done, that man.'

I thanked him and gratefully took the paper to read over breakfast, ahead of trying to get a short sleep before what was planned to be A Very Important Day.

Never mind the triumph in North Africa, after last week's excitement of Bunty announcing she was going to Wimbledon for tea with Captain Harold Thomas, the biggest news on the Home Front was that today he was returning the visit.

According to Bunty's report after they had met up, Harold had turned out to be just as nice as we had remembered, and as luck would have it, also happened to have an interest in fixing old sheds.

'He's a decent man, Em,' Bunty told me when we were on our own, 'and he's had the most awful, awful time.'

Nearly two years previously, when Harold's team were trying to defuse an unexploded bomb in north London, the foul thing had decided to finally do its job, and blown up. Two of his men had died. Harold suffered serious injuries. He had spent the next year in hospital.

He was of course invalided out of the army, and another year later, was trying to get used to a new life. Bunty said that if Bill was still alive, he would have told everyone to rally round and try to cheer up his old friend.

Now as Thel and I arrived home, excitement was rising about the impending visit.

'Can I ask him about UXBs?' said George.

'Will he know about planes?' asked Stan. 'I'd like to talk about planes.'

'You'll talk about planes anyway,' said Margaret.

'Or we could discuss how we've thumped them in Tunis,' said George. 'Emmy, is that where Captain Charles is?'

'I don't know,' I said, lightly, 'but Walls Have Ears, remember.'

'George, you're not to talk about bombs unless Captain Thomas mentions it,' said Thelma. 'He's not here to be interrogated.'

'He's coming to have a look at the shed,' said Bunty.

I quietly thought that it didn't need an expert in engineering to see that it was on its last legs, but I realised that wasn't the point.

'A captain in the Royal Engineers,' said George. 'I can't wait.'

'He's probably the bravest person ever,' said Margaret, 'after our dad.'

'And Charles,' said Stan, loyally. 'After our dad and then Charles.'

As Thel's kids held both men in the highest esteem, the bar for Harold was being set high. All he needed to do was to work a small miracle on a heap of wood in the garden.

'I'm going to polish the front doorstep,' said Bunty. 'It's a sight.'

The front doorstep was already sparklingly clean.

'I'll help,' I said, following her upstairs.

As Bunty set to work, I sat down on the floor by the front door. 'You know we won't show you up, don't you?' I said, quietly. 'He sounds a nice chap.'

'He is,' said Bunty. 'but I don't think he quite knows what to do with himself at the moment. When you're in hospital for ages, you almost forget what normal life is like. Or at least, that's how I felt. Everyone treats you differently. I hated that.'

'I bet he finds it nice to talk to someone who understands,' I said.

Bunty stopped her work for a moment.

'This might sound odd, but it's nice for me to talk to someone who knew Bill,' she said. 'Harold's told me lots of things about when they were at college. And he really has been through the mill.'

'Bunts,' I said, 'you don't need to justify anything.' Then I gave her a nudge with my elbow. 'By the way, I can already see my face in that step. Shall we go and polish the garden?'

*

The last, and only, time I had met Harold was in the spring of 1941 during a chilly walk in Hyde Park. I remembered him as good fun with an easygoing way about him.

Now, as Bunty reintroduced us, it was clear that Harold

had had a rough time. He was still a tall man of course, well over six feet, but where before he had looked like a mammoth England rugger forward, now he was thinner than his clothes wanted him to be. While the friendly smile was still there, it was obvious he had taken a pretty grim hit.

'Harold, how lovely to see you!' I exclaimed as I walked towards where Bunty was showing him the garden.

'And very nice to see you again, Emmeline,' he said, heartily. 'Old Adolf got in the way there for a bit.'

He held out his left hand, which was still the size of a tennis bat, and I shook it warmly.

'Well, I'm jolly glad you're here now,' I said, very much meaning it.

Bunty had told us, of course, about Harold's injuries. He had lost his right arm and most of the sight in one of his eyes. To hear him now, you'd have thought it was little more than a scrape.

'Last time we met, the old lugs had gone and I couldn't hear,' he said. 'Now I'm not so good on one side. God knows what shape I'll be in if we leave it another two years. And may I also offer my belated congratulations, Mrs Mayhew?' he added. 'I understand you met your husband just after I'd missed out?'

'Thank you,' I said. 'Although, if I remember rightly, it was *you* who said we should just be friends. So really it's all down to that.' I paused just for a second. 'I'm so sorry you got roughed up.'

'That's very kind,' said Harold. 'It could have been worse.'

He stopped abruptly and looked to Bunty.

'Damn,' he said. 'That came out wrong. I'm sorry. I'm lucky to be here.'

'Don't be silly,' said Bunts, knowing he meant Bill.

'There's no walking on eggshells in this house. You'll find that when you meet the children.'

'Will they be all right?' asked Harold, as for the first time his heartiness dropped. 'I don't want to scare them. Since I got out of hospital, I've petrified one or two tiddlers. I think that's been the worst thing. You feel awful.'

'Harold Thomas,' said Bunty, severely, 'you're far too nice to petrify anyone.'

When she said that, and I saw Harold's face light up, my heart jumped a little. Whatever kind of friends Bunty and Harold were, whether they were just chums or if there might at some point be something else in it, the way she stuck up for him was all I needed to know. When Bunty was on your side, you would never face battles on your own. And if Bunty was on your side, so was I.

'Anyway, we desperately need your help with our rotten old shed,' she continued, as Harold seemed a bit lost for words. 'Everyone keeps wanting to bash nails in or pull the thing down, but I wonder if we can re-build it properly. There's no pressure but we're pinning all our hopes on you.'

'Right you are,' said Harold, now beaming. 'I'm up for the challenge. Lead on.'

'I'll sort out refreshments,' I volunteered, and headed back into the house, bumping into Thelma, who was loitering just inside the back door.

'Well?' she said in a stage whisper.

'I think you'll like him,' I said.

Thel crossed her fingers.

'It's just like the films,' she said. 'So romantic. I know, I sound like a right old duck.'

'Thel,' I said. 'You're thirty-one.'

'I'm nearer thirty-two,' she answered.

'Poor old thing,' I said. 'So, where are the troops?'

'Look sharp, you lot,' called Thelma as they were waiting

impatiently in the kitchen. 'Best behaviour please, and that includes you, Stanley Jenkins,' she said, as the children now filed past. 'George, please don't ask Captain Thomas how you dispose of a bomb. If you find one, you're to run to a phone box. Margaret, he may not want to see your dancing, but you can always ask. Everyone got the glasses? Emmy and I will carry the jugs.'

She turned to me. 'I should have been in the army,' she grinned.

Half an hour later, excitement had turned into blatant hero-worship as the children had formed a Shed Restoration working party under the guidance of their new friend, and in the sunshine of the garden were all taking their roles very seriously indeed.

'Is this right, Captain Harold?' asked George, who was carefully painting numbers on the parts of the shed that weren't beyond repair.

'Spot on,' said Harold. 'Good man.'

'What about these, please? Are they straight enough?' called Stan, who had been stacking flowerpots along the side of the air-raid shelter.

'Excellent work,' answered Harold. 'Well done, Stanley. How are you getting along with the inventory, Margaret?'

'All right I think,' said Marg, who was sitting cross-legged on the floor and looking through a box of rubbish. 'I've found something that's metal, only I don't know what it is.' She held up what looked to be part of an eggbeater.

'It won't win the war sitting in the shed. It could make part of a tank,' said Stan, which was exactly what Harold had said as a joke two minutes earlier when Bunty had found a large bolt that didn't belong to anything.

'Sorry, Stan,' said Bunts. 'It won't happen again.' Then she turned to Harold and whispered, 'You do know I'm blaming you if half the kitchen cutlery disappears.'

Harold smiled widely, but didn't say anything. He could chat like anything to the rest of us, but sometimes he became tongue-tied around her.

'It's very good of you to give up your Saturday to put up with us lot, Harold,' said Thelma, filling the silence. 'I've never seen my three quite so industrious.'

'Can you tell us some more about the nurses who saved you, please?' asked Marg. 'Do you think I could be one?'

'Of course you could,' said Harold. 'It's a *very* important job.'

'That's a smashing idea,' said Thel. 'It means working hard to pass all your exams.'

'You'll be great,' said Harold to Marg.

Margaret nodded enthusiastically. Harold had been happy to be quizzed on his time in hospital and had told everyone that without the nurses he would probably have died. It was quite clear he had said this as a tribute to the hospital nursing staff, but all it had done was convince the children that he was even more of a hero than they had previously thought. Now, Thel gave him the thumbs-up and mouthed, 'Thank you.'

As Stan interrupted his sister to ask Harold what subjects he had liked best when he was at school, Thel turned to me.

'I hate to tell you,' she said under her breath, 'but I think your husband has just been booted out of second place after their dad.' She looked at the children almost wistfully.

'I don't think he'll mind,' I whispered back. 'Thel, is everything OK?'

'It's fine,' said Thel, 'I just miss Arthur. So do they. He'd be in his element here. That shed would be down and in bits all over the garden before you could say "knife". He and Harold would make a good team.'

'They'll all be home soon,' I said. 'Won't be long.'

'I know,' she answered. 'Look at them, they're like ducklings. We'd better count them when Harold leaves, or they'll follow him out. Thank you, Captain Thomas,' she added. 'They're having the time of their lives.'

'Harold, please,' said Harold. 'Really, the pleasure is entirely mine. I haven't had so much fun in ages.'

'Then you'd better visit again,' said Thelma, quick as a flash. 'But of course I'll leave it with you and Bunty to sort out.'

'Can it be soon?' asked Stan, before either of them could say anything. 'Only, George can be very bossy about things and if we're going to get the shed ready in case we get pets, it'll be loads better if you're here.'

'I'd love to help,' said Harold immediately. Then he added, 'If that would be all right with Bunty, of course.'

He looked at her and smiled.

Stan now turned his attention to Bunts. It was hard to tell who was waiting for her answer with more interest, him or Harold.

I glanced up at the bright blue sky. There wasn't a cloud to be seen.

'Do you know,' said Bunty, 'I think Harold visiting again soon would be a very good idea indeed.'

CHAPTER TEN

Mrs Porter Moves In

NOT ONE TO hang about, Stanley helpfully suggested that Harold could come back the next weekend. Also, and entirely coincidentally, a boy at school was selling guinea pigs, just in case any of us wanted to know. Harold stayed for most of the day, and as well as making excellent progress from a construction point of view, there was no doubt that he had been a gigantic hit with us all.

'What a nice man,' I said to Bunty, after he'd gone.

'Isn't he?' she said. 'I think we cheered him up.'

'Well, someone certainly has,' I replied. Bunty ignored me, but she looked ever so pleased.

As I had hoped, the jolliness with Harold followed by another double shift at the fire station made for a non-stop weekend, and helped me put the madness of Mrs Porter to the back of my mind. I may have been tired from lack of sleep, but on Monday morning I felt ready to brace up and attack whatever wild notions might arise. After all, my job was writing for a magazine. It was not as if it involved dismantling bombs.

As I made my way up the stairs at Launceston House and then turned left towards our offices, I noticed that the pictures that hung on the wall either side of the double doors had been replaced. On one side was a smart metal sign which had *WOMAN'S FRIEND* engraved on it in rather beautiful, modern lettering, and on the other was a very large, framed photographic portrait. Below it, as if I was in any doubt at all, was a bronze plate, which read, '*THE HONOURABLE MRS PORTER, OWNER AND PUBLISHER*'.

It was a posed studio shot, with Mrs Porter in a black frock and pearls sitting at a right angle to the camera and looking over her shoulder and into the lens in a thoughtful and intelligent way. She looked very lovely, as well as very young. It gave the entrance to our modest offices a very glamorous look.

'Gracious,' said a voice behind me. It was Mrs Shaw. 'That must have cost a bob or two. Mrs Porter looks smashing.'

'It's like she's out of the films,' said Hester, joining us with Mr Newton.

'Like a young Greta Garbo,' said Mr Newton, which was taking things a bit far.

I hung back, thinking how odd it was that while we were now all well aware that Mrs Porter was not exactly as lovely as she had first appeared, even her picture seemed to have the ability to turn people slightly giddy.

'I wonder if she's moved in?' said Miss Peters.

There was only one way to find out.

Mrs Shaw pushed open the heavy doors and we all took the few steps to the office opposite mine. It had been Mrs Bird's when she was Editress a couple of years ago and had always been a rather dour room. Guy had preferred to stay in his own office when he had taken over, and I was sure Mrs Porter would now have made major changes to it. But when I gently knocked and then opened the door, the austere furniture of Mrs Bird's tenure was all in its place. Nothing had moved an inch.

'That's a damp squib,' said Mrs Shaw.

'Sorry everyone,' I said. 'I thought Mrs Porter said this weekend, but I must have been wrong.'

With a few 'Ah wells,' and as Mrs Mahoney arrived, asking what we were all doing, I shut the door on the disappointment and followed the team to the journalists' room for our usual post-weekend chat.

Then I stopped dead. Instead of being in their usual two neat rows the desks were now all squashed together in half the space. They had been joined by the long table from the meeting room which had been pushed up against the window. A stack of mismatched chairs sat precariously on top. Everyone looked at each other.

Still in my hat and jacket, I spun round and opened the door to the meeting room.

And there it was. Or rather, it wasn't. The tired and scuffed off-white walls had been freshly painted in a pale coral and there were a number of framed modern art prints at eye level. The floor had been newly re-stained and polished, and at the far end was a beautiful burr-walnut desk with a matching chair on wheels. An elegant art deco lamp sat next to an ivory telephone with matching cord, and on the other side of the desk a young woman in bronze danced with abandon on top of an alabaster base. In the centre, facing out for any visitor to see, a name plate said, '*The Hon. Mrs Porter.*'

As everyone crowded in to look, I noted that there were no chairs by the desk but instead, two sofas had been positioned further away at the other end of the room, with a low coffee table between them. A new set of magazines – not including *Woman's Friend* – were displayed.

'Bloody Nora,' said Mrs Shaw, speaking for us all.

'I don't think we should be in here,' said Mr Newton.

'I agree,' I said. I felt as if I had broken into someone's hotel suite. 'Let's wait in the journos' room. Mr Collins will be in soon for the editorial meeting.'

Quietly, everyone retreated to what now looked like a neglected, uncared-for storeroom. That the furniture had been pushed around was bad enough, but far worse was that piles of readers' letters which had been carefully sorted on Friday had been shoved to one side so that they were now in muddled, half-collapsed heaps. A full postbag that was due to be opened was stuck in the far corner under the meeting-room table, and someone would have to crawl across the floor to get it out.

This room had never been fancy, but in recent years it had been brought to life by the women who worked in it. I wasn't one for lots of rules, but everyone knew that the readers' letters had to be looked after properly. Stacked, logged, the stamps cut off and put to one side, and then once dealt with, the letters carefully destroyed. People shared their lives with us. They would be treated with respect.

Everyone knew that. Everyone agreed with it. Everyone followed the rule.

The oohs and ahhs about the new office had completely died down. As we tried to assemble some sort of a meeting in the higgledy-piggledy mess, the comparison was more than obvious.

Mrs Porter's room was like an oasis, an apparition of pre-war loveliness. In contrast, the rest of the *Woman's Friend* offices were drab and battered, a hotchpotch of mis-matched office furniture where the only 'art' was magazine covers which had been cut out and stuck to the walls with drawing pins. Each cover just had one pin at the top as anything metal was in such short supply, so when the windows were open, the covers would flap untidily in the breeze.

Mrs Pye arrived, looking swish in a new hat that was strikingly similar to the one Mrs Porter had worn the last time she was in the office.

'Our publisher will be in soon,' she announced. 'Mrs Porter is keen to see her new room. It is a triumph, of course – I assume you've all looked. I did suggest to Mrs Porter that she might wish to invest in a lock.'

'You've already seen it, then?' said Mrs Shaw.

If someone had told Mrs Pye to hide the Crown Jewels up her jumper on personal request from the King, she could not have looked more full of herself.

'I myself personally directed the refurbishments over the weekend,' she replied. 'Mrs Porter did not trust it to be done exactly as she wanted unless I was here.'

'It's a shame she didn't ask you to make sure this office was left exactly as it should be,' said Mrs Mahoney, quietly.

Mrs Pye gave a silly, tinkly laugh. 'Oh, Mrs Porter isn't interested in where the awful old furniture goes.'

I bent down and picked up a photo frame that had been knocked onto the floor. It held a picture of Hester's little brother, and usually sat proudly on her desk.

'It's not broken,' I said to her, as I carefully put it back where it belonged. 'And I'll call the Facilities Department to come up as soon as they can. We can sort things. It doesn't matter.'

The thing was, though, it did.

Bags of fudge and flattery could get you so far, but I could see by the look on everyone's faces that they were shocked.

'Good God, what's happened here?'

It was Guy.

'Mrs Porter has moved into the meeting room,' I said, calmly.

From the way Guy didn't answer, but just pursed his

lips, it was clear that this was as much news to him as it had been to us.

'She's had it redecorated,' said Mrs Shaw. 'Mrs Pye was in charge.'

Guy glanced at Mrs Pye, but unlike the rest of us, showed no interest in seeing the work that had been done.

'That's up to Mrs Porter,' he said, looking at the letters lying in disarray. 'It's this room I'm concerned about.'

'We'll sort it,' I said. 'I'm going to call . . .'

'No, no,' interrupted Guy, in a very controlled tone that didn't sound like him at all. 'Leave it for now, thank you. I'd like to get on with our meeting. Let's gather some chairs together. When we've finished, I'm sure Mrs Pye can find time to sort out the removal of anything that doesn't belong in here. If you would, Mrs Pye.'

For the first time, her face lost some of its smugness. Despite his calm, no one could be in any doubt that Guy was far from impressed.

There was no cheery conversation or happy hubbub as the team gathered. Everyone did as they were told, making a wonky attempt at a circle of chairs to form a meeting. I watched Guy take a deep breath. I realised that I had been too wrapped up in my own concerns about Mrs Porter to give anything like enough thought as to how he must feel. It was one thing to have promised Lady Overton to help look after her niece, but to have his authority and position increasingly ignored by the day was another. I wondered how much he would put up with out of loyalty to the magazine and to the people about whom he very much cared.

Now however, he gave us something approaching a normal smile and called the meeting to a start.

A few minutes later, as I started reporting on "Yours Cheerfully", doing my best to sound upbeat rather than enraged at Mrs Porter's editorial approach, I ground to a halt as I heard her high-pitched chatter in the corridor. It was accompanied by a man's voice and what seemed to be the yapping of a dog.

Mrs Pye immediately leapt to her feet.

'Please continue, Emmy,' said Guy, steadily, 'and do sit down, Mrs Pye.' He gave her a look and she reluctantly did as he had requested.

'We've been getting a lot of letters from . . .' I began.

'Now, that *is* better. Look my darling, look.' Even with the door shut, it was clear that Mrs Porter was inspecting her new office. Mrs Pye smiled.

'You've been getting lots of letters from?' prompted Guy.

'Oh no. No, no, no, that won't do. It's entirely in the wrong place.'

Mrs Pye's smile wavered.

'Where *is* everyone?'

At this point I gave up, which was just as well, as the door was flung open and Mrs Porter walked in.

'Oh,' she said.

'Good morning, Mrs Porter,' said Guy. 'Are you joining us for the Editorial Meeting?'

'Good morning,' said Mrs Porter, resplendent in a cream suit and a hat so small it needn't have bothered. 'How lovely. No, thank you. Where is Mrs Pye? Oh, there you are.'

Mrs Pye had given a small wave. 'Good morning, Mrs Porter,' she said. 'I trust you find everything as you wished?'

First prize in the Fishing For Compliments Contest to the lady on my left.

'Oh yes, very good,' said Mrs Porter, vaguely, and not appearing quite as grateful as Madame Pye had perhaps hoped. 'But Small Winston's cushion is in the wrong place

114

entirely, and he's upset enough as it is. My goodness,' she said, finally drawing breath. 'This room is a fright.'

'It's the furniture from your office,' said Guy.

'It's awful,' replied Mrs Porter. She paused and turned her smile onto full beam. 'Look at you all. Working so hard, and it's still virtually the middle of the night. And Mr Collins running everything so beautifully. I can't thank you enough. And now I'm here. It's terribly exciting.'

I wasn't sure if Mrs Porter was expecting some sort of ovation, but everyone just stared. Also, it was twenty to ten and most of us had been up for hours.

'Oh dear,' she said. 'Have I interrupted something important? Don't mind me, I shall go and sit in my office. Mr Collins, might I borrow Madame just for the tiniest moment, please? Oh, and then I must introduce you to Mr Elliot who starts today, although I am afraid he is currently indisposed as poor Winston did not feel himself in the lift.'

And with that, she swooped out of the room, followed obediently, if perhaps nervously, by Mrs Pye.

Now everyone looked to Guy. I wondered if we had seen the straw on the camel's back. Would he finally snap?

But he merely shook his head. 'This is ridiculous,' he said, under his breath. He was silent for a moment and then he began to speak. 'You know, I've always tried to be not entirely dreadful as your Editor, and I hope you've felt in safe hands. But I have to say I wouldn't blame you for currently having your fair share of doubts.' He gave a brief smile. 'Quite frankly, this is a poor show and you deserve better.' He looked at the mess of letters and papers, and pushed his spectacles up to the bridge of his nose. 'These are disconcerting times for us all, and this is the last thing any of you need. I promise I will do everything in my power to make working here as decent as I can.

Things are very odd at the moment, but I will always be honest with you, which I hope might help. You've all been absolutely top drawer.' He hesitated. 'No one could ask for more from their team.'

'Don't you worry, Mr Collins,' said Mrs Mahoney. 'We're made of stern stuff.'

Everyone nodded and several people said, 'I'll say,' and 'Hear, hear.'

'Thank you. I couldn't agree more,' said Guy. He cleared his throat. 'Now, before we get to meet Mr Elliot and someone I can only hope is a dog rather than a man who has let himself down in a lift, let's get on with running this magazine.'

CHAPTER ELEVEN

Over Four Guineas For a Frock

As GUY HAD correctly guessed, Small Winston was a dog, although generally not allowed to behave like one. He was a stocky, almost pure white little fellow who I guessed would far rather be out chasing rabbits than being carried around or having to have a nap on his own special cushion. Winston's expression was always one of stoic despair at having to put up with the utter idiots with whom he had been lumbered. I couldn't say I blamed him.

The other new arrival, Mr Elliot, was a tall, thin, snooty man in his fifties who smelt of aniseed. To date he had spent the duration of the war in the accounts department of a ladieswear company where he had been paid to be cross with people who had not paid their invoices. From his first day in the office it was obvious that he was not the warm and friendly type, but if Mrs Porter was present, a transformation of miraculous proportions took place. Then Mr Elliot would ooh and ahh, and say, 'Yes, Mrs Porter, no, Mrs Porter' to the extent that Mrs Shaw immediately named him Three Bags Full Mrs Porter.

If he knew about his nickname, Three Bags didn't care as he had been installed in Mrs Bird's old office where he sat all day waiting for Mrs Porter to need something from him, and in the meantime, glaring out of his open door with the grim air of a headmaster looking forward to giving someone the cane.

The only upside was that one person in particular took an instant dislike to him, and that was Small Winston Porter himself. However fast Mr Elliot moved, Small Winston would seek him out and try to bite him, more often than not, really quite badly. By his third day at *Woman's Friend*, the dog's popularity had soared.

'You could get rabies,' said Mrs Mahoney after a nasty incident when Winston didn't appreciate being carried outside to visit the lavatory in the rain. 'I'll get the iodine, which I must warn you is going to sting.'

'Small Winston wouldn't give him *rabies*,' cried Mrs Porter.

'He would if he could, Mrs Porter,' said Mrs Mahoney. 'He's a very good dog.'

*

Once she had moved into her office, Mrs Porter had required the next two days to recover and meet up with a number of friends before she had found the time to actually sit down and do any real work. The rest of us were kept waiting and guessing as to what would stay in the magazine and what previously very popular item would be taken out and replaced with a new, far better idea. A meeting was finally called for first thing on Thursday morning, which meant that at half past eleven the whole team diligently filed into Mrs Porter's office and perched on the fancy sofas which were not quite as comfortable as one might have hoped.

After some time, Mrs Porter made her entrance with Small Winston. Following the upset with Mr Elliot, who had been reprimanded for not carrying him nicely, Hester had been given the role of accompanying the dog on what his owner referred to as Master Porter's Personal Appointments.

Now they had just returned from such an event, and Hester had earned top marks as Mrs Porter, who had waited anxiously in case Small Winston missed her too much, declared she could tell from his eyes that Hester Would Do. With the meeting ready to begin, the tiny squash-nosed tyrant was placed on his cushion where he scowled darkly until his special biscuits were produced.

'Good morning, everyone,' said Mrs Porter, even though it was now ten past twelve.

'Good morning, Mrs Porter,' we replied in unison, apart from Mrs Pye, who chimed in with, 'Bonne après-midi,' which showed the rest of us up.

Then Mrs Porter gave a short but inspirational speech about how it wasn't our fault *Woman's Friend* was so terribly dreary, but not to worry as it was already perking up now that she was here.

'I think we can all agree,' she cooed, 'that my first innovation, the evening-wear feature in this week's issue, has been an enormous success.'

'People have called it un triomphe,' interrupted Mrs Pye, having apparently forgotten that she was the one who had said it.

'So true,' said Mrs Porter, modestly.

The rest of us weren't quite so sure. The double-page spread had featured pictures of the most beautiful long dresses, all of which were shop-bought, which admittedly *was* an innovation as previously we had always featured sewing patterns so that readers could make clothes for themselves. The dresses weren't from any old shops either. Guy and I had tried hard to disguise how extraordinarily exclusive they were by calling the article "Frocks for *Very* Special Occasions" rather than Mrs Porter's suggested

"Dinner With Friends" which was only really accurate if you had a friend who owned half of Northumberland.

Within days, readers had responded.

Dear Woman's Friend

Who's Harvey Nichols and are his frocks made from gold because by the price of them they must be. I've never seen anything like it.

I did try your economy pie recipe though and it was smashing. More savoury tips please!

Yours,

Hilda Young, Birmingham

And the slightly more brusque:

Dear Woman's Friend

I don't know how many millionaires read your magazine but I for one wouldn't know a BEST FASHION HOUSE if I was on the bus and it drove into it.

Over 4 guineas for a frock? Don't make me laugh.

Not Made Of Money, Balham

'Just ignore them,' said Mrs Porter, when I showed the letters to her. 'Fashion is like modern art. Lots of people just don't understand it.'

The discussion was then closed.

'First things first,' she now said, as the meeting continued. 'From today we are replacing one of the short stories with the most delightful page that I am calling "Weddings We Love", and which Miss Lake has been given the thrill of writing for us. You may be excited to see some of the photographs already here.'

Mr Elliot solemnly handed round a selection of very fine pictures of just-married or recently engaged couples with their names and details pasted to the back. Everyone had at least four names each and looked absolutely lovely. Almost all the men were in uniform and some of the women as well, and only an absolute killjoy would begrudge any of them their happiness. I certainly didn't. I just wondered what on earth it had to do with the rest of us. I would find out when I began interviewing them.

There were various murmurs of, 'Very pretty,' and no one mentioned that the short stories we ran in each issue were one of the most popular features of the magazine.

Much encouraged, Mrs Porter moved on.

'We will continue our series of war-work articles,' she said, 'even though, and I know Miss Lake won't mind me saying, they are a horribly dry read, so they will now be one column rather than a whole page. But the new *Woman's Friend* will not shirk from her duty. If the Ministry depends on our help, then That Is What We Shall Do.'

She tapped her fingers on her desk to emphasize each word. Small Winston looked up at the noise, frowned, but let it go as a minor irritation when he spotted a bit of biscuit that he could just about reach with his tongue without having to move.

As Mrs Porter single-handedly took over any credit for helping the war effort, there was not a flicker of reaction from Guy.

'Although,' she continued, 'I do want us to improve the calibre of people in the war-work photographs. Look at the article about the poor women who work on the trains. The Ministry want us to attract workers, not put them off.' She turned to me. 'Couldn't the ghastly looking one have stood at the back?'

There was a sharp intake of breath from Miss Peters. Mrs Shaw tutted, and Mrs Mahoney said, 'Come now,' in what the rest of us knew to be her most unamused tone. But Mrs Porter seemed quite unaware of how rude she had been.

'I'm sorry, Mrs Porter,' I said, 'but none of the women looked remotely ghastly. And if they had been, they still would have stood wherever they wanted. Those girls are doing a terrifically good job, especially as it's not at all easy being a train guard. They have to put up with all sorts, which is why the Ministry needs help in getting more women to apply.'

'Well, I saw one,' replied Mrs Porter, sulkily. Then she turned to Guy. 'Speaking of the Ministry, Mr Collins, when is our next meeting? I must make sure it is in my diary.'

'Usually first thing on a Monday,' said Guy, fully aware that despite her enthusiasm about the new office, Mrs Porter was likely to continue to prefer a longer weekend than Saturday and Sunday could provide on their own.

Her face fell. 'Could it be moved?' she asked. 'Mondays aren't really me.'

'No,' said Guy. 'It could not.'

'Hmm,' said Mrs Porter, looking sad. 'Bit Mis.'

'Would you like to update everyone on Mr Elliot?' suggested Guy, swiftly finding a diversion. 'I believe there is good news.'

'Ooh yes,' said Mrs Porter. 'Thank you. Now he has settled in, our dear Mr Elliot is ready to take on the arduous duty of looking after our editorial contributors. This means Madame can spend her time entirely on Fashion and Beauty, where she belongs.'

Mrs Pye bowed her head. Mr Elliot stood to attention, and Mrs Shaw rolled her eyes so much she looked as if she was having some sort of attack.

'Your wonderful Production Update, Mrs Mahoney now, if you would,' said Mrs Porter, gamely bracing herself for several minutes of intense boredom. 'Just the overall idea will be fine.'

Mrs Mahoney, who everyone else knew had no intention of giving anything other than the full required report, shifted slightly on the sofa and then gave her publisher a Simmer Down stare.

'Thank you, Mrs Porter,' she said, 'although I'm afraid I'm not so sure you'll think it exactly wonderful once you've heard the information I have compiled.' Mrs Porter blinked in a non-eyelash-fluttering way but held firm as Mrs Mahoney continued. 'I have looked into the availability and costs of a heavier, glossier paper and in a nutshell, there isn't any. I'm sorry to disappoint you, but it's just as well as we'd have had to quadruple our cover price. Which of course, would be the move of a complete lunatic,' she added, pointedly.

'A shilling,' said Mrs Porter, gaily, and as if they tended to grow on trees. 'That's not too much, is it?'

'Yes,' said everyone else who wasn't entirely mad.

'Mrs Porter,' said Guy, 'we quite simply would not sell a single copy.'

'Oh,' said Mrs Porter, discovering a disappointing new reality. 'How about just doubling it? Everyone has sixpence. As your publisher, I must remind you that profits are very important.'

Mrs Mahoney looked at Guy, who took a deep breath.

'Again, I am afraid not, Mrs Porter,' he said, politely as Mrs Mahoney shuffled on the slightly slippery sofa and looked as if she suspected she was the victim of an elaborate joke. 'We can't just pick prices out of the air. And everyone doesn't have sixpence. I'm afraid it just doesn't work like that.'

'How do you know?' said Mrs Porter, a pout looking imminent. Small Winston growled. 'Have you ever tried?

It's about having vision, Mr Collins. I don't think you quite understand.'

'I do understand,' said Guy, showing levels of patience beyond normal human capability. 'But we can't just double the price of *Woman's Friend*. We'd lose thousands of readers overnight. And quite honestly, I wouldn't do it to them. It's not fair.'

'It would be like Claridge's doubling the price of their suites,' I said.

Mrs Porter gave me a look that had What Do You Know About Suites At Claridge's? written all over it.

'Talking about money is so distasteful,' she said, with a shudder. 'But I am a business woman, so Mr Collins I would like you to come up with a plan to increase our profits. Good. Thank you. Let's talk about something with a dash more pizazz.' Having told Guy to magic a business plan out of a hat, Mrs Porter lost interest and moved on. 'Now,' she continued, getting out her impressive leather notebook, 'As you know, I'm cutting down "Woman's Friend to Friend". Miss Lake, no more letters from readers expecting free facilities and paid-for holidays just for having a baby.'

She wrinkled her nose at the thought.

'We do get a lot of letters from readers interested in how things will change once we've won the war,' I said, calmly. 'It's been in the news magazines for months. People want things to be fairer, especially after everything they've been through.'

Mrs Porter looked at me blankly.

'Which is where a national system that helps everyone comes in,' I said, watching her attention ebb away. 'The readers are keen to share their ideas.'

Mrs Porter sighed heavily as if she was only halfway through double Maths. Small Winston crunched on his biscuits.

'I don't think so,' she said. 'I have already penned my first edition of "Your Publisher's Week", which has some super photographs of a charity luncheon I managed to fit in. It replaces Mr Collins' "Editor's greeting", which I'm sure he won't mind, and half of Miss Lake's letters from depressing people and communists. So that's lovely. And finally,' she said, 'and this is my favourite thing of all. I will be ending each issue with an Encouraging Word in the form of a poem.'

'Dear God,' said Guy, under his breath.

'I intend to inspire,' said Mrs Porter, who was now looking into thin air just above everyone's heads as if someone had given her some sort of award.

'Yes,' exclaimed Mrs Pye, immediately so inspired that she forgot to speak French.

'Poetry?' repeated Guy. 'I had no idea that you . . .'

'I have just taken it up,' said Mrs Porter, airily, 'and find that I have a natural ability with rhymes. I know not everyone can manage it, but if a poem doesn't rhyme, it's not really a poem, is it? It's a sentence dragged out. And that's just not me.'

'I do so agree,' simpered Mrs Pye, nodding thoughtfully at Mrs Porter's insight.

Guy put his head in his hands.

I wanted to scream. *Woman's Friend* was being turned into Cressida's personal scrapbook, and our readers were expected to both still want to read it and actually pay more for it.

'Mrs Porter,' I said, trying very hard to remain polite, 'I'm sure your poetry will bring much joy to people, but doesn't this mean our readers will only have half the usual space to share their thoughts and hopes for the future? Aren't they more important than pictures of people having lunch?'

Mrs Porter's smile disappeared like a shot. 'Do you

have a problem, Miss Lake?' she said, her tone switching in an instant. 'I was unaware we were all voting on my innovations. This is London, not Leningrad.'

'Not at all,' I said. 'It's just that readers care about issues that affect them, and they're pleased to have our support. We've been helping to push for more Government nurseries for war workers for over a year now and things are beginning to get better. We *can* help. I had a horribly sad letter just last week from a reader whose son has been killed in action and she's been made to give back two weeks of his pay that had already gone into his bank account. I'd very much like to put that in "Woman's Friend to Friend" as this sort of thing goes on all the time and it shouldn't. But now there won't be enough room. I'm not trying to be difficult, Mrs Porter, but there are so many topics our readers are keen to talk about.'

Mrs Porter had lifted Small Winston up from his cushion and was now feeding him biscuits as he sat on her lap.

'Ah, yes, the readers,' she said. 'There are still too many gloomy letters. From now on I shall personally approve everything that is printed in the problem page. Miss Lake, you always side with the women and I fear it makes us look as if we are bitter, which is horribly unattractive. Most men are perfectly harmless if one knows how to manage them.' She looked fondly at her dog. 'After all, the men they complain about can't *all* be in the wrong. They're probably just being silly sausages.'

I opened my mouth but words refused to come out.

'If I might, Mrs Porter,' said Mrs Mahoney, who had been biting her lip for some time, 'but if we don't stand up for our girls, who will?'

Mrs Porter sighed. 'It's just . . . *so* mis. No one wants that.'

'Mrs Porter,' said Mrs Mahoney, 'sometimes women

write to us because there's nobody else. We've all read hundreds – *thousands* – of letters and if a reader is being daft, we tell them.'

'The problems we help with aren't trivial,' I said, quietly. 'There are no "silly sausages". Honestly, Mrs Porter, we can show you tons of letters.' I was being as polite as I possibly could. 'I'd be so pleased for you to read them yourself.'

Mrs Porter was now a picture of concern. She put Small Winston on the floor.

'Hester,' she said, 'I fear Master Porter has some Urgent Personal Business to attend.' Then she turned to me. 'I have of course read the letters in the magazine. They're horrid.'

'It's real life,' I said, passionately. 'You don't need to take my word for it, just listen to the readers.'

I could hear the pleading in my voice, but Mrs Porter was running low on patience. She surveyed her desk, frowned, and moved the dancing statue slightly to the right.

'Mrs Porter,' said Guy, carefully. 'Ensuring the readers are happy is central to our business. If nothing else, I would point you to our circulation figures. Can I suggest we end this meeting so that you and I can discuss this in a more conducive setting?'

Mrs Porter looked up at him, but not in her usual coy mode.

'Mr Collins,' she said, 'I think Miss Lake overestimates the importance of her views.'

I had expected her to be angry, or for the famous pout to come into play, but this version of Mrs Porter was different. The spoilt little girl act was nowhere to be seen. She was now perfectly calm.

'As it appears that we are saying what is on our minds,

let me tell you all what is going to happen,' she said, looking around the room. '*Woman's Friend* is my magazine. I decide what goes in and what comes out. If the readers, for their thruppence a week, do not like it then they can read something else. We will attract new readers, and they will be the right sorts. Mrs Pye will lead the way with what is actually fashionable fashion, Mr Newton will turn his efforts to attaining a better class of advertiser, and I shall decide whether or not we include a problem page at all. Currently, I think not.'

Mrs Pye inclined her head in modest acceptance of Mrs Porter's announcement. Mr Newton gulped. Then, and to the entire room's surprise, Miss Peters spoke up.

'But what about us, Mrs Porter?' she said, in her soft voice. 'If there's no problem page, what shall we do?'

Mrs Porter smiled at her, far more like her usual electric beam.

'That, Miss, er . . .' She hesitated.

'Peters,' said Guy.

'That, Miss Peters,' said Mrs Porter as if she had remembered her all on her own, 'is up to you. Indeed, your futures are up to you all. Either you are *for* these exciting changes, or you are not. It is quite simple. Now then, I must go to my dear Winston as I fear he has over-indulged. Good day.'

Mrs Porter lifted her chin, and with her nose in the air, swept victoriously out of the room.

. . . Darling, I am writing this in haste before I leave for the station. Bunts and I are having a lovely time now that Thelma and the children are living with us. I just wish you were here too.

All the children are madly in love with Captain Harold (I think Bunty quite likes him as well!), and their campaign to get guinea pigs is getting up speed. Thel is bound to crack soon and I am secretly hoping she does. What are your views on guinea pigs? I can't believe I don't know.

Pooling food/coupons etc is turning out v well, and I am like a sponge learning every trick in the book (if sponges could read books) from Thel who makes everything taste better than you think it possibly could. I thought I was a fairly decent cook, but by the time you get home, I shall be so much better. (Mind you, don't expect cordon bleu – the bar was fairly low to begin with.) Thel says Bunts and I are better than her at baking, which probably says a lot about our priorities! After the war I am going to specialise in making anything that contains POUNDS of sugar. My aim is that our teeth all fall out by the time we are forty.

But how are you, darling? I know you say you like hearing about everyday things but I hope I am not being madly dull. The newspapers are full of HUGELY encouraging reports about how well you are all doing, (I know you can't say but I am guessing) and I keep wanting to nudge people on the bus and tell them how proud I am of you. Don't worry about writing if work means things are too busy. Our version of busy here is silly really. Mrs Porter is rather mad, but Guy is very good with her – patience must run in your family! Her dog bit Mr Elliot again which shouldn't be funny, but of course, was. I was sent to interview a very upper-class girl who is working in the ATA – she was decent and very dedicated. She is marrying a chap in the RAF . . .

CHAPTER TWELVE

A Day Out at the Zoo

IS IT BETTER to always be truthful to your husband, or to lie through your teeth so he doesn't worry about something he can do nothing about?

I wasn't at all sure, but I did lie to Charles, and hoped that I lied well, partly because he loved to hear about life at home, and partly because when you got down to it, any worries I had about my job couldn't possibly be as concerning as his. Nevertheless, Mrs Porter's declaration that we were either behind her, or not, shook everyone at *Woman's Friend*.

'I feel a fool,' said Mrs Shaw. 'She had me taken right in with all that handing out fudge and telling us we were the bee's knees. This is a very different side.'

Mrs Shaw was far from alone.

It was a subdued team that spent the rest of the week getting on with their work. If Guy said that Everything Was Going To Be Fine once, he said it a dozen times.

'Do you really think Mr Collins is right?' Hester whispered to me.

'Oh, gosh, yes,' I said, vehemently. 'Absolutely.'

Is it better to always be truthful to your colleague, or to lie through your teeth so she doesn't worry about something she can do nothing about?

I was more than grateful when Saturday finally turned up.

Bunty and I had decided to go to the zoo.

Thelma was going to see her mother in East Grinstead for the weekend. It was only thirty miles away and didn't take long on the train even with the stops and starts that were part of wartime life. Things weren't easy as her mum had a dicky ticker and her sister who lived there as well had an enthusiastically complicated love life which made it worse. Bunty and I had volunteered to look after the children while Thel tried to talk sense into their aunt and stop their granny worrying herself into an early grave. As the children were disappointed not to be going with her, I had suggested a trip to London Zoo as a treat. Bunty had asked Harold along, and Guy was joining in too. The children could hardly wait.

At eleven o'clock on a bright and clear mid-May morning when summer was beginning to pick up some speed I was determined to put work worries to the side for the day. George, Margaret, Stanley and I caught the number twenty-four bus and having bagged the best seats, upstairs at the front, we headed northwards from Pimlico. Morale was high, particularly about the possibility of seeing Ming, the panda.

As the bus made its way up into Camden, heavily battered by the Blitz but, as always, unbowed, excitement really began to rise, with everyone fighting to show they knew the most about the animals we might see.

'There are no fish and no snakes,' announced Margaret, matter of fact. 'Ginger Belinda at school said.'

'Oh, I like snakes,' said her younger brother.

'I'm afraid they had to kill them all, Stan,' said Marg, failing to sugar-coat the sad news. 'In case they got out during an air raid and bit people. The snakes, not the fish.'

'What a waste,' said George. 'They could have sent

them to Germany in spies' pockets, and trained them to kill Hitler.'

'Who said they didn't?' I replied. 'Perhaps they just said they're dead to put people off the scent.'

Three mouths dropped open.

'That,' gasped Marg, 'would be the best thing ever.'

'I bet Hitler's scared of snakes,' Stan said, confidently. Stan very much looked down on anyone who was afraid of animals. 'And spiders. Mr Armstrong at school doesn't like spiders and he's the spit of Hitler.'

'Everyone hates him,' confirmed George, as the family's elder statesman.

'Shall we not talk about that?' I suggested, aware I should probably not encourage them to be rude about their teachers. 'We're on Camden High Street and any minute now you might see Guy. Look out to the left. You should see the barrage balloons in the park as well.'

The children hurtled to the window, shouting, 'There he is,' as they spotted a variety of people, none of whom looked anything like Guy, and then as the bus slowed down, took no encouragement to head to the stairs at the back.

'Don't jump out until the bus stops,' I called as George expertly negotiated the high steps that led downstairs to the open platform, and rang the bell to tell the driver we wanted to get off. To my slight amazement, all three children did as they were told and waited, which was more than I would have done when promised a panda and the possibility of espionage snakes. 'And wait for me,' I yelled as we finally came to a halt, and unable to contain their excitement a moment longer, the three of them flung themselves out and onto the pavement.

'Mr Guy!' cried George, finally spotting him, and in the heat of the moment unsure of the appropriate term with the result that Guy sounded like a faithful old servant no one had the heart to retire.

'Morning, George. Everyone,' said Guy. 'Ooof.'

Stanley and Marg had hurled themselves at him, nearly winding him in the process.

'Steady on, chaps,' said Guy, happily. 'Now then, who knows the way? First one there buys the ice creams.'

'Hello, Mr Guy,' I said, as the children all cheered. 'You do know there's a war on.'

'Ah well,' said Guy. 'We'll just have to pinch some of the peanuts off the monkeys. That's assuming they're still there. I know they got rid of the snakes.'

'Here we go again,' I said.

'They're all dead,' said Margaret.

'Or in hiding with our spies,' whispered George, loudly.

Stan nodded. 'We probably shouldn't say that,' he warned. 'Not when people can hear.'

'I haven't the faintest idea what any of you are on about,' said Guy, cheerfully. 'Come on.'

With the children leading the way, the five of us headed towards the zoo. Guy was on good form, joining the effort to have a proper day out. He offered me his arm and we chatted as we walked towards Gloucester Avenue and then onto Regent's Park Road.

'Now,' I said, 'Bunty and Harold are meeting us at the entrance. She asked him to come, which Thel and I think is A Significant Move.'

'Ah ha,' said Guy.

'Anyway, I don't want to frighten her off by being too enthusiastic,' I whispered, 'and don't say anything to the children as we're trying to keep it low key.'

'I see.' Guy dropped his voice. 'You make it sound as if you're stalking a gazelle.'

'Shhh,' I said, as Marg had stopped to tie her shoelace.

'Well, good for her,' said Guy, doing his best, but clearly not finding Bunty's personal life half as fascinating as Thelma and I did. 'He sounds a decent chap.'

'I think he is,' I said. 'Oh, I say, there they are.'

We had walked round Outer Circle and were now near the main entrance to the zoo where a little way behind at the back of a sizeable queue stood Bunty and Harold, chatting in an animated way. The children spotted them immediately and dragged us over. Bunty of course introduced Harold to Guy which was all very nice, and by the time we had got into the zoo and Marg had been put in charge of the guidebook, after which there was a small kerfuffle over what to see first, anyone would have thought we had all known each other for years.

Harold was even more chipper than when he was talking about sheds, and I noted that he had a little more colour in his cheeks than the other day. He said he had started going for walks to try to get his full strength back.

'I think they're good for me,' he said.

'You enjoy walking, don't you, Bunts?' I said.

'Oh yes,' replied Bunty, 'especially in the summer.'

At that point I decided it was imperative for me to slow down and check for something important in my handbag. Guy, who was more on the ball than I had given him credit for, hung back with me.

'I think the gazelle knows exactly what she is doing,' Guy laughed as Bunty and Harold walked on, chatting. 'Good for old Bunts. They look very nice together.'

I agreed. I also thought how easily Harold fitted in with everyone. He didn't even mind when a short while later George told an unpleasant boy who had been making nasty comments, that Harold only had one arm as the other one had been bitten off by a lion.

'You're lying,' said the boy. 'You'll go to hell.'

'You're not allowed to say that word,' said Stan, horrified.

'Actually, young man,' interrupted Harold, now looking very tall and speaking in an authoritative voice, 'it's the first rule on safari. If a lion attacks, you have to ram your arm down its throat so it can't grab you by the neck and kill you.' He shrugged, as if he did it all the time. 'You'll lose the arm of course, but it's worth knowing, just in case one should escape.'

The rude boy looked suitably reproached, which cheered Stan up no end.

'Are you sure that the elephants aren't here?' he asked his sister, who was sharing information from the guidebook on a strictly Need To Know basis. 'They're my favourites.'

'I'm sorry, Stan,' said Margaret, 'Ginger Belinda said they moved out to the country ages ago.'

Poor Stan looked disappointed and I did feel this Belinda character was rather a damp sort. Harold pitched in to help.

'I say, old chap,' he said, 'I'm keen on monkeys, but I may be a poor shot at throwing nuts for them these days. Do you think you could help me out?'

'Yes, please,' said Stan. 'And then would you like to go to Pets' Corner? Mum says they tell you how to keep goats.'

'There goes the garden,' said Bunty.

Over the next hours we wound our way around the zoo, becoming part of the crowds of families keen to see their favourite animals and make the most of a day out. If you ignored the sandbags and the air-raid shelters, and the fact that the glass houses had all their windows covered in tape, it was almost as if there wasn't a war on. Even the aquarium had re-opened which, as George kindly said to Stan, was one in the eye for Belinda, who clearly had not kept up with the news.

A llama pulling a small cart brimming over with hay was led past by a friendly keeper who told George even animals had to make an effort what with petrol being unavailable these days. When it was followed by a camel similarly doing its bit for the war, Harold said that from experience it was true they could spit. Then, when we got to Pets Corner, Guy rather rashly said he was reminded of a friend's parrot which had been taught a very rude song about a goat.

At this point, Harold let out a mighty guffaw, with immediate and obvious regret.

'Do you know the rude song, Harold?' gasped Margaret. 'You DO. I can tell.'

Harold looked at Bunty in a panic.

'I can't help you,' she said, trying not to laugh.

'Sadly,' said Harold, 'I have forgotten the words.'

'And I've never known them,' said Guy, quickly.

'Don't worry,' said Stan, helpfully. 'Everyone knows it at school.'

And then as one, to the tune of 'Men of Harlech', the children burst into song.

'I'm the man who comes from Scotland,
Shooting peas up a nanny goat's bottom.'

It was a miracle we weren't asked to remove ourselves from the zoo.

Harold was now well and truly part of the pack.

We very quickly moved on from Pets Corner with Stan leading the charge to the Monkey House.

'It's nice to see you having fun for a change,' I said to Guy as we walked after the children. 'You've been looking a bit tired recently. It's entirely understandable, but are you all right?'

Guy nodded, unconvincingly. 'Long old stint fire-watching last night,' he said. 'I'm knocking on, you know.'

He stopped and stood on his toes to look over a crowd of people gathered around the penguin pool.

'If Mrs Porter is the death of you,' I said, 'what on earth am I going to tell Charles? He'll be furious.'

'I'm fine, Em,' said Guy. 'She won't be the death of anyone. Well, possibly *Woman's Friend*.'

'Guy!' I said, surprised. 'You can't say that. You've just spent the last two days telling everyone it's going to be all right.'

Guy removed his spectacles and rubbed his eyes. 'I could hardly do otherwise,' he said.

I fixed him with a stare. 'This isn't like you.'

'I'm sorry,' he said, and then in a far heartier voice added, 'I was being self-indulgent. Where are the monkeys? Come on, we're getting left behind.'

'We can catch them up,' I said. 'What's going on?'

We were standing by a bench and now I leant back against it and folded my arms. 'I'm not moving,' I said.

Guy put his spectacles back on and perched beside me. 'The truth?' he asked. Then he paused. 'I don't know what to do. So much for Lady Overton thinking I was the capable hands that would keep it all going.' He shook his head. 'Emmy, nothing works with Cressida Porter. And believe me, I'm trying.' He gave a huge sigh. 'I'm also failing. Nothing I say or do is stopping her from turning our dear old magazine into her personal folly. She's impervious. But we said we weren't going to talk about it. Today is supposed to be happy.'

I wasn't sure what to say. Guy had been so admirably calm around her. Worse, I had never known him admit defeat before. It was completely disarming.

'You'll work her out,' I said. 'You're clever like that. I mean obviously you hide it well,' I added, nudging him and trying to make him smile. But it didn't work.

'I hate letting people down,' he said, fiercely. 'It's the worst thing in the world.'

'So don't give up,' I said. 'As you've been saying, we just need to keep on her side, and then come up with something. And I know I've not been very good at that, but I did a wedding interview and it wasn't as bad as I'd feared.' Now I was clutching at straws. 'The page could be all about what brides are doing for the war effort. Mrs Porter might be all right about that as long as there are nice pictures.'

It wasn't a bad idea. Guy nodded, but hardly look convinced.

'Come on, Guy,' I said. 'This isn't like you.'

'Well, what about "Yours Cheerfully" then?' he answered, challenging me. 'How are you going to get round her on that? Emmy, the most pressing problem in the next issue is a woman who wants to find a present for her husband's birthday. The answer to which is a bloody two-guinea cravat.'

'I know,' I said. 'But I thought we might be able . . .'

'Emmy, I was on the phone with her for an hour and a half yesterday,' said Guy, cutting across me. 'Trying to persuade her to change her mind about readers' letters. An hour of buttering her up to avoid her ringing off, and then for the short time we actually discussed anything editorial, I had to run through my entire repertoire of cajoling, negotiating, flattering, and in the end, more or less begging. Which got me absolutely nowhere.' He almost spat out the words. Then he added, quietly, 'I'm sorry. I shouldn't be telling you this.'

'Of course you should,' I protested. 'And honestly, Guy, you always find a way to sort everything.'

Guy didn't answer, but the look on his face scared me to bits. For the first time ever, he seemed utterly defeated.

'Emmy,' he said, finally, 'your faith in me means a huge amount, but I am drawing a blank. Perhaps it's time to call it a day. Do you know, last week Simons mentioned a job going at the Ministry. They come up relatively frequently and I never give them a thought. But for the first time ever, I didn't immediately say no. I will of course, but this is the first time, I've actually considered it.'

Now I really was shocked. 'But what about the readers?' I asked. '*Think about the readers.* It's what you always say. And it's what we do. It's what we're good at. We can't just give up.'

Guy looked at me and broke into a small smile. 'Of course,' he said. 'I'm sorry. An off day. I've run out of ideas at the moment, but I'll buck up, Em, I promise.'

Shrieks and shouts of laughter wafted over from the penguins, where feeding time had officially begun.

'No, I'm sorry,' I said, 'you've been taking the whole weight of the Mrs Porter situation. All I've done is moan and cross swords with her. I'm going to think of something. I don't know how good it will be but we'll turn it into a decent plan and find a way to stop her. Somehow we'll find a way. Mrs Porter will not be the death of *Woman's Friend*.'

CHAPTER THIRTEEN

A Germ of an Idea

I HAD BEEN taking it for granted that Guy would be able to bring Cressida around – pull something out of the bag as he always did. The thought of him begging her not to change the magazine that thousands of readers loved, and her ignoring him, was horrible.

'You should have told me,' I said after we had disappointed an elderly lady who asked if we knew the way to the baboons. 'I know you're the Editor and in charge, but I'm always here for moral support, if nothing else. Every time she's come up with something awful, I've just thought that somehow you'd talk her out of it.'

'So did I, to start with,' said Guy. 'But I underestimated her. My fault. I need to brace up. Perhaps an ice cream would help.'

'War on,' I reminded him, pleased he was having a go at levity. 'But what was Lord Overton thinking when he left it all to *her*? He wouldn't have wanted this, would he?'

'God, no,' said Guy. 'He could have packed in *Woman's Friend* years ago if he'd wanted, especially when it was in the doldrums and losing money for all those years. But he didn't. It was one of the few things he was sentimental about. Lady Overton liked it, so on we went while he propped us up.'

'Are you sure you can't speak to her?' I asked. 'How about writing?'

Guy shook his head. 'Lady Overton's just lost her husband of fifty-five years, and she believes that I will look after Cressida, and I assume, *Woman's Friend*. What would I say? *Dear Lady Overton, So sorry I've let you down, but can you help me stop your uncontrollable niece?*' He shook his head. 'I can't do that. The alternative of course is to appeal to their son – the new Lord. The man who once referred to our magazine as "that rag full of bellyaching and bloomers."'

I winced. 'Did he really?'

'Oh, yes. I might have been friends with his brother, but Johnny Overton couldn't give a fig. In fact, that's probably our answer as to why his father left *Woman's Friend* to the Egg. Johnny wouldn't care if we went under tomorrow.' Guy bit his lip and stared over to the top of the aviary. 'Dammit, now that I say that, it does make sense.'

For several long moments, we sat in silence, until finally, Guy spoke.

'I can't apologise enough for lumping all this on you on your day out.'

'Don't worry,' I said, trying to be hearty, 'we're giving Bunty and Harold lots of time on their own. They'll probably be engaged by the time we get to the antelopes.'

'Good man,' said Guy. 'No point hanging about.'

'Are you absolutely sure the new Lord Overton won't listen?' I asked. A large exotic bird screeched dramatically. This was an odd place to be having a serious conversation.

Guy narrowed his eyes as he thought. 'I know he won't care. Doug Hemmings at the *Chronicle* says Overton thinks his cousin Mrs Porter will lose interest by Christmas.' He reached into his pocket for his cigarettes. 'Apparently she's never stuck at anything in her life.'

Douglas Hemmings was one of the senior editors on Launceston's *Evening Chronicle* and was so famous for having his ears to the ground that he was known in press circles as The Bloodhound.

'But that's great,' I said, astonished that Guy hadn't mentioned it. 'All we have to do is wait, and then when she gets bored and leaves us to it, we can change everything back. We'll carry on doing all the work, Mrs Porter will get lots of lovely profit without doing anything, and everyone will be happy. It'll be a rotten seven months until Christmas, but if we can stick it out, then it'll be worth it. Why didn't you say this before?'

A wave of hope flooded over me.

A cheer went up from the crowd as a zookeeper shouted out that he needed some volunteers.

'Well?' I prompted. 'Isn't this good? Why are you still looking low?'

'Because if Mrs Porter continues to make all the changes she's planned, in seven months' time there won't be a magazine to save,' said Guy, now looking at me intensely. 'Emmy, you know how many other magazines our readers and advertisers could move to. You've said yourself that the complaints have already started. We don't have until Christmas. If we don't do something well before then, *Woman's Friend* won't exist.'

I tried to think on my feet. 'Right-oh,' I said, refusing to accept defeat. 'How about this: if Mrs Porter is likely to lose interest by Christmas, why don't we hurry things up?'

It would have been easier to sound inspirational if I wasn't now battling against a flock of honking penguins, but as Guy raised a not entirely despondent eyebrow, I pushed on.

'We can try to put her off, before it's too late,' I explained. 'Let's look at what we know.' I felt like a detective as I started counting off things on my fingers. 'She likes all the snazzy, glamorous things, she wants to show off to her friends, she certainly wants to make money . . . but she's not interested in what publishing actually involves and she gets bored at the drop of a hat. So,' I concluded, 'why don't we introduce Mrs Porter to Important Publishing Things she'll think are terribly dull? If she wants to go to the Ministry, let's take her to one of their most unexciting meetings. She adores having lunch so let's invite some of the most, well, *least* interesting people we know.' Now I was picking up speed. 'What about an hour or two with Herbie Garson from the printers? Herbie once made Mrs Mahoney actually watch paint dry while he talked to her about ink. She said after three hours she was seriously considering throwing herself into the vat. My point is, the more Mrs Porter sees, the more uninterested she'll become. And then she might leave us alone.'

Guy looked thoughtful. 'Hmmm. We'd have to work out how to stop losing readers at the same time,' he said, half to himself.

Now I spoke more slowly. It was little more than a germ of an idea, and I was working it out as I spoke. 'Just after the Blitz, when I hadn't been at *Woman's Friend* very long, the Editress of one of our biggest competitors did a sort of plea in her column directly to the readers. I've never forgotten it. They'd been bombed out, but not mentioned it to the readers so some of them had had to wait ages for their letters to be answered. People had got really cross and complained. Anyway, the Editress wrote an apology in the magazine and explained that they'd been having a pretty steep time of things but that they were all very sorry and it wouldn't happen again. I asked Monica about it once. She said the complaints dried up overnight and readers actually wrote in to thank them for their honesty. Guy, even if we only have half the magazine we used to, they're still our readers. We're still their friend. We'll just have to try harder.'

Guy stared across to the aviary again. 'So, are you saying we apologise to the readers?' he said. 'The Egg will go crackers.'

'Sort of,' I said. 'Obviously we can't say, "sorry, we've gone a bit mad", but we could talk to them. If Cressida won't let us print their letters, let's write back to more of them instead. We could print something like, *We're sorry but due to space, we can't feature as many letters in the magazine as we'd like, but please keep writing and we'll write back.* And even if she cuts down "Woman's Friend to Friend" we can still pass on readers' views to the various Government departments – Housing, Employment, Pensions – you know, as we always do. It'll be hard work, but we can try,' I said. 'The only thing I can't work out is helping people who can't tell us their address, and that's awful. But at least this is something. At least we'll be showing we still care.' I looked at Guy hopefully.

'All right,' said Guy, slowly. 'And meanwhile I'll keep trying to rein in Mrs Porter.'

'That's right. We'll protect as much of the old *Woman's Friend* as we can so we still actually sell some and make her money. The main aim being she realises she can go back to doing nothing while we do all the work and she gets even richer.'

'A three-point approach,' said Guy. He was now pacing around the bench, as if he was in a board meeting. 'One: ensure publishing is crashingly dull to put CP off job. Two: protect as much of the original magazine as we can. Three: ensure readers know we're still listening and aiming to help, potentially increasingly directly.'

He threw his cigarette on the ground and squashed it out with his foot. I had to smile. No wonder Guy was in charge. He'd taken my waffle and put it into something that actually resembled a plan.

'Well, when you put it like that,' I said. 'Do you think we might have a chance?'

He looked a hundred times more positive than before. 'We might. We need to think it through properly, but I think you've got something here. Running a magazine is all A Bit Mis, but we're the dullards who enjoy it, so just leave it to us. Yes. I like it.'

'Hurrah!' I replied. 'Here's to being a dullard. Now will you please promise me you're not going to give up?'

'Would I?' said Guy, smiling broadly. He had stopped pacing around and now offered me his arm. 'Come on,' he said. 'I'm rather keen to see a gnu.'

*

It was extraordinary how having a tiny glimmer of hope lifted our spirits. When George came running up to tell us we were missing out on all the best animals, Guy and I put work to one side and very happily joined in. Guy found his gnu, Stan learned how to keep goats, and Marg was able to win in the one-upmanship stakes over the infamous Belinda as Bunty had brought her camera and took a very good photograph of her outside the newly re-opened aquarium. George spent his pocket money on a book explaining how to build your own fish tank, and Harold immediately promised that he would help. Best of all, Bunty was beginning to look the happiest I had seen her in years.

As we all headed to the bus stop to make our way home, tired and with noses now red from the sun, everyone agreed that the only thing that would have made it better would have been if Thelma had been there too. I had the feeling that after she had listened to a full re-enactment of the day by the children, my friend would feel as if she had been there every step of the way.

When Guy and I returned to the office on Monday, it was with a new optimism. We also knew that we couldn't possibly try to launch a covert campaign without the rest of the *Woman's Friend* team. Or, at least, those who we knew and trusted.

With Mrs Porter as usual unable to face the 'beastly horror' of returning from the country on a Monday, things were made even easier when Mr Elliot called in poorly. ('That'll be the rabies taking hold,' said Mrs Mahoney.) When Mrs Pye had to go out on a Very Important Research Trip to Fortnum & Mason, Guy called an emergency team meeting.

If I had had any doubts that my on-the-spot ideas were too wobbly to try out, they disappeared immediately. Everyone, it seemed, was keen as mustard to give them a go.

'I'm in,' said Mrs Mahoney, straight off. 'I'll call Herbie Garson and ask him about lunch.'

'I don't mind typing up more letters to the readers,' said Miss Peters. 'Mrs Shaw and I are both very fast.'

'There won't be Minutes from this meeting, will there?' asked Mr Newton, nervously.

'Absolutely not,' said Guy.

'In that case,' continued Mr Newton, 'if I may speak entirely off the record, I know some rather robust advertising agency people. A meeting with them might be useful. They're awful.'

'Excellent,' said Guy. 'Although we do run the risk Mrs Porter will think they're top hole.'

'I've been working on some cover designs,' said Mr Brand, reaching for his portfolio case. 'I think they may help maintain a certain level of happiness.'

We all gathered round to see a series of utterly lovely illustrations. Six entirely different but enormously attractive women, all with different hair colours, styles, clothes and occupations, and all somehow looking like idealised versions of Mrs Porter.

'Good God, Mr Brand, you're a genius,' said Guy.

'They'll go down a storm,' I grinned.

Ever modest, Mr Brand deflected the praise. 'You're very kind,' he said, 'I'm just glad if they are of help. I think Miss Lake has come up with a jolly good plan.'

'Hear, hear,' said Mr Newton, boldly.

'Thank you,' I said. 'Guy and I did it together. I know it's a long shot.'

'But it's all we've got,' said Mrs Mahoney and Guy at the same time, which made everyone laugh.

'Excellent,' said Guy. 'Well done everyone. Remember, not a word outside this room. Operation It's All We've Got is go.'

Ten minutes later, I had made the first step.

YOURS CHEERFULLY

Don't forget, we're here to help! As you may have noticed, there's not always as much room to print your letters as we'd like, so why not write to us for help privately?

A stamped, self-addressed envelope will do the trick, or chum up with a pal and we can send our reply to you at another address.

What's that old phrase? "A problem shared is a problem halved!" We think so and we want to help out.

We are, and always will be,

Your friends at *Woman's Friend*.

CHAPTER FOURTEEN

If I Won The Pools

FOR THE NEXT three weeks, a game of cat and mouse began to emerge. Mrs Porter and her allies, Mr Elliot and Mrs Pye, pushed ahead with making changes to *Woman's Friend*. The rest of us did our best to appear entirely on board, while surreptitiously trying to protect the magazine that our readers knew and loved.

Mr Brand's strangely familiar illustrations were a hit as expected, and Guy scored further points by telling Mrs Porter that he was joining Mr Newton to push for the sort of advertisers that would befit the magazine's new look. There was little we could do about the sudden emphasis on unattainably expensive fashion but Mrs Stevens, who was in charge of knitting, stepped up to the mark. To Mrs Porter's surprise, she produced patterns that copied and even improved the sort of rig-outs worn by the aristocracy in articles our publisher followed in the fancier press.

For my part, I did my best to toe the line, even when Mrs Porter told me to provide a selection of 'the least depressing' readers' problems, from which she would pick a few lucky people for us to help. It wasn't easy to keep quiet, especially as I felt that 'It's Not My Fault I'm Prettier Than All Of My Friends' was not the most pressing concern during a war.

The was no doubt however, that the readers were

wondering what was going on. Some were nice about it, others more to the point. We put all of their messages into Mrs Porter's in-tray. Invariably Mr Elliot tried to take them all out again, but if we timed it properly and mixed the few favourable ones in with the complaints, some did manage to get through.

Dear Woman's Friend

Please can you tell me when the short story you usually have by the gardening is coming back? It's my favourite as I'm lucky if I can get five minutes to myself to read anything in one go.

Also, please can we have normal food? If I ever see a real egg again, I'm not risking it on "The Art of a Soufflé", even if the Duchess of What Not does enjoy it when she's at home.

Yours faithfully
E. D. Brown (Mrs), Aberdeen

Dear Woman's Friend

Last month in your column "Woman's Friend To Friend" you said you wanted to know what readers thought about a new 'family allowance' after the war. I wrote in, but you don't seem to have printed any answers? I'm all for it and think it would give us parents a real boost.

Thank you in advance,
Mrs Marjorie Willis, Brighton

Dear Mrs Porter

I hope you don't mind, but I saw the pictures in your magazine of your dog wearing a hat and eating a cake. I work at a veterinarian's and I'm afraid that even if it is his favourite, if you keep feeding him this way, he will most probably die.

Yours,
Miss B Tully, Newport
PS: And it's a waste of sugar.

Mrs Porter had to spend the rest of the day at home after she read that one. Some people didn't know anything. It upset Small Winston as well, and she said he only cheered up after a double helping of suet dumplings for being a brave boy.

To be fair, not all of Mrs Porter's ideas missed the mark. The wedding pictures did cheer some readers up.

Dear the Honourable Mrs Cressida Porter
    I do like your pictures of weddings. Can anyone send in a photograph? Here's mine. It was such a happy day.
    I hope it might be one that you choose.
    Yours sincerely,
    Evelyn Howard (Mrs)
    PS: I enclose an envelope and stamp. Please do return it to me.

Mrs Howard sent an absolutely beautiful picture.

Mrs Porter laughed and said, 'No.'

In the meantime, Mrs Shaw, Miss Peters, and I worked out a system to try to privately answer more letters than ever. Mrs Porter didn't mind, or possibly didn't notice that we encouraged readers to ask for personal replies. Taking it in turns, the two ladies would bring a bundle of problems into my office where I would quickly read them and then dictate an answer. They both had world champion speed shorthand, and while one took dictation, the other typed like fury, and then they would swap. Over and over again, all day, every day.

Hester would open the envelopes but as she was far

too young to read what might be inside, Guy volunteered to help out. Unused to the sheer volume and often troubling problems that readers were trying to cope with, after a week he was heard to say that someone should resurrect the suffrage movement.

Mrs Mahoney told him that while she was delighted he finally had a clue about what it was like to be female, if he said 'bastard' in front of Hester again, she would walk straight out of the office and never come back.

Guy apologised profusely and admitted he had let himself down.

Moments of jollity, though, were few and far between. Everyone was working as hard as they could, but if we were trying to hold the line, those holds were few and far between.

Woman's Friend was moving inexorably into a different world.

*

When I wasn't at the office, I was working shifts at the fire station. These days lots of girls had two jobs, but it wasn't easy. I only managed due to Guy being terrifically understanding about me working some very odd hours, and Captain Davies being equally decent and quite happy to have someone who worked more weekends than anyone else. Along with most of the population of Britain I was also an excellent cat-napper. All the same, other than the trip to the zoo, I hadn't had a day off in weeks.

'What you need,' said Roy, one night shift when he found me in the bunk room, nodding off over a small pile of readers' letters, 'is a night out. That'll pep you up.' He did a little soft-shoe shuffle. 'Get you moving.'

Then he thrust a piece of paper into my hand.

'*A Grand Celebrity Concert at the Royal Albert Hall in*

aid of the London Fire Service Benevolent Fund,' I read out loud.

'It's on Sunday. Me and Fred are going with a couple of the boys. I've just asked Thel and she says she's keen if she can find a babysitter. I'm not taking no for an answer, Emmeline, you can't be put to shame by a bunch of old geezers like us.'

'You're hardly even forty, Roy,' I said. 'That's not an old geezer.'

'I'll take that as a "yes",' said Roy.

It was a smashing excuse for a rare group night out.

Thirty-six hours later, Mrs Harewood from next door, who had taken quite a shine to the children, was comfortably installed in the kitchen so we could all go and make an evening of the event. The four of them were enjoying the end of *Children's Hour* on the BBC Home Service, and Marg in particular was looking forward to a talk on 'nerves' by a medical psychologist at seven o'clock.

Thel, Bunty, and I had just finishing getting ready, Thel and me in our uniforms and Bunty in a very pretty pale green cotton frock.

'I can't remember the last time we all went out together,' she said, as the front doorbell rang and Roy and Fred were revealed. They were immaculately turned out – parade ready of course.

'You two do scrub up well,' said Bunts, as she let them into the house.

'You're looking very nice yourself,' said Fred, gallantly, only to be interrupted by a thunder of feet as Stanley and Marg came racing up from the kitchen and looked imploringly at their mother, who was adjusting her cap in the hallway mirror.

'Hello, Uncle Roy and Uncle Fred,' said Stan. 'Can we show them, Mum, can we?'

'Five minutes,' said Thel, without turning round, 'and don't let Roy get dirt on him.'

'Excuse me, ladies, important matters, thank you very much,' Roy said as Stan cheered. Marg grabbed Roy's hand and dragged him off to the garden.

As if Harold wasn't already something of a hero to them, over the last two weekends, he had cemented his place in the family history books by leading a huge team effort to turn the dilapidated old shed into a perfectly serviceable and safe home for pets. With Bunty and the children all mucking in, not even the hardest heart could have said no when Stan asked if they could finally get two guinea pigs.

'Roy's honoured,' I said. 'Visits are by invitation only because Stan Laurel and Oliver Hardy are still settling in.'

'They couldn't come up with another name?' said Fred, laughing. 'What with there already being a Stan.'

'Hasn't even occurred to them,' said Thel. 'Right, I'll just go and check with Mrs Harewood that she's happy and then we should go.'

'We're meeting Buzz and Hilda there,' said Bunty, 'so we'd better get a move on.'

Beryl 'Buzz' Berkeley and her friend Hilda had been lodging with Mrs Harewood for several months. Both in the ATS and members of an all-female big band, we had become friends, and Buzz had recently started giving Margaret lessons on the trombone. When we'd heard that one of the acts on the bill tonight was Ivy Benson and Her All-Girl Band, naturally I'd given them a shout.

Five minutes later, Roy reappeared as promised, with not even a blade of straw to let his spotless uniform down.

'How were they?' I asked.

'Healthy looking pigs,' said Roy. 'Your Harold did a

good job on the shed, Bunty. It looks like new. You could get half a farm in there. Chickens at least.'

Bunty beamed at him and didn't dispute the 'Your' Harold.

'Let's see how we get on with Laurel and Hardy first,' said Thel. 'Now, is everyone ready?'

There were agreements all round that we were, although Roy was looking suspiciously smiley since mentioning the potential for poultry.

'You heard Thelma,' I said to him. 'Don't even think about it.'

'Would I?' said Roy. 'Come on, we don't want to be late.'

There was no time to ask what he meant, as we yelled our goodbyes to the children and headed off to the bus.

Roy had been right. A night out was exactly what I needed. It was a lovely June evening and with Double Summer Time it would be light for hours to come. The ride to Kensington had a party atmosphere with everyone talking and joking, especially Fred and Roy who were having a lovely time teasing Bunty about Harold.

'Did he not want to come?' asked Fred.

'He's busy,' said Bunts. 'One of his old army friends is visiting.'

'He's not gone off you, has he?' said Roy.

'We could call Frank,' said Fred. 'He'll be here like a shot.'

'I'm perfectly capable of spending an evening out with my friends,' said Bunty, pretending to be prim.

Roy and Fred laughed, and we came to our stop and joined other concertgoers making their way towards the Royal Albert Hall. Roy offered Bunty his arm, which she gladly took, as Thelma and I got in the way of everyone else by walking arm in arm with Fred. We were far from alone in our National Fire Service uniforms, as not unnaturally the concert had attracted large numbers of NFS members. When the war had first broken out, all the boys had been given a rough time by more than a few people as it was said in some quarters that joining the fire service was a soft route compared with joining the military. The Blitz had changed all that. Now no one would ever question how brave they were. Night after night, firemen had faced unimaginable horrors, and often still did. To say I was proud to be associated with the Service was the biggest understatement in the world. And as far as Roy and Fred and the rest of the boys at Carlton Street station were concerned, they were the absolute best.

When we arrived at the Albert Hall, Bunty patted the bag that was slung over her shoulder.

'I've got two pictures left on the film in my camera and I thought I could take a photograph of the four of you outside,' she offered.

'Ooh, yes please,' I said. 'Although it's a shame Your Harold isn't here to join in.'

Bunty smiled but didn't rise to the bait.

Ever since London Zoo I had been stopping myself from asking about him, as I wanted her to be able to tell me in her own time. But Roy had set it up too well for me to not take up my chance. 'Is he then?' I asked. '*Your* Harold, that is?'

We carried on walking, looking around at the crowds. No fuss, no teasing, just me and my best friend on a night out.

'Yes,' she said, simply. 'Yes, I think that he is.'

★

'A pleasure to meet you. I'm Buzz, this is Hilda. Bunty's told me all about you. Did the chap with the teeth not come? Another time. Have you seen Ivy Benson before? They're crackerjack. Hilda knows one of the girls, don't you, Hil?'

Having congregated outside the giant venue, enthusiastic introductions were made. Bunty took a picture of the four of us NFS members, which raised a cheer from other fire service personnel, one of whom volunteered to use the last picture on Bunty's film to take a snap of us all.

As we thanked them, the most beautiful open-top car pulled up and a very dashing RAF officer kissed the woman sitting in the front passenger seat before she got out of the car in the most elegant way.

Fred and Roy, who were both mad keen on cars, stared.

'Derby Bentley drophead coupé,' said Fred, reverentially.

'The Silent Sports car,' added Roy, almost to himself, 'seventy miles an hour, just like that.'

'It's lovely,' said Buzz. 'I bet it cost a fortune.'

Fred nodded. 'If I win the Pools,' he said, 'that's what I'll buy. Straight down the showroom.'

He looked almost misty-eyed at the thought. It was silly, but it made my heart ache.

'If I win the Pools, Fred,' I said, 'I'll buy one for you. As long as you promise to give us all lifts.'

'That's a deal,' replied Fred.

'I'd buy everyone houses,' said Thelma.

'In the same street,' suggested Bunty, and within seconds we were planning how to spend our fortunes.

Quite quickly between us we'd spent every last penny we could possibly win.

'Thanks for saying you'd buy me a Bentley,' said Fred. 'It's a lovely thought.'

'It mainly so you can take me to work every morning,' I laughed. 'Just so I can see the look on Mrs Porter's face.'

'I tell you what,' said Thelma, 'if I win the Pools, I'll *buy* you *Woman's Friend*. The whole thing. That'll show her.'

'Thanks, Thel,' I said. 'Do you actually do the Pools?'

'No,' said Thel.

'That's a flaw,' said Bunts, thoughtfully. 'Mind you, neither do I. I say, does anyone fancy going in on it together? Then we'll have more of a chance.'

The suggestion went down well, although Thelma said that if we did win, she was afraid the children would want to buy a herd of elephants and half of Buckinghamshire to put them in.

'You can never have too many pets,' said Roy.

I gave him a searching look. 'What are you up to?' I asked.

Roy's face went blank.

'Please tell me you're not planning on getting the children an elephant,' I said with a grin.

'Me?' he replied, innocent as the day was long. 'Now why would you say that?'

Then, and as the others carried on spending the money that was definitely going to be ours, he turned his head away, so I could only just see him break into the widest possible smile.

CHAPTER FIFTEEN

The Women Publishers' Vegetable League

MONICA EDWARDS WAS laughing so much that a waiter came over and asked if she was in some sort of distress. She, Guy, and I were in a private club in Soho, where Monica was a member and I very probably never would be. It was chock-a-block with American servicemen who all had the most beautiful smiles. It was my second night out in a week, even if it was for work and only a quarter past six.

The three of us were safely settled in a small velvet booth in the corner of the club where despite the number of people we had a decent amount of privacy. Guy and Monica were on the single-malt whisky, and I was trying a vodka. As I hadn't had any lunch or very much sleep since the night before last, there was a distinct possibility I might become insouciant, or possibly, as the Americans would say, drunk as a skunk.

Guy was telling Monica about his efforts to be delightful with Mrs Porter which earlier in the day had involved a visit to the second floor at Selfridges. There he had been obliged to endure an entire hour of Cressida swooning over silk suzette nightgowns all in the name of plans for a feature on summer maternity wear.

It was fair to say, he was not getting the sympathy he felt he deserved.

'Oh, Guy,' said Monica, dabbing at a tear with a napkin, 'what have you done with the real you?'

'Bloody nothing, Monica,' replied Guy, gloomily. 'I'm being adorable. It's the most horrible strain.'

Monica said it must be. 'I'm sure you're doing it wonderfully,' she said. 'Charm like a snake and then bore the poor woman to death.'

'There's nothing poor about Cressida,' said Guy. 'She's invincible. It's like working with a Lancaster bomber in a hat.'

Monica smiled and said she had heard 'things' to that effect.

Whenever Guy invited me to a get-together with his old friend I always jumped at the chance to tag along. Now as we regaled her with stories of the Not So Honourable Egg, although we were making her laugh, Guy and I had the serious intention of asking for Monica's help.

'We're just hoping this whole thing is a short-lived indulgence on her part and when something equally Darling Fun comes up, she'll leave us alone,' said Guy. 'We're chipping away. I took her to lunch with Mrs Mahoney, our production manager, and Herbie Garson last week.'

'Gosh, you do mean business,' said Monica. She raised her glass to him. 'Was Herbie on form?'

Guy nodded. 'We were there three hours,' he said. 'Herbie's the only man I know who can eat, breathe and talk paper thickness at the same time. He was a real sport actually. Mrs Mahoney had had a word with him about our situation, so he explained five hundred years of letterpress printing to Mrs Porter over the soup. Once he'd moved onto magazine costing models, Cressida pretended to feel faint and we had to take her out to her car.'

'She said that if we ever made her have lunch with him

again, she would set fire to the restaurant,' I chipped in as Guy sipped his drink.

'Slightly dramatic,' said Monica, as a small jazz band in the far corner of the room began to play. 'I love Herbie, as long as you can keep him off paper.'

'Mrs Porter is rather sure of her opinions,' said Guy. 'If you're fun, you're in, if you're not . . .' He didn't finish his sentence.

'She was furious,' I said, 'especially when Guy told her he thought she'd done terrifically well and would only have to do it once a month to encourage Herbie to keep his prices down. Which otherwise was highly unlikely.'

'That doesn't sound like him,' said Monica.

'It isn't,' admitted Guy, 'and anyway we've got a fixed-price deal. But Cressida hasn't bothered to know that. Herbie played his part to a T. He took me to one side and said he'd had a lovely time.'

'Well played,' said Monica. 'What next?'

'In a nutshell,' said Guy, 'the Ministry. Mrs Porter is terrifically keen to get involved. I have an idea that she thinks it's all flirting with spies and getting to know the Churchills. Anyway, I asked Simons if he could come up with something helpfully dull, but he made the very good point that there's a war on and the Ministry of Information doesn't exist to sort out my personnel issues. He was impressively stern. So that's why we've turned to you.'

'Quite right,' said Monica, unperturbed to be second string.

A group of officers in the next booth were having an animated conversation and I leaned forward so that I wouldn't need to shout over the din.

'Mrs Porter would *love* to meet you,' I said. 'We've told her that you have a lot of connections in the MOI. She's also familiar with your name from what she calls fashionable circles.'

'Pish,' said Monica modestly. 'So you need her to be rather put off by it all? Well, if Simons can't help, we need to find someone else we can definitely trust. Hmm.' A smile spread across her face as she was thinking. 'What are you doing tomorrow afternoon?'

'I can be entirely free,' I replied. Guy said much the same.

'Wonderful,' said Monica. 'If Mrs Porter is available, I can set something up. I'm sure it will be enjoyably bewildering.' She paused. 'This is all such a shame. You were the talk of the town in terms of changing the fortunes of the *Friend*. I know for a fact that some of the other editors read your letters page to test the water for their own editorial. You're the best of the lot of us for rooting out what readers really care about.' She smiled at me warmly and then turned to Guy. 'I keep telling you, you've got a good one here, Guy. Make sure you keep her.'

'Pish,' I said, making them both laugh. It was the highest praise from someone I admired enormously, and I was chuffed to bits.

'The thing is,' continued Monica, becoming serious, 'now you're being talked about for the wrong reasons. Word is definitely out about Mrs Porter. We've all seen what she's doing.' She grimaced. 'It makes no sense at all. She might as well set fire to pound notes.'

'I know,' said Guy. 'We're getting more complaints every day. Newsagents have started reporting cancelled subscriptions. That's the first time in nearly two years.'

'Madness,' said Monica. 'Well, let's try to keep up Herbie's good work.' She glanced over to the bar and quickly looked away again. 'Oh goodness, I'm going to have to run. There's a chap I wish to avoid, but I'll see you tomorrow.'

She kissed us both goodbye.

'And, Guy, do try not to be *too* adorable until then.'

Then, carefully avoiding a heavily decorated colonel who was gazing at her like a schoolboy from just beyond the bar, Mrs Edwards swept out of the club.

*

The next morning, when I extended the invitation from Monica to Mrs Porter, unsurprisingly her diary became clear. Mrs Pye said that she had thought they were going to Harrods 'for research', but was told unceremoniously to stay in the office and 'answer some of those ghastly people with bad feet'.

It occurred to me that Mrs Porter was no less brutal to members of her own circle than to anyone else.

'Have you any thoughts about a fashion assistant, Mrs Porter?' I said to make conversation as Guy and I met her outside the Ministry's headquarters on Malet Street. 'We've been looking for ages.'

Mrs Porter, who had cut her luncheon short in order to join us on the dot of ten to three in the afternoon, smiled prettily. While clearly shocked when Guy told her that I was friends with the fashionable Mrs Edwards, it meant that Mrs Porter was being unusually pleasant to us both.

'We need to find the right type,' she said. 'I must say that poor Esther doesn't get any brighter, does she?'

Pleasant was perhaps too much of a stretch.

'HESTER,' I said, 'is one of the best assistants I've ever known. She's as bright as a button.'

'I don't think so,' said Mrs Porter, wrinkling her nose. 'Which reminds me, I have some more teeny ideas to tell you about after this meeting.'

She looked up at Senate House, which was blindingly

white in the sun, and then beamed at Guy. 'Now, this is what I call a proper office,' she said. 'I can't believe you've kept it from me for so long.'

Guy did his best smile back. Bunty had once christened it his Cary Grant, which had made the three of us laugh, although slightly more than Guy had said he felt fair.

'I am sure Mrs Edwards and I shall become firm friends,' said Mrs Porter. 'Just being here makes one feel patriotic. I've told everyone I know. It's all about duty, isn't it? Shall we go in?'

I wondered just how many people Mrs Porter had told about a confidential meeting with the Ministry of Information, but dutifully followed her and Guy to the front of the building to have our identification papers checked. We were then allowed up the steps and through to the personnel on reception, where Mrs Porter ignored them all and wandered off, saying in a loud voice, 'Oh yes, this is most agreeable,' as if we had just arrived at a hotel.

'Mrs Porter, if you could just . . .' called Guy, manfully going after her, before she accidentally got herself shot.

Meanwhile, I gave our names and felt compelled to be as polite as possible.

'Good afternoon. I'm sorry about that, it's my colleague's first visit. Um, the Honourable Mrs Porter, Mr Collins and Miss Lake from *Woman's Friend* magazine, here to see,' I checked the note I had made earlier, 'Mr Batley-Norris, please. Thank you.'

The receptionist, who I had seen on previous visits, kindly ignored Mrs Porter marching off and the fact that Guy was carefully leading her back, rather like a relative you couldn't quite trust to be out on their own.

'First floor, off to your left,' said the receptionist. 'Room one hundred and three. Mr Hastings here will take you along.'

'Is there not a lift?' said Cressida.

'Come along, Mrs Porter,' said Guy, firmly. 'We can't keep Mr Batley-Norris waiting.'

Guy and I hovered and herded and managed to get our publisher out of earshot and up the stairs following the man from the Ministry, before further reputational damage could be done.

Mrs Porter was dressed for a luncheon party in a nice yellow frock and another of her tiny versions of normal hats held on with an even tinier pin, and it was hard not to feel out of place among all the dark suits and even darker expressions that we passed.

'It's quite a walk,' she breathed, as if there should have been some sort of chauffeur service. 'Not that I mind,' she said, adding loudly, 'it's all for the war effort,' in case anyone wasn't sure.

Mrs Porter was now walking beside Mr Hastings, whom she asked if he might slow down.

'Remain calm,' I whispered to Guy.

'I give up,' he said.

Mercifully, we arrived at the meeting room, and Mr Hastings knocked on the door. When a voice called, 'Enter' we were ushered inside and out of almost all public view.

In terms of disappointment, Monica Edwards had done us all proud.

It was the pokiest room imaginable. Tiny and drab, with a desk at one end and a small table squeezed into the other, a sad-looking pinboard with nothing pinned on it was the only thing on the walls. There was no window.

Monica was sitting with a fair-haired middle-aged man in spectacles, and both rose as we went in. Mrs Edwards was wearing a plain jade frock, her only jewellery a quite extraordinary brooch in the shape of a crescent moon, filled to the brim with green Bakelite fruit and vegetables.

It was easily as big as the palm of my hand and managed to be both remarkable and quite dreadful at the same time.

It really wasn't like her one bit.

'Guy,' cried Monica. 'Emmy!'

'Mrs Porter, may I introduce Mrs Monica Edwards,' said Guy formally. 'Mrs Edwards, this is the Honourable Mrs Porter, owner and publisher of *Woman's Friend.*'

Mrs Porter exchanged some enthusiastic how do you do's although I couldn't help but notice an air of bafflement in terms of the way she surveyed Monica's turn-out. Then Monica introduced the gentleman in the suit.

'This is Mr Batley-Norris, Senior Executive Officer. Mr Batley-Norris is in charge of women's information and garden morale, with a particular interest in Digging for Victory,' said Monica, solemnly, 'and he has graciously agreed to meet with us today. I must tell you that as far as cabbages are concerned, we are with the right man.'

'Many people find them boring,' said Mr Batley-Norris. 'But vegetables could win us the war. Please do all sit down. Mr Collins, Miss Lake, Mrs Porker.'

'Porter,' said Mrs Porter, coldly.

'What? So sorry, my mistake,' said Mr Batley-Norris. He looked at a memorandum. 'It says Porker here.'

Monica looked over his shoulder. Mrs Porter looked at me as if it was my fault.

'So it does,' Monica mused. 'Never mind, it's very close. I do love your hat, Mrs Porter. May I ask, do you garden?'

'Of course,' said Cressida, which struck me as unlikely.

'Wonderful,' said Monica. 'How are you finding your kale?'

'Kale could win us the war,' said Mr Batley-Norris. 'Secret weapon. Full of iron. Would anyone like tea?'

'Thank you,' we all said, except Mrs Porter who was looking nonplussed.

'Mr Collins said you were very keen to see me,' she said. 'I've come especially.'

'And we're so grateful,' said Monica, smoothly. 'Mr Batley-Norris, shall I say or will you?'

'It's all about the vegetables,' said Mr Batley-Norris.

'It is!' cried Monica. 'That's exactly how I was going to put it. We're like peas in a pod. That was a vegetable joke. Do you see?'

I listened, transfixed. Either Monica Edwards had gone completely mad, or she was an exceedingly good actress. Guy was watching as if everything was perfectly normal. I'd bet a week's wages this was not the first time he had seen her do something like this. Somehow, Monica was managing to be a mixture of her usual polished and urbane self, and a total fruitcake.

'Not peas,' said Mr Batley-Norris, seriously. 'Cabbage. I'll cut to the chase, Mrs Porter. We need your magazine to do more about veg. That's the crux of it. You used to be first class on the subject, but do seem to have gone off.'

'Like a marrow,' said Monica. 'Once they start going off, that's it.'

Mr Batley-Norris pressed on. 'Would you mind if I ask you, Mrs Porter, can *Woman's Friend* do more?'

Mrs Porter was still coming to terms with the fact that this meeting was not turning out to be quite what she had hoped for.

Guy stepped in to help.

'I assume the Ministry would be very grateful if we could?' he said.

'Indeed we would,' said Mr Batley-Norris earnestly. He was a sincere man and I felt myself warm to him. 'The Ministry would be very pleased indeed. Your readers

166

are vital to winning the war. Now, shall we start with preparations for August? Planting and harvesting. Here's the list.'

He opened an enormous box folder full of typed pages and photographs of vegetables.

'It's all about doing our bit, isn't it?' said Monica chummily to Mrs Porter. 'We're doing "Ten Ways to Keep Lettuce Fresh Without a Fridge" next month. It's going to be divine.'

She said it as if she was referring to a spread on evening wear.

'Lettuce is almost entirely water,' said Mr Batley-Norris, severely. 'Same with celery.'

'You will help us, won't you, Mrs Porter?' said Monica, sounding like her normal self and entirely sane. 'For the war effort.'

'Well, yes,' said Mrs Porter. 'For the war effort. Of course.'

'Thank you so much,' said Monica. She put her hand to her throat. 'Now, what are your thoughts about fruit?'

This went on for an hour.

By four o'clock, Mr Batley-Norris had only got as far as September planting schedules and that was despite starting in July. Monica had discussed every fruit and vegetable he mentioned with a level of devotion commensurate to referring to the King and Queen themselves. From the abject misery etched across Mrs Porter's face, I felt that our publisher was jolly nearly a broken woman.

I coughed very slightly and Guy picked up on the hint. 'Mr Batley-Norris, Mrs Edwards,' he said. 'This has been remarkably informative, but with regret, I believe Mrs Porter has another engagement she must attend.'

'Thank goodness,' cried Mrs Porter, departing her seat as if she'd been shot out of a cannon.

Monica leapt to her feet too. 'Thank you so very much,'

she said, sounding quite normal. 'Mrs Porter, it has been such a pleasure to meet you, especially as a keen fellow-gardener.' She held out her hand, which Mrs Porter shook wearily. 'Can I count on you to join me in the Women Publishers' Vegetable League? Mr Batley-Norris is kind enough to meet with us at the same time every Thursday. You'll know of course that there's far more to fruit pulping than people might think.'

'Thank you, Mrs Edwards,' said Guy. 'I think that might be enough.'

'I'm always very thorough,' said Monica. 'Mrs Porter, I can see that Mr Collins is trying to protect you from my enthusiastic ways. Quite adorable,' she added, with the smallest hint of a quite wicked smile.

'We must go,' said Guy, giving her one of his looks. 'Mr Batley-Norris, it has been the greatest pleasure. Thank you very much for inviting us. I know I for one, have been hugely inspired on the vegetable front. I hope you will be happy to know we will reap what you have sown in the strongest of ways in *Woman's Friend*.'

And with that, all hands were shaken and Mrs Porter allowed herself to be escorted out of the room.

'I shall see you out,' said Mr Batley-Norris. 'Security of course.'

As he and Mr Collins led Cressida to the stairs, I lagged behind with Monica.

'How did I do?' she whispered when we were out of earshot. 'I could see Guy thought I laid it on a bit thick.'

'It was extraordinary,' I said. 'How do you know that much about vegetables?'

Monica chuckled. 'Actually I enjoy gardening,' she said. 'And I'm very fond of Mr Batley-Norris.'

'I've never met anyone like him,' I said, truthfully. 'He knows so much. I hope he didn't mind doing this.'

'Mind? He enjoyed it immensely,' whispered Monica. 'He doesn't usually get to do meetings. It's most unfair. Don't worry, I'm not being mean. He's a horticultural genius. An extraordinarily gifted man.' Now she turned to me. 'He's also my cousin. He gave me this brooch.' She looked down at the Bakelite basket. 'It's one of my most precious possessions.'

'I don't mean to be rude,' I said. 'But is this really all true?'

Monica nodded, her eyes kind. 'It is. There are all sorts of very clever, interesting people working in places like this,' she said. 'Horace is just one of them and I couldn't be prouder. I telephoned him after our lunch and he was delighted to help. Now, we'd better catch them up or we'll get marched off to the Ministry allotments.'

'Really?' I said. At this point I was ready to believe anything she told me.

Monica laughed. 'We're safe,' she said. 'Although I don't think fruit and vegetables are quite up Mrs Porter's street, do you? Let's just hope they've played their part.'

'Well,' I said, 'if nothing else, I shall go home feeling quite an expert on tomatoes.'

'I have a very good recipe for chutney,' said Monica. 'I'll send it to you.'

I looked at her for a moment. She really was quite remarkable.

'Thank you,' I said, 'for today. You really have been a brick.'

'Not at all,' she replied. 'You know how fond of *Woman's Friend* I am, and of you and Guy. And now I understand what you're up against. If there's anything else I can do, *anything*. Just let me know.'

CHAPTER SIXTEEN

We Met a Man in the Pub

MRS PORTER DID not voice her disappointment over the Ministry meeting until after we had left Senate House, which I thought was good of her, and Guy later said he thought was because she was still in shock over Mr Batley-Norris's passion for greens.

She remained in an unusually thoughtful silence until we had walked to where her car was waiting just around the corner. Finally, as Mrs Porter's chauffeur jumped out to open the door, Guy asked her how she felt the meeting had gone.

'I do hope you enjoyed your first visit to the Ministry, Mrs Porter,' he said, politely. 'I'm bowled over that we were lucky enough to meet Mr Batley-Norris. What an inspiring man.'

Mrs Porter looked up at Guy, almost pityingly. 'You said I would be meeting interesting people in positions of power, not a peculiar man in a horrid little room talking about peas. The whole event was utterly mis.'

'Mr Batley-Norris is one of the country's leading horti-culturalists, Mrs Porter,' I said. 'Mrs Edwards thinks very highly of him.'

Mrs Porter looked even more unimpressed. 'That was another matter,' she said, getting into the Daimler and holding up a hand to stop the driver from shutting her door.

Guy and I stood on the pavement and leaned forward like two children looking into a baker's with not quite enough money for a jam tart.

'I was of the impression that Mrs Edwards was quite somebody to know. I planned for us to become lovely friends.'

'You still can,' said Guy, as if encouraging a small child. 'I could tell she thought very highly of you. The good news is that we have lots of information for Mrs Fieldwick's "News from the Shed", and I am sure Mr Batley-Norris will report up to the very top. That's certainly something to let people in the know hear about.'

'No, it's not,' said Mrs Porter, looking at him as if he were mad.

'We can't let the Ministry down,' said Guy, showing commendable resilience. 'Not after we've been granted a personal meeting with Mr Batley-Norris. And Monica has invited you to join the League of Soft Fruits.'

'The Women Publishers' Vegetable League,' I murmured.

'Quite,' said Guy.

'I'm going home,' said Mrs Porter. 'I'm quite exhausted, so shan't be in the office again until next week.'

'Of course,' said Guy. 'I hope you will feel well enough for some advertising meetings. Mr Newton and I are very gung-ho.'

'Perhaps you could get on with doing them on your own,' said Mrs Porter without interest. 'Meetings are not always my thing.'

She sank back into the plush, blue-grey leather seat and waved listlessly at her driver, who quickly pushed past us to close the sedan's door.

Guy gave a spirited wave as the car drove off.

'How is she allowed to still be driven around in that thing?' he mused, cheerfully. 'The amount of petrol it must use.'

'I'd rather not know,' I answered. 'Anyway, how do you think that all went?'

Guy broke into the biggest smile I had seen from him in an age. 'In the light of "Meetings are not always my thing", I think it went very well,' he said. 'Very well indeed.'

*

Mrs Porter was true to her word and was not seen in the office again that week. This was unremarkable as she was never in on a Friday, but unusual in that no one, not even Mr Elliot, received a single phone call. She hadn't even bothered with the teeny ideas she had mentioned before our meeting at Senate House. When Guy tried to get approval on a pressing article that she had insisted she must see, he was met with complete silence. When a message was finally sent back to him, it merely said, 'Mrs Porter says, do as you wish.'

It was the first real sign that perhaps, just *perhaps*, our plan was beginning to work. With a weekend of fire station shifts and catching up on readers' letters ahead, I dared to allow myself a sliver of optimism. Having completed the Friday nightshift, Thelma and I were on the second part of a double, working on through Saturday. It had been a quiet night and now we chatted on our lunch break, eating paste sandwiches and leafing through two American magazines that Mrs Porter had brought into the office. It was impossible not to marvel at the colourful pictures and what seemed like abundance on every page.

'What's Miracle Whip Salad Dressing?' asked Thel. 'Do they mean salad cream?'

'I don't know,' I said, peering at the advert. 'Everything's different, isn't it? Look at this bra. "Superb bosom contours guaranteed".' I looked at my chest and wondered if it came up to scratch.

Thel studied hers and we both pulled faces and laughed.

'All right, ladies?' It was Fred, standing in the doorway with his hands over his eyes. 'I don't know if I should come in.'

'It's OK, Fred,' I said. 'You're safe. How are you?'

'I could do with a rest,' said Fred, and he began to give us an update on a recent air raid at the postal sorting office in north London that had needed thirty-two pumps to get the resulting fire under control. It had been quite spectacular and the NFS had worked through the night trying to put it out.

'Bloody Germans got away with it as well,' he added, darkly. 'Dodged the ack-acks and legged it. Two dead and fifty thousand parcels up in smoke. That's between you and me.'

'Of course,' said Thel as I nodded.

'Oh and now, before I forget,' added Fred, 'Thel, Leonard on A Watch says do you have those shoes you're lending his Rosie? Only it's her party this afternoon.'

'Dammit,' said Thel. 'I've left them at home.' She looked at her watch. 'I wonder if I could nip there now?'

One day, I thought to myself, the idea of talking about borrowing a pair of shoes in the same breath as saying that people had been bombed will seem very strange and more than likely insensitive in the extreme. But it was normal conversation now. Just what we did, even though there was nothing normal about it at all.

'I'll go,' I said, shaking myself out of reflections that would not do anyone any good. 'Thel, you do enough running around. I'll be back before we have to start work.'

As Thelma protested, I headed for the door. It had

given me the excuse I was looking for to sneak back to the house.

Although it was over six weeks until Thelma's birthday, the children had already started planning a surprise. This mainly involved doing things they were keen on themselves, and it had turned into a complex series of secret plans, the most challenging of which was the fact that Margaret had decided to learn to play 'Happy Birthday' on the trombone. It was a smashing idea and the only fly in the ointment was the fact that obviously Marg could only practise when Thelma was out of the house, and more worryingly, was only on lesson five.

She had not chosen the easiest instrument, especially for an eleven-year-old, and the enthusiastic tones of Marg playing 'Pease Pudding Hot' on a slightly battered but nevertheless serviceable trombone in the upstairs bathroom (Buzz said that good acoustics were key) had not sounded promising at first. But she had taken to it with her usual spirit and progress had definitely been made.

Today, I knew she was having a lesson with Buzz and from the sound of it as I let myself back into the house, they were hard at work. I galloped upstairs to the flat, where Buzz and Bunty were sitting on the sofa as Margaret played. When I arrived, though, Marg immediately stopped and quickly looked at the clock on the mantelpiece.

'You're supposed to be at work,' she cried. 'But now you have to stay and listen. It's very important.'

'We're all under strict instructions,' said Bunty, in a serious voice. 'I've been up here some time.'

'I must say, Marg is doing terrifically well,' said Buzz. 'She's a natural. Go on Marg, play Emmy your "Pease Pudding Hot".'

I smiled bravely. This particular melody and I were already close friends.

'It's the jazz version,' said Buzz, as Marg veered from note to note in a tuneful but slightly haphazard way.

'Well done, Marg,' I said. 'How's "Happy Birthday" coming along?'

'It's harder, especially the third line,' said Marg, breathlessly. 'Shall I show you?'

I noticed that she glanced at the clock again. Something was going on.

'Yes, please,' I said, and sat down on the arm of the sofa as Buzz motioned for Marg to keep her head up and take a deep breath.

Marg began, bearing the fiercest look of concentration. It was not the most recognisable version of the song I had ever heard, but as Thelma's daughter blasted her way to the end, in my opinion it was undoubtedly the best.

Buzz, Bunty and I all burst into applause as Marg's little purple face broke into the hugest smile.

'Do you think Mum will like it?' she puffed.

'Of course she will. Glenn Miller *himself* would love it,' I said, giving her a big hug. 'Marg, it's super.'

'I can't do the third line,' said Marg.

'Yes, you can,' I said, ignoring the fact it had sounded like someone letting down a balloon. 'You've only just started learning and it's bound to be tricky at first. But you've loads of time to practise, and I promise, your mum is going to be thrilled.' This was something I could safely say with my hand on my heart. 'Now, I really must find those shoes and hurry back to the station.'

'NO!' shouted Marg. 'I'll play it again. You have to stay up here.'

I looked over at Bunty who shook her head and mouthed, 'I don't know.'

'Sweetheart, I really can't,' I said. 'Captain Davies will be cross. I'm so sorry. We'll get Bunty to take your mum out somewhere and then I can listen to you practise for ages. I promise.'

Marg bit her lip. 'You mustn't go in the shed,' she said. 'It's very important.'

'That's easy,' I said, having had no intention, anyway. 'I'll go straight out. Guides' honour.' I gave her the salute, grabbed the shoes that Thelma had left by the coffee table, and after a Does Anyone Know What's Going On? look at Bunty and Buzz, said my goodbyes and left.

As I went down the stairs, going to the shed was now my heart's only desire.

I was being ridiculous. Children liked having secrets, and I was going to be late back if I didn't get a move on. When I reached the ground floor, I headed for the front door.

But Stanley was hovering in front of it, hardly aware of me as I came up behind him, and as I said a friendly Hello, he jumped out of his skin.

'Nothing,' he said, almost getting himself caught up in the heavy blackout curtains.

'That's good then,' I said, trying not to smile. 'Stan, are you expecting someone?'

'No,' said Stan.

He was a terrible liar.

There was a loud knock on the door, which sounded more as if someone was kicking it. Stanley looked at me and then at the door and then back at me again.

'Don't worry, love,' I said. 'It's all right.'

There was another kick, and a voice that very clearly belonged to his big brother, shouted, 'HURRY UP!'

'You mustn't see,' whispered Stan, urgently.

'It's a bit late for that,' I said. 'Come on, open the door. I know it's George. And I really do have to go to work.'

Stan looked mortified, but before he was forced into making a decision, the door opened and we both moved back, only to see George, partially obscured by a very large cardboard box. It meant that he didn't see me at first, but when he did, he let out an enormous gasp, nearly dropping the box in the process.

'Hello,' I said. 'Don't tell me, I'm not allowed to look in the shed.'

George and Stanley stood rooted to the spot. The box made a shuffling noise.

'Is this a secret?' I asked.

Two heads nodded.

'Is it a goat?' I said.

'No,' said Stan. 'It's chickens.'

Roy.

'Honestly, Stan, you're useless,' said George. Then he turned to me. 'Are you going to tell Mum?' he asked, looking for all the world as if his heart would break if I did.

Before I could answer, the sound of voices floated down from upstairs. It was several flights, but I could hear the others coming. Now the boys looked even wider-eyed with concern.

'Quick,' I said, 'let's get them out to the garden.'

Two minutes later, I had joined an underground world of secrecy and dubious intent.

'Well, you keep it all very clean and tidy,' I said, looking around the shed, which was indeed immaculate. There was a large hutch for Laurel and Hardy for when they weren't in their run outside, but in addition, there were several more cages and a sectioned-off area which had been neatly lined with straw. 'Quick question,' I added. 'What's going on and does it have anything to do with Roy Hodges, if I even need to ask?'

Now the boys stared at their feet. 'We bought them,' said George. 'They're for Mum's birthday, only they came early. We've got to keep them secret so we don't spoil the surprise.'

'That's quite a long wait,' I said, already thinking about the logistics. 'Well, they're here now so you'd better let them out of the box as they won't like being in there. Gently now.'

George nodded, looking more hopeful, and opened the lid of the box. Then he gently picked up each chicken in turn and put it carefully onto the straw. Stan crouched down, eager to get a closer look.

It had to be said that neither of the birds was exactly prize-winning.

'They're beautiful,' breathed Stan. 'Hello, little chickens.'

Super. There was no way I could rat on the kids now. 'Flipping heck, boys,' I said. 'Where did you get them?'

'The pub,' said Stan, calmly, sitting on his haunches and gazing at the two birds.

'THE PUB?'

This had taken a turn.

'Sssshhh,' said George.

My mouth was making shapes, but words didn't seem to be happening. One of the chickens clucked forlornly. Stan moved a saucer of water towards it.

'You've been in a pub, buying chickens?' I whispered. 'From who? Have you been talking to strangers?' Now I really would have to tell their mother.

Two heads shook adamantly. 'He's not a stranger. He's Roy's friend. His name's Scary David and he's got a wooden leg and he's really good at darts.'

It was getting worse.

'I don't care if he's really good at standing on his head,' I said. 'Why's he called Scary David?'

'Because he looks scary,' said Stan, as if I was the one being ridiculous. 'So does SB.'

'Who's SB?'

'Scary's brother,' said Stan and George together.

Dear God.

'It's not his fault,' said George. 'He's got one great big eyebrow and he doesn't smile much, but Roy said that's because of the first war. SB killed loads of Germans with his bare hands, especially after they shot off Scary's leg.'

'They're both in Heavy Rescue,' added Stan, reverentially. 'They've saved loads of people and their things AND they saved a dog. It's called Harry Houdini.'

It was a lot to take in. 'Boys,' I said, slowly. 'I'm really sorry, but I think you're going to have to take the chickens back. Does your mum even like them?'

'Not much,' said George. 'so we're going to look after them for her. She's always saying she'd do anything for a poached egg.'

I had to admit that was true. Unfortunately, I was pretty sure we might just have become the owner of two poached chickens.

'Where did Scary get them?' I asked, trying to ignore the fact I was now talking about a man called Scary as if it was perfectly normal.

'Don't ask,' whispered Stan. 'Roy said not to.'

'We can't take them back,' said George. 'Fred says that Scary and SB are very, very kind, but it's best if you don't muck them about.'

Stan nodded in agreement.

'All right,' I said, thinking on my feet. 'Perhaps we'll forget that bit.' I didn't want to encourage the children to lie to their mother, but I did feel that this particular piece of information wouldn't help.

'And we didn't go into the pub,' said Stan.

'Just the garden,' said George.

'It's more of a yard, really,' added Stan.

'Was it the White Hart?' I asked. It was one of the firemen's locals. The landlady's brother was on B Watch, so I supposed it could have been worse.

The boys nodded. 'It was meant to be a surprise,' said George. 'We only met Scary and SB once, and Roy and Fred were with us. Roy picked up the chickens today.'

'Well, that's one good thing,' I said. I was trying to think what Thel would say about it all. The boys hadn't done anything terribly wrong. Roy and Fred on the other hand, would be getting a piece of my mind.

'OK,' I said. 'Let's see what we can do. I'm assuming you've done your homework on how to look after them?'

George moved a piece of wood from beside one of the cages and brought out a slim book. *The Country Life Home Front Series for Intensive Cultivation: Poultry Keeping on Small Lines*.

'Well done,' I said, not entirely sure I should actually be praising them. 'And it does sound as if you've made quite an investment. Was it out of your own money?'

They nodded. 'We got a discount,' said George.

I didn't know if I was a soft touch, or whether the threat of having to ask for a refund from a man called Scary David had made the decision for me, but now I realised I was in on the deal.

'All right then,' I said as two small faces in a shed began to light up. 'Operation Secret Chicken is go.'

. . . Oh Charles, it was so wonderful to get a letter from you! It took six weeks to get here, but I don't care. I'm not going to think about what has been going on since then. I'll just read it hundreds of times and picture you writing it in the sun.

Now, to answer all your questions, darling: yes – we are all very, very well.

I have been learning about growing vegetables from the Ministry itself! You can quiz me about kale as I know everything. And 50 different sorts of tomato. When you come home we should probably buy a farm.

I've also become trapped in a web of lies over two chickens that the children bought for Thel's birthday. Roy got them from the Scary brothers at the White Hart. (Did he ever tell you about them…?!!!) He was very apologetic when I took him to task about it! I've had to tell Bunty, and now we've got to try to keep Gert and Daisy quiet for an absolute age.

Please come home soon as I think I may be falling in with a bad lot.

Oh Charles, do you mind that I write such trivial things? You must wonder if this is what you're fighting for. Anyway, I'm running out of room so am now writing up the side of the paper. Hope you can read this. I haven't had a letter from you in a while, but don't worry AT ALL because I think about you all the time and that gets me through EVERYTHING.

I'm sending you about a million kisses. Will write again tomorrow.

I love you.

E. xxxxxxxxxxxxxxxxxxxxxxxxxxxxxx

CHAPTER SEVENTEEN

I Believe the Term is 'The Sack'

IT TURNED OUT that we were better at keeping chickens than *Woman's Friend* was at keeping advertisers.

'I'm afraid another two have pulled out,' said Mr Newton as the team huddled around desks in the journalists' room for the Monday Editorial Meeting. 'Freezone for Corns and Mothak's Anti-Moth. They're switching to other weeklies. That's six cancellations in the last fortnight. I can't apologise enough.'

'That's quite all right, Mr Newton,' said Guy. 'It's not your fault. I'm sure things will pick up.'

Mr Newton did not appear reassured on the first point, or remotely convinced on the second. I knew for a start that Guy wasn't either, but these days the team meetings were more an exercise in diplomacy than actually getting much done. With Mr Elliot taking copious tight-lipped notes, and Mrs Pye all ears for any sign of dissent, there was nothing to be said that wouldn't go straight back to Mrs Porter herself. With this in mind, Guy took up the baton in terms of *Woman's Friend*'s advertisers heading for the door.

'I'm afraid I have very little happier news,' he said. 'We are struggling with invitations to meet with Mrs Porter, which is obviously extremely disappointing.'

Mr Elliot dragged his beady eyes up from his notes. 'And why would that be, Mr Collins?' he said, for all the world as if he, rather than Guy, was the man in charge. 'I fear Mrs Porter will be most distressed.'

I rather feared that I might punch Mr Elliot on the nose, but there we were. Not for the first time did I wish Small Winston was in the office as he was the only one who could get Mr Elliot to stop being an almighty stuffed shirt. Mrs Porter, on the other hand, actively encouraged it.

'Well,' said Guy, smoothly, 'would you care to hear our clients speak for themselves on this?'

'I would, indeed,' replied old Three Bags, still under the impression that Guy worked for him.

A loud tut came from the direction of Mrs Shaw, who spoke for us all.

'Good,' said Guy. 'As Mr Newton has been kind enough to share some of the replies with me. I shall read them aloud:

"Dear Mr Newton, Thank you for your kind invitation, but sadly we do not see your magazine as an obvious home for our clients' products. Should we represent companies of a more utilitarian nature in the future, we will of course be in touch . . ."

'That was from a well-known clothing designer, who I believe you are familiar with. Ah, and here is a more informal response from an advertising agency we have dealt with for some time.

"Sorry, Newton old man. Nothing doing. God knows what the client would say if they saw their tweeds next to an advert for Vim. Heart attacks all round. Yours etc. . . ."'

Mr Elliot stopped writing. He was one of those people who, when putting a full stop, did it with a large flourish as if he had just played the last note of an impressive piece on the piano, or come up with the Constitution of the United States all on his own.

'I rather think,' he mused, with his nose in the air, 'there would be a better response if the invitations had been sent from somebody else. One either knows the right people, or one does not.'

He might as well have slapped Mr Newton in the face. Our hard-working and dedicated Advertising Manager looked cut to the quick.

Without hesitation, a chorus of complaints rang out.

'How rude.'

'I think you should take that back.'

And best of all, 'Mr Newton, don't listen to him, he can't even control a small dog.'

Guy held a hand up for order. 'There is no need for that kind of comment, Mr Elliot,' he said, coldly, 'and I will not have it in my meeting. We are a team, and we work as a team.' Then he paused just long enough for even the rhinoceros-skinned Mr Elliot to register the very awkward silence. 'And in case you feel that communications in this matter have been from an inadequate source, perhaps you would like to hear a reply to an invitation that was sent from me.

'"Dear Mr Collins,

'Regarding your messages left with my secretary. We do not advertise in women's weeklies – you will understand of course that our clients are not interested in jam recipes and romance. We do not know of your owner, the Hon. Mrs Porter, but trust she will understand.

Yours sincerely . . "'

Guy looked at the paper with contempt. 'The worst kind of snob,' he said. 'I imagine their clients are interested in the bombs and tanks and planes and warships that our readers are building during the seventy-hour weeks that they work.' He screwed the note into a ball and threw it into a bin. 'In conclusion, Mr Elliot, I share your concerns that Mrs Porter may well have to endure a disappointment. Letters like these are hardly a jamboree read for any of us. I will of course ensure that she sees them, even though they are unlikely to impress. In the meantime, we will continue to push on and do our best to retain those advertisers who have, until now, been a source of significant income.'

Then, without his usual request for any final business, he called the meeting to an end.

Guy was not the only person who was troubled by the advertisers' response. Even though it supported our argument that *Woman's Friend* was better off sticking to what had proved a success, the rejections were harsh. It was one thing to be able to organise scenarios to try to put Mrs Porter off from the business of running a magazine, but it was quite another to invite derision at our own expense.

It was even harder to hear from the readers. Perhaps it was because we had always encouraged them to write to us about what was on their minds, but letters were now coming in thick and fast. A few were positive but they were heavily outnumbered.

Worst of all, for all our efforts to write back to more readers, it was inevitable that some of them were now being ignored.

Dear Yours Cheerfully
Please would you print my letter as I am so worried.
I'm afraid I lost my head with a young man at work who

was lovely to me. Now I think I am going to have a baby,
but he doesn't want anything to do with me.

Please don't ask me to send you a stamped addressed
envelope for a reply. If my parents see a letter from you,
they'll open it and I'm scared of what they will do.

Yours
Worried and Alone
PS: PLEASE, PLEASE PRINT THIS.

We did not print the letter. When I put it into the next
week's issue, Mrs Porter said it was depressing and took
it straight out.

Even Madame Pye herself was not finding life as part
of the smart set quite as straightforward as she had hoped.
It was all very well including fancy retailers and expensive
products in her column, but it also meant that when
readers wanted to know why "On Duty for Beauty (Pamela
Pye Reporting To Help)" suggested spending half a week's
wages on a bottle of scent that was hardly available anyway,
they knew who to write to with their complaints.

As Hester opened all the letters to Mrs Pye, even if
Madame didn't mention them to the rest of us, Hest most
certainly did. 'Mrs Pye has told Mrs Porter at least three
times that people are getting fed up, but she doesn't listen,'
she reported to me in hushed tones. 'And when I was taking
Small Winston out I heard Mrs Porter tell Mr Elliot that
she's becoming moany. She didn't call her Madame either.'

'Good going, Hest,' I said.

'I just thought I'd keep my ears open,' said Hester. 'My
mum says that when she was in service, it never crossed
people's minds that their servants could actually hear. Mrs
Porter says all sorts in front of me.'

'We're not her servants, Hest,' I said. 'Even if sometimes
it feels like it.'

186

After Hester had provided us with this information, it was no surprise when Mrs Pye began to look less buoyant about the new glamorous ways. She even grumbled that some of the West End ladieswear stores had refused her requests that they provide photographs of their upcoming new lines.

'They don't understand Mrs Porter's vision, you see,' she said. 'We can't make a silk purse out of a sow's ear overnight.'

'That sow's ear paid your wages for a long time before Mrs Porter and her vision arrived,' said Mrs Mahoney, in reply. 'It might be worth remembering that.'

Cracks were beginning to show. What we didn't know was if Cressida was seeing them too.

A few days later, that particular question was answered.

Mrs Porter had continued to stay away from the office. She was late with her copy for "Your Publisher's Week", and her inspirational poem was extremely short, which perhaps wasn't an entirely bad thing.

Chin up, it's not that bad,
No one looks attractive with a face that is sad.
If you're down, just look at me,
The happy publisher at one's favourite weekly.

It was accompanied by a new misty-eyed picture of Mrs Porter hanging onto Small Winston, who looked seconds away from biting the photographer.

'That doesn't rhyme,' pointed out Mrs Shaw.

'Unless you say week-LEE,' said Miss Peters, trying to help. 'Then it does.'

'No one says that,' argued Mrs Shaw. 'Why don't we change the third line?'

After that things fell apart as everyone came up with

increasingly idiotic suggestions, all of which were preferable to Mrs Porter's. It also meant that when Mrs Porter
did finally pop into the office, she walked in to see half
her staff laughing their heads off.

'Oh,' she said, resplendent in a lightweight cream suit
and tilt hat the size of a peanut. 'Has someone made a
funny? Do tell.'

Mr Newton looked as if he might faint.

'Good morning, Mrs Porter,' several of us said, playing
for time.

'We were just talking about poetry,' I said, wildly. 'How
it can lift the spirits.'

'So true,' cried Mrs Porter, clapping her hands together.
'I knew I would inspire.'

Hester let out a guffaw.

'COUGHS AND SNEEZES SPREAD DISEASES,'
bellowed Mrs Mahoney, trying to drown her out. 'Let's
go and look in the First Aid tin for a hankie.'

Mrs Porter gave me a look as if to say, 'What did I
tell you about Esther?' and then called for Small Winston,
who trotted in and sat down with a grunt.

'He's hungry,' said Mrs Porter.

Not for the first time I thought how much I would
love to kidnap the poor little chap and take him on some
decent walks. But Mrs Porter had moved on.

'Ah,' she said. 'Mr Newcombe. I am glad you are here.
I understand you have failed to attract any of the advertisers on my list.'

Mr Newton went pale. 'Well, I . . . er . . .' he began.

Mrs Porter did one of her dismissive waves. 'No matter.
I have sorted it,' she said. 'Where is Mr Collins?'

'I'm here, Mrs Porter,' said Guy, from the doorway.
'Is that Small Winston? I haven't heard Mr Elliot scream.'

He crouched down and looked at the dog from a safe distance. Small Winston remained largely unmoved, but Mrs Porter, who must have been in good humour, gave a twinkly laugh and told Guy he was a silly old softie.

The tiniest hesitation from Guy spoke volumes about what he thought about that, and I nearly had a Hester explosion, only just managing to keep it inside.

'Ah,' said Guy, 'I've never been called that before, but, er, thank you.' Then he switched on a full Cary Grant, shamelessly trying to encourage more of her cheerful mood. It seemed to do the trick.

'Mr Collins,' she announced, 'Mr Archie Morley is coming for a meeting. He is most interested in my plans and will be here at twelve. Perhaps you might join us?'

'Archie Morley?' said Guy, standing up. 'Goodness.' He looked surprised. 'Mrs Porter, you do know Mr Morley has a reputation for being somewhat blunt?'

Mrs Porter gave a dismissive wave of her hand and turned to leave. 'Mr Collins, he and I know many of the same people. We shall be in my office. Come along, my darling.'

It wasn't entirely clear if she had been referring to Small Winston or to her editor. Guy rolled his eyes. Small Winston didn't move.

'Biscuits!' cried Mrs Porter from the corridor. Small Winston weighed up the options, eventually got up, and to show that he wasn't easily bought, slowly followed her out.

'Well,' said Guy to Mr Newton. 'Archie Morley.'

Mr Newton had taken a neatly pressed handkerchief from his pocket and was dabbing his forehead. 'Oh dear,' he said.

'You know, you really should be in the meeting,' said Guy in a low voice. It had been painfully obvious that

Mrs Porter had completely forgotten her Advertising Manager. 'I'll have a word.'

But Mr Newton shook his head. 'Thank you, Mr Collins,' he said, 'but I'm far happier not joining in. I've, um, met Mr Morley before.'

'Wise move,' said Guy. 'OK, everyone, back to work.' He looked at his wristwatch. 'Emmy, can I have a word?'

'Of course,' I nodded, hoping he might be about to shed some light on the meeting.

I didn't have to wait long. Guy shut his office door and motioned to me to sit down. 'This,' he said, sitting behind his desk and leaning his chin on his hand, 'will be interesting.'

'Who's Archie Morley?' I asked. 'Do I know him?'

'Morley, Ticehurst and Lowe,' said Guy. 'Big advertising agency. Very high-class clients.'

'Oh,' I said. '*That* Morley.'

'Exactly. It will be some coup if Mrs Porter can make any headway there.' He fiddled with a box of matches. 'But I can't see it. Even if they do "know the same people". Morley's a hound.'

'Did you just shudder?' I said.

'Probably,' said Guy. 'I'd like to think I can stand up to most people, but I have to admit, I'd rather not with Archie Morley. I'm not sure you'd like him much, either.' He scratched an eyebrow. 'Famously fond of a female face. Famously even fonder of his own. But as far as this meeting is concerned, his least likeable attribute – and it's a long list – is that his preferred way of negotiating is to rip people to shreds. It's not even to get a better deal. It's just for the sport.'

'He sounds horrible,' I said.

'He is,' said Guy, seriously. 'I hope Cressida knows what she's doing.' He looked concerned.

'This is going to sound awful,' I said, slowly, 'but might it actually help our campaign? If Mr Morley tells Mrs Porter some home truths? It might help put her off.'

'It might,' said Guy. 'In fact, yes, it certainly could.'

For someone who was fighting for that very thing, he didn't appear at all happy about it. 'This is a rotten business,' he said, after a moment. 'I know it's for a good cause, but even so, it's not the way I like to do things at all. I'm in half a mind to try to persuade Cressida to cancel as fast as she can.'

'Gosh,' I said. 'Is he that bad? Or are you warming to the Honourable? You are a silly old softie, after all.'

Guy didn't laugh, or even smile. 'No, I'm certainly not. But I think this meeting could get rather bloody, rather swiftly. Morley's a bully. I've come across him once or twice, although I don't expect him to acknowledge it.'

There was a tap on the door and when Guy called, 'Come in,' to my surprise, Mrs Porter appeared. Cressida rarely ventured into Guy's office, and as she looked around at the terrific mess the rest of us hardly even noticed any more, I could see she had remembered just why.

'Very quickly,' she said, brightly, 'as I can see you are busy. I haven't had time to tell you about my little plan – the one I mentioned before that dreadful meeting about vegetables.'

'Of course,' said Guy. 'Would you like to sit down?'

'No, no,' said Mrs Porter. 'This won't take a moment. It's just that before I forget – my silly brain is like a sieve of course – you should know that I have decided about Mrs Croft.'

'Decided?' said Guy.

'That's right. Her "What's In The Hotpot" column. Goodness knows I've tried, but it's all just too grim. Potato this and potato that, and a hundred things to do with a carrot. I can't bear it. Anyway, this afternoon Mr Elliot is going to phone her to tell her she is no longer needed.'

'What?' said Guy. 'He's going to do *what*?'

'I believe the term is "the sack",' twinkled Mrs Porter. 'Don't worry, I shall find someone far more exciting to take her place.' She gave a happy simper. 'That was all. Do carry on. See you shortly.'

'You can't do that to Mrs Croft,' I burst out. 'She hasn't done anything wrong. Quite the opposite. She's the very heart of *Woman's Friend*.'

'Too late,' chimed Mrs Porter. 'She can retire. Mr Elliot will suggest it.'

'Mrs Porter,' said Guy, 'I must insist . . .'

But before either of us could say or do anything more, Mrs Porter disappeared out of the door.

Mrs Croft. Our wonderful, loyal, beloved Mrs Croft.

Guy could hardly speak. 'That bloody woman.'

My mind raced. Mrs Porter seemed to think it was a jape. How long had this been planned? Had Mrs Pye put her up to it?

Was she going to sack all the staff one by one? I looked at Guy.

'How could she?' I said, quietly. 'She hardly even knows who Mrs Croft is. She hasn't tried to find out.'

'And here I was worrying that a tough-talking advertising man might be unfair on her. Good grief.' Guy shook his head.

'She treats everyone the same way,' I said. 'Buttering them up if she thinks they'll be useful and then dropping them if she decides that they're not. She never bothers to learn anyone's name. We might as well be pieces of furniture. Guy, why are we trying to protect her from Mr Morley? She never does anything for anyone else. Let him say whatever he wants.'

My voice was shaking. I had had enough.

Of all the people to pick on, Mrs Porter had chosen the most decent and loyal of us all. Mrs Croft had worked for *Woman's Friend* longer than anyone. She was well into her seventies and could so easily and justifiably have used the war as a reason to retire, but she hadn't. She'd kept going – doing her bit. Never missing a deadline, never missing an issue. Magicking hundreds and hundreds of recipes for the readers out of absolutely nothing. Mrs Croft was everything we stood for. She was everything we wanted *Woman's Friend* to be.

The sound of an extravagant greeting came from Mrs Porter's office.

'You're damn right,' said Guy. 'Come on, Emmy, let's go.'

CHAPTER EIGHTEEN

An Advertiser Calls

I HADN'T BEEN invited to the meeting and I was sure Mrs Porter would not welcome me either, but I really didn't care. I would listen to whatever rudeness this Morley fellow was likely to come up with, and then as soon as I possibly could, try to convince Mrs Porter to change her mind about Mrs Croft.

'Mrs Porter, so sorry we're late,' said Guy, as he breezed into her office.

I gave a small flick of my hair, put my shoulders back, and, adopting an air of detachment, followed him in.

Mrs Porter was caught between annoyance at Guy's tardiness, and from the look she gave me, the fact that I had joined in, and a very clear excitement at the arrival of one of London's premier advertising executives. After an icy glare, she recovered and adopted the version of herself to which Archie Morley was to be treated.

'Mr Morley,' she cooed, her eyelashes going into their blinky routine, 'may I introduce Mr Collins, our Editor.'

Archie Morley nodded, and gave Guy the sort of handshake that crunches knuckles and is popular among men who find it imperative to announce their virility on sight.

'Collins,' he said, not impolitely.

'Mr Morley,' said Guy, radiating quiet confidence, 'very nice to meet you.'

Morley gave another small nod of acknowledgement as Guy continued. 'I'd like you to meet Miss Lake, our Readers and Advice Editor.'

'Good morning, Mr Morley,' I said, holding out my hand and hoping he didn't break it. For a moment he smirked at my expectation, but then he shook my hand quite normally, and looked me straight in the eye in a disconcerting manner.

Mr Morley was, I estimated, at least fifty, but nevertheless, you could tell that he still cut quite a dash. He was all a bit Errol Flynn, only twenty years older, with the same moustache and a similar amount of self-confidence. My immediate impression was that if you worked for Archie Morley, while you would very much hope to avoid being in his bad books, more than anything you would hope not to have caught his eye.

I lifted my chin a little and nodded, much as Guy had done. If the men could do it, so could I.

Mrs Porter, I presumed, did not share my reservations about her guest. Always attractive, Cressida now seemed to have become more luminous, as if she had her own volume button that could be turned up or down. I had no idea how she did it, but she and Mr Morley were certainly a match for each other. Either one made in heaven, or somewhere far bleaker.

'Shall we sit?' she purred.

We all repaired to the apricot sofas where a tray on the coffee table had been set with a desperately stylish demitasse coffee set, complete with butterfly handles which looked lovely but made trying to hold the cup virtually impossible.

'Would you, Miss Lake?' smiled Mrs Porter.

As I began to pour the coffees, Cressida launched into an effusive soliloquy that wandered from her delight at

Mr Morley's visit through to an almost religious zealotry about her vision for *Woman's Friend*. As she spoke, Archie Morley lounged on the sofa, his arms stretched across the back of it, one leg casually crossed over the other, for all the world as if he had just arrived at his club. She talked on as he hardly acknowledged her, choosing instead to watch me. I wasn't sure what he was hoping to achieve, but it was bloody rude. For a second, I wanted to tell him to at least have the decency to listen to what Mrs Porter had to say. Then I remembered Mrs Croft.

I handed Morley his coffee, thinking how easy it would be to spill it. When he winked at me, it was all I could do not to tip the whole cup into his lap.

'And that,' finished Mrs Porter, with a flourish and after some time, 'is my vision. An *élégante* magazine for an *élégante* advertising clientele.' She perched prettily on the edge of her seat, and gazed at him, her eyes the size of Betty Boop's. 'What do you think?'

Mr Morley looked at her with something approaching, but not quite reaching, a smile. It was hard to work out if he was going to laugh at her, or go full-pelt Errol and kiss her. I'd never seen anything quite like it. I glanced at Guy, who was watching the drama, entirely unreadable. I made a note never to play him at poker.

Morley looked at his watch. Then he sighed as if bored with life itself. He really was as vile as Guy had said.

'Mrs Porter,' he said, sanctifying her by even bothering to acknowledge her presence. 'I am known to speak frankly. Are you sure you want my honest opinion?'

Cressida batted her eyelashes. Previously I would have been willing her on to come up with something better than that, or even tried to create some sort of diversion to stop Archie Morley from doing his worst. But not now.

'Of course,' she breathed.

Ancient Errol sighed again, as if it was his sad, but dreadful duty to go on.

'All right,' he said, uncrossing his legs and spreading them widely, which wasn't half as appealing as I was sure he thought it was. 'I'm afraid, Mrs Porter, that you must be mad as a bat.'

Cressida blinked, once.

'It's a ridiculous folly. There is no *élégante* clientele for what you're talking about. The market doesn't need it and the audience doesn't want it.'

Cressida made a funny little noise from the back of her throat. 'But,' she said.

Morley closed his eyes. It was hard work having to deal with mere mortals. 'Look, I'll save you the time. Your lot already have *The Tatler* and *Vogue*, which are both excellent, and the country set whose houses are falling down unless Grandpa married an heiress have *Country Life*. None of them will have any interest in your so-called vision. It's a terrible idea. It's as simple as that. Sorry, old girl. You're nuts.'

Mrs Porter stared at him.

'I think that's enough, Morley,' said Guy, dispassionately.

'Oh, come on, Collins,' said Morley, 'surely you've told her this, already? For God's sake, it's bloody obvious.'

It would have been very easy for Guy to accept the invitation and twist the knife into Mrs Porter. But even though I knew he loathed her and had no intention of throwing himself on his sword, I also knew that Guy wasn't the sort of man who would take sides with a bully like Archie Morley.

'Mr Morley, thank you for your candour,' he said. 'Mrs Porter, I know you have a very busy diary, would you like to call this meeting a day?'

But Mrs Porter ignored the lifeline he offered. 'Actually,' she said, 'Mr Morley is entirely wrong. My vision is perfect.'

I had to hand it to her. She really was made of strong stuff.

Morley seemed amused. He looked her up and down, which was horrible, and did his awful Not Quite A Smile. 'No skin off my nose,' he said. 'But if you want to make money, I'd leave it as it was. Your Mr Newton is a limp rag, but he is good at what he does. Beef cubes and deodorant. That's your world, and I've got clients who are millionaires because of it, with significant advertising budgets they're happy to spend. But it's up to you.'

'It certainly is,' said Cressida, whose cheeks were now very pink.

'Just don't expect my more *élégante* clients to come in,' said Morley. 'As one of them said when I told him I was seeing you today, you'd have more chance trying to sell caviar at Wimbledon Dogs.'

Now he stood up. 'I have to go. I'm seeing *The Chronicle* boys for lunch. Sorry, Mrs Porter, but you did ask. Nice dress by the way. I'll see myself out. Collins. Miss Lake.'

And with another almost imperceptible nod of his head, the most obnoxious man known to magazine publishing exited the room.

The three of us sat in silence. Even Small Winston, who had watched the meeting from his cushion, was quiet.

For a moment, I thought Mrs Porter was beaten. I was wrong. 'Did you know?' she said. 'I rather believe you did.'

'Know?' said Guy.

'That he is the most appalling man,' snapped Cressida. 'Of course you did. You probably put him up to it.'

Seeing as Cressida had been the one to arrange the meeting, this was a bit rich. I began to put the coffee cups back on the tray.

'Leave them,' barked Mrs Porter. 'I don't pay you to be a waitress.'

'I did warn you that he's known to be blunt,' said Guy.

'The man's an idiot,' replied a quite furious Egg.

Archie Morley was a pig, but he was far from being that.

'Mrs Porter,' said Guy, 'I entirely agree that he's objectionable, and I'm sorry you had to put up with his rudeness. But Morley does know his stuff. I can't tell you how much I hate to admit it, but it's true. He's made a fortune from it. I know it doesn't match your vision, but he's worth listening to.'

'*Worth listening to*?' cried Mrs Porter. 'You sit here and watch me being treated like a fool, and now want me to take the advice of some dreadful man who's probably from Trade anyway, just because it fits in with what you all want?'

'Mrs Porter,' I said, 'I thought he was vile. I was tempted to throw coffee at him at one point. But he said he has clients who *want to spend money* with us if we stick to what we do. I know you don't like talking about money, but if you just let us get on with things, including Mrs Croft, we can make loads of it for you. You wouldn't have to put up with meetings like this, or people like Morley. You wouldn't have to do a thing.'

I thought it was a good argument. Not for the first time today, however, I appeared to be wrong.

'Money?' scoffed Mrs Porter. 'I don't need to go begging to Bovril. In fact, I don't need this magazine at all.'

Now she stood up, marched over to the door and shouted down the corridor for Mr Elliot, who arrived in two seconds flat.

'Yes, Mrs Porter,' he oozed.

Mrs Porter looked over at Guy and me, paused for a moment and then turned back to her second-in-command.

'Mr Elliot,' she said, calmly. 'Forget about calling Mrs Croft. She'll go with the rest of them. I want you to make an appointment with my solicitors. Tell them I have decided to sell *Woman's Friend*.'

CHAPTER NINETEEN

I Know This is Mad

WE HAD MADE a terrible mistake. Our assumption that if Mrs Porter lost interest in the magazine she would drift off and enjoy the proceeds of its success could not have been more wrong.

Mrs Porter didn't want to leave us to get on with it. She wanted to leave the whole thing altogether.

As Mr Elliot inclined his head in obeyance and slithered off to make the phone call, Guy leaped in and began trying to persuade Mrs Porter to think again.

Archie Morley was a bully who enjoyed showing off. He shouldn't be the one to make Mrs Porter lose faith. We should all sit down and talk about Mrs Porter's concerns.

'Mr Collins,' said Mrs Porter, now happy again having very much enjoyed the shocked response to her announcement, 'this isn't because of Mr Morley. He has barely registered with me. I can't imagine how we have mutual friends. No, no, I've been thinking about this all week. Magazine publishing just isn't me. Time to move on.'

She was really quite gay about it, as if she had tried out ping-pong and after a couple of lessons decided to switch to shuttlecock and give that a go because she preferred the shape of the bats. *Woman's Friend* was nothing more than a game to her.

'Why don't you just leave it to us, as Emmy said?' suggested Guy, with the most admirable control. 'As you know, the magazine has been very profitable. You could move on to other interests while enjoying the benefits. No harm done.'

I didn't know how he managed it. My heart was going at about two hundred beats a minute. Guy sounded as if he was happy to give a refund as the table-tennis lessons hadn't worked out.

Mrs Porter, who was still a little flushed after the trial with Mr Morley, bit her bottom lip and looked at the ceiling, which was her way of showing she was currently having a think.

'Ummm,' she mused. 'No. I do loathe talking about money, but if we must, then frankly I've always thought "a bird in the hand" is rather a good thing. The magazine is for sale.'

'But have you thought about the staff?' asked Guy, more urgently now.

'Ummm,' said Mrs Porter, who I was increasingly sure was pretending to be vague on purpose. 'Not really. I suppose that all depends on the new owners, doesn't it?'

She smiled very, very sweetly.

I smelt a rat. This wasn't something she had chewed over in the last few days. I would have placed a very large bet that we had been on probation for far longer than that. Planning to sack Mrs Croft had just been a bit of fun.

'Has this always been your plan?' I said. 'To just sell off your inheritance?'

Mrs Porter put her head to one side. 'Miss Lake,' she said in her best sing-song voice, 'that sounds almost sinister. No, I've been learning the ropes. Of course, both of you, and almost everyone here, have stood in the way of everything I've tried to do to bring new life to my dear uncle's magazine. None of you understand creativity or imagination.'

'So you'll just get rid of what your "dear uncle" had been hugely fond of for years?' I said.

Cressida wrinkled her nose. 'You needn't make it sound so horrid,' she said.

'Mrs Porter,' said Guy, 'what is your intention in terms of telling the staff? You must realise how upsetting this news will be.'

Mrs Porter pulled a face. 'Can't you just tell them?' she said.

'I can,' answered Guy, 'but I would like to have a little more detail. Your plan, your timing, most of all your thoughts on how we look after them, both now, and if and when *Woman's Friend* is sold. I might even suggest that we discuss this more formally, before the news is shared as it will be a great worry for everyone. You and I can sit down and . . . '

'Oh, Mr Collins,' sighed Mrs Porter, 'I really . . . don't want to.' She looked over to where Small Winston had been sitting. 'Now, where is Master Porter?' she said, as the dog had vacated his spot. 'I can't talk about selling the magazine when I don't know where he might be. Worrying about telling the staff will just have to wait.'

She began to look under the sofas, in case he was there. Then I heard a voice behind me.

'It's all right, I've got him.'

Hester was standing in the doorway, Small Winston in her arms. I had no idea how long she had been there, but from the expression on her face, she had heard more than enough. She carefully put the dog down on the floor. Then, the best assistant in the world turned on her heels and fled.

I didn't hesitate, but took off after her, leaving Guy to continue whatever remained of a conversation that had been going nowhere very fast. Hester ran towards the end of the corridor which led to the ladies' lavatories, but before I could catch up, her escape came to an abrupt halt as she crashed into Mrs Mahoney.

'Hester! This isn't a playground,' she began, at which point poor Hest burst into tears.

'She's going to sell us,' she managed to gasp, between sobs. 'Mrs P-Porter.'

'Oh, Hest,' said Mrs Mahoney, immediately putting her arm around the teenager and giving her a hug, 'don't be daft.' She looked over Hester's shoulder at me. There was no point denying it. Part of me rather felt like crying, as well.

But that wouldn't help anyone, so I nodded. 'That's what she's just said.'

Unsurprisingly, the commotion had attracted the rest of the team, and Mrs Shaw and Miss Peters had come out into the corridor to see what was going on. The cat was well and truly out of the bag. I took a very deep breath.

'Come on,' I said, as I herded Mrs Mahoney and Hester towards them. 'Let's all go back in here. Miss Peters, could you fetch Mr Brand and Mr Newton, please. And Mrs Pye, as well, I think.'

I wasn't sure about that. I wasn't at all sure what I was doing, full stop. Playing for time, and hoping Guy would join us as soon as possible. It wasn't much of a plan.

Everyone gathered in the journalists' room. This was the very opposite of how any of them should hear Mrs Porter's news, but it was too late for it to happen in any other way.

'Who's selling us?' demanded Mrs Shaw. 'What does that mean, anyway?'

Mr Newton looked panicked, Mr Brand frowned, and

Mrs Mahoney said, 'There, there,' to Hester who let out another sob. Even Mrs Pye wasn't fast enough to disguise a shocked look, before settling her face back into smug.

'Selling us?' repeated Miss Peters. '*Woman's Friend*?'

'I don't think it's certain,' I said, 'Guy, I mean, Mr Collins is speaking with Mrs Porter now. We all need to keep calm, and wait until he can give us more information.'

Much to my relief, Guy walked into the room, his expression suggesting he was carrying the weight of the world.

'I am terribly sorry, everyone,' he said, catching my eye. 'I assume you've heard that Mrs Porter is talking about selling *Woman's Friend*.'

There were murmurs of 'yes' and more exclamations of surprise. If Guy was saying it, it must be real. He spoke slowly, choosing his words. 'I have only had the briefest of discussions with her,' he continued, 'but I believe this is something certainly under consideration. Mrs Porter has now left for the day, and Mrs Pye, she would like you to meet her downstairs, if you would.'

All eyes turned to the Fashion and Beauty Editor, who appeared to grow several inches in height as she deigned to nod an acknowledgement at Guy, before doing a passable imitation of a glide out of the room. Guy shut the door behind her.

'Right,' he said, decisively. 'Everyone draw up a chair. I'm going to tell you everything I know, which isn't much, and then we're going to . . .' he hesitated, 'then we are going to talk about it. Not that I can fix anything at the moment, but we're a team and a family, and I am not letting any of you go home until I have tried to answer any questions you may have.'

At that moment, the unctuous Mr Elliot had the temerity to walk into the room.

'Mrs Porter has . . .' he began.

'Mr Elliot,' said Guy, with obvious dislike, 'I am in a meeting with my staff and I will not be interrupted. Please close the door behind you as you leave.'

Under a very heavy stare, Mr Elliot retreated.

Guy grimaced, but then began to tell the team, word for word, what Mrs Porter had said. When he got to the part after I had left to go after Hester, it was clear that Mrs Porter's threat was certainly not a spur-of-the-moment whim.

'Do you think she'll really do it?' asked Mrs Mahoney.

'I think she might,' said Guy. 'I'm sorry, but I want to be honest with you. Mrs Porter says there has been interest already.'

'So much for all that talk about her dear uncle,' said Mrs Shaw. 'What a load of old cobblers.'

'Yes,' said Guy, briskly. 'I don't disagree.'

'What do we do now?' asked Miss Peters. 'Will we lose our jobs?'

'We could go on strike,' said Mrs Shaw. 'We might as well if we're getting the sack anyway.'

'I don't think that would help,' said Guy. 'If Mrs Porter does want to sell, then it's likely to take some time. You don't sell, or buy for that matter, an operation like this, overnight. So we have time to get to grips with it. Please don't panic. I would understand though,' he added, gently, 'if, in the light of this very unsettling news, you might question what you're doing here. So, whatever you need to do to make sure you look after your own interests, then you must do it.' No one said anything, and Guy smiled at us. 'What I am saying – rather badly – is that I don't expect you to feel you have to go down with the ship. If that is what this is. Which it might not be,' he finished rather too cheerily. 'Now. More questions.'

I glanced around the room. Everyone looked in shock.

I was in shock. Half an hour ago I was furious when Mrs Porter said she would be letting Mrs Croft go. Now she was doing it to all of us. I couldn't help but think that I should have seen it coming. I had fallen for the My Darling Uncle lines, the lofty claims that publishing was her 'calling'. What an idiot I had been.

Hester, who was sitting quietly next to Mrs Mahoney, put up her hand. She looked very young, as if she was still in a classroom. It must have been more frightening for her than any of us.

'Mr Collins,' she said, haltingly, 'what can we do? There must be something.'

'Well, Hester,' said Guy, gently, 'I'd like you to go home to your mum and tell her everything I've said, and say that I'd be very happy if she wants to come in with you and talk to me about it all. I know this is a lot to take in.'

'No.' Hester shook her head. 'Sorry, Mr Collins, but I didn't mean that. I meant, what can we do to stop her? How can we stop Mrs Porter from selling *Woman's Friend*?'

A couple of the adults smiled, but Guy took Hester seriously.

'That's a very good question,' he said.

'It's just that, you know when Emmy answers the readers' problems? Well, almost all the time, she tells them not to give up. Especially if it's really important.'

Now it was my turn to feel tears threaten. Hester was right.

Guy smiled at her. 'True,' he said. 'Thank you. The last thing we should do is give up.' He paused for a moment, thinking, and then looked over at me. 'The new Lord Overton,' he said, with a brief smile. 'There's nothing to lose now. Let me speak with him,' he said, addressing everyone. 'He may be able to help.'

'We could see if Monica's heard anything about the

so-called "interest" Mrs Porter mentioned. That is, Mrs Edwards from *Woman Today*,' I added. 'She knows everyone. If there really have been approaches, I bet she'll be able to find out from whom.'

'Herbie Garson might know something,' said Mrs Mahoney. 'I can ask.'

As we began to come up with names of people we knew in the industry, the gloomy atmosphere lifted just a little. I watched as Guy thanked and encouraged everyone, no matter what they suggested, and bit by bit the initial panic began to die down. As each member of the team grabbed on to something that might give them the tiniest bit of control over what had been a horrible shock, things began to feel better.

'I bet that Mrs Pye is in on it,' said Mrs Shaw. 'You could see it in her face. We could get her and make her give us the information.'

'That sounds mildly threatening, Mrs Shaw,' said Guy.

'Yes, I know,' said Mrs Shaw.

'We could write something in the magazine and ask readers not to buy *Woman's Friend*. Then it won't be worth anything so Mrs Porter won't make any money. That'll teach her,' said Miss Peters.

'By the rate we're going with her rubbish ideas and fancy frocks and that, we won't have to ask them,' said Mrs Mahoney. 'Sales are worse every week. The whole business won't be worth fourpence ha'penny by August.'

'If it's fourpence ha'penny,' said Mr Newton, who had been looking sick to the gills until now, 'I'll put the money up for it myself.' He gave a brave if slightly tremulous smile, which prompted Mrs Mahoney to reach over and squeeze his hand, and at the same time, very nearly broke my heart. Mr Newton was so easily worried, and I dreaded to think what Mrs Porter's news would do to him.

'Actually,' I said, hoping to brighten him up, 'my friend Thelma has already said that if she wins the Pools, she'll buy *Woman's Friend* for us. In fact, I'll make sure I ask her, in case she's the one interested as some sort of surprise.'

It raised a bit of a grin, and then Mr Brand, always the quietest but, equally, the wisest of us all, said that his sister-in-law had won ten pounds just the week before last, which the rest of the team jumped on as proof that it could actually happen.

As everyone started to chat now animatedly about winning the Pools, the most outlandish idea came into my head.

'What if we could get the money?' I said, surprising myself by saying it out loud. 'I'm not saying I have any idea where we'd even begin to find it, but don't people start their own companies all the time?'

Guy looked at me as if I had broken into fluent Swahili.

'Is that crazy?' I said. 'Especially in the middle of a war. I don't know. Someone with financial acumen and all that sort of thing would know. Certainly not me.' I gave a small, self-conscious laugh, but now everyone was looking at me.

'What are you saying, Emmy?' asked Guy.

I had no idea really why I said it. Perhaps I had got carried away with the thought of winning a fortune, or I was just trying to cheer everyone up. Either way, I found myself making a suggestion.

'Well,' I said. 'No one knows more about running this magazine as a successful enterprise than us. If I had lots of money, I'd back us to give it a go.' I looked around at my colleagues. 'You'll probably think I've gone stark raving mad, but why don't we find a way to buy *Woman's Friend* for ourselves?'

CHAPTER TWENTY

A Pipe Dream Takes Hold

FOR A MOMENT there was silence, but to my surprise it was *not* followed by laughter. Hester was the first to speak. 'I've only got my Post Office Savings Book,' she said, 'but I can ask Mum if she minds that I use it.'

'I've a small pension,' said Miss Peters, hesitantly, 'although I was hoping not to touch it until nineteen sixty-one.'

'I put my savings into War Bonds,' said Mrs Shaw, 'and anyway, it's a nice idea, Emmy, but unless one of us is secretly the Duke of Westminster, we'd never have enough.' She looked at Mr Brand.

'I'm sorry, Mrs Shaw,' he said, 'I am very definitely not him.'

'Thank you, ladies, all very much,' said Guy, 'but I think what Emmy meant was that we would look to borrow money. No one would be giving up their personal savings.'

'It's a pipe dream,' I admitted. 'I said it without thinking. Sorry, everyone.'

'I don't know if it is,' said Mrs Mahoney. 'Every publisher has to start somewhere. Look at Alfred Harmsworth. Started out with *Comic Cuts* and ended up as a viscount.'

'That'd show Mrs Porter,' said Mrs Shaw. 'And Mrs Pye.'

'All modesty aside, between the lot of us what we don't

know about magazines you can write on the back of a stamp,' said Mrs Mahoney.

As the others joined in saying there was no modesty needed, and that of course Mrs Mahoney was entirely right, I sat for a moment and noticed how the mood had changed. Utter desolation had turned to something grittier. No one wanted to take the news lying down.

Perhaps it *was* just a pipe dream, and this was just the sort of If You Won The Pools What Would You Buy? conversation that you might have in an air-raid shelter to while away some time. But if Hester was willing to give up her Post Office savings before even being asked, and Miss Peters was considering stumping up the money that she had saved for her old age, then it did make you feel that if there was some way that it could become even the most remote possibility, the people surrounding me would do everything in their power to try to make it work.

'It's certainly a novel idea,' said Mr Newton, 'but Mrs Shaw made a jolly good point. This is the sort of thing that rich people do. Rothschilds or Rockefellers. Not normal people like us. I sometimes read *The Financial Times* on the bus,' he added in case anyone thought he was showing off.

Once again, silence fell and we all looked to Guy.

'Before anything else, we need to be absolutely sure that Mrs Porter definitely means it,' he said. 'I will try to speak with her tomorrow. I'll also try to get an appointment with the new Lord Overton. He may be able to shed light on the situation, or even,' and here Guy looked anything but convinced, 'offer some support. We must all hope that Mrs Porter isn't going to sell. But if she is,' he finished, 'then we have a very large challenge indeed.'

★

The next morning, Mrs Porter confirmed that *Woman's Friend* was officially for sale.

Mr Elliot slid into the office with a memorandum stating that we were to continue to work on the magazine as usual, and not to change or drop any of Mrs Porter's inspirational ideas. If anyone had any questions, they were to ask him.

As soon as he slid back out again, we all agreed we would not. Guy was our Editor, and as far as we were concerned, he was in charge.

Following Mr Elliot, Mrs Pye came in, later than usual, which a cynic might have said was so that she could make an entrance. Dressed in what I knew was her best suit, she staged an homage to Mrs Porter by trying out a new very false laugh and attempting to call Mr Elliot 'darling', which was an embarrassment for them both. Untroubled, she then made a rare visit to the journalists' room where we were all mucking in to help sort out the post.

'Bonjour,' she trilled. 'Why so sad?'

'Good morning, Mrs Pye,' I said. 'Thank you for your concern. *Are* we sad, Mrs Shaw? I didn't think we were.'

'I'm not,' said Mrs Shaw, jauntily, 'but that's because I don't have to answer all these complaints. There you are, Mrs Pye, today's post for you.'

She plonked a significant pile of fashion and beauty correspondence into Mrs Pye's arms.

'Mnnfff,' said Mrs Pye, who turned on her heels and left the room, saying loudly, 'It's no wonder Mrs Porter has had enough.'

The rest of us looked at each other and as Mrs Shaw opened her mouth to reply, I put a finger to my lips.

'It's all right,' I said, once Madame was safely out of earshot. 'Don't forget, we're the ones who are going to come up with a plan.'

'I bloody hope so,' said Mrs Shaw.

I bloody did too.

★

A few days later it was fair to say that we had. Or at least, we'd made something of a start. It was Tuesday evening and Guy was coming to Bunty's after work in order to share what information he had found so far over a fish and chips dinner.

I had, of course, told Bunts and Thel about the idea to buy *Woman's Friend*. Now, as I was already at home having spent the afternoon in Chelsea interviewing one of Mrs Porter's brides, Bunty and I were sitting in deck-chairs in the garden, chatting and trying to work out if we could hear any noise from the shed. The chickens had been in hiding for over a week now and as it was turning into a decent summer, keeping Thelma indoors and away from them was proving a challenge.

'I'm sure she knows,' I said to Bunty. 'The children bring them into the garden as soon as she goes out anywhere. She must have noticed bits of fluff and what have you.'

'You can definitely hear them,' said Bunty, concentrating, with her head tilted to one side.

'I'll ask Roy if he can look after them until Thel's birthday,' I said. 'I don't think I can cope with the pressure of hiding them for another whole month.'

I was joking, but Bunty picked up on an edge in my voice. 'How are you?' she said. 'Really? All this awful business with Mrs Porter must be so hard.'

I sighed, a very long sigh. 'It's horrible,' I admitted. 'When Guy told the contributors, he said Mrs Fieldwick was awfully choked up about losing her gardening column, and Mrs Croft blamed herself for the entire thing. He told them both that if we can save *Woman's*

Friend they are to be the very first people to be put on the staff.'

'He's a good man, Guy,' said Bunty. 'How's it going on that front?'

'We'll hear tonight,' I said. 'It was just a spur-of-the-moment suggestion, but it's taken on a life of its own. It was lovely to see everyone cheer up, but I can't imagine how we'd make it work.'

'Guy will know,' said Bunty. 'He always does.'

'I'm not sure,' I answered, watching a ladybird as it marched confidently up my finger and then took off into the air. 'No one simply ups and buys a company. We couldn't just walk into a bank and ask for a loan. They'd laugh at us. Anyway, the banks aren't allowed to lend money unless it's part of the war effort.'

'You're *entirely* part of the war effort,' protested Bunty. 'How many letters have you shown me from the Ministry thanking *Woman's Friend* for its support? Not to mention the fact you're helping keep Britain's women going. Can't Guy pull some strings at the Ministry for a reference?'

I wasn't convinced. '*Dear Mr Bank Manager, please can you give Guy thousands of pounds as we know him and he wants to buy a whole magazine? Lots of love, The Ministry,*' I said, pulling a face.

'Now you're just being glib,' said Bunts, nudging me in the arm with her elbow.

'Sorry,' I said. 'Maybe he'll have news when he gets in. But getting anyone to back us is a terrifically long shot. We've no background in company ownership. Why would they trust us? Anyway everyone's money is tied up in war bonds.'

Now I wasn't being glib at all. It was the truth. To my surprise, Bunty began to laugh.

'What is it?' I said, smiling. 'Banking isn't funny, Miss Tavistock. It's very serious and also incredibly dull.'

Bunts laughed even more.

'Oh, Em,' she gulped, 'did you ever think we'd end up sitting in a garden listening for smuggled chickens and saying things like *company ownership*?' She looked up to the sky and stretched her arms into the air. 'What's going on?' she yelled. Then she raised her voice even more. 'THIS WAR'S SENDING EVERYONE BONKERS.'

I stretched my arms up as well. 'I KNOW,' I shouted. 'I WISH IT WOULD END BEFORE I GO MAD.'

Bunty grinned, put her arms down and wrapped them around her knees.

'Too late,' she said, cheerily.

I smiled at my friend and thought how lovely she looked and so very well. Her face was brown as a berry as she and Harold had been on a day trip to Worthing at the weekend. They couldn't go on the beach of course because of the mines, but they'd had a lovely time walking along the prom, and then eating their packed lunches and looking past the barbed-wire fences and out to the sea.

'I sound about eighty,' she'd said when she told me.

'No, Bunts,' I replied. 'You sound happy.'

'Harold's coming over tonight, isn't he?' I asked now. 'It's good of him to offer moral support.'

'He's quite good on all sorts of things,' said Bunty, failing completely not to sound proud. 'He might have some ideas.'

'We could do with that,' I said. 'Although it's rather a trek just for chips.'

'He says he doesn't mind,' said Bunts, 'Although I feel a little bad.' She paused. 'Do you want to know a secret? Mrs Harewood's annoying lodger is moving out. She's asked him to leave.'

'That's good news,' I said. 'Buzz said he was quite odd.'

'Yes,' said Bunty, keenly.

'Is that it?' I prompted. 'Is that the secret?'

Bunty shook her head and leaned forward. 'Mrs Harewood has asked Harold if he'd like to have the room,' she said. 'As a lodger.'

This was Enormous News. I couldn't believe Bunty hadn't told me the minute I got home.

'No?!' I said. 'Do you think he will?'

Bunty nodded frantically. 'Yes.'

'Oh Bunts,' I said. 'I'm chuffed to bits. But why's it a secret?'

'I suppose it's not really,' said Bunty, sounding slightly self-conscious. 'I just didn't want to make a big thing about it.'

'Oh love,' I said. 'It's smashing news.'

Bunty nodded again. 'I know,' she said. 'I feel a bit giddy about it all.'

I leaned back and looked up at the sky. 'Everybody's going bonkers,' I laughed.

And then, although the point needed little further proof, Bunty and I both threw our arms into the air, and just as if we were still children together with hardly a care in the world, we let out the most enormous of cheers.

CHAPTER TWENTY-ONE

Monica Makes A Move

IT WAS AWFULLY hard to act normally when Harold
arrived.

'Hello there!' I said, which came out far too loudly,
giving the game away that I had heard the news.

Harold looked at Bunty and then back at me.

'HELLO, Emmy,' he said at a similar volume and
smiling broadly.

For the first time since meeting him again, he sounded
exactly the same as the cheerful, self-confident man we
had first met. It was a joy to see. I was fit to burst for
them both.

As well as Guy coming round to talk about the pie-in-
the-sky idea, tonight we were joined by Mrs Mahoney,
whose participation if we were to stand any chance of
building a realistic plan would be absolutely vital. Completing
what Bunty had jokingly referred to as the *Woman's Friend*
War Cabinet was our final guest, Monica, who had been
the first person Guy had called to check if he had lost all
his marbles to even contemplate buying the magazine.

Her answer had been, 'Yes you have. When do we start?'

Now, Harold and the children had just returned from
the chippy, laden down with our dinners wrapped in newspaper and bringing the glorious smell of salt and vinegar
into the room.

'Oooh,' breathed Monica. 'Perfect.'

Guy smiled at her fondly. 'I told you she's not as grand as she seems,' he said.

'Grand?' said Monica. 'Shoot me now.'

'I don't think you're grand,' said Stanley. 'But you do look very pretty and you smell nice, or at least you did before the chips arrived.'

'Stanley,' said Thelma, mortified. 'I'm sorry, Monica, Stan gets excited about new people.'

'Thank you, Stanley,' said Monica, entirely unruffled. 'So do I.'

Stan beamed at her.

'Tuck in, everyone,' I said. 'Nothing worse than if it gets cold.'

Mrs Mahoney gave Stan a big smile, although Thelma gave him A Look and silently tapped her wristwatch. The children had been allowed to join in on the understanding it was a grown-ups' dinner, after which they were to be off upstairs for reading and bed.

'I declare our first board meeting open,' said Guy. 'May they all involve the best grub money can buy.'

Everyone said cheers to that, and for the next half an hour no work was done as we focused on eating. Guy asked for an update from Margaret on her dancing, which she confirmed was going very well, but really she was more interested in the trombone these days.

'Not at the same time?' said Guy, which Marg took very seriously, and patiently explained that you really couldn't do that because of the breathing.

'Thank you, Margaret,' he said, 'I understand the difficulty. Now, do you think we should begin? I did an agenda on the bus. First point is from me. I managed to see the new Lord Overton this afternoon.'

Now ears pricked up all round. If anyone knew Cressida's plans it would be her cousin.

'It wasn't a great success,' said Guy. He glanced at Margaret, who was watching him with one last remaining chip stuck on her fork. 'Just to say again, this is all a big secret,' he added.

Thel took the hint and asked the children to go and make sure Laurel and Hardy were ready for bed. As they happily marched off outside, Guy picked up his thread.

'I'm afraid to report,' he said, 'that as far as *Woman's Friend* is concerned, this Lord Overton has no interest. The magazine, the staff, Cressida selling up – none of it. He's very much focused on *The Chronicle* and the other news titles, which makes perfect sense. They're an immense business. I also had the temerity to ask what his mother would think of it all. That was a mistake.'

'What did he say?' I asked.

'Quite a lot. Mostly along the lines of, "what Lady Overton thinks is not your concern . . . just lost my father . . . you may have been chums with my little brother, but get your nose out of my family's business."'

'That's disappointing,' said Mrs Mahoney. 'His parents were both very fond of *Woman's Friend*.'

'Times change,' said Guy. 'But do you know, I rather respect him for being his own man. He's paving his own way and not taking the inheritance for granted, unlike the Egg. Johnny Overton is very protective of his mother and there's a lot to be said for that. If my mother was still alive, I'd be much the same if I thought someone was pushing their luck.' Guy paused. 'But I'm sorry, everyone. As far as Launceston Press is concerned, we're on our own.'

'Well done for trying,' said Monica. 'It may actually be preferable to break away entirely.'

'Let's hope so,' said Guy, playing with a fork. 'Which brings us to number two on the agenda – raising the finances. If anyone is rolling in money, now would be a good time to say.'

Unsurprisingly, no one spoke up.

'You're not a millionaire, are you, Harold?' I asked. 'Keeping it under your hat to make sure we like you for just being you?'

'I'd have said,' he replied, 'to be on the safe side. Sorry, bit of a dud on this front. I don't even have a job yet.'

'You will,' said Bunty, softly. 'Anyone sensible will want you.'

Harold smiled at her in a way that made my heart want to burst.

'Monica?' said Guy. 'You're looking thoughtful. Which is usually a good thing.'

Monica nodded seriously. 'Actually, I've been giving this whole situation quite a lot of thought. I don't want to push in, but I can rattle on for a bit if now is a good time.'

Everyone agreed now was a *very* good time for Monica to say anything. 'All right,' she said. 'Here's what I think.'

As Bunty and Thelma got up and cleared the table, Monica began to speak. Within moments, everyone was glued to her every word. We were sitting in the family kitchen, surrounded by household items, drawings by the children, and Stan's collection of homemade aeroplanes which hovered in silent balsa-wood battle on their pieces of thread from the ceiling. But now, we could for all the world have been in a corporate board room.

Monica Edwards was the epitome of experience and knowledge. Poised as ever, she spoke in low and measured tones. Thelma quietly left to round up the children and take them upstairs, while the rest of us stayed gladly in the palm of Monica's hand.

'I've been speaking to a few of my contacts,' she said. 'There's no doubt that thanks to the success of the *Friend* over the last couple of years, and your profile with the Ministry, there's an enormous amount of gossip about what's going on. Now,' she held up her hand for a moment, 'that's both good and bad. Some of it is because, as you know, the publishing industry loves a drama, and Mrs Porter's editorial direction has obviously made quite a splash. I know this rubs salt in fresh wounds, but quite frankly, it's been like watching someone take a very nice car and drive it as fast as they can into a wall.'

Monica took a breath as I saw Mrs Mahoney frown and Guy wince.

'I'm sorry,' Monica continued. 'There is a great deal of sympathy for you and an even stronger feeling of "there but for the grace of God go the rest of us". Which brings me to where I lay my cards on the table.' No one moved as Monica paused for a moment. 'All of us are at the whim of our owners. I've been Editor in Chief and more recently Publisher of *Woman Today* for over ten years. It's fair to say, I've given my all to it during that time, including sacrificing my marriage, although arguably that was a bonus. My point is, it could all end tomorrow. With that in mind, and you should not say anything at this point, but if this is of any benefit to you, I would like to join you as an interested party. Financially.'

Monica's suggestion of not saying anything at this point was immediately ignored, as everyone broke into excited agreement that it was the best thing that we had heard. Guy sat back, watching and listening.

'Have you two talked about this?' I asked.

'A little,' he nodded. 'Monica, would you go on, please?'

'Thank you, Guy. Yes. Now sadly, rather like Captain Thomas, I am not a millionaire. However, thanks to very poor judgement on my part in choosing a now ex-husband whose hobbies were making money and philandering, I do have a certain amount of capital. With a couple of caveats, I would like to discuss being one of a select number of private investors for your business.'

Monica did not mess around.

'Caveats?' I said.

'Yes. In my view, *Woman's Friend* is only worth backing if it returns to the formula that has made it a success. That means you three. Guy, Mrs Mahoney and Emmy as a condition of purchase, as it were. And of course your team, but as far as I can see, it was you three that took the magazine to where it was before Mrs Porter arrived. *You're* central to the business plan. *You are* the magazine. Put together a strong argument that you can do what you did before and thereby save *Woman's Friend*, and I think we can take a business plan to other people who will back you as well. The second condition – and I think any investor will expect this – is that you have to do everything you can to stop the rot that is so obviously taking place. You don't need me to tell you, but every reader, subscription and advertiser you lose is going to make it harder to get the money chaps on board. But I think you can do it. I really do.'

Monica took a sip of water from her glass, and waited.

There was lots to take in. Finally, Guy spoke. 'Thank you, Monica. This is an enormously generous and supportive offer. I'm not going to do you the disservice of asking if you are sure. But it is a huge gesture.'

Monica shook her head, and swallowing the last of her water, put the glass down. 'No, Guy,' she said. 'This isn't a gesture. This is pure business.' Now she spoke with more emotion. 'This is an opportunity,' she said, 'to own a magazine. A very good one, and on our own terms, with the knowledge that a Mrs Porter could not happen again. That's a dream. If we can bring *Woman's Friend* back from where that ludicrous woman is trying to take it, then we can use it as the start of an independent publishing company. I've never had the guts to do it until now. We need to find decent backers, but ensure we have the deciding share. Of course, it may not work.' Now she looked around the table intently, the slightest smile on her lips. 'But imagine. How *exciting* it could be.'

'And you would help us find these people?' I asked.

'Yes. If you'll have me,' said Monica. 'I think there will be interest, if we can move fast. The fact is, there is money around and people want to invest. *Woman's Friend* plays a key role in the promotion of civilian morale. You're part of the war effort. That's a help too. Prove you're worth investing in. That's the key.'

It was exactly what Bunty had said.

I should probably have looked serious and muttered something about consulting with my colleagues. This did not happen.

'YES,' I said. 'AYE.'

I was sure people said, 'Aye' in this kind of situation. Mrs Mahoney clearly agreed.

'AYE,' she said, and thumped the kitchen table with her hand.

We both turned to Guy. He and Monica were looking at each other in the way that makes you realise there's a shared history you'll never entirely understand. I knew they'd become friends during the last war, and I'd heard dozens of stories about their adventures during the 'twenties. But every member of their generation had scars. For all the anecdotes and devil-may-care japes, I would bet my life that there were more stories that remained in darker shadows and would never be told.

Now, however, Guy raised his eyebrows. 'Never had the guts,' he scoffed. 'Absolute nonsense.'

Then he thumped his hand on the kitchen table. 'Aye.'

Everyone started speaking at once. From a potential list of people to target, through to the practicalities of suppliers for print and production, ideas and suggestions came thick and fast. Having settled the children, Thelma returned to a scene of intense discussion.

Bunty, whose shorthand was second to none, took notes that raced across her paper pad at a sprint. Harold turned out to know all sorts of details about Government regulations which he said he had picked up from a chap he was friendly with in hospital. Within an hour we had signed Captain Thomas up as part of the business team.

'I might turn out to be rubbish,' he said, happily, 'but I'm available, conveniently situated, and also free of charge.'

'That's our man,' said Guy.

'Not for free,' said Monica. 'This is a business. We must look into remuneration. You're an asset. And an overhead. But mostly an asset.'

'It's handy you'll be next door,' I said, grinning at him.

Bunty kicked me under the table.

'How many people will you have on the staff?' she asked, changing the subject.

I started counting. 'Guy, Mrs Mahoney, me, Mr Newton, Hester and Mrs Shaw and Miss Peters. We'll need a new Fashion and Beauty person as I think we can agree that Mrs Pye isn't our biggest ally. And an assistant too. We'd want to keep the freelancers so that wouldn't change.'

'Will you rent the offices from Lord Overton? It's going to be very tricky to find anywhere else,' said Bunty.

That was the understatement of the year. Great chunks of London's offices had been bombed out or taken over for the war effort.

'That's a very good point,' said Guy. 'Based on my meeting with him today, I think probably not.'

'So let's say ten people to start with,' said Bunty, pushing on. 'Good. So I have a suggestion. Why don't you move in here? If the team don't mind working in Pimlico rather than Fleet Street, it could work.' Without waiting for an answer she began to draw out a map of the house. 'It won't do your proposal any harm to have an office lined up. Now, Thelma and the kids are in the top flat. Emmy and I could move our bedrooms up to the floor below, and that leaves the ground floor and the first floor. Loads of these old Georgian houses are used for businesses. Embassies run entire countries from less space. And it won't cost you a penny.'

It was another extraordinarily generous offer.

'What about your granny?' I said. 'Would she mind you turning her house into an office? Strangers coming in and out every day?'

'That's the cleverest part,' said Bunty. 'You aren't strangers. Emmy, it's you and Guy. If it wasn't for you two, I probably wouldn't be here today.'

'And you wouldn't mind living above the shop, as it were?' said Guy to Thelma.

Thel laughed. 'Of course not,' she said. 'It sounds very exciting. The kids would love it and so would I.'

'That's sorted then. I'll ask Granny when I go to see her,' said Bunty. 'Or rather, *we* can ask her. Harold and I are going to visit.'

Thel busied herself with the kettle. I said a very bland, 'How lovely,' and then Guy summed up what we were both really thinking, by letting out a long, low whistle.

'Meeting Mrs Tavistock,' he said. 'I say, old man, how are you feeling about that?'

'Guy,' I said. 'Really.'

'Terrified,' said Harold.

'Darling,' said Bunty.

'Sorry,' he replied. 'I'm just not sure what Mrs Tavistock is going to think about her granddaughter going out with an old wreck like me.' He gave a wide but now slightly strained smile.

'Oi, none of that.' Thelma whirled round from where she was getting cups out for some tea. 'Harold, do you have any idea how much my children look up to you? They don't care how bashed up you are. You're a hero. So don't you go saying that sort of thing again. All right?'

Harold nodded. 'Will do,' he said, a little gruffly. 'Thanks, Thelma.'

'Good,' said Thel. 'Now can someone come and help me with this tea?'

Guy said he would and got up smartly, giving Harold the slightest squeeze on his shoulder as he went past.

'Are you definitely serious about this, Bunty?' he said. 'It would just be until we had *Woman's Friend* up and running properly again, of course.'

Bunty sat up straighter. 'If you lot can pull this off, you'll deserve to have somewhere sorted so you won't have to worry for a while. You could stay here as long as you wanted.'

Guy was now balancing cups and saucers in one hand and a teapot in the other. He set them down on the table.

'Excuse me, Harold,' he said. Then he went over to Bunty and gave her a huge kiss on the cheek. Bunty laughed and told him she hadn't persuaded her granny yet.

I was already up and heading towards the kitchen door.

'I don't want to be the sort of waste bug who doesn't

drink a freshly made cup of tea,' I called back over my shoulder, 'but last one upstairs gets the worst spot in the new office.'

And then I hurled open the door, and hurried off to see how Bunty's wonderful offer could be put to the test.

. . . Darling, you'll never guess what, but Bunty says if her granny agrees, we can have the house for W.Friend! She came up with the idea and told us tonight. We all had a meeting in the kitchen about trying to buy WF. Bunts is going to ask Mrs T this week and she's taking Harold to meet her which we are all terribly excited about.

Anyway, Guy is cock-a-hoop. And that isn't even the big news: Monica E. wants to come into business with us. She had masses of ideas + contacts re the money side. I wasn't ANY good on that count and sat there like the kingpin of flops, but I should be more helpful on the actual mag + readers etc. I hope so anyway.

I wish you were here. I'd give almost anything for you to be home even for a minute, but it won't be that long until you are. Stan says that when their dad comes home he's going to glue his feet to the floor so that he can't go away again.

Are they feeding you all right? The papers are sounding chipper. Joan at the station said her nephew had Vera Lynn sing for them. We've heard the American boys get all sorts of film stars. But we're all still reeling about Leslie Howard getting killed. Did you know? Bloody, bloody Hitler. (Sorry — my language is getting worse. I blame your brother.)

I miss you, darling. All my love. E. xxxxxxxxxxxxxxxxxxx

CHAPTER TWENTY-TWO

Stealing is a Definite No

IT WAS WONDERFUL to be able to write to Charles without having to put on a chipper face. As if Monica coming on board wasn't the most remarkable piece of good luck, Bunty's suggestion about the house gave us all a much-needed spring in our step. It was hugely supportive of her, as even though the building was owned by her grandmother, it was very much Bunty's home. We took the tea things up with us and once we had sensibly gone through the rest of the agenda and made plans for next steps, everyone spent the rest of the evening rearranging furniture in the rooms on the ground floor and taking it in turns to 'be' the various members of the *Woman's Friend* team and positioning ourselves in different configurations to see how we could all fit in.

The dining-room table was a large and impressive reminder of the days when twelve people could easily be seated at dinner to enjoy numerous courses, all of which required different cutlery. As a result, having set up a type-writer (my own, quickly brought down from my room), a container for stationery (an old cocoa box from the kitchen) and several trays for correspondence (three old vegetable crates), which we sat on dust sheets so as not to scratch anything, it was clear that there would be more than enough room for everyone to sit, and most importantly, work.

As we arranged everything, anyone would have imagined that we had procured tens of thousands of pounds and that *Woman's Friend* was already ours. Suggestions came thick and fast for obtaining basic office items which were now almost impossible to find. I wondered out loud if we could sneak out something small each day from the current *Woman's Friend* offices.

'That,' said Guy, 'is stealing, and a definite No.'

There was no doubt that despite the fun of setting up an imaginary office in Bunty's house, in all probability we would be worryingly short on some critical pieces of kit, not to mention the impossibility of trying to run a business from one telephone line. Monica, however, was a very calming influence.

'All part of the business plan,' she said, with the same level of concern as if someone had just asked if she could lend them a spare hankie. 'I don't mean to sound blasé but I'm sure Guy will back me up when I say publishers acquire, launch, close and sell off magazines at an indecent frequency.'

Guy, who was sitting in a corner with Mrs Mahoney discussing production requirements, looked up and nodded.

'They'll be circling Cressida as soon as the word is out.'

'So we need to buckle to,' said Monica. 'If Guy and I put our heads together we can come up with some pretty decent investor leads, and if Captain Thomas is game I can bore him silly with the operational side of his Business Director role. The rest of you really do need to keep the *Friend* going day to day, otherwise it won't be worth saving. What do you say, Captain Thomas?'

'Harold, please,' said Harold. 'Delighted to be on board. Not working has been driving me mad, so I'm grateful to have something to do.'

'This really is incredibly good of you, Monica,' I said. 'I'm beginning to think we might just have a chance of making this work.'

'I'm thrilled to have elbowed my way in,' she replied. 'It's going to give me a new lease of life, and you know how fond I am of *Woman's Friend*. It started my career,' she added to Thel and Bunty. 'Mrs Porter is just the worst type. You all deserve better.'

'We just have to get on with it,' said Guy.

Everyone agreed. It was time to crack on.

*

Monica had been right. Word about Mrs Porter's planned sale spread around the publishing industry as fast as a Hold The Front Page piece of news. Guy said he spent more time fielding phone calls from publishing acquaintances asking for the inside track than actually doing any work on *Woman's Friend*, let alone trying to fit in cloak-and-dagger meetings with Monica and people they hoped might become interested parties. We all agreed that the last thing we wanted was for the Dishonourable Egg to catch wind of what we were doing, so any hint of discussion was banned. None of us trusted Mrs Pye and certainly not Mr Elliot.

Mrs Porter did not come back to the office.

Her presence, however, was more than felt. Now freed from the shackles of hiding from Small Winston, Mr Elliot took to creeping around the office like a spectre, silently appearing with missives before announcing, 'Mrs Porter wishes . . .' or more often than not, 'Mrs Porter is not happy that . . .'

I buttoned my lip and kept my head down, even when war effort articles I had been planning for months were randomly pulled and replaced with photographs of aristocratic toddlers.

'Am I being a killjoy?' I asked Mrs Mahoney one morning as a rousing feature about a reader who had joined the Women's Land Army was swapped for a picture of a small child standing by an enormous front door, while holding a turnip. 'I appreciate that *Lady Barbara at Work in Her Garden* is terrifically sweet.'

Thankfully, Mrs Mahoney agreed.

'We all like to see the little ones joining in, but we're tight on paper and those land girls are feeding the country. No offence to little Lady Barbara, of course, but a kiddie with a turnip's not quite the same thing.'

We all just kept going, but it was hard to watch everything we had been working on get cut and cut and cut. "Yours Cheerfully" now hardly took up a third of the page. We put *WRITE TO US AND WE WILL WRITE BACK* in capitals at the top of the page, doing our best to keep the readers informed and feeling that it was still their magazine. We wrote back to everyone that we could.

'Have you actually had a weekend?' Bunty asked, when she returned from her trip with Harold to find me sitting on my bed, still in my NFS uniform, answering letters on my typewriter.

'How was your granny?' I said, ignoring the question. 'And did she like Harold?'

Bunts moved the typewriter out of the way and sat down.

'She looked a little tired, but, yes . . . she LOVED him!' she said, beaming at me. 'It was all I could do to get a word in edgeways. He was ever so nervous, but he came through it with flying colours.'

'Oh, Bunts, I'm so pleased,' I said.

'I know,' said Bunts. 'So am I.' She put her arm around me and gave me a hug. 'Thank you for doing your best to be normal about it all. It must be a huge strain.'

It was, but I played it down. 'I just want you to be happy,' I said. 'After everything has been so rotten.'

'I am happy, Em,' she said. 'Oh, and by the way, there's another thing. Granny said yes to the house.'

'What?'

Now Bunty laughed. 'She said yes if you and Guy need it. So you'd better tidy this bedroom if you're going to use it as an office.'

It was the best possible news.

'And Harold is taking to all this business planning like a duck to water,' she continued after I had returned the hug, nearly crushing her in my excitement. 'I think that's what swayed Granny actually. Honestly, she still doesn't see me as a grown-up. She'd have thought it a hare-brained scheme if it had come from me and you, but with Harold being all serious and throwing Guy's name in at the drop of a hat she thought it was a marvellous idea.' Bunts rolled her eyes. 'I blame Queen Victoria.'

'You always do,' I replied. 'It's most unfair. My granny's the same age as yours and she had her own bicycle by 1892.'

'Horrifying behaviour,' said Bunty, happily. 'Most unsuitable.'

'I'll tell her that,' I said. 'Oh, and speaking of unsuitable, Roy is looking after Gert and Daisy until Thel's birthday. She definitely smelt a rat. I should have made him do it from the start.'

'I hope they start laying soon,' said Bunty. 'Ooh, hold on, I think that's Thel now. Talk about something else.'

We quickly switched back to Mrs Tavistock and the house, and when Thelma appeared in the doorway, Bunts gave her the good news.

'What a relief. Well done,' she said, coming into the

room and collapsing into the chair by the window. 'It's nice to get some good news.' She puffed out her cheeks.

'You all right, Thel?' I asked.

'I'm fine,' she said, pushing her shoes off. 'It's my flipping sister that's the problem. I've just been in the telephone box feeding pennies in.'

'You should use the one here,' said Bunts.

'Thanks, but it's OK. Poor old Elsie can talk the hind leg off a donkey once she gets going.' Thel looked frustrated. 'She's just been dumped by the infamous Reg. He's decided that although he said he was married to "the wrong woman" who "didn't love him and made his life utter hell" he's had a change of heart and isn't going to leave her for Elsie after all. She's beside herself.'

'Might he change his mind back?' I asked.

'I hope not. His wife's having a baby,' said Thel. 'Poor Else. She always picks wrong 'uns, but this one's really broken her heart. He's now saying he didn't promise her anything and she's made it all up. Honestly, he's a piece of work.' Thel took off her hat and tousled her hair. 'Mum's worried out of her mind.'

'What are you going to do?' said Bunts.

'I'll have to go and see them, but I can't before Wednesday night. I've got back-to-back shifts.'

'Well, we can look after the children,' I said, quickly, 'I'm sure some of the girls on A Watch won't mind covering for you. A couple of them owe me as I've stepped in for them tons of times.'

'Thanks, love,' said Thel, looking relieved. 'Mum says Elsie has been missing work, and the last thing we need is her getting the sack. Would you mind if I stay until Saturday? I can come back first thing so I'm in time for our afternoon shift. I just hope I don't have to leave Mum if she's in a state.'

'Why not bring them back here for a few days?' said Bunty. 'Elsie can tell work she's poorly. We'll look after everyone and the kids will cheer them both up. It's school sports day next week. Your mum will love it and we can make sure we all watch out for Elsie if she wants to just hide away back here.'

'That's really kind, Bunts,' said Thelma. 'I'm sure they'll be fine where they are.'

'Honestly, bring them for a break,' said Bunty.

'I'll have to see how Elsie is,' said Thel. 'You're sure you don't mind having my three while I'm away? You'll have to get them out of bed for school – they're awful in the mornings.'

'Piece of cake,' I said. 'I'll borrow a whistle from the station.'

'You two are saints,' said Thel. 'I'm sorry to drop you in it, but I know I should go. To be honest, I've been quite unsympathetic to Elsie and I need to make up for it.'

'Tell her she's far from being the only one,' I said. 'If I had a shilling for every letter we get about this exact thing, we'd all be out eating at The Ritz. You do what you need to do. The kids will have to put up with being horribly bored with us.'

Thelma smiled. She knew I had no intention of letting them get bored.

'If they're with you, they, and more to the point I, will know that they are safe and they are loved. That's all that matters. And they must clean their teeth. I'll tell them in a minute. I bet they're in that flipping shed again, aren't they? I'd better write to Arthur and tell him too. It's ages since we've heard from him. Makes you jittery, doesn't it?'

'No talking like that, now,' said Bunty. 'He'll be home soon enough.'

'God love him,' said Thel. 'Right, I'm going to pack.'

'Cup of tea?' I said to Bunts. 'I'm parched.'

'You're off to plan how to spoil them, aren't you?' said Thel, who knew us both far too well.

'Not in the least,' I said. 'Now, who fancies another trip to the zoo?'

CHAPTER TWENTY-THREE

A Knock on the Door

HAVING THE CHILDREN for a few days meant some juggling of work schedules and several favours from the other girls at the station, but no one minded mucking in for each other, and at home there was the usual holiday feeling when Bunts and I were left in charge. Even better, Guy reported positive news from one of his meetings with Monica about investors. With Bunty's house as our new HQ, they would come over at the weekend to talk in more detail. Thel had rung to say her mum was in a real state about Elsie and so if it was all right with us she would definitely stay with them until Saturday. There was, she reported, a lot to sort out.

As we had done previously when Thelma was away, the children all bunked in the spare bedroom on the same floor as Bunty and me, and from the sound of it, there was very little sleeping and far more jumping on the beds until way after lights out.

'You do know they'll be horribly tired and cranky by the time Thel gets home, don't you?' I said to Bunts.

'Nothing to do with me,' she said. 'They can have as much fun as they like on our watch. We're the fun aunties.'

By Saturday morning everyone was exhausted, but we all calmed down and got on with our chores, which included cleaning out Laurel and Hardy's cage and inevitably losing them for some time in the vegetable patch. As Thel and I would be at the station in the afternoon, Bunty had promised a trip to the cinema, and when Harold arrived to go with them, excitement levels among the Jenkins children went through the roof.

'Roy hasn't called, has he?' said Bunty as the children surrounded Harold and bombarded him with updates about late nights. 'He said the other day that he would let me know if he's at home so we can pop in to see Gert and Daisy after the matinee.'

I shook my head.

'No, not a word,' I said. 'That's not like him. Perhaps he's in hiding after the talking to I gave him about the chickens.'

'Poor man,' said Bunts. 'We'll call in anyway. I'd better go and rescue Harold. See you later.'

I waved her off and looked at my watch. We had to be on shift in half an hour and Thel was cutting it fine. I hoped everything was all right. Her mum wasn't in the greatest of health as it was. Humming a tune that had been playing on the wireless, I was just putting some magazines for the girls at the station into my bag when there was a knock on the door.

Mr Parsons had promised to pop in with some yarn for Bunty, but to my surprise, when I opened the front door it was Captain Davies from the station, with Fred who was standing behind him.

'Oh, gosh, Captain Davies,' I said, hastily. 'I'm so sorry, am I late? I'll just get my cap.'

'No, no, it's fine, Emmy,' he said. 'Are you on your own?'

Captain Davies was always a serious sort, but he was looking really quite fierce. And he only ever called me Miss Lake. Fred didn't say anything.

'Yes,' I said. 'Bunty's out with the children. They've just left. Is everything all right?'

Other than for our wedding reception, the captain had never been to the house before. Now he didn't answer but asked if they might come in.

I didn't like his tone. I didn't like any of this at all.

'I've been waiting for Roy to phone,' I said, as I led them into the drawing room. We never used it so I quickly took some dust sheets off the furniture and asked if they would like to sit down.

Then I waited. Captain Davies had taken off his cap. His face was ashen. Fred wouldn't even look at me.

I felt my stomach tighten. I wished they would say something. I sat on the edge of my seat. Even though it was summer my hands had gone cold.

Something was very, very wrong.

'Roy is fine,' said Captain Davies. He took a breath. 'Emmy, I'm terribly sorry, but I am afraid I have some extremely sad news.' Now he came and sat beside me. 'There has been an air raid on the High Street in East Grinstead, with multiple casualties and loss of life. I'm afraid we have reason to believe that Mrs Jenkins – Thelma – was there.'

I knew the expression on his face. It was exactly the way Roy had looked when he told me about Bunty's fiancé, Bill.

'No, Captain Davies,' I said, cutting him off. 'Please don't.'

The big grandfather clock in the corner of the room ticked on.

Fred now sat down with me as well.

'West Sussex Fire Service found Thel's purse,' he said, softly. 'It had her identification in it.'

I didn't believe him. This could not be happening. Not to Thelma. Not Thel.

Fred carried on speaking.

I put my hands over my ears. If I didn't listen it wouldn't be true.

But it was too late.

Thelma was gone.

CHAPTER TWENTY-FOUR

A Bloody Awful Job

A SINGLE GERMAN aircraft dropped a single bomb on the Whitehall Cinema in East Grinstead late in the afternoon of Friday the ninth of July. Then the plane circled round, came back, and opened fire on the cinema with machine guns. Over eighty people were killed, including servicemen, women and children. Among them was my friend Thelma Jenkins, together with her younger sister Elsie and their mother Ivy Ward.

I had thought I loathed Hitler before, but those feelings paled into insignificance now. And as for whoever had done it, I didn't care that they were somebody's brother or husband, or son. I didn't know it was possible to hate someone I had never met, to such a degree.

Captain Davies was enormously kind. Fred looked distraught. When I protested that it couldn't be true, he gently explained that when the emergency services had found Thel's National Fire Service ID on Friday night they had traced her to Carlton Street station. They moved particularly fast for one of their own. Captain Davies didn't want to tell us if there was a chance the information was wrong, so Roy had volunteered to go to East Grinstead and find out. Poor Roy, what a bloody awful job.

After they told me, I couldn't think, or even move. Disbelief wrapped itself around me like a blanket, but not a nice, comforting blanket. Instead it was one that was too tight, so that I couldn't hear, or see, or understand what was going on. I couldn't even breathe.

It didn't last long, probably a few seconds.

'The children.'

It was a second, bigger wave, but now of pure panic, as I vaguely heard Captain Davies saying that he would do everything in his power to help. I fought through the fog.

'I need to tell Guy,' I said. 'I have to . . . could someone take my shift, please?'

I was stammering but dragging myself into action. I had to get things ready for when Bunty and the children came home. *I* had to be ready.

'Don't worry about your shift,' said Captain Davies. 'Don't think about the station. You're going to be needed here.'

I looked at him as the truth began to sink in. 'What do I say?' I whispered.

Captain Davies did not reply at first. Then he put his hand on my shoulder. 'I have absolute faith in you,' he said, 'and so would Thelma.'

I nearly crumbled when he said that. How quickly it had become 'would' rather than 'does'.

The captain must have been through this situation a hundred times, but I would never forget how kind he was. He had to return to the station, but Fred said he would stay until Guy got here. Fred and Roy had both been in the Fire Service for years and had known Thelma for nearly as long.

There wasn't much they hadn't seen, especially during the Blitz, but it didn't make it any easier. How much death were these men expected to be able to cope with?

I didn't properly cry until Captain Davies left. Then I

couldn't stop. I sobbed and sobbed while Fred held on to me as if I was a child. He was as tough as they came, but there were tears rolling down his cheeks too. He insisted on phoning Guy for me, and Guy said he would come straight round. I wasn't to worry, he said, Bunty and I would not be on our own.

I wasn't worried about Bunty and me. I didn't even think about Thel. Perhaps it was easier that way. I could hear myself asking Fred, 'But what will I say? I don't know what to say.'

Fred suggested putting the kettle on so we went down to the kitchen where I turned on the tap and splashed water all over my face, drying it quickly with a tea towel. My cheeks were hot and as I tried to pull my thoughts together, I covered them with my hands, which were still stone cold.

'Don't let me cry any more,' I said to him. 'I have to not look awful when they get home.' I checked my watch, trying to work out when Bunty and Harold were likely to be back. 'If they watch the B-movie, the newsreel, the feature . . .' I added it all up. 'She won't keep them out after that as they'll need their tea. They must have that. Bread and jam, and Bunts was going to give them strawberries too.'

It felt hugely important that the children should be fed. Yesterday we just had meals like normal people and nobody cared. Today feeding them felt like the most essential thing in the world.

I took out the notebook that was kept in the kitchen table drawer and began to write a shopping list for food.

'Does Thelma have any other family?' asked Fred, using the wrong tense.

'I don't think so,' I said. 'And Arthur's an only child.' I looked up. 'We have to let him know.'

'We can get word to him,' said Fred. 'I can sort that out.'

My mind started to race. 'Then there's coroners and banks, and we have to tell the schools and, oh God, there's everything for her mum and her sister, as well.'

It was overwhelming.

'I tell you what,' said Fred, his brown eyes kind. 'Let's not think about any of that. None of it. All you need to think about is you, Bunty and the kids. Everything else can wait.'

And so that became the plan. Everything else would wait. It felt as if my stomach had clenched itself into a fist. A huge, hard, immovable fist. I could convince myself that Thel was still just over at her mum's house, but the thought of George, Marg, and Stan coming home scared me witless.

When Guy arrived, shocked and desperate to help, we worked out what we would do. I needed to tell Bunty the news on her own. When we heard them come in, I would go upstairs to my room, and Guy would tell her I had come home from my shift and ask if she would go up to see me. Bunty would know something had happened, but with luck, the children would not notice. This would give us a little time.

It was horrible for Guy to have to put on a front with the children, but he told me not to worry about him. He would be fine. He looked awful.

'Don't worry,' he insisted. 'I've been in this kitchen enough times, I can sort things out if they're hungry.'

I wished Charles was here, but thinking about him made me feel worse. Somehow it might not have been as horrible if he had been here. Or if not as horrible, I would at least have felt less out of my depth. I missed him so much, it hurt. But then, so did everything.

Fred reluctantly left to return to the station as Guy and I talked about telling the schools and what would happen next. There was so much to take in. Thel, of course, but the children's gran and their aunt as well. How could young heads cope with it all?

'Forget about the office,' said Guy. 'I know there's a lot going on, but none of it matters. Don't think about anything. You have to look after yourself and the children.'

I nodded. It didn't matter. Nothing did now.

At a quarter past five I decided to go upstairs, leaving Guy to pace up and down in the hallway, waiting for the front door to open. I pressed a cold, wet flannel to my face, hoping it would make me look better. But as I sat on the stairs and listened for the front door, hot tears kept coming.

Then I heard them. High-pitched chatter and the sound of Bunty laughing and saying, 'I don't know about that.' Then a sound of surprise as she must have seen Guy and a 'Right-ho, is she unwell?' before she came up the stairs.

I got to my feet and went into my room. My heart doubled its speed. My throat felt dry and as if something was stuck. I tried to breathe properly as Bunty came in.

'Em?' she said.

Despite being adamant that I must not cry any more, the tears came faster. I put my arms around Bunty and hugged her as hard as I could. Not hugging, but hanging on to her, as if her arrival could make everything go away.

'What is it?' she whispered, into my hair.

I pulled back and pushed the tears out of my eyes.

'Thel,' I said. 'Bunty, it's Thel.'

CHAPTER TWENTY-FIVE

Don't Ever Stop The Larking About

NOT LONG AFTER he became Prime Minister, Mr Churchill gave a speech where he said that if the British Empire lasted for a thousand years, men would still call the Battle of Britain our 'finest hour'. At the time I rather doubted it. People forget. Now, most of all, I wondered if people in the future would remember the children in all of this?

Because when I looked at George, Margaret and Stanley Jenkins, as far as I was concerned, these three children were braver than anyone else I knew, and that included adults who risked their lives every day. Charles and Harold in the army, my brother Jack flying planes. Roy and Frank facing firestorms in the Blitz. They were all lions, but as grown-ups they did at least have some choice in what they had signed up for. The children hadn't signed up for anything, let alone this.

Harold came upstairs, and one look at Bunty and me meant that he didn't need to be told much. I was glad he was there. Bunty cried into his chest as I strode around the bedroom. I needed to pull myself together. Slapping my hands against my thighs, I told myself I'd had an hour . . . two hours . . . It would have to be enough.

I needed to get this right. I stopped and closed my eyes tight for a moment, talking to myself inside my head.

I don't know what to say.

You'll find the rights words.

They're children. Stan's nine years old. There are no right words.

Silence.

I have to make this better.

You can't make it better.

I can't make this better.

'I'm going downstairs,' I said. 'I'm going to tell them.'

*

George, Margaret and Stanley were in the garden, showing Guy the guinea pigs, and as far as Stan was concerned, trying to convince him that they knew how to do tricks. Guy was asking questions and nodding. It was the sort of beautiful early evening that July is really good at, when the sun is still shining and for children any thoughts of going to bed seem like days away. I stood on the steps that led down to the garden. Just a few seconds more.

'They are safe and they are loved,' I whispered. It was silly really, but I wanted Thel to know that I had listened to her. It would become a mantra for Bunty and me.

Guy looked up and saw me. I nodded.

Very gently, he told the children we had something we had to tell them and could they please come inside. George, I could tell, knew something was going on. His younger brother and sister insisted on making sure Laurel and Hardy were safely back in their hutch. I said, 'Of course.' I'd happily have let them take the whole night.

Before Bunty had come home I tried to think of all the ways the children might respond. In the past, Roy and Fred had told me stories about how people react to being told that someone is dead. None of that helped.

Harold and Bunty had come downstairs, and we all

sat with the children in the kitchen as I explained what had happened as best I could.

On that day and in the ones that followed, there were more tears and more pain than I could possibly have imagined, but by far the worst thing was when Stan looked at me and in the smallest, saddest voice, asked, 'Why?'

I knew some people said grown-ups should always set an example through stiff upper lips, but rightly or wrongly, Bunty and I cried with them.

In the face of their tragedy, all any of us had to offer the three children was ourselves. If nothing else – and there was nothing else – they would be surrounded by people who loved and wanted to protect them. We all meant it with every fibre of our bodies, but we were still a wretched substitute for their mum.

The children, though, in their very different ways, somehow coped. Over the next days, sometimes there was calm and sometimes their grief was like a storm battering them with heartache, anger and shock.

George was stoic, trying desperately not to cry, and looking to Guy and Harold who both told him he did not have to be the big, tough man of the house. On Sunday morning we were woken by the sound of hammering in the garden as Thel's eldest lad threw himself into his hobby, resolutely repairing things, consulting his wood-work book and searching for new things to build. Harold moved into Mrs Harewood's house the day after we heard the news. He and George talked for hours about the things they would make. George told him all about his dad. He wouldn't talk about Thel.

Marg alternated between heartbroken sobbing and quiet despair. She disappeared into the bedroom she had shared with her mum, and returned with a pile of *Picturegoer* magazines. She had gone off the films, she said, and didn't want to go to the pictures again. Marg didn't think she wanted to be a nurse any more, either. What was the point? But an unlikely ally arrived. On Sunday evening, Ginger Belinda stood on the doorstep with her mum, holding a Mars bar and a slightly wilted bunch of sweet peas. Belinda's dad, they said, had been lost at Dunkirk. The girls went up to Marg's room and played, and Belinda's mum, Angela, accepted the offer of tea and a biscuit.

'We'll all stick together,' she promised. 'There's a lot of us around. I'm not trying to downplay this, but the kids are used to their friends turning up at school with bad news. Or not turning up at all.'

It was the worst silver lining I had ever heard.

But the schools did help. They were sympathetic of course, but said the children should return as soon as possible. Keep them going, keep them doing what they always do. They have to get on with things. It was similar advice, if less sympathetically said, to letters I had replied to in *Woman's Friend*. But it was bloody hard taking your own advice.

'I don't know, Bunts,' I said, 'they've just lost their mother, but it's brace up and get on with your homework.'

In the days after we heard about Thel, while Captain Davies and Guy had both very generously told me not to go into work, which must have made me one of the most fortunate people in Britain, it was hard not to feel knocked for six. More than anything, we worried about Stan. I wanted to wrap him up in cotton wool and tell him that things would be fine, but I couldn't do the first and the second wasn't true.

The poor little boy was bereft. Lost. Of course he was. He was also terrified that the three of them would be taken away and put in a Home. I swore to him they wouldn't, that his home was here and we wouldn't let anyone come near him. He spent most of his time with the guinea pigs in the pantry, where we'd moved them as he was convinced they might die if left outside on their own. Stan also refused to go to sleep at night, in case 'the people' came for him. The kids stayed in the room they'd been camping in while their mum was away, and after lights out I would doze in the armchair on the landing so they knew someone was near.

'Stan, do you think I'd let anyone get in?' said Harold, very seriously. 'I'm only next door, and you know I can beat anyone in a fight, even with one arm. And if I can't, Bunty will. She's small but she fights dirty. Don't tell her I told you.'

There was the tiniest, *tiniest* hint of a smile from Stan.

It was the junior school that inadvertently helped by asking me to confirm that I knew Thelma had put me down as next of kin in the absence of their dad. I hadn't known, but it meant a sort of proof for Stan, and George and Marg too, that their mum had officially made it clear where she wanted them to be.

When the school secretary told me, I managed to get through to the end of the call without crying, and then I'd put down the phone and run upstairs to my room where I could hide, just for a while.

It meant more than anything in the world that Thel trusted me. Sometimes I spoke to her out loud. 'Thank you,' I now said. 'I'll try. I'll do my best.'

A lot of the time it didn't feel like nearly enough.

George, Marg and Stan hadn't just lost their mum. With no relatives, and their dad hundreds of miles away at sea, someone needed to be legally responsible for them until he came home. There was no shortage of people who loved them and wanted to help, but in the eyes of the law, we weren't family.

Stan's school were happy enough that my name was

on their records, but when Stan said he wanted to stay home with me and the animals, they weren't impressed. I told the headmaster that as Stan, at only nine years old, was finding things difficult with no mum, and a dad God knows where, if he wanted to play in the garden with his pets then that's what he would damn well do.

But when the little boy asked me if I was sure they wouldn't be taken away, I was scared to bits in case actually somebody could.

'They'll be fine,' Guy said as we discussed it in hushed tones. 'There's a war on. People look after other people's children all the time. Look at the evacuees. And I defy anyone to outwit you, Emmy Lake.'

'Quite right,' said Harold. 'No one is taking these children anywhere.'

They both sounded confident but Captain Davies was the person who gave us the answer. A few days after the news, he phoned the house and asked if he could come round. This time when he arrived, he handed me several letters.

'These have been with Thelma's solicitor,' he said. 'The children needn't worry. They're safe.'

Thelma, in sound body and mind, had stated that in the event of her death and the absence or death of her husband, that Emmeline Hope Lake should be the legal guardian of her children, George, Margaret and Stanley Jenkins. It had been witnessed by Captain Davies and Roy.

There were also letters to me and to each of the children, and her mum and sister too.

Dear Emmy

 I don't know why I'm writing this as you're never going to read it, but if you are then something's happened and I'm really, really sorry if this mucks up things for you.

I've thought about this ever such a lot. I hope you don't mind me putting you as the kids' guardian and it doesn't land you in it with Mum and Elsie. I've written to Arthur and I know he'll agree. The kids will be best with you.

There's no one else in the world who will look after them better than you, and Bunty too. I know the two of you will stick it out.

I haven't asked you to your face as you'll think you can't do it. But you can. You really, really can. I'm giving this and my will to Captain Davies, and he'll give it to you. He says he'll help too, if I'm not here. Take him up on that, Em. Take everyone up on their help.

They're good kids and they'll do as they're told. Tell them to be good, go to bed when you tell them to, and never, ever forget that their Mum loves them. I've written them letters too. You can read them first if you like. Whatever you need to do or whatever helps.

Oh blimey, I've gone a bit tearful. I'm only writing this as it's not going to happen. Bloody silly old fool!

Please tell them that me and their Dad love them more than anything in the world. He'll be back anyway, but tell the kids we'll be watching over them.

Thanks, Emmy. And Bunty too. As I'm writing this I can hear you both larking about with my lot downstairs. Don't stop that, will you? Don't ever stop the larking about.

Loads of love, Em. Tell them every day that I love them, won't you?

Thel xxx

Harold had taken the children out. Bunty and I sat in silence as we read it together. The penny had finally dropped. Our friend was not going to come home.

At least I very definitely wasn't alone. As Bunty worked at the War Office, her bosses weren't half as understanding as mine, and she had to go back to work after a few days off, but my mother had arrived as soon as she had heard the news about Thel, a steadying and experienced hand in the middle of our desolation.

Mother came up from Hampshire on the train, bag in one hand and half a dozen eggs in a hatbox. She didn't interfere or try to take over, but quietly brought a feeling of calm to this most horrible storm. The children, who had met her a handful of times, were shy at first, but my mother did not fuss. In the evenings she sat and knitted or did embroidery, listening or talking with the children about interesting things. I had seen her like this with my father's patients when someone was terribly ill. Serene, unafraid, making sure people knew they weren't alone.

Guy took to coming round for his dinner in the evenings. Roy suddenly had all sorts of jobs he needed a bit of a hand with for George and Stan, and Captain Davies decided that the firemen weren't good enough at cleaning the engines, so if the children wanted to help out on Saturdays that would be ever so kind. George got his first ever pay packet of thruppence as a result.

Ginger Belinda (whose mum Stan referred to as Mrs Ginger, which immediately stuck), chummed up with Marg, and Buzz insisted that Marg had to keep up her lessons on the trombone. When Marg said she only knew two tunes and one of those she was never ever going to play again, my mother quietly asked her if she would like to try something together on Mrs Tavistock's piano. Mother wasn't a bad pianist and she could play by ear. When I crept to the door of the drawing room and heard Marg singing along while my mother played Glenn Miller's 'In The Mood', having learned it while Marg was at school, I thought my heart would break.

But the most unexpected gesture of help came the week after Thel's death.

I had been on the telephone in the hall when there was a knock on the door. I wasn't expecting anyone, but when I opened it, I was met by a total stranger. He had a quite terrifying scowl and one enormous eyebrow that reached right across his face.

'Morning,' he said. 'Are you Miss Lake? Or Mrs Mayhew? One or the other?'

'Good morning. Yes, I am,' I said, wondering how he knew either my work or my married name. Then it dawned on me. 'Excuse me,' I said, 'but you're not Sca . . . ?'

'I'm David Scarey,' said the man, brusquely. 'With an E.'

I put my hand to my mouth. I'd nearly called him Scary David. It was the first time I had smiled in days.

'I do apologise,' I said. 'I think the children mixed up your name.'

'I'm one of the Scarey brothers,' he replied, matter of fact. 'Some people do call me Scary David. Don't know why.' He shrugged as if they were idiots.

'Me neither,' I said, thinking he could probably knock out a tree. 'Thank you so much for the chickens. Roy had them for a bit, but he's just brought them back. Would you like to come in?' It felt rude not to ask, even though he did look quite foreboding.

Mr Scarey shook his head.

'I'm all right, thanks all the same. I just thought you might like these. To cheer up the kiddies. Me and my brother were very sorry to hear about their mum. Bleeding Nazis. It's a fu . . . flaming disgrace.'

I hadn't noticed that he had a cardboard box under one arm. Now he handed it to me.

'Ducks,' he said. 'Ducklings really. One each. You don't

have to keep them, as the zoo'll take them for the snakes. They've still got the squeezy ones. Horrible things. At least they killed off the biters. They're even worse.'

If someone had told me that I would once again be having a conversation about London Zoo's snakes but this time with a man who in almost any other situation would have scared the socks off me, I would have said they were mad.

'Thank you, Mr Scarey,' I said, 'this is one of the nicest things anyone has ever done. Roy said you and your brother were kind, and he was right. The children will love them.'

'Kind?' said David Scarey. 'Bugger me. I'll have to have a word.'

'Deep down,' I said, with a smile.

'That's more like it,' he replied. 'Right, I'm off. Hope the littl'uns like the ducks. Oh, and if you ever get any trouble from anyone, Roy knows where we are.'

Then he gave a terrifying nod and was gone.

How are you darling? I am well. July has brought such lovely
weather. A friend of Roy's brought round some

Hello darling, how are you? Not much to report from here.
The weather is super. We have some new

I was thinking of you today, darling

Hello darling

CHAPTER TWENTY-SIX

Children Are Not Like Canaries

I FOUND IT impossible to write to Charles. For the first time in two and a half years I didn't know what to say. I wanted desperately to pour my heart out, to say how much I missed him, how awful everything was. But there wasn't a thing he could do about it other than feel awful. Equally, I couldn't find it in me to pretend everything was all right, when nothing was. The newspapers were full of the Allied forces landing in Sicily – the first to be in Europe for two long years – so it was safe to assume Charles might have other things on his mind. The last thing he needed was me all upset.

So I didn't, which felt nearly as bad. But there was enough to be getting on with as it was.

The children were cheered by the three ducklings, who they christened Huey, Dewey and Louie, and added to the menagerie in the back garden giving them a small galvanised steel tub so they would have their own little pond. The ducks were actually far too small to be alone in the world, but luckily Daisy the chicken took to them and became a model example of how to take someone under your wing.

I found myself wanting to write to Thel to tell her about it, as if she was just off somewhere with her mum and sister on a holiday. I knew David Scarey turning up would make her laugh like a drain, especially as I was fairly sure Mrs Harewood would have been round in a flash if she thought there was trouble. As Harold was now one of her lodgers she made sure he never left her house without a package for us of some sort for us. Biscuits, a jigsaw puzzle, occasionally entire meals.

'If there's anything you need. Anything I can do,' she said. '*Anything.*'

She was not alone. Buzz and Hilda dropped in whenever they could, saying they were bored and fancied going to the park if anyone was interested? Mr Bone the newsagent took to posting comics through the door almost daily. He said they were unsold copies and would be wasted if not. We all thanked him and I didn't say that I knew they could be returned to the publisher. There was a steady stream of visitors from the fire station. We were grateful to them all.

At the funeral the church was filled to bursting. If love could bring someone back, Thel would have turned up before the service had even begun. The children were surrounded by people desperate to help. The three of them were unimaginably brave.

People were all terribly nice, but I felt as though I hadn't a clue. I felt like that a lot. Looking after George, Marg and Stan for the odd weekend when Thelma had gone away had always been an excuse for outings and fun. Looking after three shocked and deeply distressed children day in and day out was a different thing altogether.

We were doing our best, but Bunty and I were out of our depth.

It kept me awake at night, *every* night. Was I doing things properly? Were we getting it right? Over the last two years I had spent a huge amount of time reading books and talking to professional people in order to learn about countless issues and problems so that I could do my very best to help the people who wrote in to *Woman's Friend*. But nothing had prepared me for this. It was all very well doing research and handing out advice, but what if I was doing things wrong?

With a house full of people and others queuing up to offer support, George, Margaret and Stanley were surrounded by love and time and commitment. But in the small hours of the morning, when I had sat up with Stan, or held Marg's hand after she'd woken up from another bad dream, the fact remained. I couldn't bring back their mum. I had never felt more inadequate in my life.

I was grateful that my own mother was there, but she couldn't stay with us for ever, and I was haunted by the one thing that none of us grown-ups ever said to each other.

What if the children's dad doesn't come home?

It was unthinkable. I couldn't even say it out loud. But as it never tired of showing us, the war was more than generous at handing out horror. How would the children bear it if Arthur was lost? How would they cope? How would any of us cope? Sometimes I hardly felt like an adult, myself. I would never let them down, but were good intentions enough?

There were too many questions. In all of this, we just had to get on with things. I hadn't even had the guts to tell Charles what had happened. One day he would come home from the war to the wife he had spent all of three days with. Would he arrive to a family he hardly knew? We would have to make it work. And anyway, who wouldn't love George, Margaret and Stan? I knew Charles would step up to whatever was needed. It would be all right. I tried not to think about it.

One evening, two weeks after the news about Thelma,

I couldn't find Stan at bedtime. It was still staying light until well after ten o'clock, but as I had often watched the children beg their mum to be allowed Just Five More Minutes in the garden, I was confident that was where he would be. It was his job to ensure that Gert, Daisy and the ducklings were safely inside at night, so it was no surprise when I heard his voice in the shed.

As there was a sign on the door which said, 'PRIVATE – ANIMALS AND BIRDS ONLY', I raised my hand to knock, but paused for a moment. Stan was putting the ducklings to bed and having a goodnight chat.

'Come on, Dewey,' he was saying, 'in you get. Well done, Huey. Where's Louie? That's it. Now, you're not to be scared when it gets dark. I'm not because I'm nine, but you're only young. Gert and Daisy are here, so you'll be all right, and I'm going to lock you in so you can't get lost. Night, night.' Then he added, 'You are safe and you are loved.'

It came from nowhere. Like being knocked over by someone you hadn't seen coming. I let out a small noise that wasn't a cry or a gasp – perhaps it was something in between. Leaning against the side of the shed, I slid to the ground.

Oh, Thel. If you could see your little boy.

It was unbearable.

I wasn't sure how long I sat there, but I could hear Stan still chatting away. For the millionth time in the last weeks, I said to myself, *Come on, Lake. You can do it.*

I took a very deep breath, and then I stood up. 'Stan,' I said quietly, knocking on the door, 'it's Emmy. Can I come in?'

'Yes.'

He was sitting on an upturned bucket, with his friends. 'How are they all?' I asked.

'All right. They're feeling a bit lonely.'

'Oh dear, that won't do,' I said. 'Can I sit with you until they feel better?'

Stan nodded and I sat cross-legged on the floor. We sat in companionable silence watching the ducklings and the chickens for a while.

Then Stan pointed at a little yellow and brown duckling. 'That's Louie,' he said. 'He misses his mum.'

★

As soon as we had heard about Thel, at the house all talk of trying to raise funds to buy *Woman's Friend* had stopped. There was a unanimous agreement to put things on hold. No one said for how long. When Guy visited, he didn't mention it, in fact he hardly mentioned work at all, other than to say all was well.

It was my mother who asked me when I was going back.

'Darling,' she said, one morning after we'd dropped Stan at school, 'I know Guy always says things are fine, but how do you think they're coping?'

I shrugged. 'I don't know,' I said.

'I understand,' said Mother, mildly, as we walked in the sunshine towards the butcher's. 'How are the rest of your colleagues, though? It must be very depressing for them. So very disappointing. You were all excited about trying to buy *Woman's Friend*.'

'It's not exactly the Brighton Pier Amusements *here* at the moment, is it, Mother?' I snapped.

'Of course,' she said, 'and that wasn't what I was trying to imply.'

'Sorry,' I said, 'I'm a bit tired. But what are you saying?' I called a good morning to someone I knew as they came out of the bank. They returned my greeting and looked sad. It was what Bunty called The Face. The Oh No, You're Bereaved And I Don't Know What To Say To You face. I hated it.

'I'm not saying anything in particular,' said my mother, 'but I know how much you love your job, even if Mrs Porter has messed everything up. When do you think you might go back? Guy looks washed out. I do worry about him. But then, I worry about you all.'

I knew she was right, but it was so soon after Thelma had gone.

'What if the children need me?' I said. 'What if I'm stuck in the office and can't get home? And it's nearly the school holidays. They can't be left on their own.'

'Well,' said my mother, 'I'm here and Harold is mostly here, and the children do have their own friends. If they're anything like you and your brother used to be, you won't see them from dawn until dusk for the next few weeks. I know this is an awful time, but you'll be surprised. Children like to have some normality. We need to be there when they feel wonky, but they need to try to find some fun. George was talking about his friends meeting up at some bombsite or another this morning.'

'That doesn't sound at all safe,' I said.

'I'm sure it isn't,' said Mother. 'That's why they like it. Figgy Brewster in the village came home from spending Easter at his granny's in Ealing with a suitcase full of shrapnel. His mother said he couldn't have been happier. He sold most of it off to the other boys in the Scouts.'

I wasn't convinced.

'Oh come now,' said my mother, seeing my face. 'Where's the girl who spent holidays at the seaside searching for deathly quicksand and getting stuck behind rock pools with the tide coming in? You, Jack and Bunty were utter horrors. Even at home I never knew where you were, or what you were up to. You'd disappear to the canal and turn up hours later, having had the time of your life. Covered in mud, demanding food and showing off a jam jar full of indignant sticklebacks.' She stopped to look in the window of Durton's Hardware. 'That reminds me, I must get some string.'

'But weren't you worried?' I asked.

'Of course I was. Permanently. But you were children, not canaries in a birdcage. You can't lock children up. Well you can, but they get very annoyed about it. Emmy darling, worrying about them is all part of the torture of being a parent, which is what you're having to be for them at the moment. It's a terrifying and awful process, and then at the end of it, even though you love them more than you ever imagined possible, the dreadful creatures grow up and leave. I honestly don't know why anyone does it. I really only wanted a dog.'

Now she was smiling. 'You're doing a wonderful job in a hellish situation. All of you. But don't give up on your own life.' She sighed. 'And darling, one day their father *will* come home.'

'It's all so desperate,' I said. 'I miss her. I really do.'

'I know,' Mother replied, 'I would give anything in the world to get Thelma back for you all. But you will get the children through. And you need to work. Even though that wretched woman is selling *Woman's Friend*, your colleagues still need you, and so do your readers. And darling, I think you need to work. Why don't you at least get Guy to send a few letters over? You've got a typewriter. You'll be here if the children need you. I shall help you as much as I can, and as much as you want me to. I need to make sure my own child gets through this as well, big though you are. That goes for Bunty too. I must say I very much approve of Harold. He is a lovely young man.'

And with that, the conversation was moved on to happier topics.

For the rest of the day I chewed things over. Mother was right. Even if it was for the very best reasons, I had just walked away from *Woman's Friend* and everyone I worked with. I was tremendously lucky that Guy had somehow enabled me to have the time off, but I was still employed and really did need to return. No one else in the country got to abandon their job when the worst of times happened. If everyone did, the war would be over already, and not at all for the best.

Captain Davies had instructed me not to return to my work at the station until further notice. When I argued that I would be breaking the law regarding conscription, he reminded me that he knew what he was talking about, and that as I was the temporary guardian of three children, it was information enough for an exemption. I gratefully agreed.

As with everything, I turned to my best friend about getting back to the office.

'I think it's a very good idea,' said Bunty. 'Try to keep things as normal and familiar as possible, that's what we've said, and normal for you is being at *Woman's Friend*. I can work nights while it's the summer holidays. We'll do shifts. Don't worry, Em, we'll do what all the other women in Britain are doing.'

'What's that?' I said.

'Cope,' said Bunty.

I decided to tell the children what I was planning. Stan in particular liked to know where everyone was. Bunty had actually taken him into Whitehall so he could see the area where she worked. She couldn't take him into the building of course, but they walked up to Horse Guards and she described how safe she was working underground. That night he had slept a little better.

At dinner that evening, which was Mrs Harewood's carrot pie, I asked the children how they would feel if I went back to *Woman's Friend*.

'I'm going to bring work back with me, so I'll mostly be at home,' I said. 'There'll always be someone here and Harold's only next door.'

The children took it in their stride.

'I have one question, please,' said Stan, putting up his hand.

'Of course.'

'Bunty,' he said, 'when are you and Harold going to get married?'

Bunty went puce and told him his carrots wouldn't eat themselves.

The rest of the evening followed its usual course of everyone straight into the garden with the animals while avoiding homework until the last possible moment, and then the wireless and some quiet before bed.

George had told me from the very start that he didn't want to talk about what had happened to his mum to anyone at school. I promised him that no one would make him, and told him that whenever he felt he might want to talk to me or Bunty or any of us at home, he just had to say. No one would force him until he was ready.

Tonight, after dinner, as Marg practised her trombone with Bunty, and Stan and Harold oversaw the ducklings' evening swim in their steel tub, George and I were concentrating on a model aeroplane, me holding it by the wings as George painted the fuselage.

'Are you sure you're all right about me going back to work?' I asked.

George nodded. 'We probably need the money with all

of us living here,' he said, seriously. 'I can give you my money from washing the engines to go towards our food. Me, Marg and Stan eat loads.'

'Don't you worry,' I said. 'You eat as much as you want. Anyway, Bunty and I get extra rations for you. Twelve ounces of sweets a week between you three. That's tons. It's astonishing you have any teeth.'

George carried on painting. 'That's what Mum always says.'

'She's right,' I said.

'I miss her,' said George quietly as he painted.

'I know, love,' I said. 'So do I.'

George nodded without looking up and carried on as I held the wings of the plane and hoped he didn't see my eyes fill up despite myself.

Oh, Thel, you'd be so proud of your boy.

That night, the children settled relatively quickly, although I knew it was likely that Stan would wake up, and Marg might have nightmares again. I crept out of their room and sat in the armchair on the landing with a book. I was so tired my bones hurt.

It wasn't long before Marg came out and said she couldn't sleep.

'What are you reading?' she asked, noticing the unopened paperback on my lap.

'P. G. Wodehouse,' I said. 'He's very funny. I can read you a bit if you like. It's not a children's book but I don't think your mum would mind.' Marg squeezed into the chair with me and I read her a part that I thought might make her laugh. It did a bit, and then she asked if she could ask me something.

'Of course, fire away,' I said.

Marg chewed on her fingernail for a moment.

'When you move the magazine here,' she said, 'can me

and George work for you? It's just we've been talking about it. Stan's too young at the moment, but we'd like to, because it's only fair as you're taking care of us and Mum said looking after us can be exhausting.'

'That's a lovely idea, Marg,' I said. 'It would be great fun. It's just I don't know if *Woman's Friend* is going to move here after all.'

'But why not?' Marg asked. 'You had that meeting and we worked out where you'd all sit. And Mum said Guy would be here every day and we could see him after school.' Her face fell. 'Is it because of us? Is it because you're too busy having to make sure we're all right? That's why you were worried about going back to work, wasn't it?'

She was eleven years old. I put my arm around her and gave her a hug. 'Don't be daft,' I said. 'Looking after you lot is the best thing ever. Just look at Harold. He's practically moved in. He loves being with all of you. Don't tell Bunty, she thinks it's because of her.'

Margaret giggled. 'So why won't you buy the magazine, then?'

'I don't know,' I said, truthfully. 'Mrs Porter might have already found someone.'

'That's not fair,' said Marg, hotly. 'What about all your friends who you work with? You have to stop her.'

'I don't know,' I said again, and beginning to feel a bit lame. 'I have to admit I've sort of given up.'

Marg frowned. 'Mum told us giving up is for people who are weedy knickers,' she said, and then put her hand over her mouth.

I gasped at her. 'You said "knickers",' I said, and poked her in the ribs. Marg wriggled and laughed.

'Please don't give up, Emmy,' she said. 'If George isn't busy at the fire station he'd like to be a post boy, and I want to meet Nurse McClay.'

'Oh, do you, now?' I said. 'Why's that then?'

'I've been thinking,' said Margaret. 'I went off it for a bit because I was sad about Mum, but most people do get better, don't they? When they get lots of help?'

'What do you mean, Marg?' I said, not cottoning on.

'People get better. Like Harold has. He's really happy now. So, I've changed my mind back again. I'm going to become a nurse.'

CHAPTER TWENTY-SEVEN

Have You Read Winnie-the-Pooh?

MARGARET SOUNDED JUST like her mum. Thelma would definitely have called me a weedy knickers. In fact, as soon as I started to think about it, I knew she'd have been furious at me for giving up on *Woman's Friend* and the team. Worst of all, though, was what Marg said next.

'If you're worried about looking after us we could probably find somewhere else to live. George and I can take care of Stan. Big children do it in books all the time.'

'Oh, Marg, not in a hundred years,' I replied, appalled that this was what she might think. 'It's got nothing to do with you and the boys. You're all lovely. And *The Children Who Lived in a Barn* isn't real life,' I added, now regretting the discussion we'd had about her favourite book the previous week. 'Is this where George wanting a job is coming from?'

Marg denied it, but pressed home her view that having *Woman's Friend* here would be the most exciting thing in the world, and actually if I could get on with it that would be good, as she was already planning her own novel called *The Children Who Lived in a Magazine Office*, and needed to do the research.

'Now I think I'm tired enough to go to sleep,' she finished. 'N'night, Emmy. Don't worry, it will be all right. Will you come and tuck me in?' Then she gave me a big hug and I followed her back to their room.

After I was sure Marg was asleep, I sat on my own on the landing. Here were three children going through the most dreadful time in their short lives, but doing everything they could to cope and get on with things, whereas I had sort of just stopped. Marg shouldn't be the one giving me the hug and telling me things would be all right. It was supposed to be the other way around.

'She's so like you, Thel,' I said to myself and then I pressed my nails into the palms of my hands because I missed my friend so very much, and crying about it wasn't going to bring her back. 'Bugger you, Hitler.'

It was what Thelma and Joan and young Mary and I used to say whenever the raids got a little unruly when we were on duty during the Blitz.

*

The next evening after dinner, I dragged Guy into the garden to marvel at Bunty's tomato plants, which were now thriving thanks to Horace Batley-Norris's plant food advice.

'Guy,' I said, 'if it's all right with you, I'm going to come back into the office. I'm sorry I've neglected everything.'

I had hardly mentioned *Woman's Friend* since Thelma had died.

'That's good,' he said, mildly. 'As long as you're sure.'

'Entirely sure,' I said. 'Thank you for letting me just wander off.'

Guy frowned. 'It's not wandering off,' he said. 'You've been doing the right thing. We all want to help and God knows I've felt useless. Giving you a little time is the least I could do.'

'I haven't even asked about Mrs Porter,' I said, apologetically. 'How is she?'

'Largely absent,' said Guy. 'And not giving a hoot. That's why it's been easy for you to be off work. I'm assuming she's moved on to her next whim.'

'Is there any news about the sale?' I asked. 'We'd just got going with our plan.'

'And it was right that we decided to stop,' said Guy, firmly. 'Frankly, I'm not sure that anyone would want to back us now, even if they took the briefest look at the accounts. *Woman's Friend* is a dog's dinner. We're losing readers hand over fist and I'm not surprised. The issues coming up are dreadful and the decline is painfully clear. The odd decent short story and a nice cover picture, but other than that, it's hardly worth the paper it's printed on, let alone thruppence a copy.'

Guy was right. He had brought me the new issue, and calling it a dog's dinner was being kind. Mr Brand's cover was, as ever, lovely, but once you opened it up, nothing made any sense.

A small paragraph on becoming a bus conductor (cut down from an informative two columns) was stuck in the corner next to a photograph of a thoughtful looking Mrs Porter holding a pen, which took up the rest of the page. There was only one piece of fiction instead of three, and an article on Errol Flynn's hair had replaced Nurse McClay's popular series "Coping with Baby". Mrs Fieldwick's "News From the Shed" column had survived, but was far shorter than usual and now accompanied by pictures of expensive brooches shaped as bunches of grapes. That at least made me smile, as clearly the only inspiration taken from Monica had been on the sartorial front. But there were hardly any paid advertisements either, which probably explained Guy's concerns.

Woman's Friend wasn't one thing or another. It felt rather like going to the greengrocer and finding potatoes and greens as normal, but next to them, an elaborate hat that cost fifty pounds, while the lady behind the counter was dressed like Queen Mary and wanted to know if you were planning a holiday in Biarritz. You couldn't help wondering where the nice helpful man in the apron had gone.

It was a mess.

Our magazine had had its ups and downs, but it had always come back in the end. It was awful to see everyone's hard work reduced to a nonsense. The "Yours Cheerfully" page was a shadow of itself with just a handful of letters ranging from the trouble in finding domestic staff to someone vaguely missing their five-year-old who was boarding at school. I wondered if Mrs Porter had written them herself. Worst of all, it no longer included the message to readers asking them to send in letters so that we could write back. As for "Woman's Friend to Friend", which three months ago had been a page full of optimistic letters about plans so that one day anyone might get to see a doctor for free, now it didn't exist at all.

I couldn't blame the readers if they had gone off us. I wondered if we could get them back. I wondered if *we* could get *Woman's Friend* back as a start.

There was, however, one tiny spark of hope.

'Guy,' I said, 'did you say that the accounts are looking groggy?'

'Groggy?' he scoffed. 'Virtually unconscious.'

'Do you think they could be revived?'

'Actually, I do. We've overhauled the *Friend* before, so we can certainly do it again. If the readers aren't all happier having jumped ship to other magazines. It's a crowded playing field.'

'Perhaps that works in our favour,' I said. 'Maybe no one else will be interested in Cressida's sale. Have you or Monica heard anything?'

Guy shook his head. 'Rumours, but nothing concrete.'

'Well, then,' I said, starting to perk up, 'that may not be the disaster we think. After all, who's going to want to invest in a dud? Anyone with half a brain will look at the books and see that the magazine's not working. As you said, there comes a point when it will stop being worth buying.'

'This isn't cheering me up,' said Guy, throwing a tomato into the air and catching it as if it was a tennis ball.

'Well, maybe it should,' I said. 'What if the playing field doesn't have anyone else trying to play?'

'True. But it would also mean we'll struggle to find anyone to back us,' argued Guy.

Now I sighed, heavily. 'Have you read *Winnie-the-Pooh*?' I asked.

'No.'

'You should. You're just like Eeyore. He's lovely, but not terrifically optimistic.'

Guy raised an eyebrow.

'Oh, come on,' I said. 'Help me feel hopeful.' Now I cut to the chase. 'The children think we're buying the magazine. Marg told me they're looking forward to us working at the house and they'd all like to help out. Properly, with jobs. I have to admit she gave me pause to look at myself.' I felt my words catch in my throat. 'Guy, I know I've taken my eye off things since Thel died, but if no one else has made an offer to the Egg, and I'm not coming back into this far too late, do you think we could still give it a go?'

Guy looked at his tomato for what felt like ages. Finally, he slowly nodded.

'Monica and I did speak with a couple of people who were interested. We can go back and see. It might be too late, though,' he warned. 'Cressida may still have found someone herself.'

'Why don't we call Monica?' I said, trying not to look jubilant at bringing him round.

'Good idea,' said Guy. 'But you have more than enough on your plate. Between going back into the office and looking after the children, if we do try to get financing, I'd like you to leave the work to Monica, Harold and me. You can't do everything, Em.'

As his answer, I gave him a big hug which he put up with manfully.

'Eeyore,' he said, once I'd let go, 'what kind of a name is that?'

*

Before I returned to work, there was something I needed to do. That evening after Guy had gone home, I went up to my room, sat on my bed, and got out my writing set.

'*My dearest, darling Charles,*' I wrote, '*I am not sure where to begin . . .*'

It was true. Finding the right words was still almost impossible at first, however, I kept going, doing my best not to dwell on the awful desperation of the last weeks. Sometimes I had to stop as tears blurred my eyes, but agonising though it was to have to re-live even the most general of details, finally telling him lifted a weight from my shoulders. It was one thing to have avoided saying how awful Mrs Porter was, but keeping the news about Thelma from Charles had felt like a betrayal of our relationship. He was my husband and he deserved to know the truth.

'*The children are being enormously brave,*' I wrote, '*and everyone is being so helpful and kind.*' I thought for a moment. '*Darling, you must promise not to worry about us, or I shall be ever so cross.*'

Then I told him how much I loved him.

'*Come home safely, my darling.*' I paused, my pen hovering in mid-air. '*I don't know how I could bear it if you don't.*'

But on the paper I said nothing like that. I just drew kisses until the end of the page.

First thing Monday morning, I left the children having breakfast with Bunty, and headed off for my bus. It was August the second. A new month. The first without Thelma.

As the children were now all on summer holiday, Bunty had managed to take the week off. The War Office had been kind. She and Harold were taking them to Parliament Hill Lido. Thel would have loved it.

I felt almost guilty as I ran up the steps into Launceston House. Waving a Good Morning to Miss Poole on reception, I dashed across the shiny floor and into the lift, just as the doors began to close. It felt good to be back at work, even if I wasn't quite sure what I was about to walk into. For the last weeks at home, I had felt so out of my depth. At least here I knew what I was doing.

'Someone's keen,' said a grizzled-looking man in the lift.

'Yes, I am,' I replied, which he hadn't expected.

It had been three weeks since I was last in the office, and it felt like three years. Oddly, I expected things to have changed, perhaps because so much had at home, but of course it was exactly the same.

Exactly, that was, other than the stacks and stacks of letters that covered my desk, and it turned out, all the spare desks in the journalists' room next to Mrs Shaw and Miss Peters.

'Welcome back, Emmy,' said Guy, appearing behind me.

'We've been trying our best,' said Mrs Shaw.

'I'm so sorry I've been away,' I said. 'I'll make up for it.'

Mrs Mahoney and Hester had both been over to the

house several times, Hester in particular being a hit with Marg. It made it easier to come back but it was still a welcoming and overwhelmingly sympathetic team that offered condolences and kind words. Even Mrs Pye managed a 'So sad,' without lapsing into schoolgirl French, which was a relief. Mr Elliot did not appear.

'It's like working with one of those amphibians,' said Mrs Shaw. 'My Gerald used to keep a lizard when he was a boy, and Mr Elliot's just like it.'

'You're right,' said Mrs Mahoney. 'He's always there, just lurking.'

Miss Peters and Hester nodded in silent agreement. Clearly relations with Mrs Porter's second-in-command had not improved while I was away.

'I have missed you all more than I can possibly say,' I smiled.

'You're back now,' said Mrs Mahoney, kindly.

'Shall we go through some letters?' said Mrs Shaw. 'We've got ever such a lot to catch up.'

By the end of the day, I felt better. Here were problems I had answers to. When I returned home, the children all talked at the same time, keen to tell me about the lido. In turn, I told them about a lady who had a cat in a basket on the bus.

'That's nice,' said Marg. 'When are you buying *Woman's Friend*?'

*

For the next two weeks everyone at the magazine worked flat out. It was a peculiar job, partly working on what Mrs Porter wanted, but also desperately trying to keep the old version of *Woman's Friend* in the best health we could.

Guy still did his best to be civil to Mr Elliot even though he had become even more unbearable, acting as

Mrs Porter's gatekeeper and hardly deigning to communicate. The upside to this was that as we worked diligently on, he could gain little idea that we were actively trying to buy out his boss.

I did as I had promised Guy, and let him, together with Monica and Harold, shoulder the bulk of the business plan needed for Monica's contacts. I still pulled my weight, however, compiling editorial plans for *Woman's Friend*, combining what I knew readers loved as well as new ideas I was confident they would take to. None of them involved ten-guinea frocks.

I certainly had enough on. I still felt uneasy about being away from the house, although for the first week, as Bunty was off work, I went into the office full time, and brought more letters home. Bunts and I worked out a schedule so that one of us was always nearby after the children had gone to bed, with me two flights down in the kitchen, typing away like mad, while Bunty and Harold stayed quietly upstairs. My mother went home to check that my father was fine, which of course he was, even if she did say that in her absence he had forgotten to have a haircut. He had cheerfully reported that someone had said if he wasn't careful he would start looking like Grigori Rasputin, so he now was thinking of starting his own cult.

There were good days and bad. The children, as Mother had predicted, seemed to enjoy as much normality as they could. Marg was now firm friends with Belinda and they started their own society called The Orphans' Association which you could only join if at least one of your parents was dead, or officially missing. I thought it the saddest thing I had ever heard, but Mrs Ginger said that Belinda was full of chat about belonging to something that involved a homemade badge and secret meetings, as well as a special, if wobbly, crest that spelt out the initials T.O.AST.

She and Marg and a quiet boy called Terry were the founding members. The rest of us hoped, more than anything in the world, that they would stay the only ones.

Stan hurled himself into looking after the animals, where, without doubt, he came closest, at times, to being happy. Both he and George did sometimes go off to play on the bombsites with their friends, at which point Bunty and I had to hold our nerve and not think about them being crushed to bits by piles of falling debris. We were not much comforted when George said that if anything did happen, the Scarey brothers were the best Heavy Rescue men in Britain.

'Did someone mention the Scareys?' boomed Harold, who was in the next room. 'Don't worry, darling, if anyone can get the children out it'll be them.'

'Good grief,' said Bunty.

'This is hypothetical, George Jenkins,' I said, sternly. 'Not a challenge to see if you can get yourselves stuck.'

George smiled. It made my week.

Harold had been hard at work helping Guy and Monica put together a business case for investors. He had quickly become invaluable, and from his increasingly cheery and hearty appearance, his claim that it had given him a real boost certainly looked true. It was my feeling that falling in love with Bunty probably had something to do with it as well, but I knew better than to mention it, even though it was screamingly obvious. I understood why they didn't want to make a show of it at the moment, when so many things felt dark, but it was an enormously welcome little light that I hoped one day would be allowed to shine brightly, as they both deserved.

For now, Harold set about collating all the information we would need to persuade investors that *Woman's Friend* had a future, and we were neither amateurs nor entirely mad. Guy brought home the magazine's accounts, Mrs Mahoney met with him secretly, Monica phoned him with ideas and suggestions, and Harold wrote everything down in longhand, then checked and edited it, before Bunty typed it all up. In triplicate. It was just like planning the design for a building, Harold said. Now we had become architects of *Woman's Friend*'s potential future.

Thank goodness for Captain Thomas. While the rest of us juggled our day jobs with hurried conversations and surreptitious meetings, he set up a war office of his own in the dining room at the house. Every day he was either at his 'desk' there, or with one of the children, building or listening, or cheering them on with their hobbies. From applauding wildly as Marg played a trombone duet in her lesson with Buzz to studying military plane recognition booklets with Stan. And of course, woodwork with George. He was always building things with George.

Slowly and surely, Harold had become part of our world and a very big part of Bunty's.

One day, when Bunty was at work, Mrs Harewood asked if we needed a typist. She was rusty, she said, but soon our neighbour was part of the team. The junior members, meanwhile, were now doing their bit. Once George built his first set of pigeonholes for 'the post room' out of bits of old beer crates, the pressure was on. Now we really did have to make sure we bought *Woman's Friend*.

CHAPTER TWENTY-EIGHT

Mrs Porter Returns

WE WERE READY to do battle, and when it came to it that's exactly what we did. Dressed in our best bib and tucker, Guy, Monica, Harold, Mrs Mahoney and I threw everything into our presentation to the private investors Monica had brought into her confidence. There were two of them. Mrs Southern and Mr Shorthouse. Both were rich and had what they called portfolios of interest in publishing, retail and what was vaguely referred to as The Arts.

Monica chaired the meeting and one by one, like a financial music hall, we did a turn, me painting verbal pictures of how our magazine had always been based on listening to the readers and understanding what was important to them, rather than what might be important to us. We had all practised our parts well. I over-ran on mine, but we took it as a good sign that nobody said stop.

I couldn't work out if Monica's colleagues were interested or not. Their faces gave nothing away. We pushed on regardless. Afterwards, they were given copies of our plans. Then, questions came back. Guy and Monica held their nerve as negotiations took place. The waiting was interminable.

They gave us the money.

We were told two days later, after they had had time

to consider our plans. The children and I went to the bakery and bought as many buns as were allowed. Harold instructed the solicitors we had engaged to notify Mrs Porter's representatives that a consortium wished to register their interest in the sale. No names were mentioned at this stage.

'It isn't ours yet,' I said, again and again and again. 'We have to outbid all the other people. We can't get excited yet.'

Guy had heard a rumour that there were other interested parties, as he put it, but we didn't know who they were, or how much they were prepared to pay. It felt as if we had found a car to borrow for a race, but did not know if we would need to out-run a Mercedes-Benz Torpedo, or just the local double-decker bus. Nerves all round felt frayed.

It was, however, a gigantic step forward, and when the agreement in principle was signed, which seemed to take years, but was actually not long at all, Guy called a secret meeting in a pub in Covent Garden and gave the good news to the rest of the team. We planned to tell Mrs Porter that we were making an offer.

The next morning, we were given our chance. Mr Elliot had informed us that the Egg would be visiting the office on her way to see Lord Overton at twelve o'clock, and wanted to check on the progress of a special feature entitled "Fun On The Four-Legged Front". This consisted mostly of pictures of Small Winston in a variety of military themed hats, and was a jolly idea, but possibly didn't need to take up four entire pages, with the reminder to Cut Out And Keep. Small Winston hadn't looked as if he thought the idea was up to much either as by the time he was photographed wearing a sailor's hat with HMS Barker written on the brim, he had clearly fallen asleep.

Either way, it was with a mix of anticipation and nerves that we all waited for her appearance.

Mrs Porter's arrival was heralded by the frenzied cry of, 'DO BE CAREFUL, MR ELLIOT – HE HAS BRITTLE BONES.'

Guy had been waiting with me in my office.

'Brace yourself,' he said.

The doors to the office creaked open followed by a thunder of paws as Small Winston charged down the corridor to the journalists' room, where he liked to hide in the salvage box. This was followed by the clickety-clicks of Cressida's heels and an enthusiastic call of 'Good morning, Mrs Porter,' from Mrs Pye. Mrs Porter paused long enough to tell her that she would like to see Mr Brand and his designs, and then continued down to her office.

'Good morning, Mrs Porter,' Guy and I called as we heard her walk past.

A gay reply of, 'Good morning, Mr Collins,' surprised us both. 'My office, if you would.'

'Good mood?' I mouthed at Guy.

He shrugged. 'Come on,' he said. 'No time like the present. I'll get Mrs Mahoney.'

I hastily followed him out.

'Mrs Porter,' he said as we followed the heady scent of her perfume into the splendour of her room. 'I hope you are well. What a lovely hat.'

'This old thing?' she purred. 'Silly.'

She gave him a wide-eyed smile. It was almost like the olden days of a few months ago.

'Might we have a moment?' said Guy.

'I'm in rather a hurry, I am afraid,' she answered. 'Can't Mr Elliot help you?'

The Editor of *Woman's Friend* ignored the indirect snub and carried on.

'It won't take a minute, I promise.'

Mrs Porter sighed, as if burdened with the tribulations of the world, and without asking us to sit down, placed herself behind her enormous desk.

'Of course,' she said, graciously. 'How can I help?'

'It's a courtesy thing, really,' said Guy. 'Our solicitors will be communicating through the appropriate channels, but I wanted to tell you myself, that as part of a consortium of investors, we – that is the *Woman's Friend* management team – are entering the bidding to buy the magazine.'

Mrs Porter stared at him.

'That was all,' said Guy, in a friendly way. 'We won't take up any more of your time. I'll ask Mr Brand to bring in Small Winston's feature.'

'Oh dear,' said Mrs Porter, airily, 'why didn't you say? I'm afraid I have already accepted an offer. But how sweet that you tried.'

Guy, Mrs Mahoney and I stared at her. 'But the closing date for the proposals isn't until Monday,' I said.

The Honourable Egg turned her huge eyes to me. 'Oh gosh,' she said, 'I must have forgotten.'

'And you don't know what we are proposing,' added Guy, with admirable composure. 'Mrs Porter, we have some very serious backers involved.'

Mrs Porter sighed and looked at her nails. She frowned and rubbed one of them with her thumb, which seemed to solve whatever the problem had been as then she smiled.

'The thing is,' she said, almost conspiratorially, 'that wouldn't really help.' Now she stood up. 'It's been sold.'

'And your solicitors did not think to inform other investors who had registered their intent?'

Guy's face was beginning to colour.

'Whoops,' said Mrs Porter. 'So sorry. Now I really must get on.'

'Might I ask what the time frame is for the sale?' asked Guy.

I stood there, rather uselessly, as the reality began to sink in. We had lost our magazine.

'Oh, goodness,' sighed Mrs Porter, weary from putting up with the demands of being Businesswoman of the Year. 'The legalities are of course very arduous, but they should be sorted within the month.'

'Who have you sold to?' I asked, finally finding a voice.

'Ah,' beamed Mrs Porter. 'A very jolly newspaper owner. Bobby someone of West London Press.' She put her hand to her silk dress, somewhere in the region of where humans had a heart. 'Rather down to earth. Not my sort of person. Never mind. They're going to give it away for free on Saturdays with their paper. I can't remember the details but they like the name and said something about being able to sell what he called space around the war effort. Between you and me, he said it is very lucrative. Of course, I told them how terrifically "in" with the Ministry we are.' Now there was a clear glint in Mrs Porter's eyes. 'Oh, you'll find this rather fun. Apparently, all that boring old business about cabbages was a key factor in their interest. So it has served me rather well.' She paused for thought. 'I should probably thank you, really.'

So much for Mrs Porter not caring about money. She had sold *Woman's Friend* to someone who would use what remained of its name to sell adverts. 'Bobby Roberts is slippery as a snake,' said Mrs Mahoney under her breath.

I wasn't worried about that. Mrs Porter had not mentioned the most important point of all.

'What about the team?' I asked.

Cressida, who was having a lovely time, pushed on. 'I am going to tell them now,' she said. 'The legal people said not to yet, but you're bound to tell them, so I might as well.'

'No, Mrs Porter,' said Guy. 'We must talk before you tell them anything. I need to know what will happen to the staff. If, as I assume, the West London Press will not continue to employ them, then I want to tell them myself.'

Cressida gave him one of her blank looks.

'Mrs Porter,' he said, 'if they are to lose their jobs, there is a right way to let people know.'

Mrs Porter put her head to one side and gazed at him. 'Oh, Mr Collins,' she said. 'I've had staff my entire life. I do know how to speak to them. And anyway, they've known about the sale for weeks.'

'Mrs Porter,' said Guy. 'This is not the right way. Let me tell my team.'

'They,' said the least Honourable Person I knew, 'are *my* team.'

Short of wrestling her to the ground, there was nothing Guy could do to stop her. She swept past him to the door, where she clapped her hands.

'Everyone! My office, if you would,' she called, cheerfully. 'I have an announcement.'

Within moments, the entire staff had assembled in Mrs Porter's office. Even Small Winston came along, chewing on a piece of paper.

'Good morning,' Cressida cooed. 'I know you have all been waiting to hear about the future of *Woman's Friend*. Oh, now look at my little man, what's that in your mouth? Mr Elliot, do something.'

In the middle of the most important announcement, Mrs Porter crouched down to fuss over her dog.

Mr Elliot inched towards his nemesis, aided by Mrs Pye who was trying to help stop Small Winston. Winston ignored them all and swallowed part of an envelope.

The *Woman's Friend* team looked at Guy.

Guy shook his head. 'No,' he said quietly. 'I'm sorry.'

'Master Porter may need veterinary attention,' said his owner, standing up, 'so I must be quick. I have sold *Woman's Friend* to West London Press so I'm afraid your services will no longer be required. There will be three or four more issues to complete, isn't that right, Mr Elliot? And I shall of course need you all to carry on. I am going on a short holiday, due to exhaustion. That's all. Thank you.'

There was an awful silence. Guy looked sickened, and I felt the same. I could tell that Hester, who was standing next to me, was fighting as hard as she could not to cry. I didn't say anything, but I reached for her hand and held on to it tightly.

We had let everyone down. I should have come back to work sooner, refused to let our bid for the magazine be put on hold. We should have kept going. Not that I would have changed looking after the children for a second, but I hadn't thought about the others enough. I bet Thel would have told them to crack on. I just hadn't had room in my head. Worst of all, we had got everyone's hopes up, and now they were dashed.

The silence didn't last long. From the back of the room, a strangled voice spoke.

'West London Press?' croaked Mrs Pye. 'But you said you would sell it to someone in Fashion. Who would understand our vision. Not chip-paper people. What about me?'

'Ah yes,' said Cressida. 'Or rather, no. All things must come to an end. I've moved on from my vision. Mrs Pye, I am sure you will find a role very quickly that you will enjoy.'

'But,' said Mrs Pye.

'Mmm?' replied Mrs Porter.

'But you said I would go with the magazine,' said Mrs Pye, utterly stricken. 'That someone of my calibre would be needed. "On Duty for Beauty" by Pamela Pye.'

Of all the people to elicit sympathy, I would never have thought that Mrs Pye would be the one. Now though, her shock and disappointment were awful to watch.

Cressida didn't give a fig. 'Oh, I did, didn't I?' she said. 'Silly old mind like a sieve.'

'This meeting is over,' interrupted Guy, as Mrs Porter blithely destroyed her most loyal supporter.

I squeezed Hest's hand again and said quietly, 'Let's go.'

'Come along, Mrs Pye,' said Mrs Mahoney. 'I'm sure you have lots to do.' She gently guided Mrs Pye towards the door, with as much dignity as the situation could allow.

We all headed to the journalists' room as Mrs Porter began issuing Mr Elliot with the order to take Small Winston out for his ablutions. For once the sound of teeth snapping at heels and then a very loud, 'Ouch,' did not raise a smile.

'I believe you are late for your appointment,' I heard Guy say to Cressida, the disgust in his voice more than clear.

Then I heard him close the door to her office, as our Editor came to look after his team.

CHAPTER TWENTY-NINE

News From Us To You

WE HAD ALL known that there was always a good chance we wouldn't be able to save *Woman's Friend*. From the moment Mrs Porter began changing the things that meant anything to anyone, it had been a downhill slope, and the fact that she had sold it out from under our feet should not have come as a surprise.

But when it did happen, and she had spelt it out so very carelessly, it was still the worst ever shock. Other than Mrs Pye, who despite Mrs Mahoney's kind gesture had picked up her handbag and rushed out of the office, the rest of us convened in the journalists' room, just as we always did when something was up.

'Are you all right, Hest?' I asked her. 'I'm very proud of you. You did ever so well in there.'

Poor Hester was now tearful, and I didn't blame her one bit. 'Why was she so horrible?' she whispered. 'Even to Mrs Pye?'

'She's a very spoilt, nasty lady,' I said. 'Whatever happens, we're better off without her.'

Hester nodded bravely, but I couldn't help but think that I didn't have the first clue of what 'whatever happens' meant.

Guy shut the door. I had never seen him so entirely beaten, but with head held high, he addressed his colleagues. His friends.

'I want to apologise,' he said, 'for everything. I'm so sorry it has come to this, and even sorrier that I wasn't able to manage Mrs Porter, either in the way that she gave you this awful news, which was unforgivable, or indeed, over the last few months. From what I understand, the late Lord Overton thought I might be able to have some form of influence over his niece. I'm afraid I failed.'

Mrs Mahoney began to say something along the lines of 'don't be daft', but for the first time I could remember, he didn't accept her view.

'Thank you, Mrs Mahoney,' he said. 'You're very kind, but I had wanted to do better for you all. As you know, I'd hoped we could somehow keep *Woman's Friend.*'

'Excuse me for asking, Mr Collins,' said Mrs Shaw, 'but if you've got the money sorted out, can't we set up a new version?'

Guy smiled, the wrinkles around his eyes looking deeper than usual. 'Mrs Shaw,' he said, 'you are remarkable. Undefeatable. But setting up a completely new magazine is a very different project. *Woman's Friend* was sold for its name and reputation. Beginning from scratch would take far more money. And launching magazines is a tricky business. Many more fail than succeed.' He paused and then cleared his throat. 'I think we are at an end,' he said. 'I cannot tell you how sorry I am.' His voice broke slightly. 'Please do not feel you must work until the sale is finalised, as Mrs Porter expects. If there is anything at all I can do to help, then of course, I will.'

Everyone looked even more disconsolate after Guy finished speaking. We all felt wretched, and we knew that he understood.

As we sat in silence, there was a knock on the door and when Guy said, 'Come in,' Clarence appeared with a sack from the post room.

'I'm sorry to interrupt,' he said, seeing our dejected expressions. 'It's the post. I'll just put it down here.'

Seeing Clarence was the last straw for Hester, who promptly burst into tears. No more *Woman's Friend* meant no more seeing our Post Room Junior Administrator every day. It really was too much. Clarence looked mortified.

'Blimey, I'm sorry, Hest,' he said, not knowing what he had actually done. 'Do you want a hankie?' He fished a nice clean one out of his post-room uniform pocket and handed it to her, which she managed to accept, although the chivalry of the moment now reduced her to helpless sobs. 'What's happened?' asked Clarence, looking as if he was ready to punch whoever had upset Hester.

'We've had bad news about *Woman's Friend,*' I said. 'Mrs Porter's sold it.'

Clarence was a bright young man and it didn't take much more than a second for him to realise that this would mean Hester had lost her job. It also meant he wouldn't get to see *her* every day either.

'She can't do that,' he said, his ears going very red, very fast. 'It's not on.' Then he looked embarrassed at his emotional response, and added, 'I mean on the readers. It's not fair on them.' He gave the postbag a kick, which was what we'd all have done, given half a chance. 'It won't be the same,' he ended sadly, and not meaning the readers at all.

By now everyone was beginning to look as if they wanted to join in with Hester's tears. There had to be a bright side, somewhere.

'We've still got a little while,' I said. 'Four more issues. That's something we can work on together. And Mrs Porter said she's going on holiday so we can pretend it's like old times. It can be our last hurrah. I fully intend to ignore anything Mr Elliot says, for a start.'

'Three Bags Bloody Full,' muttered Mrs Shaw. 'Miserable old git.'

'That's the spirit,' I said, 'and we still have the readers.' I nodded towards the slightly dented sack. 'I know we used to get three times as many letters, but we can still do something. And don't forget all the people we've helped. All the times you've typed up replies, written letters, *listened* to them. Or answered the phones when people rang in. Mr Newton, look at how you kept *Woman's Friend* going when it was hopelessly out of date and very few people wanted to advertise with us. You've been doing that all over again these past weeks. Any magazine would be proud to have you. I know we'll all have to go our separate ways, but it doesn't mean we can't stay friends. And until then, I for one am going to try to say goodbye to the readers properly. Not for Mrs Porter. Not to keep things going for her – she's never cared about anyone, let alone the women who write in. She's done everything she can to put them off. Well, bugger Mrs Porter – sorry, Hester, don't listen – but I'm not bloody well giving up on the readers until the very end of the last day.'

'Well said, Emmy,' said Mrs Mahoney. 'Although do you know what sticks in my throat? It's that when we get complaints about the sillinesses she's put in our magazine, the readers don't know that we agree with them. I've a mind now to tell them. Put in a little note when we write back to them. PS, we're as sorry as you are that it's all gone on the wonk.

I nodded. It had been driving me mad, too.

'So why don't we?' I said. 'Every letter we send, we say that we're really sorry but *Woman's Friend* has been sold – thanks for sticking with us, and goodbye.'

'I like that,' said Mrs Shaw.

'So do I,' said Miss Peters.

'I might write to the advertisers,' said Mr Newton. 'Politely of course.'

Guy had been quiet for some time, chewing his bottom lip and looking miles away. I knew he was as crushed as the rest of us. Now, though, he finally looked up.

'I agree,' he said. 'The readers deserve an explanation. And we deserve to get to say our goodbyes.' He pushed his spectacles up his nose and turned to his Head of Production. 'Stop the press, Mrs Mahoney,' he said. 'Let's tell the readers exactly what has gone on.'

★

WOMAN'S FRIEND TO FRIEND

News From Us To You

Some of you have written to us over the last few weeks with questions about the recent changes that have been happening to your magazine. I am sure lots more of you had similar thoughts too. If we're honest, actually, so did we.

Some of you have liked the changes, some of you haven't, but what we at *Woman's Friend* didn't do was talk to you about them – here – in one of the parts of the magazine that particularly belongs to you. We really should have, so, please forgive us for being slow on this matter, but now that's exactly what we'd like to do.

You'll see on this page a selection of the letters we've received from you with views on a range of subjects, from the sorts of fashions we've been telling you about, through to the things we haven't been doing. We are glad that almost all of you like the dog pictures – you'll see in this issue there are rather a lot more! We all know Small Winston well. He is a lovely chap, although occasionally gets out of his bed on the wrong side.

We also want to tell you, with the very greatest of sadness, that *Woman's Friend* is moving on. It will still be available for you every week, but the magazine is getting new owners, so your team here will be saying goodbye. We had hoped to buy the magazine ourselves – but sadly got pipped to the post. We want you to know that we tried.

We are sure that there will be lots of interesting things to look forward to in the magazine, and the good news is that the current team have four more issues with you, so do keep writing in! We promise to answer every single letter that we can, either printing them in our pages, or writing back to you. We apologise if our replies are a little short, or even handwritten rather than typed, but we're going to do our best to help you out if you have any worries.

We would love to hear from you. The *Woman's Friend* readers are the best in the world. Through thick and thin over the years, we have loved writing to and for you.

Thank you for letting us into your homes.

With fondest wishes,

Your Editor, Guy Collins, and all your friends at *Woman's Friend*.

CHAPTER THIRTY

The Readers Respond

WHILE MANY PEOPLE might have said we should have just walked away, none of us wanted to give up. There was no loyalty to Mrs Porter, of course, but we all felt strongly that we should do what we could for the remainder of our watch, as it were. Until the West London Press took over, *Woman's Friend* still felt as if it was ours.

The Exhausted Egg was, for once, true to her word, and went on holiday. As far as she was concerned, *Woman's Friend* could ebb away until WLP did with it whatever they wanted. From a business point of view, this didn't make the least bit of sense, but there we were. For a month, we would almost get our magazine back.

This was helped in no small part by the fact that Mr Elliot had become rather unwell. While it would have been poor form to wish illness on anyone, the fact that Small Winston had made quite an impression on him in the shape of a not-insignificant bite, cheered everyone up. More to the point, as Mr Elliot had been extremely rude and told Mrs Mahoney she could stick her bottle of iodine in her ear, no one felt that he had anyone to blame but himself when his ankle turned nasty and he was laid up in bed.

'I shall miss that dog,' said Mrs Mahoney, and we all agreed that Small Winston had done himself proud.

The other obvious victim was, of course, Mrs Pye. Even though she was still almost entirely unlovable, no one had taken any joy from the humiliation handed out by her former mentor. It had been cruel and unnecessary, and we all felt a good deal of sympathy, even if Mrs Pye didn't appreciate it. It probably didn't help that Mrs Shaw started referring to her as Marie Antoinette.

'Poor old duck,' she said, the day after the news, 'one minute you're the Queen of France, and the next, your head's in a bucket and nobody cares.'

Mrs Pye continued to come to work, almost in a state of shock, but kept mainly to her office and seemed to dislike everyone even more now that they were trying to be nice.

At home, I had to break the news to George, Margaret and Stan. It had been something to look forward to, to plan and join in with, and now it was gone. They listened quietly.

'Will Guy still come round and will I still get to see Hester?' asked Marg.

'Does it mean Harold will move away?' asked George.

'This summer's rubbish,' said Stan. 'I hate it.'

I said yes, no, and agreed completely with Stan. Then I suggested we start our own magazine and call it *The Pimlico Gazette*. It could be especially for children and we could fill it full of pets and hobbies and where the best bombsites were. Three pairs of eyes looked at me.

'It wouldn't be the same,' said Marg. 'Nothing is ever the same.'

Now that things were coming to an end at Launceston, and there was no Mr Elliot to keep check, I began to spend more time at home, bringing letters back with me and answering them by hand. Mrs Harewood sometimes helped out and Miss Peters, who lived nearby, occasionally came round and typed for me, too. It meant I was there for the children whenever they needed me. It also meant that we could sort of run an office from home, in a poorer version of what we had hoped for and planned. I would go into *Woman's Friend*, pick up my sorted-out correspondence, and then hail a cab and take a sack of letters home. As Guy said, 'Damn the expense – take it all out of the petty cash.'

Two days after the new issue of *Woman's Friend* hit the newsstands – the one where we had included the letter telling everyone what was going on – Clarence had delivered a slightly fuller postbag than in recent weeks. It was no surprise, seeing as we had invited readers to write in before things came to an end, and we all set to sorting them out. There were more for "Yours Cheerfully" as well as for Mrs Pye's "On Duty for Beauty", which we had expected, but more surprising was the volume of letters addressed to Mr Collins, or the Editor, or "Woman's Friend to Friend".

'This is very nice,' said Miss Peters. She began to read one out.

'*Dear Mr Collins, I just wanted to say I'm sorry that Woman's Friend is changing hands. Please can you ask them to keep Mrs Fieldwick and Mrs Croft? Good luck in the future, Mrs J W Mason.*'

'I've got an interesting one here,' said Mrs Shaw.

'*Dear Woman's Friend, Thank you for telling us what is happening,*' she began. '*I'm really sorry you didn't manage to keep Woman's Friend going. I imagine someone rich is trying to buy it. Please find enclosed a postal order . . .*'

Mrs Shaw looked in the envelope, and took out a postal order. She went back to the letter.

'*. . . enclosed a postal order for half a crown, which I hope you can put towards still trying to beat the other people. Don't give in! Me and my friend Mavis have read your magazine* *for years and we don't want it to change. Yours sincerely, Mrs Iris Baird.* Fancy that,' said Mrs Shaw. 'Bless her.'

'Hold on,' said Miss Peters. 'This one felt like it had something in it as well.' She rummaged through a pile of letters and picked one out, ripping it open and revealing a letter and two pieces of card which had a shilling hidden in the middle.

'*Dear Mr Collins,*' she read, '*I saw your letter to the readers and felt very sorry. I know this isn't much, but I hope you can put it towards trying to buy the magazine. Your problem page lady helped my sister when she was in a right state last year, and we'll always be grateful. Wishing you all the very best, Mrs E. Bell.*'

As the three of us continued opening the letters, we found more and more of the same. Readers writing to say how sorry they were, and several of them enclosing postal orders or coins. It was the kindest thing I could imagine.

'Make sure we put all the ones with money back in their envelopes,' I said to the women. 'We can't possibly accept it, even if we were still in with a chance of buying *Woman's Friend.*'

By the time we got through to the bottom of the postbag, the pile of sympathetic letters was the largest one of the lot, and as we had started to note them down, we calculated that the donations had added up to twelve shillings and sixpence, which was a quite enormous amount, easily as much as if we had sold fifty copies of *Woman's Friend.*

I told Guy, of course, not least to make sure we were being entirely above board with the readers' money, but also so he could see how much his letter meant to them.

'We have to send it all back, or find a charity if people haven't included an address,' he said, leaning on a desk and reading one of the letters. 'Goodness me,' he said, 'this is really very nice indeed.'

297

'That great big pile over there is all for you, Mr Collins,' said Mrs Shaw. 'Not all with money, or you could go and live in the Bahamas like the last king, but lots of very nice messages, which might cheer you up.'

'Thank you, Mrs Shaw,' said Guy, 'they very much will.'

At that moment, Mrs Pye walked in. Madame's usual joie de vivre and random outbursts in French had all but disappeared, but it was unusual for her to converse, even in English.

'Ah,' she said, 'Mr Collins, there you are. A reader has sent in tuppence.' Mrs Pye said it as if she had opened an envelope filled up with mud. 'I thought you should know.'

'Thank you, Mrs Pye,' replied Guy. 'People are very generously trying to help.'

'How odd,' said Mrs Pye, like everyone else, not used to public displays of support, but unlike everyone else, apparently unmoved. 'I've also had many letters saying pleasant things and even more asking for beauty advice, before – and I quote – "*Woman's Friend goes to the dogs, probably that one in the hats.*"'

That made the rest of us laugh, and Mrs Pye looked up from the letter, entirely bemused.

'They're most kind,' said Guy. 'But we can't have people sending in money. I'll write another message. I must say,' he said looking around the office, 'it is nice to be busy. It rather makes one forget for a moment that we're on borrowed time.'

Mrs Pye gave him a look as if to say she was never going to forget any of this for as long as she lived.

'Actually, Mrs Pye,' said Mrs Shaw, 'there's one here you might enjoy.' She handed it to Guy, who scanned it and grinned.

'*Dear Whoever is selling Woman's Friend*,' he read aloud. '*I am writing to say that we were very happy with your magazine the way it was. Is it too late to stop the sale? Also, I don't know what you've done to Pamela Pye "On Duty for Beauty" but she has always been a great help and very informative, and actually me and my sister's favourite part of the magazine. Recently she seems to have inherited a fortune or married a millionaire. But anyway, good luck to you all. Yours, An Old Reader.*'

Mrs Pye pursed her lips. 'I've done my best,' she said, tartly, and left the room.

'She's not herself,' said Mrs Shaw.

'Non,' said Miss Peters, which was the wittiest thing I'd ever heard her say.

'I tell you what,' I said, 'let's run a double-page spread answering all the questions we get asked the most. In the next issue. In fact, two double-page spreads. Beauty, fashion, love lives, careers, you name it. Try to go out with a bang.'

'There isn't room,' said Mrs Shaw. 'Mrs Porter's written a very long poem and sent it in with some photographs of her looking about eighteen.'

I rolled my eyes.

'What a shame,' said Guy. 'I do hate it when things get lost in the post.' He got up from where he'd been slouching on the desk. 'Run the piece, Emmy. Turn it around, double quick.'

WOMAN'S FRIEND TO FRIEND

A Thank You

Following our message in last week's issue we would all like to thank you very much indeed for your kind letters and messages about *Woman's Friend*. We read every single one of them.

We are also glad you enjoyed the pictures of Small Winston the dog. We have sent on your letters to our current publisher, who is his proud owner, and she will tell the young man himself.

On a serious note, while we have been very moved by those of you who have wanted to help us try to buy the magazine, we must ask you not to send contributions. We are extremely grateful for your concerns but are not seeking to raise funds and will only be able to pass any donations on to The Children's Society if you have not enclosed your return address.

Do join us next week for what promises to be another issue full of features we hope you enjoy, and don't forget to send in any last problems or concerns by the third of September as after that we will not be able to reply.

With fond wishes,

Your Editor, Guy Collins, and all your friends at *Woman's Friend.*

When the issue was published, something strange began to happen.

Mr Newton noticed it first.

'I don't know how we're going to fit everything in,' he said. 'I've had three clients telephone me since yesterday, all wanting to place adverts in our final issue.'

'We've had almost no returns this week from news-agents,' said Mrs Mahoney.

'I think we may have overstretched ourselves on the "We'll answer all your letters" promise,' I said.

And then things really took off.

CHAPTER THIRTY-ONE

The Grim Reaper Himself

TWO VERY DIFFERENT things happened.

The readers who had not given up on *Woman's Friend* began to write in, in droves.

Mrs Porter picked up a copy of the magazine.

The two events did not exactly mix well.

We had definitely overstretched ourselves in terms of our workloads, but if nothing else it meant I didn't think about what I would do after Mrs Porter shut us down. I needed to find another job, but it would have to be something I would be able to fit around the children until their dad returned from sea. In the airgrams he had sent since being given the news about Thel, it was painfully obvious that he was more desperate than ever to get home.

We had no idea when that would be, so launching myself as a freelance journalist could be ideal. It was something, at least about work, to feel hopeful about. If I tried. Really hard. I would find another job, even if not with a magazine that meant as much to me as did *Woman's Friend*.

I still brought my work home with me and now that time was running out on *Woman's Friend* Bunty helped too, typing up my shorthand notes while I handwrote other letters. Stan liked licking envelopes so he got to do that, under pain of death not to look at the correspondence inside. Marg and George were both learning to type. They were enormously disappointed that we wouldn't be running a publishing company from the house. Even Huey, Dewey and Louie, who now ruled the garden in a tyrannical pact with Gert and Daisy, couldn't raise morale.

It was now two months since Thel had been killed and I still expected to hear the front door open and see her walk down the hallway and the kids hurl themselves at her. Sometimes, I'd find myself thinking, *All right, Thel, enough's enough. You've made your point, we all miss you. You can come back now.*

Other times – and this made me feel dreadful – I'd get angry. One night, after George had woken up screaming from a nightmare in which his mum had been trying to get through the window but no one would let her, we all went down to the kitchen and had hot milk and Horlicks to try to calm down. Early autumn had begun to make itself known, so it was chilly enough to warrant dressing gowns and blankets all round. As we sat together in various states of tiredness and upset, I just wanted to tell someone, *anyone* with more power or authority than me, that this wasn't fun any more. As if it had ever been.

There were odd moments of course. When the children played, or laughed at something on the radio, or one of the pets did something silly. Actually, the children were good at having bouts of normality. But Thel's absence never left any of us.

In a way, it was now worse, as the initial shock had worn off but the pain and sadness hadn't, and really it never would. Bunty said you didn't miss someone any less, you just made room for other things to surround the gap they had left.

All I knew was that it felt as if everything was slipping out of my grasp. Above all else, Thelma of course, but I missed Charles dreadfully and worried about him more and more each day. And now *Woman's Friend* and the team that meant so much to me would soon be gone. It was like tent pegs coming loose, one by one. At some point, perhaps not yet, but if the wind got up, the whole structure was going to collapse. There was nothing I could do, but just like every other person in the country, stick my chin up and keep going. After all, hadn't I written to thousands of readers telling them that there really wasn't a choice?

So, I followed my own advice and pushed on.

★

The closure of *Woman's Friend* as we knew it came around quickly.

A few days after the issue was published with our special questions and answers features, I made my way in to work. We had to put the final edition to bed and try to answer all the post that had come in, and then that would be it. Even though we had tried to give readers a deadline for their letters, they kept coming. There was tons still to do.

I reached the top of the stairs and rounded the corner, to see Mrs Mahoney and Mr Newton reading a typewritten notice that had been taped up on the doors to the *Woman's Friend* offices.

I said, 'Good Morning', and joined them.

THESE PREMISES AND THEIR CONTENTS
ARE THE PROPERTY OF LAUNCESTON PRESS LTD
AND THE HON. MRS CRESSIDA PORTER.
DO NOT ENTER.
SIGNED: *W. Elliot* W. ELLIOT

'This is ridiculous,' I said.

'What is?' It was Guy. 'Oh for heaven's sake. Just ignore it. Excuse me, please.'

We moved out of his way and Guy flung open the double doors, only to jump back in surprise.

There, sitting bolt upright on an office chair in the murkiness of the corridor, was Mr Elliot, looking not unlike the Grim Reaper himself.

'Good God, man,' said Guy, 'you frightened the life out of me. What are you doing sitting there in the dark?'

Mr Elliot, stood up, with, I noticed, the help of a walking stick. 'I thought this would happen,' he said. 'I trust you saw Mrs Porter's notice.'

'I did, thank you,' said Guy, briskly. 'It's a nonsense. We've got a magazine to get to press. How's your foot, by the way? It sounded painful.'

'My ankle,' said Mr Elliot. 'I have been quite ill. Which explains the present state of anarchy here.'

Guy snorted. 'Anarchy? This is a publishing company, not the Spanish Civil War. Now come on, let's get this thing done, and then it's over to you.'

Mrs Shaw and Miss Peters had now arrived with Hester and Mr Brand.

'Oh look, it's old Gloom Bag,' said Mrs Shaw, not entirely helping the diplomatic standoff. 'What's he doing?'

'There's a notice,' I said.

'I haven't seen it,' said Mrs Shaw correctly, as now the doors were open it wasn't obvious.

'This office is closed,' said Mr Elliot, pompously. 'By order of Mrs Porter.'

'Well, I need to go in, for a start,' said Mrs Shaw. 'I've got a full jar of plum jam in my desk and you're not having that.'

'There you are,' said Guy, as if Mrs Shaw had just

given a compelling closing argument at the Court of Appeal. 'I must tell you, Mr Elliot, that as no notice has been given, the staff have every right to retrieve their personal belongings. You can check the legalities of the Launceston employment policy if you wish, but I must insist we go in.'

I was sure Guy was bluffing, but he was ever so good at it and Mr Elliot hesitated.

'Good-oh,' said Guy, and walked in past him. 'Can someone put the lights on, please?' Then, and I was sure just to be annoying, he added, 'Happy for you to remain on guard, Mr Elliot.'

Guy walked down to the journalists' room and rather than going to our specific offices, we all followed. Now his breezy demeanour had gone. 'Pathetic,' he muttered. 'I'll lay ten bob it's because of the latest issue.' He took a deep breath. 'Right, everyone, you really must ensure you have collected anything that is yours. I am going to make a couple of phone calls as I'm pretty sure Mrs Porter doesn't have the authority to do this. Contractual obligations and all that.'

Mr Newton nodded. 'The clients have all paid for their advertising space.'

'Can he actually turf us out?' asked Mrs Mahoney. 'Legally?'

'I shouldn't think so,' said Guy, 'but I can't guarantee it. You've all gone way beyond what you could have over the past weeks. If any of you would like to go straight home, then please do.'

No one moved.

'It just gets my goat,' said Mrs Mahoney, 'to have to end like this. After all these years.' Her voice trembled and it took me aback. Mrs Mahoney was never over-dramatic and to hear her upset for the first time I could remember was awful. 'It's always been more than just a job, here. I'd have liked to have been able to finish things properly,' she said.

For a moment there was silence. Mrs Mahoney had spoken for us all. *Woman's Friend* had always been more than just a job. If this was going to be the last time we were here, it was a pretty rum way of ending things. No proper celebration of all we had done. No cups of tea or plans to go to the pub.

'We've still got masses of letters,' I said. 'I wonder if I can get them out past Elliot and finish them at home? I've nothing else to do.'

'I can come round and help,' said Hester, immediately. 'And I can help Marg and George with their typing.'

'Thanks, Hest,' I said. 'That would be nice.'

'Hold your horses, for a moment,' said Guy. 'There's a decent chance we can come back in on Monday. I need to speak with Legal upstairs. I'll call them now.'

But Mr Elliot appeared in the doorway. 'I must ask you to all leave,' he announced, 'and do ensure you take only what is yours. Nothing else.' He shot me a look and then turned to Guy. 'I have asked Security to come up.'

'Mr Elliot, we need half an hour,' said Guy, sternly. 'I have been here ten years. I will not be rushed into leaving anything of personal value behind.'

He walked over to the corner of the room where several empty postbags were neatly folded, waiting for Clarence to collect them. It was unbearable to see him pick one up and take it with him to collect his things. I left the others checking their desk drawers, and went back to my office.

I shut the door behind me and sat down. Although we had all known it was coming, the notice, and Mr Elliot trying to bar us had come as a shock. It was jolly hard not to feel wobbly. I ran my hand over my desk, as if it was a trusty old carthorse that was being moved on.

'Daft,' I murmured to myself, but it wasn't really. Ever since I had blundered quite by accident into a job at the magazine, *Woman's Friend*, and more than anything the people who worked here, had become a most enormously important part of my life. They were my friends. My family. This was a vile situation all round.

I opened the drawer to my desk and took out the spare fountain pen that I always kept there, and two clean hankies. Then I decided to steal two pencils. As anarchists went, it wasn't of historic proportions, but it made me smile. I stood up and walked over to the noticeboard, which was still covered in the readers' letters and photos that I had been sent, and held dear. One of a family at the seaside – the Burtons – and another of a middle-aged woman and her mother – Mrs Skinner and Mrs Wade. They had both been through difficult times, and I had been very happy to try to help out. I wasn't leaving without them. I quickly began to take everything down, finding it hard to believe what was happening.

And then that was that. I looked at the clock on the wall, as I must have done a thousand times in the past. I still had twenty minutes.

I could hear the rest of the team talking in quiet voices, including to Mrs Pye, who had come in late. While everyone else sounded muted, I heard her clipped tones say, 'Well I do hope one will still receive one's outstanding pay,' which was not quite in the spirit of the moment, but understandable nevertheless. Then Mrs Shaw told her to shut up. I had a little smile.

My word, I was going to miss them.

I pulled out a buff folder and decided to extend my kleptomania and take it to keep the photos and letters in.

Then I paused to read a memorandum that Guy had given me the previous year. It was from the late Lord Overton and was just two lines.

Collins
V. well done re The Ministry. Have heard Miss Lake's work v. well received, esp. in your absence. Pls pass on my appreciation. Good work.
O.

It had been one of the absolute highlights of my career to date. I had wanted to put it in a frame, but thought that too showy. I would take it home and perhaps do it now. The publisher of the entire Launceston Press, a man I admired immensely.

What would he make of all this? It was too depressing to think about.

I closed the folder and put it safely in my bag. There was still a pile of letters on my desk waiting for replies. Out of habit as much as anything, I took the lid off my fountain pen, and reached for the *Woman's Friend* note-paper for what was likely to be the very last time.

CHAPTER THIRTY-TWO

It Was Never In Doubt

NONE OF US returned to the office on Monday. Mr Elliot had been quick to call Mrs Porter, and she had been even swifter to seek legal advice. Although Guy had been right about contractual obligations to publish the final issue of *Woman's Friend*, Mrs Porter dug in her heels. Finally, and after missing the regular print deadline, she relented, but only to the extent that Guy, Mr Newton and Mrs Mahoney would be allowed into the office to deliver the magazine for production. Mrs Pye had also been included. Even after everything Mrs Porter had said, she still expected Madame to turn up. My hunch was that she didn't trust Guy.

The rest of us were banned from going in.

It was a final, petty act on the part of Mrs Porter. She did, of course, know from reading the magazine that we had told readers to write in if they wanted our help. We had not heard a peep from her. Now, I was sure Mr Elliot would have reported about the stacks of unopened post. It was why she didn't let us back in to finish the job.

Instead, I stayed at home with very little to do. The children were back at school, and Harold had set himself the task of finding a new job, so the house was empty, which was not what I needed at all. I finished off the few "Yours Cheerfully" letters I had at home and then phoned

Captain Davies at the station and explained I was free if he needed me. After that I got out the notes Horace Batley-Norris had kindly sent, and set about sorting out the cold frame in the garden to sow cauliflowers for next year.

It all took me until Monday lunchtime.

Talk about going from sixty miles an hour to nothing. Three months ago Thelma and I had been sitting at the fire station cheerfully moaning to each other that we were tired and could do with a holiday.

I bet she'd tell me what I should do now.

I got out my notebook and started to write out a to do list. That took ten minutes. I wandered around the quiet house and then checked on the animals who were still as well as they had been an hour ago. I couldn't wait until the children got home from school.

On Friday lunchtime, Guy came round. The last issue was done. Mr Elliot had paced around all week like a prison warden, but Guy had been able to go through his office properly and make sure he had taken home everything he needed. He, Mr Newton and Mrs Mahoney had agreed they would all meet up again very soon, and with everyone else as well.

And that was it. I had never seen him look so down.

I found a bottle of stout and handed it to him. He didn't even drink stout, but it was all we had, and anyway, he looked as if he needed it. We sat in the garden in the September sun and said very little.

'This is absurd,' he said after a while. 'It was just a job.'

'Absolutely,' I said, flatly.

'It was about time I had a change. Been there too long.'

'True.'

'I was thinking I might see if there's anything at the Ministry.'

'So was I.'

We both laughed, without much enthusiasm.

'Talk about switching sides,' said Guy.

'I just wish we could have finished things properly,' I said, failing in my determination not to torture us both. 'As Mrs Mahoney said. I wish we'd got the bloody letters out. I should have thought it through. I hate the idea of them all going into the salvage without even being opened.'

Guy took a large sip of his drink. 'I tried to see Johnny Overton again,' he said. 'He refused to meet.'

'What will happen to the office?' I asked.

'I imagine they'll close it all up. I assume Porter doesn't want anything, so there's a good chance the *Chronicle* journos will sneak in and nick any supplies. I know I would.'

'I took two pencils,' I said, coming clean.

'A hole punch and two bottles of ink,' said Guy and raised his glass to me. 'Highly unlikely to ever need a hole punch, of course, but I thought I'd take it anyway.'

'Quite right, too,' I agreed. 'Although, won't they lock up the offices to stop that sort of thing, now?'

'I don't know,' said Guy. 'They hadn't changed the locks on the doors when I left. I don't think they care. She's just waiting for WLP's cheque.'

I nodded vaguely and watched Laurel and Hardy in their run. I envied their contentment.

'So,' I said, after a few moments, 'anyone could just walk into the office?'

Guy nodded. 'As long as they can get past reception.'

'And they have a key,' I said.

Guy nodded again. 'Oh, I nearly forgot,' he said, reaching into his pocket. 'I got you a present.'

He threw something at me, which I easily caught.

'A lot of people are still waiting for help,' he said.

I uncurled my fingers and looked at the large metal key.

'Tomorrow?' I asked.

'It was never in doubt,' answered Guy.

CHAPTER THIRTY-THREE

A Hive of Industry

IT WASN'T BREAKING into an office if one opened it with a key. And even if it was breaking in, how many people did that in order to work for free? All in all, and morally at least, there was nothing wrong with the plan.

Guy and I talked through the details. He said there were at least two sacks of letters still sitting in the office. Mr Elliot had watched everyone like a hawk so there had been no chance to take them, he said, apologetically.

'The thing is,' said Bunty when she got home from work, 'technically if you bring anything home, it's stealing. Whether you have a key or not. Even if the receptionist is nice enough to look the other way, if you get caught, especially lugging out a sack of post, it would look awful for her.'

That was our biggest concern. Getting into the building was one thing. Getting out was another. The other suggestion had been to go via the post room, but again, it would put someone's job – we all knew that probably meant Clarence – in danger.

It was a definite no.

In the kitchen in the house, we were all listening to the wireless. Marg was practising doing bandages on my ankle, and Stan and George had just tried – unsuccessfully – to persuade everyone that if the Scarey brothers *happened* to come across a piglet, it would be perfectly sensible to keep it in the back garden.

'Honestly, between you two stealing letters from your old office, and the boys trying to hide a dubiously sourced pig, sooner or later someone is going to get caught,' said Bunts, 'and frankly, I don't think I can cope with that. It's bad enough I know about the hole punch.'

'You've all done your bit,' said Harold. 'You should be terrifically proud. This is quite a risk.'

They were both right. I'd always taken the job seriously and done my best. Perhaps I should just move on. But it didn't feel right and the thing was, I knew exactly why. Bunty did too. She asked me to help her make up the children's room but when we got upstairs she sat down on one of the beds.

'What's *really* going on, Em?' she said. 'I know you hate admitting defeat, but you've done all you can. Is this about Thel?'

'I'm not sure,' I said. 'I just hate that I can't make things right. I know that's obvious, and I know I'm no different to anyone else, but it eats at me. I hate that I can't fix the important things – like when Bill died. I couldn't make it better for you. I think that's why I've loved "Yours Cheerfully". I got to solve problems. I know I couldn't fix all of them, but most of them, I could try, and if nothing else, people knew that someone cared. You know that folder I brought home?'

Bunts nodded. I'd shown her the file of photographs and letters, and Lord Overton's memo.

'It's proof,' I said. 'That we helped. Sometimes I sit up here at night, hoping the kids aren't having bad dreams, because I know there's nothing I can do. We can't bring Thel back, we can't promise that their dad will come home safely. We can't guarantee anything for them.'

Bunty nodded, but said nothing. She was a good listener.

'Bunts, sometimes this is just too big, but at least I know I can talk to you and you'll understand. I know you're feeling exactly the same as me and somehow we'll bumble through and it'll be as all right as it can be. I don't know how I would cope if I was trying to do this on my own. Without you, or Guy, or Harold. Or Roy and Fred calling in, or even the Scarey brothers coming up with the ducks.' I paused and rubbed my eyes. 'Bunts, there are so many people just trying to get through this bloody war who don't have this kind of support, and I just don't know how they manage.'

Bunts put her hand over mine.

'And that's what I keep thinking about,' I said. 'We said we'd help the readers right to the end, and we haven't. Hundreds of people hoping someone will hear them. What if a letter in there is from a reader who has lost someone like we lost Thel, only they don't have a family or best friend to help? War's bad enough as it is. Imagine if you're trying to get through this on your own.'

We sat together in silence, but I knew Bunty understood. She always did. In the end she spoke first.

'You're right,' she said, quietly. 'They can't just sit there being ignored. We'll come up with something.'

She said 'we'.

It was going to be all right.

*

There were two ways to do it. Bit by bit, or all at once.

We chose all at once.

Saturdays at Launceston House were not as busy as the rest of the week, but because the news staff worked around the clock, there was still enough bustle to be able to blend in. The other factor in our favour was something that had irritated me over the years, and that was the fact that the *Woman's Friend* had always been the small cousin hidden away in a corner of the fifth floor. Had *The Evening Chronicle* been closed, the organisation would have been in disarray. Today, though, it was a decent bet that most of the people coming in and out of the building were not even aware that our magazine had been sold, if they had ever given it much thought in the first place.

Having left the children enjoying breakfast with Harold and Mrs Harewood, Bunty and I arrived first thing, Guy having said he would meet us there. Bunts and I were both dressed in smart office clothes as if it was any normal day of the working week.

'There is absolutely nothing unusual about this,' I said to her, as we walked up the steps of the building and through the large doors. 'Just keep talking. Good morning,' I called to the receptionist as we walked past and straight to the lifts. Bunty gave a confident half-nod, as if speaking might give her away, and as the lift doors shut behind us, we both breathed a sigh of relief. 'Weekend shift,' I said. 'They're used to all sorts coming in and out. *The Chronicle*'s motto is We Never Sleep.'

When we got to the *Woman's Friend* offices, the doors were shut, as they usually were. Nothing to worry about, so far. What was a surprise though was that waiting for us wasn't just Guy. With him was one of the leading publishers in the country.

'Monica!' I said, delighted.

'I thought I could help open envelopes or something,' she said, giving me a hug. 'This is all perfectly awful, but I know how you feel about not finishing a job. It's just not cricket. Hello, Bunty, good to see you. This is quite a party.'

'How did you get into the building?' I asked.

Guy looked at me as if I had asked them to explain how to suck eggs.

'Guy and I have been wheedling our way into places we shouldn't for the last twenty years,' said Monica. 'Now, who's got the key?'

I opened my bag and looked for my 'present' from Guy.

'Good morning.'

It made us all jump out of our skins.

'Mrs Mahoney,' I said, 'what are you doing here?'

'A spot of work, given half a chance,' said Mrs Mahoney. 'Mr Collins happened to mention he still has a key.'

'Technically, we're all still employed,' said a voice behind her. 'Until the last issue is in the shops.' It was Mr Brand with a nervous-looking Mr Newton. 'I've just mentioned it to Mrs Fraser on reception.' He smiled. 'In case anyone else just happens to be passing as well.'

Mrs Shaw and Miss Peters arrived, saying they had been doing just that.

Now it *was* beginning to feel like a party. The next guests to arrive, however, really did take me by surprise.

There, together with Hester and Clarence, were Harold, George, Margaret and Stan.

'You forgot your key,' said Stanley. 'It was by the telephone in the hall.'

'Chump,' whispered Bunty.

'Some of us were supposed to wait outside,' said Harold, handing me the office key. 'But then Hester and this very kind gentleman took us round to the service lift.'

'It's an honour, sir,' said Clarence.

'I've told Clarence everything,' said Hester, blushing slightly. 'He wants to help.'

'The post room thinks what's happened is a disgrace,'

said Clarence, gravely, and, one felt, on behalf of his department. 'You're our best customer. We get more letters for you than anyone. There's still post sitting downstairs.'

'We can stay, can't we, Emmy?' asked Marg. 'Mr Boone said he wouldn't tell anyone.'

Clarence nodded and looked chuffed to be referred to as Mr Boone.

'Well,' I said.

'Let's just get in,' said Guy. 'Go on, Emmy, you do the honours.'

I stepped forward keenly, ignoring the fact I had already fallen at the mission's first hurdle by leaving the key at home, and unlocked the doors.

As we led our visitors down to the journalists' room, I felt almost like a visitor myself. I remembered the very first time I had come here. It had been for an interview, and I had met my future brother-in-law for the first time. Guy had been untidy, unconventional and covered in ink. Nothing much had changed on that front, but *so* much else had.

In stark contrast to the usual relaxed and chatty starts to a day, we were quiet as everyone got to work. It was one thing to come into the office even though none of us worked here any more, but it was another to waste unnecessary time.

Mrs Shaw, Miss Peters, Mrs Mahoney and I set to the letters, just like we always had. Dictating replies, the typewriters going at nineteen to the dozen, and now with Bunty joining in as if she had worked with us all her life. Monica did far more than opening envelopes, within seconds taking on the role of additional advice columnist and declaring that it was 'nice to be back in the saddle at this sort of thing'.

Hester opened envelopes and the men sorted the letters,

while the children followed Clarence and Hester around like very helpful lambs, George in his school uniform so he could look like a Junior Post Boy if anyone asked. Stan sharpened pencils, whether people needed them or not. Marg was allowed to put advice leaflets into envelopes, although she caused a stir by going against orders and starting to read one. After she asked Mrs Mahoney what a prolapse was, she was relegated to stamps.

We wrote to everyone we could. To the scared, the confused, the lonely and the lost. The readers who felt just as I did, but weren't surrounded by people who cared. Keep going, we said, don't give up. Talk to your friends, or your workmates, your family or to our fellow magazines. We can't always understand just how bad things are for you, but we believe you and we stand with you, and we are willing you on.

My initial feeling of euphoria at actually getting into the building and seeing everyone else there calmed right down. It had always been part of the job that you couldn't read letter after letter and not feel thoughtful. Even the children understood that this was not a jolly. When Clarence momentarily disappeared to the post room, they helped the rest of us as much as was practical, and when it wasn't, they sat quietly, on best behaviour. Their mum would have been proud.

We worked fast, everyone in silence other than Mrs Mahoney, Monica and I as we dictated answers to the readers. It felt like the days when I had worked with Mrs Mahoney on "Yours Cheerfully", learning more from her than I could possibly have got from any book.

After a couple of hours, we had made good progress. Clarence had even brought up another bag of post.

Not all the post was from someone writing in about a problem. There were large numbers of letters wishing us good luck. Guy wrote notes of thanks back, although it was unlikely anyone would understand his handwriting. And of course there was nothing we could do for people who hadn't given their addresses. The others we got through as best we could.

Then, just as we thought we were winning, there was a noise outside and a woman I didn't recognise walked in. Everyone stopped what they were doing.

'Goodness. What's going on?' she said, staring at our tableau of a hive of industry. 'I thought *Woman's Friend* has been closed?'

'We're just finishing things off,' said Guy, calmly. 'Guy Collins. Editor.' He shot a look at the rest of us. Don't say a word.

'And who are they?' asked the woman, looking at the children. 'They really shouldn't be here.'

'The children are with me,' said Guy. 'There were a few loose ends to tie up and now it's all safely under control. In fact, I was just about to send my staff on their way. And I'm so sorry, I didn't catch your name?'

It was an extraordinary performance on his part. Still the Editor. Still suggesting everything was in hand, and implying that he was the one who should decide who was in his office.

The woman ignored his question, but she seemed not to intend harm. 'It's nothing to do with me,' she said. 'But you're all barmy.'

Then she walked out.

No one just *happened* to wander into the *Woman's Friend* offices on a Saturday, out of the blue. The game was up.

'Right,' said Guy, as soon as she had left. 'Time to go.'

'Clarence,' I said, 'please leave straight away. No argument. Don't even think about taking anything else to the post room. You're the only one who still has a job here.'

Clarence hesitated, but Guy backed me up. 'Emmy's right,' he said. 'We've done everything we can. Clarence, thank you. You have done an incredible job today. You all have. But now we must look after ourselves. Nobody touch another thing. We need to leave.'

No one argued. The room was something of a mess, but we had done as much as we could.

As we gathered our things and began to file out down the corridor, a phone rang in Guy's office. Through habit, Hester stopped and looked round. I put a hand on her arm.

'No, Hest,' I said. 'We have to go. And George, Margaret and Stan, I want you with me, or Bunty and Harold. If anyone asks you anything on the way out, you're not to say a word.'

But before we could get to the doors, they crashed open with a bang. A serious-looking man in a suit strode in.

'We're just leaving,' said Guy.

'Not yet,' said the man. 'Would you mind going back inside. Please wait where you were.'

He didn't look as if we should argue.

'*Now*, if you would,' he said, and as we turned round, we heard him add, 'they're all in here ma'am. We caught them just as they were going to leave.'

CHAPTER THIRTY-FOUR

A Letter from Woman's Friend

I HAD BEEN holding Stanley's hand but now I gripped it tighter.

Clarence put his arm around Hest.

'Damn,' said Guy, under his breath.

'Don't worry,' I said to Stan. 'We're not doing anything wrong.' Bunty and Harold stuck like glue to the other children and nodded.

Why on earth did I think this would be a good idea?

As directed, we all returned to the journalists' room.

'Emmy, are we in trouble?' whispered Stan.

'Gosh, no,' I said. 'I might stay with Guy, to talk to the gentleman, but I think Harold and Bunty are going to take you children out for some lunch.'

'I'll say,' said Harold, cheerfully. 'You know me, I can eat.' He didn't take his hand away from George's shoulder.

'Me too,' said Bunts. 'Hungry, Marg?'

'We don't mind staying,' said Margaret, 'even if it is the police.'

'It's not the police,' I said, firmly.

'Shall we call Roy?' asked Stan. 'It's just that the Scarey brothers said if we ever needed them, he'd know where they are.'

'No, no, darling,' I said, lightly, as the rest of the team stared. 'It's all fine. I don't think the Scareys would help.'

'But they did say,' insisted Stan.

'I know, love,' I said, still appearing carefree. 'Not now, though. It's Scarey with an E,' I added because Mr Newton looked as if he might faint. 'They're very nice.'

'Massive,' said Stan. 'They can lift up a house.'

'And kill Germans with one hand,' added Marg, unhelpfully.

'Oh dear,' said Mr Newton, who was finding it all a bit much.

The doors into *Woman's Friend* opened again.

'It's this way, your ladyship,' said the man who had told us to stay put.

'Thank you,' said a woman's voice.

Nobody moved an inch. We just waited. A moment later, she walked into the room.

'Good morning, Lady Overton,' said Guy. 'Perhaps you might allow me to explain.'

*

This was not what anyone had expected. Most of us had never met or even seen Lady Overton in person before, but even if Guy had not tipped us off, we could probably have made a good guess. For a start, there was a huge portrait of her in the entrance hall to the building that most of us had walked past hundreds of times, but more than that, her appearance confirmed that this was not just anyone who happened to have wandered in.

Lady Overton cut a very impressive figure. She was dressed in the sort of outfit one might see on Queen Mary. Not quite modern, not quite Edwardian, but modestly longer than was fashionable, and beautifully cut. Her grey hair was perfectly set, and a double string of pearls suggested a certain station in life. Now she looked around the room, a slight smile on her lips.

As none of us had ever met a Lady before and I for one had no idea of the socially acceptable response, there was a great deal of shuffling, nodding, a slight curtsy from Hester and Miss Peters, and very respectful, 'Good morning, Lady Overton's from us all, including the children, although they were now looking more excited than anything.

'Good morning, everyone,' said Lady Overton. 'Yes, Mr Collins, an explanation would be most appreciated. I was led to believe that *Woman's Friend* had been closed.'

'It has, your ladyship,' said Guy, 'but unfortunately it was done so before we were able to finish all the reader correspondence. My staff have come in, voluntarily and unpaid, to try to wrap up our responses. At my suggestion,' he added. 'I should clarify that any concerns are entirely my responsibility.'

'Thank you,' said Lady Overton. 'Now then, let me see.' She looked to the woman by her side, who I recognised as the one who had come in earlier. 'Might I have the letter, please, Miss Taylor? Thank you.'

Now Lady Overton looked briefly at the piece of paper handed to her.

'May I ask if there is a Miss Hester Wilson here?' she said.

Hester, unsurprisingly, gave a small gasp from beside me. As she did, Clarence straightened his back and stood taller by her side.

'That's me, ma'am,' said Hest, in the tiniest voice as everyone stared. Without thinking, I moved closer to her.

'Might I guess that you are Miss Lake?' said Lady Overton, turning to me, and as I nodded, she handed me the letter. 'I received this just the other day.'

Dear Lady Overton

I am very sorry to bother you, but I wanted to write so that you know how ever so sad we all are that Woman's Friend has been sold, and also that we are very sorry we couldn't save it from the new owners who I have been informed confidentially are not up to scratch.

Miss Lake told me that you started the magazine with the late Lord Overton, and Mr Collins says how kind you were to him when he was in the first war, and have been ever since, and we all hoped very much that we could keep it going for you.

This probably doesn't sound very important, but I also wanted to tell you how much it has changed my life. I am sixteen and it is my first proper job. I work for Miss Lake and Mr Collins and they have taught me everything I know, other than what my mum already has.

Miss Lake says we have to keep going until all hope is lost. I think it probably is now, as Mrs Porter has sacked us, but I wanted you to know that we tried.

Also, please may I offer my sincere condolences about Lord Overton. When my grandad died, my nan wouldn't let any of us even say his name for ages as she was so sad. Some people say that when you're old and someone dies it's not so bad, but Nan said that after fifty-two years she didn't know what she would do without him.

So, I do hope you are all right. I know the new Lord Overton is very busy now, but I hope he will still be able to visit you in Scotland sometimes.

Getting my job at Woman's Friend was the best thing that has ever happened to me and I will never forget it.

Yours sincerely
Miss Hester Wilson
Woman's Friend Editorial Assistant (Retired)

Hester was now looking absolutely terrified.

'Well done, Hest,' I said to her. 'That's the loveliest letter.'

'That's exactly what I thought, Miss Lake,' said Lady Overton. 'Please don't worry, Miss Wilson, you've done nothing wrong.'

Hester thanked her and looked at the floor.

'May I ask, Lady Overton, how you knew we were here?' said Guy.

'You're rather hard to track down, Guy,' replied Lady Overton. 'Your charlady told my assistant that you had gone to work.'

At this point, Margaret, who was standing near the postbags which had been making her wheeze all morning as she seemed to be funny around hessian, let out an enormous sneeze.

'Bless you,' said half the room at the same time.

'Lady Overton, we're helping too,' said George, pre-emptively. 'In case you wondered why there are children here.'

'George was going to be the post boy when we bought the magazine,' said Stan, informatively. 'The office was going to be at our house but Mrs Porter said no. It's a shame as it was our mum's idea and Guy is our friend, and we like seeing him after school. Hester's teaching Marg and George to type,' he added, now in something of a reverie, 'even though George is a boy.'

'Stan,' said Bunty, quietly.

'I might learn too, but at the moment I prefer animals. I'm Stanley,' he continued. 'We live with Emmy and Bunty, and Harold lives next door although he's always round at ours and he and Bunty aren't married even though they should be, but that's all right and nobody minds because he's a lot happier now and not as sad about getting blown up.'

Having brought Lady Overton fully up to speed on the key issues taking place in his and almost everyone else in Pimlico's lives, as well as making Bunty and Harold look as if they had let themselves down, Stan gave her a large smile, pleased that he had covered everything.

Bunty swallowed and Harold said, 'Ma'am,' as if Lady Overton reminded him slightly of Queen Mary too.

'I see,' said Lady Overton. 'Goodness. It's all go.' She turned back to Guy. 'Guy, we need to speak. Until Miss Wilson's letter, I had no idea you were trying to buy *Woman's Friend*. I very much wish I had known.'

Guy nodded. He was more than a bit stuck. The last thing he could say was that Lady Overton's son had told him in no uncertain terms not to contact her.

'I'm afraid, Lady Overton, that Mrs Porter preferred to follow another route,' he said. 'If my colleagues might be able to leave at this juncture, I could explain?'

Lady Overton surveyed the room again. 'And you are all here even though the magazine has been sold?' she asked. 'That's extremely good of you. Might I see some of your work?'

An hour later, Lady Overton was still sitting at one of the desks, reading letters and listening intently as Mrs Mahoney, Monica and I, continued to dictate advice. The others had also stayed, carrying on with what they had been doing, oddly safe in the knowledge that we were unlikely now to be thrown out. Clarence continued to come up and down from the post room, and it was safe to say that if anyone in the building had not previously been aware that Lady Overton was in residence, they certainly were now.

After a spirited chat with her ladyship about poultry

(an unexpected area of happy common ground) Bunty and Harold had taken George, Marg and Stan off for their promised lunch. All things considered, the children had behaved impeccably on this oddest of days, but it was best for them to go and have some fun, in case someone got carried away and mentioned buying chickens in pub gardens.

As Lady Overton had told her assistant to arrange a tray of refreshments, by lunchtime we – the soon to be redundant *Woman's Friend* team – found ourselves in the unexpected position of sitting in an office, somewhat awkwardly taking tea and biscuits, and discussing the week's post with the matriarch of Launceston Press.

'So you see, Lady Overton,' said Guy, 'many of the letters are from readers simply saying how sorry they are about the sale. At one point we had to stop them sending in donations. But it looks as if we're very nearly there in terms of answering those that need it. I am aware our actions have been unorthodox. Thank you for supporting us today.'

'I should like to say something,' said Lady Overton. 'An apology is in order. No, Guy, not from you, but from me. Clearly you have all had a most regrettable time of things recently. My husband believed in giving people a chance. Invariably he was right,' now she looked at Guy, 'but on this occasion . . . well. I will just say he would be both proud of you all, and I believe, not entirely happy with how things have turned out. For my part, I had no idea anyone wished to preserve *Woman's Friend* as the magazine it was. I had thought the time had come for it to move on. Thank you for your work. You will of course be paid for today at weekend rates.' She paused and smiled. 'Yes, I do know how we run the business. Now then, I am required elsewhere, but if some of you are happy to continue until all these letters are cleared, I would be most grateful. I very much wish things could have worked out differently.'

Then, as I for one regretted just having taken a mouthful of biscuit, we all said our goodbyes, and with Miss Taylor accompanying her, Lady Overton left.

CHAPTER THIRTY-FIVE

Return of The Egg

AFTER LADY OVERTON had gone, the day really did feel as if it had turned into a celebration of sorts. As we all worked on finishing everything up, now no one felt worried, only pleased that they had come into the office, and perhaps sadder than ever that things really were at an end.

'Blimey,' said Mrs Shaw. 'That was a turn-up.'

'Fancy her joining in,' said Miss Peters. 'Opening envelopes and everything. I'll be dining out on this for years.'

'A Lady, opening the post,' marvelled Mr Newton.

'Lady Overton is human,' I said. 'She's not from the moon.'

'Socialist,' said Mrs Shaw. 'Old Joe Stalin would love you.'

'I'm not sure about that,' I said. 'I think he'd find me too argumentative.'

'Don't we all,' said Guy, making everyone laugh.

Just then there was a noise outside.

'What now?' said Mrs Shaw. 'I don't know about finding a new job – come Monday, I'm having a rest.'

'I'll go,' said Mr Newton, getting up.

'It's like Piccadilly Circus,' said Mrs Mahoney. 'It was never this busy when we actually worked here.'

'I do feel I missed out,' said Monica. 'I like being part of this team. Guy, why didn't you ever offer me a job?'

'Couldn't afford you, Monica,' said Guy. 'Nobody can.'

'I'd have done it for biscuits,' said Monica. 'Would anyone else like the last one?'

No one had the chance to say yes, as Mr Newton came rushing back in.

'It's her,' he said. 'Mrs Porter is here.'

For the first time in weeks, Mr Newton didn't look worried at her arrival and if nothing else, today had been worthwhile just to see him back to his old self, and possibly even better.

A beefy man in overalls looked in.

'Removals,' he said.

'Editorial,' replied Guy.

The removal man tutted, went back out and shouted, 'There's people,' down the corridor. 'What do you want me to do?'

'If he so much as touches you,' said Monica to Hester, 'hit him as hard as you can. We'll all swear on the Bible you slipped.'

Hester giggled.

'I wish you *had* worked here,' I said.

Then the Honourable Mrs Porter arrived. None of us moved.

'What,' she said, 'is this?'

'Good afternoon, Mrs Porter,' I said. 'Ah, Mrs Pye.'

'We've just had lunch,' said Mrs Pye, who was standing behind her.

'Go on, I bet it was scallops,' said Mrs Shaw.

'Merci, madame,' said Mrs Porter, ignoring her. 'You were absolutely right.'

'C'est scandaleux,' said Mrs Pye, whose French had clearly recovered itself. 'They shouldn't be here. Ils trespasse.'

'Do you mean *ils transgressent*?' asked Monica. '*Trespasse* is Portuguese.'

'Who are *you*?' said Mrs Pye, rudely.

'This is Mrs Monica Edwards,' said Guy. 'Mrs Pye is a big fan of yours,' he added to Monica.

'Bless you,' said Monica.

'I'm not,' said Mrs Pye.

'Oh, do shut up, Pamela,' said Mrs Porter, tiring badly as she wasn't the centre of attention. 'Go and get Mr Elliot. We need the police.' Now she began to motor. 'You – Mr Collins, Miss Lake, Mrs Edwards – all of you – shall be arrested. You're trespassing on my property, having no doubt lied your way in, and I am confident you have been stealing my things.'

When no one looked remotely concerned, she moved up another gear.

'Do you not hear me?' she shrieked. 'You will all get criminal records. Thank God this is nearly over and I can retire to where I am appreciated. You, on the other hand, will all be in court.'

'Mrs Porter,' began Guy, in a reasonable voice, 'we were just finishing our work. It's not a crime.'

'YES IT IS,' shouted Mrs Porter. 'YOU'RE ALL NASTY COMMON PEOPLE WHO HAVE NEVER UNDERSTOOD ME. I CAN HARDLY STAND THE SIGHT OF YOU.'

'Cressida, that's enough.'

Lady Overton's calm voice stopped Mrs Porter in her tracks.

'Aunty,' she said, suddenly babyish. 'What are *you* doing here? These awful people have broken into my office and are stealing . . . er . . . things. It's quite dreadful. Mr Elliot is calling the police. Thank God Small Winston isn't here. He'd DIE. They'd have murdered my dog.'

'Well, he's not here and they haven't,' said Lady Overton, sounding just like anyone's long-suffering family when they're related to a prize idiot. 'Please calm down.'

'Aunty,' continued Mrs Porter, ignoring her completely, 'you don't realise. They've been awful from the word go. My whole life has been Entirely Mis. It's a wonder I haven't had a nervous breakdown. In fact, I could be in a sanatorium now, only the best ones are in Switzerland so I can't even do that. IT'S ALL JUST UTTERLY MIS.'

Mrs Porter, knocking forty years old, stamped her foot.

'Cressida,' said Lady Overton, quietly, 'please will you come with me.'

'NO,' insisted Mrs Porter. 'Not until they've been thrown out.'

The Honourable Mrs Porter was being given every opportunity to leave with a shred of dignity intact, but was having none of it. She continued to hurl unfounded accusations about her dreadful experiences at *Woman's Friend*. It was becoming embarrassing.

'I give up,' said Lady Overton, evenly. 'You've been like this since you were four years old. Mr Collins, would you and your team care to join me, instead?'

That brought her niece to a halt. 'What?' she said. 'Aunty?'

'Have you signed the contract yet?' asked Lady Overton. 'With West London Press?'

'Yes, I have,' said Cressida. 'Well, nearly. We're signing over lunch at The Savoy on Monday. It's going to be lovely.'

'Then you must consider the new bid before that point,' said Lady Overton. 'I understand you haven't even looked at it.'

'No, and I'm not going to,' said Mrs Porter. 'They can't afford it, anyway.'

'I'm sure they can,' said Lady Overton, 'if they wish.' There was a moment's silence. 'Mr Collins, might we speak?'

Mrs Porter may have been spoilt and hysterical and ridiculous, but when it came down to it, she was no fool.

'What do you mean, Aunty?' she said. 'You're not thinking of trying to keep this wretched magazine? If you are, then speak to Johnny, because he doesn't want it. I'm actually doing everyone a favour by selling it.'

'No, I'm not suggesting *Woman's Friend* stays as part of Launceston,' said Lady Overton. 'I think it's time for it to have a new home. Guy, I really would rather have discussed this with you privately, but as things appear to be coming to a head, might you be interested in a partner? Not a working one, as you clearly don't need that, but on your executive board?'

'NO,' shrieked Cressida.

'Mon Dieu,' gasped Mrs Pye.

'Goodness,' said Guy, very much taken aback. 'Emmy? Monica? Mrs Mahoney? Everyone?'

'I am very ancient,' continued Lady Overton, not exactly telling the truth, 'and I haven't been involved in the business for a long time. But I did so enjoy it once, before I had children and it was temporarily acceptable for me to consider having a job. I remember my husband telling me about you, Mrs Edwards, when you worked with us some time later. I was so envious that you could have a career. I rather wished I was thirty years younger.'

Monica looked touched. 'His Lordship gave me my first big break in journalism,' she said, 'even though I was completely green. I've never forgotten that.'

'Nor have I,' said Lady Overton. 'My husband always knew a good journalist when he saw one.' She smiled at the memory. 'Anyway, everyone, do have a think. We have to move swiftly of course, by Monday, clearly. But should it be required, I will finance any shortfall in your bid, and whatever more is required. That is if you and your backers are interested, of course.'

'It's too late,' pouted Cressida. 'There's a verbal agreement.'

'Ah,' said Lady Overton. 'Miss Wilson, could you possibly place a telephone call for me, please? I should like to speak with Sir James Robinson-Gilbert. Might I use someone's office, rather than go all the way back to my son's?'

'Of course, your ladyship,' said Hester.

'Mine's quite tidy,' I said, aware that Guy's was bound to be a disaster and by the expressions on everyone's faces, no one wanted to put Lady Overton off at this point.

'Lady Overton,' said Guy. 'Just one thing. May I apologise that I didn't come to you about this sooner. I had no idea you might be interested. I'm so sorry.'

He still didn't mention her son.

Lady Overton smiled warmly. 'I'm glad you didn't, Guy. I fear I would not have replied. Miss Wilson's letter was insightful. It doesn't matter if one is old. Losing someone dear is not easy.' She looked at Hester. 'It was very pleasant to feel understood,' she said. 'It reminded me of why people write to magazines like ours. And seeing you all at work today has been rather good for me. I should like to do more. But that is entirely up to you. Now, if Miss Wilson wouldn't mind, I think Sir James should be at home.'

Lady Overton was escorted out of the room by Hester, and for the first time since we had met her, Mrs Porter was lost for words.

'Well, I've never heard of this James chap,' she said, eventually.

'Sir James Robinson-Gilbert is a High Court judge,' said Guy, when no one else spoke up. 'The general consensus is that he'll probably be the next Lord Chief Justice.'

'Crikey,' I said. 'Mrs Porter, I don't think your aunt is messing around.'

'He sounds Utterly Mis,' said Mrs Porter. 'This is all horrid. Madame, find me a taxi. I think I'll take tea at The Ritz.'

My darling C

I hope you are VERY, VERY well.

This in huge haste, but I just have to tell you that we won!!! It was an absolute battle but WF is ours!

I hope you are safe my dearest. You are so very much loved.

Always yours,

E. xxxxxxxxxxxxxxx

CHAPTER THIRTY-SIX

Snowballs in Pimlico

January 1944

THE BANGING COMING from the shed suggested that George had not quite finished his latest round of renovations. It was Sunday afternoon and Bunty and I were looking out at the snow-covered garden from the window of the *Woman's Friend* office.

'I can't help but think the chickens are quite snug enough as it is,' she said, 'what with the amount of newspaper the children have already wadded in there. The salvage man would have a fit.'

'Laurel and Hardy look very nice in their jumpers,' I said. 'You'll be knitting for the duck brothers next.'

Bunty laughed. 'Speaking of knitting, how's the new Fashion Editor getting on?' she asked. 'I like her, don't you?'

'She's super,' I said. 'I mean she's no Pamela Pye, of course, but needs must. War on and all that.'

'How is Mrs Pye?' asked Bunty. 'Has anyone kept in touch?'

I let out a guffaw. 'Oddly enough, no,' I answered. 'But I would imagine she's far too busy at her salon for socialising. Dermatologique by Madame won't run itself.'

'Dermatolo . . . ?' said Bunty.

'It's French,' I said. '*Naturellement.*'

'Of course,' agreed my friend. 'But who in their right mind would let Pamela Pye at them with an ultraviolet light? Aren't they supposed to be rather intense?'

I shook my head. 'She puts a piece of cotton wool over your eyes before she switches it on,' I said. 'Monica showed me an advert in the back of a fancy magazine. It had a picture of Mrs Pye holding an alarm clock and looking angry about skin.'

'Ah well,' said Bunty, 'as long as she's happy.'

'I hope so,' I said. 'There's a rumour that the salon has been financed by the Honourable Mrs P. Which sounds, well . . .'

'A Bit Mis,' we said at the same time.

Bunts and I laughed as I looked around the office.

'Can you believe this actually happened?' I said.

'I'm so glad you and Guy made Harold your Business Director,' Bunty replied.

'He's terrifically good,' I said. 'Mr Newton adores him. I'm far happier with readers and words. That world, I understand.' I turned back to the view out of the window. 'Oh goodness, poor Guy needs to move much faster than that.'

Outside, the Editor in Chief of TJP Limited, Pimlico, was being battered with snowballs from the company's typing and post-room trainees, who were also known as Margaret and Stan. Our Business Director was making a far better show of it, lobbing snowballs back at them, and effortlessly winning, despite only having the use of one arm.

'To think we were worried about them living at a publishing company,' Bunty said, fondly. 'I know a lot of kids live above the shop, but this place isn't exactly normal, is it?'

'No kids are exactly normal any more, Bunts,' I said, watching them all. 'Lost parents, siblings, homes, even the luckiest have lost the chance to just feel safe and have fun. There isn't a child in the country who is having the childhood they deserve. I think our lot are doing all right. I hope so. At least we got through Christmas. We can try to look ahead a little bit now.'

'Their dad'll be back soon,' said Bunts. 'You'll see. And Charles.' She put her arm through mine. 'We've got *Woman's Friend* sorted, the children are coping . . . now we just need to get the boys home.'

'Nineteen forty-four, Bunts,' I said, perking up. 'Charles and the chaps are thundering through Italy. Arthur's ship is in the Med too. It won't be long now. They'll all be home before you know it.'

'Damn right,' said Bunty.

For a moment we were quiet in the rare stillness of the office. Usually, typewriters were hammering away, people were writing articles, designing pages, opening letters or trying to find the best way to help readers on the "Yours Cheerfully" problem page. Mrs Mahoney would be chivvying everyone about deadlines, and Mr Newton was likely to be announcing the return of an advertiser, to cheers from the rest of the team.

I glanced over to the front of the room where I had set up shop at one end of the long dining-room table. A large postbag sat between my chair and Mrs Shaw's, waiting to be sorted first thing in the morning. On the wall was a home-made noticeboard covered in letters and photographs, including one of two babies dressed as Easter chicks. In pride of place, however, was an airgraph featuring a quite awful drawing of a Christmas tree. It had arrived just before the new year.

Happy Christmas my darling.
    Just you wait – one day we'll have a tree that's even better than this!

Thinking of you, my dearest love, and looking forward to
the masses of Christmases we'll have together.
Yours always, C xxxxx

'Damn right,' I said back to my best friend.

Bunty and I were silent for a moment as we looked at the higgledy-piggledy office set up in what had once been the fanciest room in the house. Everything was entirely second-hand, begged, borrowed, or, in the case of two of the pencils and the only hole punch we owned, stolen. We had the finances, but we were careful, intent on putting everything we could into the future of our magazines. Mismatched furniture had been brought from a dozen different homes, filing racks and staff pigeonholes proudly made by George were prized possessions.

Just one thing in the whole company was brand spanking new. A metal sign that had been fixed, with the hugest of care, by the front door.

TJP Limited.
Publishers of *Woman's Friend*
and *The Pimlico Gazette*.

George, Margaret and Stan had proudly made the announcement at an unveiling ceremony just a few weeks previously.

'Ladies and gentlemen, we name this company Thelma Jenkins Publishing, after our mum who came up with the idea.'

Now, shrieks of laughter floated up from the garden, as George had finished his woodwork for the day and joined the others in their snowball fight.

I thought of Thelma, as we all did, a hundred times every day.

'What are we doing in here, Bunty?' I asked her, mock-seriously. 'It's Sunday, and there's an opportunity to shove snowballs in the faces of people we love. Come on, my friend,' I said, taking hold of her arm. 'Last one to get there misses out on the larks.'

Acknowledgements

While *Mrs Porter Calling* is a work of fiction, as with the previous books in the series some parts of the story and many of the readers' problems have been inspired by both real-life events and letters to wartime magazines. In particular regarding Thelma's story, the Whitehall Cinema in East Grinstead was bombed on the 9th of July 1943. One hundred and eight people died and over two hundred more were injured. Reading about this horrific event inspired the tragedy that takes place in the novel, but all details about Thel and her mum, sister and the children are entirely fictional.

As ever in writing this book, I am hugely indebted to the many people who have shared their memories or expertise. My thanks go to Professor Mark Harrison, Ian Jones, and Susan Scott for very kindly helping with my various questions. Any errors or mistakes in this novel are completely mine alone.

Gigantic thanks to my brilliant agent Jo Unwin, who makes this whole adventure even better, and whenever I am in a right old flap, significantly less terrifying. It means the world. Massive thanks also to Nisha Bailey and all the team at JULA for looking after me.

To everyone at Picador and Pan Macmillan, thank you so much for your support, especially Jeremy Trevathan and Mary Mount, Emma Bravo, Elle Gibbons and all in marketing. Charlotte Williams, Jade Tolley, Becky Lloyd, Nicholas Blake and Rosie Shackles. Katie Tooke, Emily Sutton and Stuart Wilson for the wonderful artwork. And

Christine Jones, Emily Bromfield and all in sales. Special thanks to Gill Fitzgerald-Kelly for your belief in me and your championing of Emmy and Bunty – whatever I come up with for them to do!

To Emma Draude, Annabelle Wright, Rebecca Mortimer and all the team at the EDPR. You are the absolute best. Thank you for everything you do and for making it all such fun. Here's to the road trip!

To my US agent, Deborah Schneider at Gelfman Schneider, I still can't believe I get to learn from your wisdom and kindness. Thank you so much. You are, as we say over here, a total legend.

To Nan Graham and everyone at Scribner, thank you so much for making my American dream come true! Ashley Gillam, Jason Chapell, Jaya Miceli and Joie Asuquo, thank you all for putting up with Britishisms and 1940s slang – and that's just from me, never mind Emmy and Bunts! I also know there is a huge team of people I never get to meet, but who champion my books all over the US. Thank you for all you do. The hugest thanks to Kara Watson for going way beyond the call and working deadline defying magic while making it look easy! Thank you also for understanding the stuff I worry about. I am enormously grateful.

A whacking great Goes Without Saying Thank You to all my friends who more or less live every book with me! Massive thanks to my SBC sisters: Judy Astley, Katie Fforde, Milly Johnson, Catherine Jones, Jill Mansell, Bernadine Maxwell, Janie Millman, Jo Thomas, and never forgetting Jane Wenham-Jones, who is so very much missed.

To Gail Cheetham, Rachel Fieldwick, Penny Parkes, Janice Withey and the mighty warriors of the Not Zoom Book Club: Mary Ford, Brin Greenman, Nicki Pettitt and Linda Taylor. Thank you for being amazing and keeping the wheels on this bus going round and round, even when there's a flat tyre.

Special mention to Kathryn Croft-Baker. During my research for this book I discovered that the famous *Savoy Cocktail Book* included a cocktail called the KCB. Several of us were thrilled but obviously mortified that we had missed out on twenty years of gin-based enjoyment in the name of one of our own. KCB said if I put it in the novel she would give a donation to charity. Well, my friend, I think your cocktail deserves its own paragraph. Chin, chin – see you and the Seahorses at the bar!

Biggest love to my family, and especially my brother, to whom this book is dedicated. We were incredibly lucky kids, but I know that if we'd had to experience anything remotely as horrific as the children do in this novel, somehow you would have got us through it. Along with Cyril and Elephant, of course.

I named two of Thelma's children (George and Margaret) after my parents. The Jenkins children are totally made up, but I bet my dad could give Captain Harold a run for his money in the shed-building stakes, and I know for a fact my mum would totally nail tap-dancing, trombone-playing and nursing if she wanted. And all at the same time. You're both the absolute best.

Finally, to the booksellers, librarians, reviewers and bloggers who spread the word about Emmy and Bunty, and to all the readers who are kind enough to read these books when there are a million others you could choose, thank you. Without you I'd just be sitting here talking to my imaginary friends. Thank you for sticking with me and Emmy, Bunty, Guy and the gang. I really hope you've enjoyed this one.

PILLGWENLLY

Credits

Managing Director, Pan Macmillan Adult Books: Jeremy Trevathan

Publisher, Picador: Mary Mount

Commissioning Editor: Gillian Fitzgerald-Kelly

Editorial Assistant: Rosie Shackles

Finance Director, Pan Macmillan: Lara Borlenghi

Finance Director, Adult Publishing: Jo Mower

Commercial Finance Manager, Picador: Sarah Parry-Jones

Head of Contracts: Clare Miller

Contracts Assistant: Senel Enver

Audio Publishing Director: Rebecca Laura Marlow

Associate Publisher: Sophie Brewer

Managing Editor: Laura Carr

Editorial Manager: Nicholas Blake

Art and Design Director: James Annal

Art Director, Picador: Stuart Wilson

Jacket Designer: Katie Tooke

Jacket Illustrator: Emily Sutton

Studio Manager: Lloyd Jones

Head of Adult Production: Simon Rhodes

Senior Production Controller: Helen Hughes

Production Controller: Bryony Croft

Text Design Manager: Lindsay Nash

Digital and Communications Director, Pan Macmillan: Sara Lloyd

Communications Director, Picador: Emma Bravo

Publicist: Emma Draude

Head of Marketing: Elle Gibbons

Audience Development Manager: Andy Joannou

Digital Publishing Senior Executive: Alex Ellis

The UK Sales Team

Head of Trade Marketing: Ruth Brooks

Trade Marketing Designer: Katie Bradburn

International Director: Jonathan Atkins

Head of International Sales, Picador: Maddie Hanson

Sales Director: Leanne Williams

Marketing and Communications Director: Lee Dibble

Senior Metadata and Content Manager: Eleanor Jones

Metadata Executive: Marisa Davies

Operations Manager: Kerry Pretty

Operations Administrator: Josh Craig